RITUAL MAGICS

The blood flamed, coursing through his fingertips but not burning him. The copper wheel spinning around him in astral space resounded, and its tone increased in pitch. The ritual had found its target and flashed again. Then Kyle felt the presence coming against him grow. It was almost upon him when he collapsed the ritual. The blood in his hand burned away, reduced to ash and smoke. The wheels faded, the connection, the path to Mitchell Truman's body dissolving.

In his mind and far off in the distance, Kyle then heard a wail. A terrible, alien cry of anger. Frustration as the bridge it had been following dispersed, leaving it nothing to travel. The howls died away, fading with the magic.

Kyle stood, his left hand smoking, the final traces of the ritual folding in on itself. The candles around the ritual circle faded, and Kyle nodded to himself, satisfied.

"I found him," he said.

Before there was a
Sixth World of Shadowrun,
there was a Fourth.
Discover the origins in
EARTHDAWN.
Read *The Immortals Trilogy*
by Caroline Spector.
Volume 1, *Scars*,
on sale in mid-March 1995
from ROC.

SHADOWRUN

BURNING BRIGHT

Tom Dowd

A ROC BOOK

ROC

Published by the Penguin Group

Penguin Books USA Inc., 375 Hudson Street,
New York, New York 10014, U.S.A.

Penguin Books Ltd, 27 Wrights Lane, London W8 5TZ, England

Penguin Books Australia Ltd, Ringwood, Victoria, Australia

Penguin Books Canada Ltd, 10 Alcorn Avenue,
Toronto, Ontario, Canada M4V 3B2

Penguin Books (N.Z.) Ltd, 182–190 Wairau Road, Auckland 10, New Zealand

Penguin Books Ltd, Registered Offices: Harmondsworth, Middlesex, England

First published by Roc, an imprint of Dutton Signet,
a division of Penguin Books USA Inc.

First Printing, November, 1994
10 9 8 7 6 5 4 3 2 1

Series Editor: Donna Ippolito
Cover: Peter Peebles

 REGISTERED TRADEMARK—MARCA REGISTRADA

SHADOWRUN, FASA, and the distinctive SHADOWRUN and FASA logos are
registered trademarks of the FASA Corporation, 1100 W. Cermak, Suite B305,
Chicago, IL 60608.

Printed in the United States of America

BURNING BRIGHT

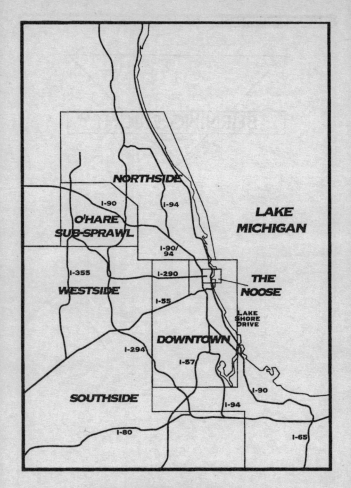

NORTHSIDE

I-90

I-94

O'HARE
SUB-SPRAWL

LAKE
MICHIGAN

I-90/
94

I-355

I-290

WESTSIDE

THE
NOOSE

I-55

LAKE
SHORE
DRIVE

DOWNTOWN

I-294

I-57

SOUTHSIDE

I-90

I-94

I-80

I-65

CHICAGO
AREA MAP

0   3km

CIRCA 2054

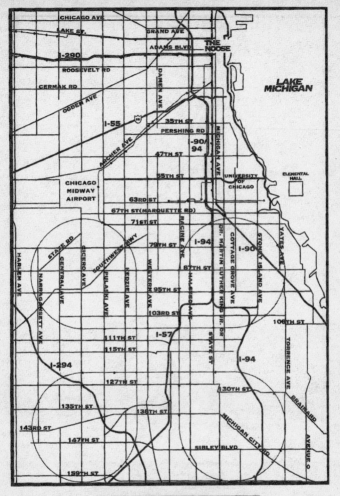

CHICAGO AVE
LAKE ST.
GRAND AVE
ADAMS BLVD
THE NOOSE
I-290
ROOSEVELT RD
LAKE MICHIGAN
CERMAK RD
OGDEN AVE
DAMEN AVE
I-55
35TH ST
PERSHING RD
ARCHER AVE
I-90/94
47TH ST
MICHIGAN AVE
55TH ST
ELEMENTAL HALL
CHICAGO MIDWAY AIRPORT
UNIVERSITY OF CHICAGO
63RD ST
67TH ST (MARQUETTE RD)
71ST ST
RACINE AVE
79TH ST
I-94
DR. MARTIN LUTHER KING JR. DR
COTTAGE GROVE AVE
STONEY ISLAND AVE
I-90
YATES AVE
HARLEM AVE
STATE RD
CENTRAL AVE
CICERO AVE
SOUTHWEST HWY
PULASKI RD
KEDZIE AVE
WESTERN AVE
87TH ST
HALSTED AVE
NARRAGANSETT AVE
95TH ST
103RD ST
106TH ST
111TH ST
I-57
115TH ST
STATE ST
I-94
TORRENCE AVE
BRAINARD AVE
I-294
127TH ST
130TH ST
AVENUE O
135TH ST
136TH ST
MICHIGAN CITY RD
143RD ST
147TH ST
SIBLEY BLVD
159TH ST

CHICAGO

— ● ELEVATED SUBWAY STATION

— ● ELEVATED SUBWAY LINE

0   .5km

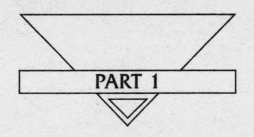

PART 1

Chicago
14 August 2055

1

Watching her, he thought of the thunderstorms of his childhood ...

He'd grown up on the Plains, far west of the Mississippi, but not far enough that the Rockies were anything more than an imagined wisp on the horizon on the clearest days. Thunderstorms were common the year round by then, and he and his friends would run along the edges of those freak storms as they raged across the prairies. It was thirteen years since the Great Ghost Dance had broken the power of the United States of America, and Kyle Teller was nine years old.

The storms were a sign the Great Spirits were pleased the land had been restored to the People, the tribal shamans said. Running, yelling, and chasing each other in the cool of early evening, Kyle and his friends would each take the part of one of the powerful totems that had returned to rouse the people from their oppression.

Listening to the growing winds and gauging the smells in the air, they'd celebrate the re-Awakening of magic, and watch to see from where a powerful storm would spring and in which direction it would run. Then, energies spent with the storm's, they would return home, finish their chores, and prepare for the next day at school. Kyle didn't need to study as much as the others did, but he still had to prepare. His mother was Anglo, which meant having to face worse things than classwork at school.

When it came to running a storm, though, Kyle was the best. There were times when he could feel its energy deep within him long before any clear signs of it appeared. And when the storm finally did rise, to him it was an elemental flower unfolding, slowly, inevitably, until nothing could keep it from bursting free over the land. He saw the progression, felt the patterns, and could see how the storm would arise and how long it would last. In the games of the children, he was always Coyote, for only the Trickster would gift such sight upon a half-breed.

Often he heard the elders sing powerful songs of how the great Winds and Rains were spirits beyond the control of Man and unfathomable by Reason. Once, Kyle had even seen one of those spirits with his own eyes at a Calling near Salina that he and his sisters had attended with their grandfather.

There, the spirit had been summoned by three young shamans. Proud and brash, they reveled in their new power to make the legendary spirit appear at their call. This was a great and mighty being, full of the heart of the air and the sky, one of the shamans had said. A power to be respected and honored, said the other. Kyle had watched as the supernatural tower of swirling, glistening air, vapor, and majesty that was the spirit became visible to the thousands gathered in the decaying parking lot of an abandoned K-Mart.

The spirit, one of the shamans said, danced with the energy of life. Unbound, the spirit was the storm, inexplicable and beyond comprehension. Even as an awed and frightened child, Kyle had thought their words strange.

He had watched many a gathering storm back home, out in the weed-choked fields behind the house, felt them as they raced across the plain, and seen only forces he could understand. It was true the storms were beyond anyone's control, but he could see how they grew from changes in temperature and the play of other forces. He could see the lightning build, feel it jump from ground to sky, and understand. That knowledge thrilled him, but he felt no mystery, no urge to dance in its presence.

It was only years later that he would know why he saw things as he did, as few others could. Even the shamans to whom his parents took him when they finally realized his

talent at first refused the ultimate truth. Could the Great
Spirits have been so cruel as to put a boy of power among
them and not give him the gifts of dance and song?

They could, and perhaps had. The boy had the ways of
magic Awakened within him, but where inspiration and
spontaneity fueled the shamanic magic of his people, he
used logic, reason, and deliberation. Kyle Teller, to the final
humiliation of his father, was a mage.

The forces shifted, the balance changed, and he felt the
storm in her quiet.

"Ironic, isn't it?" she said, her voice calmer than he'd expected as she scooped the last of the bread crumbs from the
counter and into the long, outstretched fingers of her other
hand. "For years we barely saw you because of your work."

The stark lights of the kitchen made her pale and darkened her hair to nearly black. He knew she hated the lighting
in the room but that it was too expensive to change the fix-
tures.

"And now you only see me when I'm in town on business," he said.

She nodded, now busily brushing away the wrinkles
creased into her fashionable suit from sitting. The fabric responded, its freshness jumping back to life at her touch.
Kyle wasn't used to seeing Beth dressed for the corporate
world. It was wrong for her—too restrictive. She was an art-
ist, a dancer, not the secretary she now pretended to be.

She spoke, but had already turned to another task. There
were, after all, dishes to be done. "Sometimes I think we see
you more now."

"You know that's not true."

She bent carefully to rearrange the contents of the dishwasher. "Maybe not. But it does seem that way."

Something was bothering her. He could sense it in the timbre of her voice, in the way she avoided his eyes, in the attention she paid to tidying up after dinner. And whatever it was
had to do with her, not him, or else she'd have said something
by now. Kyle played back in his mind all the events of the

past hours: his arrival, his surprise at seeing Beth in a business suit, the gifts for Natalie, the details on Beth's new job, playing with Natalie and talking with the two of them, eating dinner, after dinner . . .

"I saw a bottle of your sister's medication in the bathroom," Kyle said. Beth stiffened, but something made him blunder on. "How's she handling things?"

Beth turned toward him slowly. She didn't snap at him and her eyes showed only the barest sign of the anger Kyle knew he'd evoked. "All things considered, Ellen's probably managing better than I might have."

He tried to force himself to wait. There was more. He thought he knew what it was, but he'd let her tell him. Let her speak her own words. For a change.

She crossed her arms and leaned back against the kitchen counter. "But I *am* worried. She's—"

"It looks like they increased her dosage."

Beth nodded. "I don't think she's taking it, though."

"She left the bottle here."

"Exactly. And I think she's started meeting with some of the people from her group. She says she needs someone to talk to."

That didn't surprise Kyle. "The conditioning she was subjected to is hard to erase. The drugs should reduce most of it, but if she's stopped taking them . . ."

"I don't understand why she won't talk to *me*," Beth said, her anger turning to pain. "I've told her to stop by or call anytime. But instead she *sneaks* off . . ."

Kyle took a step toward her and gently laid one hand on her shoulder. Beth didn't look up. "She goes to them because—right or wrong—she thinks there's no one else who understands. You read that report I had sent to you. That's exactly the kind of dependence the Universal Brotherhood tried to create in people to keep them vulnerable and believing the Brotherhood was their one and only hope.

"They taught their followers that the government and the corps were *never* to be trusted, but that's exactly who shut down the Brotherhood and had the leaders thrown into jail. None of the UB members believe any of the official statements that have been given out. They think it's all part of a massive cover-up. And now that all the Brotherhood chapterhouses have been closed, Ellen and the others believe *they* are all that's left of the Brotherhood."

"I went with her to the government meeting," Beth said. "We both saw the same trideo. How couldn't she believe?"

"Because it really doesn't make a hell of a lot of sense on any level. Ask yourself, why in god's name would the Universal Brotherhood be conducting illegal medical experiments on the homeless? Financially, it makes no sense. Not scientifically either. They didn't have the resources to *really* do much of anything. That story could have been—and probably was—faked because the corps don't want anyone threatening their hold on things. The Brotherhood was starting to get mighty powerful."

He took her hand. "She thinks she's going to be alone again and doesn't want that to happen. She's not going to shake off their influence easily."

Beth nodded. "I know. I'm just worried she'll do something desperate."

"I doubt it. The Brotherhood taught dependence, not escape."

Beth looked up at him with a hesitant smile.

"Do you want me to talk to her?" he asked.

"Would you?"

"Of course. My work here shouldn't take up all my time."

She looked visibly relieved. "Thanks, Kyle. It means a lot."

"I know you're worried, but I don't—"

"*Daddy!*" They both looked up at the childish shout from the other room.

"Yes, honey?" Kyle called back.

"Daddy! I need your help! I'm at the sixth level and the Corrupted Ones keep chopping me in half even though I hit them with the ashes!" From where he was standing Kyle could see his daughter sitting on the couch. She looked frustrated and was madly adjusting the sim-reality glasses on her head, apparently hoping that doing so would somehow help her win the game.

"I'll be right there!" he called out, then said softly to his ex-wife, "Do you think I should have gotten her a doll instead?"

"She'd only have traded it away for the chip."

Kyle laughed. Beth was right. He gave her shoulder a squeeze. "Be right back." He turned toward the living room, but his attention was inexplicably diverted down. It must have been the flicker of motion, the scurrying passage of a small cockroach almost underfoot. Kyle took a step forward to crush it, but the insect darted clear and behind a cabinet. Kyle wondered idly if he knew a spell that could reach back there and incinerate the bug, but Beth spoke, distracting him again.

"Did you know she wants a datajack implant so she can play the games 'right'?" she said.

"Great Coyote," Kyle said, his fingers unconsciously jumping to the datajack in his own temple that had been implanted only after he'd begun his hermetic studies at Columbia. "She's only eight!"

Beth frowned as Kyle turned and walked off down the hall. "I didn't say I was going to get her one, did I?" she said.

No, maybe not. But Kyle was sure she would. For Christmas, if he knew his ex-wife at all.

2

A suite had been arranged for him at the Marriott SkyTower down near where I-57 crossed 103rd Street at the edge of the financial Core, and Kyle had ended up there earlier than he'd expected. Both Natalie and Beth had tired early, and he could see Beth wrestling with her own desires about where she wanted him to stay that night. He'd solved the problem by saying he had an early-morning meeting and some research still to prepare. He'd also wanted to ask if she needed more money, hating the idea of her jacked in a desk at Fuchi America. But she hadn't mentioned money problems, so he resisted the urge to offer. There would be time enough later.

Kyle knew Chicago fairly well, but let the autopilot on the Ford Americar he'd been provided do the driving. Moving through the night, the car took him south from Irving Park Road on the Northside, down a short distance along Lake Shore Drive, past the rows of ritzy lakeside developments that barely hid the blight of the sprawl stretching to the west. Traffic was light, and except for the fly-over of a police helicopter, its lights blazing and clearly illuminating the Eagle Security logo on the side, uneventful.

At North Avenue, the view changed as the Drive wove itself along the eastern edge of what had come to be known as the Noose. Victim to the migration of Chicago's economic heart to the south side after the fall of the IBM Building in 2039, the area was a mecca for the city's criminals and underclass. Kyle turned away to watch the faintly rippling waters of Lake Michigan, not looking west again until the Drive crossed the Chicago River.

There, in the now black and dead former heart of the city,

he could just barely make out the Shattergraves area among the rubble of the hundreds of buildings destroyed or burned when terrorists had demolished the IBM Building following the anti-metahuman Night of Rage. Even more than the Noose, the Shattergraves was ungoverned and left to rot. Few lived there, for not many could retain their sanity against the thousands of ghosts and lost souls that haunted those broken, deserted streets. Still, small fires and other lights were visible in the area flanking the river. Despite the horror of the place, some apparently called it home.

The Noose continued past the Shattergraves, but now the near horizon was dominated by the new corporate towers of the transplanted Downtown area. The car continued on to the end of the Drive at 67th Street and then continued down Stony Island Avenue to 103rd. There it turned right and approached the northern edge of the corporate Core.

The sleek corporate vehicle in which he rode traveled unrestricted into the area of chrome, steel, and glass. Here and there, Kyle saw a local vehicle being checked out by Eagle Security, but everyone knew better than to delay a car bearing the ID tags this one had. Truman Technologies was *the* Chicago corporation, and even the police were smart enough not to play games with them. Perhaps the biggest non-multinational corporation in the United Canadian and American States, Truman Technologies all but dominated segments of the mega-nuyen entertainment industry. It produced, marketed, distributed, and sold the technology for the truer-than-life sensory-encoded simsense chips that had replaced CD-video decades earlier. In Chicago, there were few more powerful than Daniel Truman and his corporation.

Kyle's room on the ninety-second floor of the Marriott was high enough to give him a view of the lakeside campus of the University of Chicago near where Lake Shore Drive ended. He could also see the mist-shrouded lights of Elemental Hall, the corporate-sponsored metaphysical research park half a kilometer offshore from the University. Though Kyle had a standing invitation from a former classmate at Columbia to visit the Hall anytime, he wasn't sure whether he'd take him up on the offer. The idea of visiting Elemental

Hall was more than intriguing, and he would certainly profit from a grand tour of the U of C's metamagical and conjuring facilities, but Kyle wasn't that anxious to renew his former classmate's acquaintance. He'd decide later. There'd be plenty of time.

It was long after midnight as he scanned the on-screen catalog of the programs offered by the hotel's in-house trideo system, and Kyle wondered if he really did need to do any research for the morning. The meeting was set for ten o'clock, which left him more than enough time after break-fast to refresh his memory on information pertinent to Truman Technologies and the situation the powerful Truman family had hired him to remedy. Despite the gravity of the situation, Daniel Truman didn't seem to be in any hurry. Kyle decided to set his notepad computer to browsing sev-eral pertinent online services and databases while he slept.

The hold-image for the United Canadian and American States Federal Bureau of Investigation's Department of Par-anormal Affairs faded from the screen to be replaced by the image of Dave Strevich as he approved the telecom connec-tion. "Sorry about that," the burly man said as he dropped heavily into the chair behind his desk. "I was taking a crap."

Kyle chuckled and leaned back in his own chair as the im-age of his friend, cybernetically superimposed over his nor-mal vision, rose ghost-like through the air to sit among the vines that hung down from the ceiling over the cafe in the Marriott's courtyard atrium. The system took a moment to compensate and darken Strevich's image against the brighter background.

"I hope I didn't rush anything," Kyle said.

Strevich shrugged. "Nothing the next guy can't clean up."

"Pleasant image."

Strevich waved the compliment away. "For you, only the best."

"Thanks, Dave. That's why I'm calling to ask a favor."

"You mean you aren't calling to find out how my love life is going?"

Kyle smiled. "I know it's touchy, but I need you to cross-reference a name in the FBI's files on the Universal Brotherhood mess."

Strevich raised his eyebrows. "Touchy?" he said after a minute. "You have no idea."

"Care to tell me why?"

"Can't."

Kyle sighed. "Look, I understand it's sensitive. I wouldn't ask, not even for my best client, except that it's personal."

Strevich's eyes softened. "Your sister-in-law?"

"Ellen Shaw."

"Okay, hang on." Strevich leaned forward and Kyle could just barely see his hands tapping at the flat keyboard built into his desk. He was done quickly and then leaned back. "I've only got a membership listing for her ... address, personal data, financial contributions, that sort of thing. Nothing deeper."

Kyle felt himself tense slightly. "You pulled that data up fraggin' fast, Dave. Have the computers gotten a lot wizzer since I was there?"

But for the slightest narrowing of the eyes, Strevich's face would have been unreadable.

"Why's the file in your direct access pool, Dave? You should have had to request—"

Strevich held up one hand. "Don't," he said. "Look down."

Kyle fought the impulse to do just that, but he'd known his friend long enough to recognize one of his figures of speech. He glanced down.

"See that?" Strevich continued. "It's a land mine. Please don't set if off. I'd be grateful."

"Okay, okay. But I'm going to be doing my own checking. Please let me know next time one drops in front of me."

"If I can. You know the scan, Kyle—sometimes you swat ..." Uncharacteristically, his friend let the metaphor trail off. "If I can," Strevich finished instead. "If I can."

Kyle nodded. The message was clear enough, and he knew not to push. "Understood." he said. "Look, I gotta go—meeting to take, money to be had."

Strevich nodded and punched what Kyle knew was the command key that took him out of whatever file he'd been scanning. "I see you're calling from Chicago."

Kyle nodded.

"The Truman boy?"

"Hey, hey, hey," Kyle said, holding up his hand. "Look down." Strevich just grinned.

"See that?" Kyle told him. "It's your shoe. That's all you need to know."

"Got it."

Kyle reached toward the portable telecom unit sitting on the table. "Feed me anything you can," he said.

Strevich was just saying "Don't hold your breath" when Kyle cut the connection. He pulled the self-coiling cable connecting the datajack in his temple to the pocket phone, then sat for a while, staring at the Marriott's waterfall and pouring the last of the kaf from the self-warming carafe. It was, of course, real coffee.

So, his old teammates in the FBI's Department of Paranormal Affairs were handling the Universal Brotherhood investigation. And since that fact wasn't public knowledge, it had to mean the case involved some metaphysical matter the government didn't want anyone to find out about.

And that fact Kyle Teller found very interesting indeed.

3

The Truman Tower, its two longer sides sloping nearly to a point, jutted three hundred and fifty-two stories into the stormy Chicago sky. With the IBM Building gone, it was the tallest building in the city, but far short of holding that record for the world, despite its owner's wishes. Molded from blue glass and darker steel, it reflected and distorted the gray of the threatening sky and the bright orange and white wedge of the twenty-meter-long, lighter-than-air transport moored to its upper deck.

Kyle took it all in as his car turned smoothly off the street, then angled up the main entrance ramp and onto the open promenade of the building's east side. The almost rural landscaping of the enormous grounds would have surprised him except that his computer notepad had just been feeding him images of it and other things Truman. Its programming had ranged far and wide as he'd slept, gathering information on the Truman family and empire from various online services and databases. That done, a pair of special smart programs in the computer had analyzed, compiled, and compressed the most important and relevant data into usable form. Then, as Kyle dreamt on, the notepad had downloaded the ready-for-viewing file into the tiny amount of cybernetic headware memory he'd dared risk as a mage. The data was sitting there awaiting his examination when he woke.

Kyle had considered bringing along his special equipment, but ultimately rejected the idea. He'd amassed quite a collection of powerful magical foci for augmenting his own mystical abilities in the course of his career, yet he generally shied away from their use, fearing to create a psychological crutch. Better to do without, saving the foci for the rare emergency. An active magic item or spell—or even a magician's own use of astral perception or projection—created a bridge between normal space and the astral plane that could permit a spell or spirit originating in astral space to harm him. That peace of mind alone was worth the loss of potential power. Kyle's foci were currently stored in the hotel's secure vault, in a special box protected by a spell that would immobilize anyone who tried to open it without uttering a certain phrase. Kyle sincerely hoped members of the hotel staff would heed his warning not to tamper.

The car slowed and stopped automatically at the curb in front of Truman Tower's three-story glass entrance. The gull-wing passenger door rose upward with a barely audible hiss, and Kyle stepped out, slipping his Meteor sunglasses into place. Already, an ork male attendant and a breathtakingly lovely woman in an angled suit of the latest corporate fashion were approaching him.

The woman was tall and Nordic, with white-blond hair stylishly chopped to collar-length. She stopped a proper distance away and extended a perfectly manicured hand.

"Mr. Teller?" Her voice was soft, surprisingly throaty. "I'm Hanna Uljakën, special assistant to Mr. Truman. We're very pleased you could come so quickly. I hope your trip has been pleasant so far." She smiled, and Kyle felt a warm tingling in his belly.

He nodded, shaking her hand just as properly, but letting the contact linger slightly longer than custom. Without taking his eyes from her, he stepped aside to give the ork attendant access to the car. "I'm pleased to meet you, Ms. Uljakën. The trip so far, especially your company's arrangements, has been excellent."

She smiled again and clasped her hands behind her back. "Good. But let's go right in. Mr. Truman and his wife will see you immediately." As the two began walking toward the glass entrance, the car pulled away from the curb in response to the attendant's spoken orders. It would await Kyle in the car pool, ready for him again when he was finished upstairs.

"May I ask a question?" Kyle said casually.

"Of course." The strong breeze ruffled Hanna Uljakën's hair and blew some strands into her face. She brushed them back into place with what looked like a well-practiced gesture.

"Despite certain statements to the contrary," Kyle said, keeping one eye on her and another more cautious one on the building entrance, "there seems to be a decided lack of haste in all this." He paused to study her for a moment. "I was ready to begin from the time I arrived late yesterday afternoon."

Hanna Uljakën held his gaze for a moment. "I'm sure Mr. Truman can brief you on any details that are still unclear." With that she passed through the automatic doors into the main lobby, Kyle only a step behind.

"Welcome to Truman Tower," Uljakën said, pausing to gesture around the opulent lobby. "I'm sure we can arrange a special tour if you'd like." It was a smooth move, one she'd probably performed a thousand times for a thousand different guests, and it set him up perfectly.

Beyond her, the lobby's glass ceiling sloped away from its three-story base to finally peak eleven stories later. Two enormous trees rose on either side, flanking a spacious reflecting pool and fountain. Light, it seemed, sprayed with the water, making a brilliant cascade down the fountain's many tiers. A small flock of birds wheeled above them, darting in and out of the trees. The scene was remarkable, and distracting enough to draw Kyle's attention away from the tall woman at his side. He removed and pocketed his Meteors.

The fountain had him wondering if it was magic that created the light. Carefully shifting the focus of his perception from the physical world, Kyle let his senses extend into the astral realm. But what he saw was not quite what he'd expected.

Except for the mundane auras of the two dozen or so people present, the lobby was painfully dull and lifeless. No sign of magic radiated from the fountain, nor was any energy present in the trees. They were lifeless, artificial, but stunningly real to the unAwakened eye. In fact, Kyle could see only one source of magic in the whole lobby, and that was the single earring worn by Hanna Uljakën. Shifting again, he let his astral senses slip away and focused on her once more. Nothing in her expression indicated that she'd noticed his astral viewing, but then nothing about her aura or astral appearance suggested to Kyle that the woman was a magician.

"It's all very impressive," he said, returning her smile. "Perhaps I'll take you up on the tour later."

As they resumed their approach toward the elevators he returned to the subject most on his mind. "The reason I asked you about the lack of haste was so that I wouldn't have to ask Mr. Truman."

"I'm sure Mr. Truman would prefer to speak about that personally," she said as they stepped into a wood and brass-trimmed car guarded by a hard-looking elven woman in a starched Knight Errant uniform. Kyle had learned from his data-gathering that Truman Technologies had recently begun using the security subsidiary of Ares Macrotechnology. The Knight Errant guard was apparently unarmed, but Kyle didn't doubt she had a weapon of some kind within easy reach. And considering her tactical position he also had little doubt that her reflexes, once cybernetically triggered, would be so lightning-fast that a weapon might as well be in her hands. He idly wondered what magical security was present in or around the building, suspecting he'd find out soon enough.

As the elevator doors shut noiselessly, Kyle moved to the rear of the car and leaned against the wall. Hanna Uljakën stood about midway in, her body half turned away from him. With a barely perceptible motion the elevator began to rise upward, but Uljakën had neither touched a control panel nor spoken a command before the car began to move. The two of them were either being monitored by building security, or she had some form of cybernetic datalink to the building's systems. Kyle suspected the former, which might also explain why, beyond corporate propriety, she'd evaded his questions.

The ride was fairly long, just shy of two minutes. He

knew most megacorp elevators were capable of shuttling employees between floors at much higher rates of speed, but that also meant subjecting them to the effects of acceleration. Which was fine for the wageslaves or during emergencies, but for executives and their guests, any form of discomfort was to be avoided.

Kyle took advantage of the ride to re-open his astral senses for a closer look at Hanna Uljakën. She was silent, apparently content to avoid further questions and simply escort him to her boss while offering him her exquisite profile. He had no problem with that. It would make his astral viewing a lot easier if he didn't have to worry about keeping up a conversation while his attention was elsewhere.

First, he scanned the elevator itself, but saw no source or aura of magic. The car's interior was fairly dark, the only real light coming from the shimmer given by their auras and the faint, diffuse glow from the microscopic life in the air around them. Even that, though, was duller than Kyle would have expected. Truman Technologies, it seemed, had serious air filtration systems. He shrugged mentally. Interesting, but not particularly significant.

Next he focused his attention on her aura, trying to see whether Hanna Uljakën was really a mundane or a magician skillfully masking the telltale evidence usually present in a magically active aura. Hers was erratic, chaotic, exactly as it should be. He watched carefully, studying it for any signs of regularity that would reveal the masking. When none appeared, he turned his attention to the earring.

That item was clearly magical, obviously enchanted. Its aura was solid, with only the barest color hint of cycling energy. The item looked to be of fairly low-power or under only a simple spell, unless it were masked. He probed deeper with his senses, carefully exploring the lattice of magical energies that made up the enchantment. He wasn't likely to learn anything concrete using only his raw senses, but he might get a clue as to the—

She turned slightly, looked at him, and gave him a small, seductive smile as she tilted her head slightly. He felt the involuntary warm tingle again, but he also saw the pattern of energy in the item shift with her gaze. Comprehension dawned and he returned her look with one displaying as much lustful will as he could muster. Considering the effects the item's magic was having on him, he suspected she suddenly felt like a fine head of beef placed before a famished dragon.

Both Uljakën's own aura, and the item's, flickered for different reasons as she again turned away slightly. Kyle grinned. The woman certainly had no need of magic to boost her natural charisma and beauty, but she probably thought it gave her some edge in the fast-track corporate world. The idea made him suddenly think of Beth.

The elevators doors opened, and Kyle followed Hanna Uljakën into a wide, finely carpeted hallway. "Mr. Truman's office apartments are at the end of the hall," she said, her cool smile and composure intact. "Come."

The corridor leading to the pair of carved mahogany doors was lined with paintings of various sizes, hung without apparent regard for period or style. Kyle noticed in passing that all seemed to be originals, or at least original copies. Though some looked familiar, he couldn't place or name any of them.

When they came to the doors, Hanna Uljakën reached down and just barely brushed the golden handles with her well-manicured fingertips. The doors opened instantly, swinging outward in unison. She motioned him forward.

Kyle stepped through, and the doors swung shut behind them. He paused as if giving the room a glance, but was in fact listening to the faint metallic click of some mechanism engaging when the doors actually closed. He suspected that his and Uljakën's progress through the building *was* being carefully monitored and assisted. He wondered how far into the offices and residences that surveillance reached.

The room he had just entered was five or so meters wide, and twice that deep. And it was done in pure white. Finely veined white marble was the material of choice, accented by a pinker variety and gold and copper ornamentation. Directly ahead was a short staircase leading up to an area carpeted with a deep red and gray oriental. In each corner was a marble pedestal bearing a vase in tones matching the carpet. An open archway stood on either side. Hanna Uljakën led Kyle up the stairs, and through the archway on the left. In the distance, he could hear the faint sounds of a piano.

As they walked down another corridor, the music grew louder. Kyle recognized Chopin, but not the name of the piece. The pianist was, to his ears, very skilled.

Walking a few steps ahead, Uljakën led Kyle into a brightly lit room. One wall, facing east and the lake, was solid glass that let in the strong, but diffuse sunlight. There was a central area, furnished with a circle of couches around a sunken, glass-topped pond alive with brightly colored fish. On each side of the room stood two tall pillars, supporting nothing, but reaching to the entrance level where he and Ms. Uljakën were standing. The entranceway looked down on the room, which at first glance resembled a cross between a medieval hunting lodge and a Greco-Roman temple.

On the far side were a series of consoles made of white wood and hints of silver. He suspected they contained media equipment and possibly a bar. Below them, as he followed Hanna down the steps, he could begin to see a large white Bösendorfer piano, the source of the music. Kyle could also see that the musician was a woman apparently in her thirties, dark-haired and dressed in a simple but obviously expensive skirt and sweater. He recognized her as Elaine Annworth Truman, Daniel Truman's wife of forty-five years, mother of their three children, activist for the underclass, a classically trained musician, and like her husband, a regular user of a variety of cellular cleansers and genetic rejuvenation therapy.

Daniel Truman himself was seated on one of the sofas in the center of the room, next to a young girl who had to be his daughter Melissa, a dark-haired, dark-eyed beauty of sixteen who was beginning to make a name on the international modeling scene. She looked up, most disinterested, as Kyle and Uljakën entered, but her father had not, intent instead on the datapad display on his lap.

"Mr. Truman," Hanna Uljakën said just as they reached the foot of the stairs. "May I present Mr. Kyle Teller?"

Truman set the display aside and stood up. He was a powerfully built man with thinning dark blond hair and sharp blue eyes. "Pleased to meet you, Mr. Teller," he said, walking toward Kyle with outstretched hand. "My brother-in-law recommends you highly."

Kyle knew he should respond. Not doing so was a grave breach of etiquette, but he found his attention distracted by what hung on the wall opposite the windows. He stopped, in fact, and stared.

Truman only smiled, undoubtedly accustomed to such a reaction. "Stunning, isn't it? But it's best viewed from the middle of the room. From there you can see the dots very clearly."

Kyle moved to that spot, still gazing in wonderment. "Wasn't this lost in the looting of the Art Institute after the IBM Building went down?"

"Liberation, Mr. Teller," said Elaine Truman, "not looting. When the IBM tower fell and the city government foolishly decided it couldn't protect the museums any longer, the insurance companies declared the collections too great a risk and revoked their policies. It was either allow marauding hooligans to walk off with this country's greatest art treasures or move them to safer locations."

Kyle reluctantly looked away from the enormous painting. "My apologies, Mr. Truman," he said. "Seeing this caught me utterly by surprise."

"That's all right. As I said, my brother-in-law spoke very highly of you."

"I was glad to be of help to him, though I must say his security people had already made a good deal of progress in finding your niece by the time I stepped in."

Truman started to reply, but was cut off by his daughter. "And Anna-Marie thanks you for all you did, Mr. Teller." Her tone dripped sarcasm. "I'm sure she sends her love."

He turned his head slightly toward her. "I'm glad it turned out well for everyone involved."

Truman laughed, and Kyle was surprised at the family's overall demeanor. He'd expected something more forbidding. "This, of course, is my charming daughter Melissa," Truman told him. "She's in from Europe for a week or two."

Kyle inclined his head in acknowledgment. "My pleasure." The girl gave him a squinty smile.

"And this," Truman said, extending his hand toward his wife, who rose gracefully to take it, "is my wife Elaine."

Kyle bowed slightly. "Your playing is excellent. It makes me regret not having continued with my own piano training."

Elaine Truman smiled graciously. "From what they tell me, you have your own art to be proud of."

Interesting turn of phrase, Kyle thought. "I think it's probably more a craft than an art, Mrs. Truman."

Daniel Truman placed his hand on Kyle's shoulder. "And that's exactly why you're here, Mr. Teller," he said, guiding Kyle toward the sofas in the center of the room. Truman motioned him to the spot next to his daughter, while he and his wife settled themselves opposite.

Kyle sat down and straightened his jacket, acutely aware that he'd overdressed for the obviously casual Trumans. He pulled his Sony datacorder from a pocket and placed it on the arm of the couch. The flashing green light told him it was recording. Kyle wanted to get straight to business. "The information you sent indicated that you need help in a matter involving your son Mitchell."

Truman nodded, picking up what looked like a tumbler full of real scotch from the small table next to his seat. He swirled the ice and liquid as he spoke. 'Yes ... Mitchell."

"Our son has, to put it very simply, run off," said Elaine Truman.

"Alone or with someone?"

Truman looked up again. "With someone ... A girl named Linda Hayward, I believe."

Kyle nodded. "A romantic interest?"

"So it seems."

"He met her at some club," his wife added. "About three months ago."

"I take it you are opposed to this relationship?"

Husband and wife replied with their eyes and facial expressions, but Melissa laughed sharply. Kyle turned toward her. "And I take it you are not."

Melissa shrugged. "I think they're overreacting."

"Please don't make this harder, Melissa," Truman said.

Kyle turned back to him. "What makes you believe your son has run off with this woman?"

"He said he would."

"How long has he been missing?"

"Just under a week," Mrs. Truman told him.

"And when did you first realize he was missing?"

"He didn't show up for his father's birthday party three nights ago."

"And that's when you first tried to contact him?"

Elaine Truman nodded. "I called him at home. There was no answer."

"And you sent someone to his apartment the next morning?"

She blinked, and Kyle saw a smile cross Truman's lips. "Yes ... but he wasn't there. There were apparently a number of e-mail messages waiting for him on his system too."

Kyle turned back to Daniel Truman. "I was first contacted yesterday morning by a Mr. Davress."

"He's on my personal staff and handles my private business contacts."

"He asked me to fly out here to Chicago immediately, but when I checked in at my hotel, I found a message indicating that I should wait until contacted. Did something happen to make you believe your son wasn't really missing?"

Elaine Turner's eyes flew to her husband, but he kept his gaze on Kyle. "My security advisor wanted some time to check you out."

"Of course." Kyle knew it must have squashed some toes at Knight Errant when they found out the senior Truman had gone outside their organization for assistance. Which brought up another question. "Was anyone from Knight Errant assigned to watch or protect your son?"

"No."

"Then you believe he was in no danger?"

"Danger?" asked Mrs. Truman, her face showing alarm.

"I'm concerned about the safety of all my children, Mr. Teller," Truman said firmly, his eyes darting toward Melissa. "Mitchell, however, didn't want protection. Only my daughter Madelaine has constant protection."

"The producers have guards around when I'm working," said Melissa, a hint of annoyance in her voice. "I don't need an army following me around."

"Mitchell expressed similar sentiments," said Truman.

"Do you have any reason to believe he was in danger?"

"No."

"Have there been any threats to you recently that your security people have taken particularly seriously?"

"No," Truman said. "At least none I've heard about."

Kyle nodded. "Then you have no reason to believe your son's disappearance is connected to anything beyond this woman, Linda Hayward?"

"No."

"You said that he'd told you he was going to run away with her?"

"We didn't like her, quite frankly, and he knew it," said Mrs. Truman. "He indicated that he'd disassociate himself from us in order to be with her."

"Can you think of any event or argument that might have precipitated his running off with her?"

Mr. and Mrs. Truman both shook their heads. Kyle turned toward Melissa, who said, "Nothing I know of."

"Did he speak to you about her?"

"Only once, a month ago. We talked by telecom," Melissa told him. "She was there with him."

Kyle turned back to the Trumans. "This may seem like an odd question, but can you tell me why you called me in?"

Both of them seemed surprised. Mrs. Truman spoke up quickly. "To find our son, of course."

"I understand you want him found. But why me? Why not simply use the more conventional resources of Knight Errant? Why the need for a magician? Or why not use Knight Errant's magical assets?"

Elaine Truman seemed confused, but her husband stiffened a little. "I'm not sure I understand the point of your question, Mr. Teller, but I'll answer it: We want to find our son. Quickly.

"As I understand it, you used your magic to find my niece

directly rather than following the slow steps involved in a normal investigation. I want that speed."

"Very well," Kyle said. "I simply wanted to know if you had some reason to believe magic was already involved." He paused and then said, "Can you give me any information on Linda Hayward?"

Truman shook his head. "We don't know anything. Only her name."

Kyle looked at Mrs. Truman. "There was nothing in his apartment? No address or phone number?"

Her face flushed slightly. "No."

Interesting, he thought. When he glanced over at Melissa, she just shrugged. "All I know is that he met her in a club."

"Do you know which one?"

"The Kaleidoscope, near Fullerton and Halsted."

"In the Noose."

"Yeah. Interesting place. If you're into jet core rock."

Kyle turned back to the older Trumans. "Finding Mitchell shouldn't be a problem, but I'll need access to his apartment. Did he provide a ritual sample to Knight Errant?"

Truman frowned. "Ritual sample?"

"A blood or tissue sample gathered using a special magic ritual. The sample can be used in a ritual, like the one I'll do, to find the subject."

Truman looked over to Hanna Uljakën, who was standing silently near the window. "Hanna, do you know . . ."

"I'm sorry Mr. Truman, but it's my understanding that he refused."

"Damn," said Truman. 'That boy's too stubborn."

"Mrs. Truman looked concerned. "Will this be a problem?"

Kyle shook his head. "Shouldn't be, but it will take more time."

He stood and smoothed down the sides of his suit jacket. The others also stood up. "If you can get me into his apartment, I'd like to perform the ritual as soon as possible."

Mr. Truman nodded. "Of course. Hanna will take you right away."

4

There was a royal blue and black Mitsubishi Nightsky waiting for him and Hanna Uljakën when they came out front. Behind the limousine was a second car, this one a rather mundane-looking ToyotaCorp Traveller. Leaning against it was a big, bulky ork in a dark suit and long coat. Kyle couldn't see past the limo's tinted windows, but he was sure at least one other person was inside. As he and Hanna Uljakën approached, the ork stepped forward.

"Mr. Facile," she said. "I take it you're to be our escort?"

The ork nodded and turned toward Kyle. "Mr. Teller?" he said. "I'm Lieutenant William Facile."

"Knight Errant, I take it," said Kyle.

"Yes, sir. Mr. Truman thought it would be a good idea if we tagged along."

Kyle preferred to conduct his business without their presence, but Truman was paying him enough, just, to ignore the inconvenience. He decided to play it frosty. "Yes, a good idea. Have you and your partner worked with magic before?"

"To a limited extent, sir. We've worked in operations with magical assets attached."

"But you've never directly interfaced with a practitioner?"

"No, sir," said Facile. "But I wouldn't expect it to be a problem."

"Nor I." Kyle turned to Hanna Uljakën. "Let's get going," he said.

Mitchell Truman lived in a high-rise condominium on the lake, almost directly east of Truman Tower. On the short ride over, Kyle watched the sun struggling to penetrate the clouds. It looked like Chicago's famous weather was as changeable as ever.

Both cars of the little convoy drove directly into the underground garage, where Hanna Uljakën's palm print got the four of them access to the private elevator and then to the Mitch Truman's fortieth-floor apartment.

Kyle was mildly surprised to see that the place was furnished in modern oriental, sparse and efficient. There were six rooms: master and guest bedrooms, living room, dining room, kitchen, and a spare room that the Truman boy had turned into an exercise room. The view of the lake was stunning, the window canted slightly north to show the shoreline. Again, Kyle could see the greenery and brick of Elemental Hall off a short distance along the lake.

"How long has Mitchell lived here?" Kyle asked Uljakën.

"Just over a year. The condo was a gift from his father on Mitch's sixteenth birthday."

"Rather young for his own crash, don't you think?"

Uljakën tilted her head and smiled cooly. "I suspect Mr. Truman would be a better judge of that than I."

"But he was surprised Mitch ran off."

"I'm not privy to Mr. Truman's emotions, Mr. Teller. You'd have to ask him."

Kyle sighed. He was standing in the slightly raised dining area looking out over the lake, but turned back to face her. "I'm not asking you what Mr. Truman *did* think or feel, I'm asking what *you* think was going through his mind."

"I don't believe I'm qualified to make those kinds of judgments, Mr. Teller."

"Of course you are—you're his personal assistant," Kyle insisted, trying to catch her eyes. "You're expected to make such judgments all the time. And if Daniel Truman wasn't totally pleased with your ability to read him he'd probably have found someone else long ago."

She seemed to be formulating a reply, but Kyle didn't give her an opening. "Mr. Truman also told you to assist me in any way you can. Answering my questions with your best professional opinion is one of the best ways to do that."

Uljakën nodded, and he could feel the shift in her resolve. "You're right, of course." She glanced over at the two Knight Errant guards. "If you'll excuse us?"

Facile looked uncomfortable, and the second man, shorter and even darker-skinned, glanced at him for instructions.

"Nothing's going to happen for a few hours, Lieutenant," Kyle told him. "It will take me that long to prepare my magics. You can wait in the hall."

Facile's eyes narrowed, but he gestured to the other officer to follow him out the door. As the two security men were leaving the room, Kyle quickly shifted to astral perception to view their auras. Both had strong auras that almost sparked in some spots and darkened to virtually nothing in others. As the door closed behind them, he slowly scanned the room. It was dull, the only strong sources of mana being himself, Hanna Uljakën and her earring, and some leafy tropical plants. His senses returned to normal.

"You did that in the lobby of the Tower too," she said. "Are you looking at things magically?"

Smart girl, Kyle thought. More so because he hadn't caught her noticing what he'd been doing.

"Yes, I am," he said. "Magicians have the ability to perceive the energy wavelength that magical and living items emanate. You can learn a lot from that."

She nodded. "And the two guards?"

"Both human and unAwakened. No sign of magical talents, though it's always conceivable a magician could mask his aura. In the case of these two, I seriously doubt it. All that cyberware would keep them from being able to use magic."

"Could you tell what kind?"

Kyle shook his head. "Not really, except for certain guesses based on the location and appearance of deformities in the aura. I'd say Facile and his man are fairly standard muscle-boys: enhanced reflexes and maybe some neuromuscular augmentation and combat cyberware."

"You come pretty close on Facile," Uljakën said appreciatively. "I've seen his file. He's got a Richmond series-twelve nueromuscular accelerator, a Fuchi MPX-R headware comp and data-access package, Mitsuhama-Zeis ocular light-amplification systems, and a recent upgrade to level two for his Ares smartlink combat system."

"Quite a package," Kyle said, "for a lieutenant."

"My sentiments exactly," she agreed. "Facile is part of the team that's been attached to Truman ever since Knight Errant bought out Winter Security's contract with Truman Technologies about three months ago."

"That's unusual."

"Very. It seems Knight Errant has decided to magnify its profile here in Chicago. The city's law enforcement contract with Eagle Security comes up for renewal in eighteen months . . ."

"And KE would love to pick up that juicy contract, so they're jacking up their local presence and commitment."

"Precisely," she said.

"Interesting. And Mr. Truman was agreeable to having KE buy out Winter's contract with Truman Technologies? Couldn't he have just voided the contract?"

"Our contract with Winter was nontransferable. But I think Mr. Truman was flattered."

Kyle paused a moment before changing the subject. Now that Hanna Uljakën seemed more willing to talk about her employer, he was leery of any big questions that might make her clam up again. But he had no choice. "How would you characterize Mr. Truman's relationship with his son?" he asked. "Good, bad, indifferent . . ."

Hanna Uljakën blinked and glanced away before answering. "I'd say that things have been pretty dismal lately."

"Mitchell bucked under the authority and demands of his father?" It was a reaction Kyle understood all too well.

"Yes, but it goes deeper than that," she said quietly. "Mitchell is bisexual, and it's been a strain on his relationship with his father ever since Mr. Truman found out."

"How long has that been?"

"Two years. The truth came out after an unfortunate incident in London."

"Then why is Truman so opposed to his son's involvement with this Linda Hayward?"

"She's supposedly older than I am."

Kyle grinned. "Damned if you don't and damned if you do."

She grinned back. "Looks that way, doesn't it?"

Kyle took off his suit jacket and tossed in on the sofa. "Well, now that we're here, we'd better get this started."

Hanna Uljakën showed some surprise at the sight of the Ceska light pistol tucked into the holster under his left shoulder. He grinned again and shrugged as he unslung the holster and tossed it next to the jacket. "So you have no reason to believe or suspect that Mitch Truman has done anything other than run off with this woman?"

"No, I don't."

"And there've been no ransom demands or mysterious contacts with the Truman family that you know of since Mitchell was last seen?"

"No."

"Then my first step is to try and locate him. Did Mr. Truman tell you anything about the techniques I'll be using or how I tracked down his niece?"

"No, but I did read the *Omni* and *Popular Mysticism* articles on the subject."

Kyle laughed. "Well, don't be surprised if reality is a tad more boring than what the press makes out."

"But you *were* with the FBI section described in the *Omni* article, weren't you?"

"If you know enough to ask the question, you already know the answer."

Uljakën smiled slightly. "KE's background check was fairly exhaustive."

Kyle looked at her thoughtfully for a moment. "Have you ever seen ritual magic performed up close, Ms. Uljakën?"

She shook her head. "No, I haven't."

"Then I'd like you to assume, unless I tell you otherwise, that everything that happens is intended and expected."

"All right."

Kyle turned and looked up slightly, shifting the focus of his thoughts. "Come to me," he said softly to the air . . .

In that instant a swirl of gold light appeared next to Kyle, and Hanna Uljakën jumped visibly. The light quickly coalesced into the figure of an Amerindian man of just past middle age. He wore black denim pants and a wide tan leather belt with a bold silver and turquoise buckle. Over his clean white cotton shirt was a tattered blue denim jacket with the sleeves torn off. Two silver bracelets hung from his right wrist, and a wide band of brown leather circled the left. His hair, its glossy black touched with silver, was bound into a single, unbraided pony tail that hung down from under the wide brim of his black hat. Tied around the hat was a band of cloth woven in red, white, and black. The man's appearance was striking, even handsome, but his eyes were translucent and tinged with gold. Somewhat incongruously, he was also wearing black canvas sneakers.

Kyle turned toward her. "Hanna Uljakën, this is Seeks-the-Moon. Moon, this is Ms. Hanna Uljakën."

"I know," the spirit said, bowing gracefully, "and I am charmed."

"Seeks-the-Moon is my *sociare spiritus*—my ally spirit."

The spirit looked askance. "I see your Latin is still quite lacking."

Kyle ignored him. "He will be assisting me in the ritual."

Uljakën nodded, but had maneuvered herself slightly away from Seeks-the-Moon. "Will you need me to do anything?" she asked.

"No, but I'd like you present to verify any information that develops."

She pointed to a chair in the far corner. "Can I sit over there?"

Kyle nodded, then turned to his ally spirit, who was standing with arms crossed over his chest.

"Interesting earring," the spirit said quietly in Sioux, and Kyle could see Hanna Uljakën react, though she kept on walking. He scowled at the spirit. "Yes, but it's not a concern," he told Seeks-the-Moon in English.

The spirit shrugged slightly in deference. "As you wish." Just past the spirit Kyle could see that Uljakën had settled into her chair and was studying them intently. "How are the boys?" Kyle asked Moon.

"Complaining as usual."

"That's good. It's when they start saying nice things about me that I'll be worried." He paused and looked over the room. "This will be a simple direct-progression ritual. I need to locate and tag a missing boy, Mitchell Truman."

"Should be simple enough," Moon said matter-of-factly.

"I'll be using a Kellehoff circle as the basis."

The spirit shrugged. "You say that as though my opinion on the matter would carry any weight."

Kyle chuckled. "I just thought you'd like to know."

"Very thoughtful."

Kyle reached for his jacket and pointed at the small, round black lacquer table in the center of the room. "Would you move that and the rug under it for me? That's where I want to build the circle."

The spirit rolled his eyes skyward for a moment, then complied. "Moving furniture is, of course, the eternal aspiration of all ethereal beings."

"Good. I knew you wouldn't mind," Kyle said as he pulled two flat leather cases out of his jacket's special pockets.

Hanna Uljakën laughed. "Are they all like this?" she asked.

Kyle smiled, and the spirit looked up from where he was guiding the table across the floor with the motion of his finger. "No," Seeks-the-Moon said. "Some of us actually have complete, fulfilling existences, complete with rewards and respect."

"No, they're not all this way," Kyle interjected, ignoring Moon's sarcasm. "In creating Seeks-the-Moon I used the Rigetti formula. The only problem is that Rigetti was a Jungian, a fact I didn't attach quite enough importance to at the time."

"I don't understand."

"Seeks-the-Moon is, in a sense, or in essence, a reflection of my 'shadow', the repressed and often nefarious aspect of my personality."

The spirit winked. "Indeed."

"So it's part of his nature to be at odds with my conscious

desires, which generally makes him a pain in the butt." But Kyle smiled almost benevolently as he watched his ally rolling up the small rug.

Uljakën thought about that for a bit. "And yet, If he is a direct, or even symbolic connection to your subconscious, the fact that Seeks-the-Moon is expressive could be extremely useful."

Both the spirit and the mage stared at her. "Yes," Kyle said.

"Except that he usually finds me embarrassing and doesn't let me out much in public," the spirit said as he resumed his work of clearing away the rug.

"We can talk more about it later if you're interested," Kyle said.

"I am."

"Good. I can also tell you something of what I am doing here, though I can't afford to go into much detail because it would distract me."

Kyle unzipped the two leather cases. Both were slightly larger than his hand and each contained a number of small, flat gold objects, some thin gold thread wrapped around a piece of copper, a small sheaf of parchment paper, and a pen.

"A magical spell," Kyle told her, "is cast by harmonizing, adapting, shaping, and constructing patterns of magical energy—mana—according to a specific formula."

Seeks-the-Moon squatted down and blew away the faint border of dust that lay around the empty space where the rug had been.

"Each formula is finite in its potential, though segments in the formula are left open for elaboration," Kyle explained as he carefully removed the gold items from the cases. "If I were to create a spell with 'X' potential, its formula would have 'X' complexity. If I were to increase the spell's potential to, say, twice 'X', the formula could very easily, and very quickly, reach a complexity of four or eight times 'X'."

Hanna Uljakën nodded understanding. "Potential and complexity are geometrically related."

"That's right." Kyle gathered up the gold objects and walked into the center of the room. "But you must remember that I'm talking generally and abstractly.

"The complexity of the formula is what ultimately determines the difficulty of casting the spell, that and how much raw energy must be channeled in the casting. So, instead of trying to cast a spell with a four-times potential but a sixteen-times complexity, and probably failing and getting hurt in the process, we cast the normal-potential spell but use a ritual to amplify and expand those parts of the formula left open for elaboration. The casting takes significantly longer, but the complexity is minimized, the potential increased significantly, and the danger limited."

"Makes sense," Uljakën said.

"That," said Seeks-the-Moon, "is the grossest oversimplification you are every likely to hear, short of 'I snap my fingers and it goes "poof." ' "

"Well, it will do just fine," she told him.

"Really?" Seeks-the-Moon turned toward Kyle and raised an eyebrow archly.

Kyle ignored him. "I'm going to use a simple detection spell to find Mitchell. Normally the spell's range is so limited that if he wasn't, say, on this floor of his building, the spell wouldn't find him. But the ritual will let me cast the spell over a wider area.

"But I must cast the spell in a metaphysically 'balanced' environment, which these items are going to let me create. I'm going to do this silently, if you don't mind. Building the circle takes time and concentration."

"I, however, would be more than pleased to keep you amused," Seeks-the-Moon told Uljakën, smiling broadly.

She started to reply, but Kyle spoke first. "You must both be silent for this. I'd suggest you go off to another room to chat, but I'd like you to stay close to Seeks-the-Moon for the attunement.

"Truthfully," Kyle added, "I don't trust him."

"That's an interesting bit of self-observation, Mr. Teller," Uljakën said, and the spirit laughed loudly. "I'll have to keep it in mind."

Kyle shrugged and smiled sheepishly. "Now, if you'll excuse me, I have a space to initialize." And with that he knelt and began placing the gold items upright at the edges of a circle he was slowly building around himself.

5

"Each stand sits on either a cardinal or subordinate point," Kyle said while examining the completed circle from the outside. "Those are metaphysical points of correspondence that different traditions and theologies have assigned definitions and importance. I studied hermetics primarily at Columbia, which was also about as secular as you could get. Nonetheless, association of the cardinal points to something greater definitely allows a certain degree of conceptual and procedural centering."

"A common starting point, and so on?" Uljakën said.

"Exactly." Kyle pointed at each of the primary upright stands in turn as he spoke. "For example, north corresponds with the element of earth in many Western traditions, east with the element of air, south with fire, and west with water. There are theological correspondences as well, but I don't want to get into that."

"Coward," said Seeks-the-Moon.

Kyle ignored the jibe. "When I begin, I'll stand at the center, which corresponds to spirit. Some argue that that's the fifth element. I'm not so sure. I'll begin the ritual facing north since we're looking for a physical body."

Uljakën looked around at the eight upright stands marking a rough circle in the center of the room. "Doesn't the circle have to be closed?"

Kyle nodded. "It will be, but only once I'm inside. Before that I need something of Mitch's to focus on, something that will pick up his resonance for use in both the spell and the ritual."

"That's what the ritual sample you talked about earlier would have been for."

"Yes. Any random samples around here—hair, body fluids, and such—would be long 'dead' by now, so I'll have to go with something symbolic or associative of Mitch instead. Can you think of anything here that might be particularly important to the boy?"

Hanna Uljakën's eyes widened slightly as she cast her gaze around the room. "Um ... I'm not sure. Maybe we should call the Trumans."

Kyle laughed. "Considering the state of their relationship with him, I'm not sure they could tell us any better than we could guess."

"But I'm not so sure we actually could guess. Mitch always seemed very cold and distant to me."

"Even with your earring?" asked Seeks-the-Moon, now seated casually on the couch. He smiled innocently when both looked sharply over at him.

"Yes, even with that," Uljakën said tersely, but Kyle thought she had paled slightly at Moon's comment.

He began walking toward the bedroom. "Well, then, we look for something he had frequent contact with."

The bedroom, unlike the rest of the apartment, was a shambles.

"I was going to ask if anyone had cleaned in here since the boy disappeared, but I think I have my answer," Kyle said.

"The cleaning service only comes when they have his permission."

Kyle stepped carefully toward a pile of clothing. "And since no one could get hold of him, they didn't." He pushed through the garments with his foot, using the toe of his boot to lift out a black T-shirt. The cracked holographic logo of the band L'Infâme was just barely legible. "The Infamous?" said Kyle.

Ms Uljakën shrugged. "I don't know the group either." Her eyes, though, widened suddenly as she pointed at it. "He used to wear that all the time! I think he said it was autographed. He was very proud of it."

Kyle smiled in satisfaction. "Then I suspect this will do quite well." He flipped the shirt up off his foot and caught it. "Frag," he said, "I've had less."

Back in the living room, he surveyed the casting circle with his astral senses. Dormant lines of force were visible around the edge of the area, connecting each of the stands. He checked each closer, making sure the links and locks of energy were correctly prepared. They seemed to be.

"All right," he said. "Let's do it."

"Should I call the two guards in?" asked Uljakën.

Seeks-the-Moon snorted and Kyle shook his head. "No, they won't be able to handle the kind of problems we might have in here. Seeks-the-Moon will take care of anything unexpected that might occur."

The spirit nodded stoically, then tipped his hat as Kyle stepped within the area of the circle. Draped over his left arm was the black T-shirt and held in the same hand was a small piece of parchment that he'd taken from his case and on which he had written the words "Mitchell Gregory Truman". Taking his place in the center of the circle, he bowed his head and closed his eyes. Minutes passed as he stood there silent and still.

"Isn't he awfully quiet?" Uljakën whispered to Moon. "I thought magicians had to chant when casting spells."

"Some do." Seeks-the-Moon was watching Kyle carefully. "Shaman or mage, it makes no difference. They seem to need the universe to hear them. I think he's quiet because the magic of his people isn't."

"I'd have never guessed he was Amerindian if I hadn't read the Knight Errant report."

The spirit snorted. "You obviously haven't taken a good look at his nose."

Uljakën started to laugh, but stifled it quickly when she saw that Kyle had lifted his head and was slowly stretching out his right hand toward the east coordinate. "Now we must be quiet," the spirit said as Kyle suddenly turned his hand palm up and opened his eyes.

An argent flame appeared on the east stand, turning gold as it jumped to the coordinate stand next to it going clock-

wise, and then finally brilliant scarlet as it jumped to the
south stand. It jumped again to the next coordinate, changing
to violet and then bright sapphire when it reached the western stand. Kyle was turning to face north as the flame leaped
again, became deep emerald, and then coppery as it reached
the north. Finally, a white flame flickered to life at the northeast coordinate.

Uljakën looked wide-eyed at all the flaming stands. She
could see no wick nor any other source for the flame.

Seeks-the-Moon leaned slightly closer to her. "It's
magic," he said in a stage whisper.

"This is amazing."

"Wait." The spirit stretched out his hand toward the big
windows overlooking the lake. He gestured, and the heavy
vertical blinds moved across and rotated, blocking the light.
The room dimmed, and in that near dark it was possible to
make out a faint aura of energy, a globe it seemed, surrounding the circle area.

"The ward," said Seeks-the-Moon. "It keeps bad things
out and good things in."

"How long will this take?"

Seeks-the-Moon shrugged. "At least two hours. I hope
you brought something to read."

Inside the circle, the weave of the forces at play radiated
outward from Kyle into astral space like wheels within
wheels of colors the same as the flames marking the circle.
Each rotated in a different direction, at a different speed; and
was positioned at different angles from the rest.

Kyle, though, was at the mystical and physical center, attempting to link the energies of the ritual to those of Mitchell Gregory Truman, wherever he might be. Serving as the
focus of the synchronization was the boy's shirt, which still
held a metaphysical impression of him burned into it from
prolonged contact.

Kyle reached out mystically and changed the rotation of
one of the wheels, the copper one. To his astral senses it began to emit a low, quiet tone whose resonance soon matched
the shirt. Kyle smiled. Now it was only a matter of time. He

changed the position of the silver circle until it matched the
copper one, which pulsed and began to rotate on its axis
around Kyle. Then Kyle touched the shirt hanging from his
arm with his astral senses and completed the last link between it and the copper ring. The wheel flashed and a
ghostly image of it shot outward beyond the circle in all directions. A copper wheel still rotated around him, but Kyle
knew that an aspect of it, being in synchrony with Mitch
Truman, was being drawn to the boy's physical body. And
when it arrived, Kyle would be able to cast the detection
spell and learn the boy's location. The search could take a
while if Mitchell wasn't in the city. Meanwhile it would take
all of Kyle's concentration to keep the wheels spinning.

Outside the circle, Hanna Uljakën and Seeks-the-Moon
watched carefully. Physically, Kyle had moved little, but
Moon was quietly narrating each step of the ritual as it pro-
gressed.

"The Sending involves sychronizing the spell being cast
with the target, much in the same way that the Linking synchronized the ritual's energy with the target."

"But if he's been found, why is the spell necessary?" she
asked.

"The energies are linked, but the magician has no way of
knowing where they lead. He is forcing a connection that
should not be. It is not until the Sending that the flow of energy is sufficient to be traceable, in either direction."

"So you could trace a Sending back to its origin?"

The spirit smiled. "That's why I'm here."

"I see."

"But we're not at that stage—yet." The spirit seemed to
tense suddenly. "Something is wrong."

"Are we in danger?"

"No, it's too early in the ritual for *that* . . ."

Inside, Kyle felt the change in the energy rhythms. The copper wheel was vibrating. Soon its vibration would spread to
the other wheels and unravel the entire ritual. He was just
reaching out mystically to strengthen it when, with a loud

bell tone, it shattered. The others quickly followed suit in a blinding cascade of color and sound. Kyle braced for the psychic backlash, but it was only minimal when it came, easily countered by his training. He restored his physical senses as half the paper with Mitchell Truman's name on it drifted slowly to the floor, smoking. The name had been divided cleanly in two.

"What happened?" asked Seeks-the-Moon, stepping up to the edge of the still-active circle. Kyle held up his hand as he scanned the last vestiges of the ritual, searching for more clues to the reasons for its dissolution.

"The paper is torn," Uljakën said. "Does that mean he's dead?"

"No," Kyle said, letting the shirt drop to his feet. "He's not dead."

"Then what?" asked Seeks-the-Moon.

"The boy is within a protective ward."

The spirit's eyes widened slightly and a mischievous smile came to his lips. "Really?"

"Inside a what?" Uljakën asked.

"A ward or circle of some kind," said Kyle. "Maybe much like this one."

"And that means?"

Kyle gestured and all the flames vanished, plunging the room into near darkness. "That means that either Mitchell has very powerful friends"—a ball of silver rose from his hand and filled the room with light—"or very dangerous enemies."

6

"I'm using the term ward generically," Kyle explained. The Truman family, Hanna Uljakën, William Facile of Knight Errant, and two other corporate assistants were all gathered back at Daniel Truman's condo. "It could be any kind of mystical barrier—a hermetic circle, medicine lodge, barrier spell, or ward of some kind."

"There's no way to tell?" asked Lieutenant Facile.

Kyle shook his head. "No. If I'd been able to lock the first part of the ritual onto him, then I could have followed the magic astrally to his location. But the ward is blocking the ritual."

Facile nodded and turned to the senior Truman. "Sir, Knight Errant can assemble a larger ritual team using multiple mages. That should be enough to overcome this kind of resistance." He glanced over at Kyle. "More capable than one man at least."

Truman looked ready to speak, but Kyle had already cut in. "Maybe so, but it would also alert whoever set up the ward that trouble was coming. By doing it alone, I reduced the risk of tipping off whoever's got Mitchell that someone is using magic to find him. They should still think he's safe."

"Doesn't all this assume Mitchell wants to be found?" put in Melissa Truman, looking as bored as ever.

Facile's tone was impatient. "We have to assume that."

"It's true there hasn't been any contact with the family, let alone a ransom note," Kyle said, "but I agree with the lieutenant, Ms. Truman. Unfortunately, we have to assume the worst. Because this involves a family as important as yours, its very likely magic is being used in some negative manner."

"Then why don't we just take Lieutenant Facile's suggestion and find the boy?" asked Truman. Kyle sensed his opinion shifting toward immediate action.

Kyle stood up from the couch where he'd been sitting. "In this case, Mr. Truman, ritual sorcery is a lot like a commando raid. By initiating the ritual we're beginning a magical assault against your son and those who may be holding him. It can get very dangerous, very quickly."

"I assure you, Mr. Teller, that Knight Errant has the best combat mages in the business," said Facile, irritation edging his voice. "There's little chance that something will go wrong."

"I don't buy that," said Kyle. "We have no intelligence on what we're up against. If we aren't dealing with anything more than some wiz-kid mage gang, then I'd agree there's probably nothing to worry about." He paused for effect. "But what if, for some reason, we're facing, say, Aztechnology magicians . . ."

"Ridiculous," cut in Facile, but Kyle could see that invoking the name of the corp which politically and mystically ruled what had once been Mexico and parts of Central America had provoked the desired response.

Elaine Truman's face was ashen. "You don't think . . ."

"No, I don't," said Kyle. "The point is that we simply don't know who might be on the other end. So, just as you wouldn't stage a commando raid against some place you'd never seen before, with no clear idea of what forces were opposing you, to initiate a high-powered Sending now is foolish."

"Then your solution is. . .?" asked Mr. Truman.

"I suggest that we investigate conventionally for a few more days. Gain as much information as we can before deciding to take any direct actions." Kyle deliberately looked toward the Knight Errant lieutenant, who returned his gaze with one of challenge. "If we can't uncover anything more by then, initiating a powerful ritual may be the only choice."

Truman looked over at his wife. "What do you think, Elaine?"

She looked down at her hands, which were knotted together in her lap. Her voice was barely audible. "If anything were to happen . . ."

Truman took one of his wife's hands in his own. "All right, Mr. Teller, you have three days to investigate. If you don't turn up enough by then, we go with Lieutenant Facile's suggestion of bringing in Knight Errant full-power."

"Excuse me, sir, but I would suggest we begin that right now," Kyle told him.

"Oh?" Truman looked completely baffled.

"I don't think you can risk the possibility that something very dangerous is going on. Knight Errant should increase its personnel and site-based security on the family." Kyle looked pointedly at Melissa. "All members of the family." She flushed and looked away.

Truman nodded. "You can arrange that?" he asked Facile.

"I can have increased security here within the hour," the lieutenant said smartly.

"Excellent."

"I'd also like to add some elements of my own, if you don't mind," Kyle said.

Truman must have noticed Facile's scowl, but he shook his head. "Not at all."

Without further ado Kyle cleared his mind and let it fill with the sound and sensation of rushing air. He reached out with his thoughts, then called out both astrally and physically, "Charlotte!"

The air in the room cooled slightly and a breeze began. All present began to look around, and Melissa Truman stood up quickly. Kyle place his hand on her shoulder. "It's all right."

The breeze seemed to come to the center of the room, where it hung swirling, an almost transparent vortex of air about the size of an average-sized dog. *"Yes?"* it said in a sharp, almost feminine voice.

"This is an air elemental," explained Kyle. "It's mine. I created it. I command it."

The vortex seemed to shift slightly, but spoke no more.

"It's name is Charlotte," he said, and Mrs. Truman, though obviously frightened by the experience, managed a laugh. "I'm going to leave her here to protect this place."

He focused his attention on the air spirit. He spoke its name and the spirit stilled. "The area of your concern are these two floors of this building, and the objects of your concern are these people." Kyle moved around the room and placed his hand on each of the Trumans in turn, naming him or her. He also indicated Lieutenant Facile, who was not amused, and Hanna Uljakën, who seemed distressed but nodded at Charlotte. Without moving, the spirit seemed to focus its attention on each one. "No one else is allowed on this floor unless accompanied by one of these people or one of them has given his permission.

"And you will deny entry to all spirits and all magic except mine," Kyle said. "You will continue with this task until I, and only I, command you otherwise."

"I understand," Charlotte said.

Kyle gestured with a quick pattern of calling, and a small ball of ethereal "fuzz" appeared above his hand. It hung there, rippling with white and dark blue energy for a moment before two huge silver and black eyes opened in it. The onlookers gasped as the fuzzball gazed quickly around the room. "This is Delta, one of my watcher spirits," Kyle said. The eyes blinked.

"Don't bother trying to communicate with him," Kyle told them. "He's barely smart enough to hold himself together. Watcher spirits do, however, make good messengers."

As Kyle again turned his attention to the elemental, the watcher spirit suddenly seemed confused, as though trying to remember its own name. The contempt flowing from the air elemental toward it was palpable.

"Charlotte, if this place or these people are endangered, you will send Delta to find and alert me," Kyle commanded.

"I will," said the elemental. *"But do not hold me responsible when that one fails."*

"He will not fail." Delta, the watcher, bounced up and down in place. Melissa laughed.

"Charlotte, you will now begin you duties."

The elemental seemed to nod, then faded from view. The air in the room stilled. The watcher spirit glanced around and then disappeared as well. Kyle sighed.

Facile looked annoyed, but it was a few moments before anyone spoke.

"I thought you were leaving it to guard . . ." Truman began.

"I am. The spirit is present in astral space. To manifest in the physical world is uncomfortable for it, so Charlotte will only do so when necessary. Rest assured that she is completely capable, if not more so, when in astral space."

"But isn't that somewhere else?" asked Mrs. Truman.

"Astral space? No. It's all around you—you just can't see it. Actually, if the light was bright enough, you might be able to see a slight area of 'distortion' indicating where Charlotte is."

"Oh," she said.

"If it's easier, think of her as being invisible," Kyle said kindly.

Mrs. Truman tried to smile. "I'll try."

Kyle smiled back. "Suffice it to say, Charlotte's here and if you need her you have only to speak her name." Kyle walked toward the windows, whose view of the darkening sky was now smeared by a light rain. He watched it for a few moments, then turned back to the others.

"Lieutenant, could you get Knight Errant's extra security in motion?" Kyle's tone was more an order than a request. Seeming startled by the command, Facile looked over at Truman, who nodded.

"All right," the lieutenant said grudgingly.

"Good," Kyle said, then asked Truman, "Is Ms. Uljakën still available to assist me?"

Truman nodded once more.

"Good," Kyle repeated. "Now, as a first step, I'd like to talk to Melissa in private." Kyle addressed her directly: "If you don't mind."

He could tell it was the very last thing she wanted, but after a sharp glance from her father, the girl said, "No, of course not. Anything I can do."

Melissa Truman and Kyle moved out onto one of the balconies, where a retractable, hardened plastiglass bubble protected them from the rain. "You think I know something about where Mitch is, but I don't," she said angrily.

Kyle motioned her to one of the Amazonia-style chairs and sat down in the one opposite. It creaked ominously under his merely average weight. "I know very little. That's why I want to talk to you."

"I *told* you. I really don't know anything."

"You seem to know more than your parents about Linda Hayward."

She shrugged. "Not really."

"I'll bet everything they do know they learned from you."

Melissa looked away. "They don't pay much attention to us."

"Is that why Mitch ran off?"

She sighed. "Partially."

"So he told you he was planning to."

"No," she said, scowling. "It seems obvious, though."

"Why?"

"Dad was slinging him drek and Mom refused to meet her."

"You only saw her that once, in the background on the telecom screen."

She turned away and seemed to blush slightly. "I never said she was in the background. She and Mitch were quite friendly."

"But that was the only time you saw her?"

"No, not exactly . . ."

"Then you did see her other times? Did you meet her?"

"No, I only saw her. From a distance, at the club."

"The Kaleidoscope?"

"Yes."

"She was a regular?"

"I guess. But I'm not, so I can't really say."

"Were you there when Mitch met her?"

"No."

"Do you know how it happened."

"No."

"Has she been seen there since Mitch disappeared?"

"Sh—" Melissa stopped herself. "I don't know," she said after a pause, almost quietly.

Kyle shook his head. "Look, Melissa, were it not for the fact that magic was involved, I'd agree with you about leaving your brother alone." She seemed to cringe slightly, and Kyle suspected she was reacting to the fact that she might have blundered. "But the fact is, your brother is still a minor under your parents' protection. Add to that fact that your father is going to be paying me a lot of money to find him, and what you get is the unavoidable fact that I *will* find him."

He leaned in closer to her. "Despite what aspersions Lieutenant Facile might want to cast, I am not exactly a weak magician. The ward that protected your brother was mighty powerful. *That's* got me concerned."

"All right, all right," she said, unable to meet his gaze. "I checked around. She's been at the Kaleidoscope at least once since my parents lost contact with Mitch."

"And your brother was with her?"

Melissa winced. "Yes."

Kyle leaned back. "Thank you, Melissa. I know you don't like any of this, but I swear I'm going to try make it all come out all right."

She nodded, then hesitated as though having something to say but not sure she wanted to say it. "There's something else you should know," she said finally.

"Oh?" said Kyle.

"She's in a gang."

7

"Melissa described Linda Hayward as taller than average, maybe one hundred and eighty centimeters," said Kyle. It was late that evening, and he was stretched out on the couch in the sitting room of his hotel suite. Hanna Uljakën sat with a tray of snack foods at her side, writing notes on her datapad. Seeks-the-Moon was nearby, carefully inspecting a large bowl of fruit. "Black hair, shoulder length, bright blue eyes, pouty mouth," continued Kyle.

Uljakën looked up at the last bit of description. Kyle shrugged. "Her words, not mine. Melissa also said Hayward had a good body, and that she thought it was all hers."

"Meaning?" said Seeks-the-Moon, looking up from his investigation.

"That it wasn't cosmetic or surgical."

"Ah," said the spirit. "And here I thought we might have something kinky."

"Give it time," Kyle said. "The kicker is the gang affiliation." He sat up. "Ms. Uljakën, did the database search come up with anything on the gang name 'Desolation Angels' that Melissa gave us?"

"Nothing that our search programs could find in any of the public records. Mr. Truman has agreed to have someone from research and development look into it. Knight Errant is also investigating."

"Truman's loaning us a decker?"

She smiled. "Were he not working for us, I suppose that's what he'd be." She glanced down almost shyly, then back up at him. "You know, it's all right if you call me Hanna." She smiled.

Kyle returned the smile. "Would that be appropriate?"

"It could be."

"Should I leave?" asked Seeks-the-Moon, biting loudly into an apple as he took a seat next to Kyle.

Uljakën glared at the spirit, then turned back to Kyle. "I thought you said spirits didn't like being, what did you say, 'manifest'?"

"Some of us don't," Seeks-the-Moon said before Kyle could answer. "Unlike those poor elementals who must force themselves into an ill-fitting physical body to be manifest, *I* have an actual physical form. Courtesy of him." The spirit smiled and gestured at Kyle. "Sculpted from the primal potential, cast by the grace of will, and kept extant by the simple fact that banishing me would truly be a pain in the ass."

Kyle laughed softly. "It's true. I've let him get too powerful."

Seeks-the-Moon doffed his hat.

Hanna laughed, and just then the telecom beeped.

Kyle looked at Seeks-the-Moon, then sighed and pulled himself up from the couch. "I'll get it."

"Hate the things," said Seeks-the-Moon to Hanna. "Won't touch 'em."

Kyle sat down at the desk, swung the arm holding the flat screen out to a more comfortable viewing position, and hit the Connect key. William Facile's face appeared on the screen.

"We checked on your 'Desolation Angels'," the ork said, "but no one's got any record of it being a gang name. Not Eagle either or the Feds."

"Any other occurrences?" Kyle asked.

"Yes, an old one. Apparently it was the title of a music disk back eighty years or so. A rock and roll band named Bad Company recorded it. There was also a note that the cover image became a popular design on motorcycle jackets of that era."

"So Melissa Truman may simply have seen Hayward wearing one of these vintage jackets and assumed a gang affiliation."

Facile nodded. "That would be my guess."

"And what about the Kaleidoscope Club? Anything on that yet?"

"Not really. Just the usual drek. Every organized crime faction in town is said to own it, but it's actually controlled by a local corp called the Caleb Group. They own four clubs."

"Who owns them?"

"They're public. About eight hundred and ninety-two investors."

"Who're the principals?"

"Three people, all with four percent."

Kyle sighed. "Dead end. Nobody with enough ownership worth tracing. I assume they're all legit."

"I'd really rather not bog down Knight Errant's computers conducting background checks on nine hundred people."

"Your call," Kyle said, "but is Linda Hayward on the list of investors?"

Facile blinked, and then reached down to work his computer. A moment later his eyes narrowed. "Yes, she is."

"Great. Let me know who else interesting turns up on that list." Kyle reached for the command keys, said: "I'll check in again later", disconnected, and Facile faded to black.

"Interesting," said Hanna.

"Very," Kyle agreed. "Could you do me a favor and have your datapad re-read the profile we got on her."

Hanna nodded and keyed in some commands to the pad. A moment later, it spoke in a clear masculine voice: "Results of a public records search-check on Linda Hayward. Information gathered: one correlation. Linda Kathleen Hayward. Date of birth, 8 March 2029, Rush-Presbyterian Hospital, Chicago. Parents, Nancy Arnold Hayward and John Michael Hayward, deceased 2039. Economic records show employment with Davidion Financial until four years ago. No registered employment since. Residence records show rented housing at 3121 West George, Chicago, until four years ago. No residence record since. Education records show a degree in management and finance from the University of Illinois, Chicago, 2043. No other records found."

"Again," said Hanna, "not promising."

"It's like information on someone who's slipped off the edge of the world," Kyle mused. "Everything on her is four years old. She's completely dropped out of public record."

"What do you make of it?"

"Well, if we'd found nothing, I'd have said for sure she'd gone over to the shadows," Kyle said.

"Become a shadowrunner?" asked Hanna, almost incredulously. "Is it that easy?"

Kyle laughed. "No. If she were good or smart, there'd be no records by now. They're four years old, which is starting to leave a cold trail. But she's still using her own name." He shrugged. "I just don't know."

He sighed. "But if I run into her at the Kaleidoscope tonight I'll be sure to ask her."

"That wasn't necessary," Kyle told Seeks-the-Moon through the telepathic link they shared as master and ally spirit. Kyle disliked this method of communication with the spirit because, in his own mind, Seeks-the-Moon's voice sounded too much like his own voice. Standing at the rail overlooking the Kaleidoscope's main dance floor, besieged by untold thousands of watts of grinding, pounding, abrasive jet core rock and roll, it was the only way to talk.

The spirit shrugged even though he too spoke telepathically. "The doorman was a joker. We were obviously far more genuine than the fakers he let in ahead of us. I simply proved it."

"You didn't have to burst into flames."

"We're in, aren't we?"

"Yes, but odds are we've been noticed. Being inconspicuous is out of the question."

"Why didn't you tell me you wanted subtlety? It's not the approach you usually favor."

Kyle held up his hand to silence Seeks-the-Moon's bantering. "Okay, okay," he said. "We have a decent idea of who we're looking for, so let's split up and see what we can see."

The spirit shrugged again. "As you wish. If I locate Linda Hayward, should I call you?"

"It would be appreciated."

Seeks-the-Moon stuck his hands in his pockets and moved out through the crowd. Kyle knew the spirit was uncomfortable amid the chaos of music and dancers, but he also knew that Moon's ability to see in both the physical world and the astral one simultaneously would be invaluable in case of danger.

Kyle himself wasn't that comfortable, his musical tastes tending toward subtler techno-phasic harmonies. Jet core was too loud, too dissonant, and, combined with the billions of swirling and spraying multi-colored lights in the club, too fragging frantic.

The crowd was young—older than either Melissa or Mitchell Truman, of course, but by only a few years. There was a younger element, but they tended to orbit each other in small cliques near the edge of the main floor. Kyle wasn't sure if he should simply observe first or start working the crowd for clues to either Linda Hayward or Mitchell Truman.

Below him, the thrashing mass changed its pattern of motion as the music changed beat and pace. He thought he recognized the piece as a version of a more lyrical song from maybe a decade before, but the music wouldn't hold still long enough for him to place it. He moved forward, against the flow of the crowd, toward the bar.

The Kaleidoscope attracted a clientele that apparently considered the "magical" look to be in. He passed a pair of female elves guarded by a troll, but of the three, only the troll seemed real. In their finery, twist-dyed hair, and metallic-flake makeup, the two elves seemed artificial and posed. They ignored him, as bade their pose, while the troll gave him a polite nod. Kyle wondered for a brief moment what the truth behind the three really was.

An ork, garbed as one of the sorcerers from a recent simsense version of the *Arabian Knights,* threw what seemed to be a rainbow of color into the air. Kyle didn't need his astral senses to know it was a trick, light refracted through a handful of microcrystals. Fakery, apparently, was all the rage in the Kaleidoscope Cl—

"It would seem I am not alone," said Seeks-the-Moon in

Kyle's mind. Turning quickly, Kyle surveyed the club, trying to pick the spirit out from among the throng.

"What do you mean?"

"Well, if I'm not mistaken, the young woman near the red neon tube, across from you, is a spirit as well."

Kyle leaned against the rail and strained to see that far across the club. He could make out a cluster of figures near a red neon pillar, but not much else about them. He braced himself against the rail and shifted into astral perception. The room snapped into vivid, energetic focus, a blare of living color and energy. Despite the brilliance, the accumulated energy of the packed dancers and their emotions, there were very few mystical auras to be seen, except by the pillar.

There, Kyle picked out two powerful auras, neither masked. Both were females and they strobed with real, primal power. Spirits manifest in human form.

"Can you get a good look at them." Kyle asked through the mental link.

"No, and I don't think I should get any closer. They, like me, will have dual sight. I don't think you wish me to alert them to our presence."

"You're right. Let me try and get closer." Kyle let his physical senses return and moved quickly around the outer rim of the dance floor, keeping his eye on the red pillar. He was nearly there when Seeks-the-Moon spoke again.

"One of the two has moved away," the spirit said. "She is heading toward the rear of the club."

"Can you follow her?" asked Kyle, trying to push his way through the crowd without causing an incident.

"I believe so, but how daring do you wish me to be?"

"Could she be Linda Hayward?"

"Not unless she's disguised. This one is black."

"Follow her if you can."

"I will."

The red-tinted faces of the revelers signaled Kyle's proximity to the tube. He paused a moment and centered himself, boosting his own shielding, and perhaps most important, the masking that dampened his mystical aura. But if this woman, whoever she was, was as powerful as her own unmasked aura implied, he doubted his attempts to suppress his own would be very successful. He circled left, to come up behind her.

Her hair was the same color as the unnatural light, her flesh pale and waxen. The clothing she wore seemed to be real leather, dark and glossy, tight up along her long legs and then loose in the form of a vest across her back and shoulders. Her arms were bare, except for coppery bracelets on each wrist.

What slowed him, just for a moment, was the image on the back of her vest. It was the figure of an angel, definitely feminine and vengeful. One of the arms was extended upward, toward the sky, and wielded a bright sword. The other gestured downward across one hip, modestly hiding what the tattered rags of her clothing did not. The angel's face, rimmed by a halo of shining hair, was downturned, but her gaze looked outward—direct, provocative, and challenging. The words "Desolation Angels" arched over the angel and across the woman's shoulder blades.

"Desolation Angels," Kyle told Seeks-the-Moon. "Emblazoned across her back."

"This one has the same thing," the spirit replied, "though I haven't been able to see her—*slot!*"

Now Kyle paused. "What?"

"She just went into the rest room," came Seeks-the-Moon's voice. "I don't dare follow her in. That would get me too close."

"Then wait her out," Kyle had already started walking toward the other woman again. "Let's see what I can do with this one."

"Is it Linda Hayward?"

"No." Kyle stepped up alongside her, suddenly wishing he had a drink in his hand. He looked out over the dance floor for a moment and then casually to his left.

The woman's hair hung loosely down and across one shoulder, and this close he could see that it was actually red, but very light, almost blond. Her eyes were large and round, the color of emeralds, her mouth was small but expressive, the lips a color like blood. Her gaze shifted and she eyed him with amused disinterest. He noticed a black choker around her neck. Set against it in gold was a single pale gem.

He smiled, let his gaze wander away and then back again to her. Her smile widened ever so slightly and her lips parted the barest distance. Then she closed her eyes and slowly leaned back against the red neon pillar.

Kyle tensed. Had he been looking at another magician, he'd have taken her actions as a sure sign she was astrally projecting, releasing her spirit to roam on the astral plane. But Seeks-the-Moon had said she was a spirit like him. Not only could she *not* astrally project, having no true body from which to separate her spirit, but neither did she need any because she could see into both congruent realms without effort.

"Moon," he said quietly in his mind.

"Yes?"

"Can you see me from where you are?"

"Yes, I can."

"What's she doing?" Kyle asked, hazarding a glance at her. She hadn't moved.

"Nothing," said the spirit. "At least as far as I can tell."

"Ah," said Kyle.

"Worried?"

"Yes."

"You're closer," Seeks-the-Moon said. "You can tell more than I."

"I can't risk revealing myself."

Kyle looked at her again, but for all he could see, she was frozen there. A waitress moved nearer to him through the crowd. Deciding, he stepped in closer to her and carefully placed his hand on her bare upper arm. Her flesh, in stark contrast to the room, was cool.

Her eyes opened and she regarded him without expression.

Kyle managed a smile, pushing back an unfocused, growing unease. "Can I buy you a drink?" he said as smoothly as was possible while half-shouting over the din.

Her expression did not change. "Why?" She did not raise her voice, forcing him to partially read her lips.

"It's so warm in here. I thought maybe you were thirsty."

"I am," she said, and he was about to gesture for the waitress when her words and her strong hand on his wrist stopped him. "But I don't want a drink."

He paused, his body temperature dropping suddenly at her touch, then rising again. "What can I get you?"

She smiled. "Nothing tonight."

"Then can I—"

She let go of his wrist and began moving away. "Good night." She was walking toward the rear of the club.

"Moon!" Kyle said mentally, moving quickly to keep up with her, yet staying far enough back to duck for cover into the crowd if she turned suddenly.

"Yes?"

"She's coming your way along the rail."

Ahead of him, Kyle could just make out the figure of the woman as she approached the ladies room and then went in.

"She went in," Kyle told Moon.

"Come and guard me. I'm going to try and get a look in there."

A moment later Seeks-the-Moon appeared alongside his master. "Just like the old days, yes?"

"Quiet," Kyle snapped. "I'm going to use a far-sight spell to have a look-see. They shouldn't be able to notice, regardless of how powerful they are."

"Presumably."

Kyle looked at him. "What do you mean, presumably?"

The spirit shrugged. "We don't know exactly what we're dealing with."

Kyle nodded. "Guard me." He stepped back against a support column. The casting wouldn't require the special concentration of using his astral senses, but he wanted to be careful.

The forces of magic swirled around him. He reached out with his mind and began shaping them, connecting them to his own aura, to those elements of himself that dealt with sight. He created a node of mystical energy, the new centerpoint for his vision, and projected it forward, past the crowd, past the closed door, and into the room.

It was large and bright. Mirrored counters lined half of each wall, strip-lights tacked to the wall above them casting a hard, sharp light over the women lined up there. All the spaces were taken, and even more women waited their turn near the overflowing trash bins. An attendant was standing by, but apparently chose to ignore the obvious illegal dealings going on in the first toilet stall. There were about two dozen stalls, all at the rear of the room. All were in use, with at least one woman awaiting entrance. There was no sign of either of the female spirits.

Cursing to himself, Kyle willed his sight forward as one of the stall doors opened and women changed places. He paused a moment, uncertain, and then lifted his point of view to quickly scan the interior of the stalls on the left side.

Neither of the two women were in any of the stalls. He shifted over to the side and did the same.

Not there, either.

Cursing again, Kyle cast modesty aside and carefully checked each stall's occupant at eye level before searching through the rest of the room again.

The two spirits simply were not there.

He dropped the spell.

"Gone?" asked Seeks-the-Moon.

"Yes."

"I feared as much. I was watching, but no spirits came out."

"They must have ducked out through the rear wall. I think there's an alley back there. They wouldn't risk being seen moving through the crowd."

"So what do we do now?"

"Now," said Kyle, "we tell the Trumans that I'm getting worried."

8

As Kyle's car slowed and pulled into the pool of light at the curb of the Truman Tower, Hanna Uljakën suddenly appeared from the deep shadows near the entrance and rushed out to meet him. He was pleased to note the increased presence of Knight Errant checking his ID on the brightly lit ramp leading from street level, and equally glad to see the two troopers near the doors shift to better protect Hanna as she came toward him.

The Ford's gull-wing door popped open and he stepped out quickly, moving around the front of the car to meet her.

"I contacted Mr. Truman as soon as Seeks-the-Moon showed up," she told him as they walked toward the building entrance. "He and Mrs. Truman were entertaining on their yacht, but they're en route by helicopter. They should be here any minute."

"And Melissa?" Kyle asked as they passed through lobby doors flanked inside by three more guards.

She grimaced. "That's a problem."

Kyle stopped walking. "Why?"

"She ducked her guards a few hours ago."

"Son of a bitch!" he said, shaking his head in anger. "Is Facile upstairs?"

"He wasn't but I've notified him."

Kyle turned toward the nearest Knight Errant guard in his finely tailored high-impact body armor, full tactical communications headset, and not-so-casually slung combat rifle. Kyle pointed at him. "Let Facile know we need him upstairs." The guard seemed startled by the order, but he reached for his commlink, surprising Kyle with his quick compliance.

Kyle and Hanna continued on toward the elevator banks. "You said earlier that Melissa had provided a ritual link?"

She nodded. "Yes, it's in cold storage."

"Under the family's control?"

She nodded. "Locked in security in the basement."

"We'll need it." As they reached the elevator, the guard stepped aside smartly. Kyle noted that it was the same woman he'd seen posted here earlier, but now she was garbed for war.

"Command," Hanna said as the doors closed behind them. "Penthouse. Express." The elevator quickly accelerated to what Kyle guessed was probably its maximum speed. "Command," she said again. "Communication line to security."

A moment later, a clear male voice spoke through the elevator's speakers. "Security Control here, Ms. Uljakën."

She looked up to where Kyle guessed the hidden microsurveillance camera was. "On my authority, I need Melissa Truman's ritual biosample material brought up from cold storage immediately."

"All of it?" the voice asked as the elevator slowed.

Hanna glanced at Kyle, who shook his head. "No," she said, "only one sample."

"It's on the way. Security out."

The elevator doors opened, and the two stepped into the long corridor that led to the Truman apartment. No guards were present, but Kyle wished there were.

"Is it that serious?" Hanna asked as they approached the mahogany doors.

"Let's put it this way," Kyle said, "if I'm right, this Linda Hayward isn't from anywhere on this earth."

"Excuse me?" Daniel Truman's face had gone white. Next to him, still in her evening clothes, his wife grabbed his arm and gasped.

"I'm sorry, but it's a definite possibility," Kyle told them. "I saw two women wearing vests showing the words 'Desolation Angels', and both were spirits of some kind."

"You're sure they weren't just powerful mages?" asked Facile, who was also wearing slightly bulky evening wear. Kyle had been pleased to see him exit the helicopter with the Trumans, though he suspected the senior Truman was beginning to chafe under the increased security presence. "You could have misread their aura—"

"Lieutenant," said Seeks-the-Moon from where he was studying the tiny points of color on the huge wall painting. "Trust me when I say that I know the difference between a powerful spirit birthed in the blazing chaos of the metaplanes and the aura of Awakened meat." He turned slightly toward Kyle. "No offense, of course."

Kyle ignored him. "No, we're sure," he told Facile. "An unmasked spirit's aura is distinct. And there's also the fact that both vanished through a back wall in the ladies room."

"Could they have slipped out invisibly somewhere else?" asked Facile.

"Not likely."

"But it's possible?"

Kyle turned toward Truman. He was angry. "Mr. Truman, these are the facts as I understand them. Your son is missing. We've proven that he's either protected or blocked by a powerful ward. We have a connection between him and a woman named Linda Hayward, who appears to be part of a gang, possibly all-female, called the Desolation Angels. We have seen that at least two members of the Desolation Angels are spirits of some kind. That's enough to have me worried."

Truman nodded slowly, his mind carefully analyzing everything Kyle was telling him. "If they're spirits of some kind—and forgive me, but I'm no expert—doesn't someone have to be commanding them?"

Kyle shook his head. "There are many different kinds of spirits. Some are like Seeks-the-Moon, Charlotte, and Delta, who are conjured, shaped, and given form by magicians. These and other similar types are all commanded and can only operate within certain restraints."

Still standing by the painting, Seeks-the-Moon cleared his throat.

Kyle glanced over at him. "Some are given a great deal of

flexibility, even autonomy, because of their nature and the fact that they've proven trustworthy. All, however, have distinct personalities, sometimes with unwanted idiosyncrasies. Depending on how they're treated, some spirits may even be angry, insolent, or vengeful toward their masters. They are all, once conjured, living creatures.

"There are other spirits, generally classified as 'free spirits,' whose wills are their own. A conjured spirit can become free if its master dies or if the spirit becomes powerful enough to turn on its master and defeat him. There are also spirits in the world who are free simply by their own nature. They have their own goals, own desires, and some are quite difficult to understand.

"There are a number of different categories of free spirits, as we understand them. We could be dealing with tricksters, shadows, anima, or players."

"Christ," said Facile. His face had gone white.

"I'm afraid you've all but lost me," said Truman.

"Well, to make a long story short, I'm certain we're dealing with spirits, but I can't be certain what kind."

Facile looked at Truman, then asked to be excused for a moment. As he was going out, one of Truman's own security personnel entered, escorted by a Knight Errant trooper. The building guard was carrying a cold-storage container. Hanna Uljakën gestured toward Kyle. "Please give that to Mr. Teller."

The guard nodded, walked over, and handed Kyle the case. It was heavy and only slightly larger than a tool box, but Kyle knew it held enough coolant and battery power to keep the enclosed sample frozen for weeks. "Thank you," he said.

"What's that?" asked Truman.

"Your daughter Melissa's ritual sample. I think we should locate her as soon as possible. Were Lieutenant Facile here, I'm sure he'd agree."

"The hell with Facile," said Truman. "*I* agree."

"Good," Kyle said, hefting the container. "I'd prefer if Knight—"

The telecom against the far wall beeped, and Hanna Uljakën hurried to answer it.

"As I was saying, I'd prefer that Knight Errant handle it," Kyle went on. "There are a couple of other avenues I'd like to pursue, and since the ritual will take several hours, it would be better if someone else performed it."

Truman nodded. "I'm sure that won't be a problem." He looked around the room. "Where the hell *is* Facile?"

"He hasn't come back," said his wife.

"Well, I want him in here." Truman started to stride toward the door, but Hanna interrupted him.

"Excuse me!" she called from across the room. Everyone turned toward her. She'd taken the incoming call on audio— only to avoid distracting the others and was cradling the handset against her head. She was waving at them.

"It's Eagle Security," she said, wide-eyed. "They've found Mitch!"

"Are they sure?" asked Mrs. Truman, suddenly breathless.

Hanna nodded. "The retinal ID matches!"

"Where is he?" asked Truman. "Where's my boy?"

"Is he all right?" cried Mrs. Truman.

Hanna paused and spoke quietly into the phone. "He's at Harold Washington University Hospital," she reported. Then her voice caught suddenly and she stared at the Trumans before she could finally get the words out.

"They've put him in the psychiatric ward."

9

The man stuck out his hand as the Truman entourage entered the hospital lobby. "Lieutenant Breslin," he said, "Eagle Security."

Daniel Truman took shook his hand, and then held on to it. "Lieutenant, I want to see my son." The rest of the group entered quickly behind him, looking very out of place alongside the streeters and squatters already waiting there.

"Of course," Breslin said and motioned to an older, dark-haired woman approaching them in the distinctive white coat of a doctor. Her hands were in her pockets and they stayed there. "This is Doctor Stansfeld. She's been examining your son."

"Doctor," said Truman.

"Mr. Truman, I'm sorry to report that there's very little I can tell you about your son. Eagle brought him in about four hours ago and we've run just about every one of our passive tests on him, with little result."

"I don't understand," said Mrs. Truman.

"He's—your son, I presume?—in a unresponsive state. All indications are that he is conscious, possibly aware, but unable or unwilling to respond."

"How can that be?" Daniel Truman seemed barely able to restrain his anger and pain. "What happened to him?"

"I don't know for sure. Any number of possible mental or emotional traumas. He's been physically abused, beaten perhaps, but beyond those bruises and scrapes he's relatively uninjured. It may have been something he saw or experienced."

"Can we see him?" asked Mrs. Truman.

The doctor nodded. "Of course. Come this way." The two Trumans followed Stansfeld out of the lobby, leaving Kyle, Hanna, two staff assistants, and three Knight Errant guards standing there with Lieutenant Breslin. Facile of Knight Errant was off trying to locate Melissa Truman.

"Lieutenant Breslin," Kyle said, extending his own hand, "I've been part of the investigation on this. Might I ask you a few questions?"

The police lieutenant laughed. "That's usually my line." He was a short man, a head less than Kyle, with a mop of brown-red hair and a short mustache. His gaze was clear and direct. "I take it you're with Truman's staff?" He eyed the three obviously armed troopers surrounding the group. "Or is it Knight Errant?"

"Neither. I was called in to find the boy."

The lieutenant smirked. "Guess we made your work a little easier."

"Up to this point," said Kyle, "but I strongly suspect Mr. Truman is going to want to find out how this happened."

The officer nodded. "He was picked up on the northside, near Western and Irving Park. Squad car reports he came mad-dashing out of an alley and ran straight into the car. He fought them at first, then just collapsed. A crowd had gathered and they checked around to see if anyone knew him, but no one would admit to anything. Not a surprise in that neighborhood."

"What was he wearing?" asked Kyle.

"Jeans, shoes, and a shirt," said Breslin. "The hospital's got it all."

"Was he carrying any IDs or money?"

Breslin shook his head. "Nope, or we'd have ID'd him faster. Had to run prints and retinals to tag him."

"And his injuries?"

"Like the doc said. But I only came on the case after he'd been ID'd. All I saw were cuts and scrapes, which he could have gotten from hitting the squad car. Nearly broke the window, I hear."

"Did he say anything to anyone?"

"No. Nothing. The report said that up until he collapsed

he was trying to yell through clenched teeth. But it wasn't words, just yelling. Seems pretty obvious to me."

"Oh?" said Kyle.

The lieutenant shrugged. "Sure. Wacko behavior, then catatonia. He beetled his brain to Mars."

Kyle nodded. Mitchell's description did fit the template for someone who'd burned his brains out on BTL chips. Better Than Life, a high-powered, technological hallucinogenic that was the high of choice for many on the streets. The problem was too much or the wrong kind that could fry the user's mind. Permanently.

Kyle thanked Breslin for his help, then walked back to Hanna. "Do you know of Mitchell having a chip problem?" he asked her quietly, suddenly feeling terribly weary.

She shook her head. "No. The only simsense gear he had in his apartment was stuff the company made. All within legal limits. He hated it and rarely used it. Maybe it was because of who his father is."

"That would be the ultimate irony, wouldn't it?" Kyle said. "His father is the owner of one of the biggest multimedia conglomerates in the world and his son turns out to be a chiphead."

"I suppose," she said, but he could tell she didn't believe it.

"Mr. Teller?"

Kyle turned to see a nurse standing there in a starched white uniform and cap.

"Yes?"

"Mr. Truman would like you to join him."

"All right." He turned to Hanna. "Check with Facile and see if they've located Melissa yet. If not, see if you can find out whether she knew about any chip habits Mitch might have had."

Hanna said she would, and then Kyle followed the nurse down the corridor. The room was brightly lit with virtually no shadows. It contained little else besides a bed and the three people clustered around the figure lying on it.

Mrs. Truman was obviously distraught, but to Kyle she seemed to be holding up better than her husband. Looking as pale and battered as his catatonic son, Daniel Truman was like a man whose life had been torn away from him. Only their eyes differed. Daniel Truman's were full of sadness and fear. Mitchell Truman's eyes were empty. He simply stared.

"Mr. Teller," the elder Truman said as Kyle entered. "Please tell me that you can do something for him."

Doctor Stansfeld also turned toward him. "Are you a doctor?"

Kyle shook his head. "No, I'm a mage."

Her lips tightened slightly. "I see. Are you certified?"

Kyle stopped. "Certified?"

"By the UCAS Medical Association," she said, as if it were the most obvious thing in the world. "To use healing magic."

Kyle almost laughed. "No ma'am," he said. "I wasn't aware that there was such a thing." That was a lie, but Kyle knew that licensing was rarely enforced except as a requirement for employment in an institution like this. He had always considered it mainly a safeguard against charlatans and quacks.

"Well, there is." She turned brusquely to Truman. "I'm afraid this man can't use magic on your son while he's a patient here. It's against the rules."

"Against the rules?" echoed Mrs. Truman, aghast.

The doctor nodded. "We're not insured for noncertified magicians operating within the hospital."

Truman was practically shaking. "If you think I'm going to let your damn rules stand in the way of my son getting the treatment he needs—"

The doctor took an involuntary half-step back, but held her ground. "Mr. Truman, if you wish to take your son elsewhere, that is your right. But while he is here, he will not be treated by a non-staff mage. And you can rattle the rafters as much as you wish, but when you finally get to the top of the pile you'll find that Harold Washington University Hospital is ultimately owned by Fuchi Industrial Electronics. And, with all due respect, Mr. Truman, I don't think you'd have much success intimidating them."

Truman's eyes narrowed and he leaned in toward the doc-

tor. "Very well. We'll move my son to where he can be
cared for properly. But I don't think you'd like to know just
how much hell I could raise with Fuchi. And regardless of
the fact that we're leaving, I am going to rattle the rafters till
they fall down on your pretentious head."

Within an hour, Mitchell Truman had been transferred to
a private medical facility known as the Handlemann Institute, located just south of the Core. It was owned by friends
of the Trumans, who ordered that every effort be made to accommodate them. Even as Mitchell's own room was being
prepared, an adjacent suite was also being set up for Mr. and
Mrs. Truman so they could remain near their son.

By then, though, they'd seen one change of behavior in
Mitchell. Shortly after arriving at Handlemann, his body
jerked, his eyes seemed to focus, and his gaze darted around
the room like he was following the path of something flying.
Concerned, Kyle had immediately checked the area with his
astral senses, but found nothing. When he looked back at
Mitchell, however, what he saw was even more frightening.

For all intent and purposes, Mitchell Truman had no aura.

He was speaking with Doctor Anna Douglas, who would
handle the Truman boy's case during his stay at Handlemann. Kyle learned that in addition to her medical degree, she also held a degree in metaphysical research. She
was short and frail-looking, with thin, dark hair bundled on
top of her head. Her features were small and showed the
faintest trace of Asian blood.

"Were it not for what you've observed about his aura, I'd
agree that BTL burnout is the most likely cause," she said
with a sigh, "but I've certainly never seen any effect like
what you describe."

Kyle nodded, and sipped from the cup of soykaf cooling
in his hands. "I haven't either," he said. The two were seated
in a small waiting area just down the hall from where the
Truman family, including wayward daughter Melissa, whom
Knight Errant had finally found sneaking back into the
Truman condo, was waiting. Also present was daughter

Madeleine, just flown in from Denver where she managed her father's trideo syndication service. Hanna Uljakën was asleep in a chair across the room. The two Knight Errant guards at either entrance were not.

Doctor Douglas leaned back in her chair and closed her eyes. "I suggest we look for the signs of an essence-drainer in the aura that remains."

"Vampire?" he asked.

"Possibly," she said, "but that doesn't explain the catatonia, unless the actual act was so terrifying that his mind refused it."

"I think he might be involved with one or more spirits, probably free, but of a type I couldn't determine."

Her eyes opened and she leaned forward. "Really?" That gave her pause for thought. "An essence-draining spirit of some kind. It certainly makes sense."

She thought about this and then shook her head. "We don't have enough information." She looked in the direction of Mitchell Truman's room. "I think it's time to look deeper . . . if I can get them to leave him alone for a minute . . ."

"The D-CAT scan showed nothing abnormal, nor did the encephaphasic or neurochemical batteries," she told him some hours later. "His brain is normal. It's just not working." Dr. Douglas and Kyle were reviewing the results of the medical and magical tests they had run on Mitchell after persuading the Truman family to go home and rest.

Kyle studied the boy lying listlessly on the bed, the sheets twisted slightly around him. Moments ago his eyes had sprung open as he searched the room for something unknown and then collapsed.

"Seeks-the-Moon," Kyle said, and the spirit slipped into physical existence alongside him. Doctor Douglas looked up from where she was watching the small monitor screen that displayed the boy's vital signs. She frowned, squinted, and then looked back at the screen.

The spirit stood regarding Mitchell for a moment, then stepped forward to look at him more closely. Moon's lips were pursed. "Excuse me a moment," he said, then grew translucent and faded away to nothing.

"Your ally spirit?" the doctor asked.

"Yes."

She nodded. "I thought I saw a resemblance."

"Gee, thanks."

"You're welcome."

Seeks-the-Moon returned, fading back in a meter or so from where he'd been standing before. He was facing away from the bed, and when Moon turned, Kyle could see that he had visibly paled. That took him by surprise. He'd never seen his ally spirit react that way before.

"What's going on?"

The spirit shook his head. "I've never seen anything like it."

"We thought maybe a vampire or some other essence-draining spirit was involved," the doctor said.

"No," said Seeks-the-Moon. "This is not the work of one of those."

Kyle was startled. "When have you seen the result of a vampire attack?"

"Never," he said, staring at the limp form on the bed.

"Me neither," Kyle said. "So how could you—"

The spirit raised its hand. "You formed me from the loose energies of astral space, yes?" When Kyle nodded, he said, "The world remembers."

"What's that supposed to mean?"

"It means that sometimes I know things that you do not. And sometimes I know things that I perhaps *should* not know. This is one of those times."

"Of course!" said the doctor. "It only makes sense!"

"I'm sorry?" said Kyle, turning toward her.

"Where does the collective unconscious reside?" she said, her face bright. "Why, in astral space, of course! He said the 'world remembers', and he's formed of those same energies, the same energy that interfaces with every living thing on the planet. It only makes sense that he can somehow tap into that."

Kyle turned back to his ally spirit, somewhat disturbed by the discussion. "You've never been able to do that before."

Seeks-the-Moon nodded. "I've not been allowed to."

"Not been allowed to!" said Kyle. "This is getting absurd."

Seeks-the-Moon held up his hand again, and it seemed to be shaking slightly. "Please, I understand this less than you and find it equally disturbing. All I know is that Mitchell Truman was not attacked by a vampire."

"Then what?"

"It was a spirit, yes," Seeks-the-Moon said, "but when it tried to devour his soul and failed, the boy went mad."

"His soul?" asked Doctor Douglas.

"His primal spirit, his Self, his *ka*—the names are endless," said the spirit. "But I do not believe the spirit wanted his soul, rather it wanted his body. His soul was simply in the way."

"A failed possession?" asked the doctor.

Seeks-the-Moon shrugged. "I don't know. I've told you what I sense."

"That would explain much about—"

A ball of deep blue and white exploded into the room, moving at blinding speed, hitting Kyle in the chest and rebounding across the room. Instantly, a gray-green shield sprung up around him as he tried to protect himself from another attack. Seeks-the-Moon moved with the speed of thought across the room and placed himself between the ball of energy and Mitchell Truman.

"MASTER!" the ball screeched as it careened across the room, finally slowing to a comprehensible speed.

"Delta?" said Kyle as he lowered his hands.

"I FOUND YOU! I FOUND YOU!" the watcher spirit squealed as it quickly hovered near him.

"Great Coyote," muttered Seeks-the-Moon, relaxing.

"I told Charlotte I could find you!" It darted around him, obviously pleased with itself. *"She didn't think I could! But I did!"*

"Yes, you did, Delta," Kyle said sternly. "Now why did you come here?"

The watcher spirit paused and regarded him wide-eyed. *"Um . . ."*

"Delta . . ."

"Oh!" it said, bouncing again. *"Charlotte said another spirit came!"*

"Another spirit?"

"Yes!"

"Did she fight it?"

"I don't know." The watcher sounded concerned that it didn't know. *"She just told me to find you!"*

Kyle sighed. "That's good, Delta. You did fine."

It jumped into the air again. *"I told her I could! I told her I could!"*

Kyle turned to Seeks-the-Moon. "I'm going to see about the Trumans," he said. "Guard my body and the boy's while I'm gone."

The spirit nodded. "Of course."

Kyle sat down in one of the room's chairs and relaxed. He turned his astral senses inward and examined his own body and spirit. His form was tired, running on hyperkaf and adrenaline, but soon that would not be enough. His spirit, however, was alight with energy. He willed himself to be solely spirit, to loosen the connection to his physical body and float free, and he did.

Kyle's spirit separated, and he stepped clear of his body and into astral space. The room, filled with plants, was bright with life. Both Seeks-the-Moon and Doctor Douglas also glowed warm, strong, and healthy. Mitchell Truman was the only living source not radiating brightly. He was dim, a meat shell barely holding life.

Seeks-the-Moon, who could sense simultaneously in both the physical and astral realms, regarded Kyle in his astral form. As an expression of Kyle's idealized self-image, his astral shape sparked energy off its lean, muscular form. For a moment he was unmasked and his aura showed all his potential as a mage initiated into the higher mysteries of the world. A single throbbing silver cord connected his astral body with his physical one. He knew he could see that connection clearly now, but as he moved away from his body, the cord would dim into insubstantiality.

"*I'll be back quickly,*" he told Seeks-the-Moon, and the spirit nodded.

Kyle turned toward the window, which, along with its frame, was dull and lifeless in astral space. His astral form would be able to pass through it easily. The plants in the room, however, being now or once alive, he'd have to fly over.

And fly he did with the speed of thought.

10

Kyle flew out beyond the medical facility and high into the still-dark morning air. The city was alive beneath him, stretching away in a glowing haze to the north, west, and south. To the east it abutted the vivid glow of Lake Michigan, which hummed with life almost as brightly as the city.

Kyle also saw many patches of dark, places in the city where the creations of man were strong enough to dominate the living auras that inhabited them. The Shattergraves of old downtown Chicago was a dark blight, a scar across what had once been the heart of the city. That, however, was not Kyle's destination, but Truman Tower, still south of him.

He soared that way, high above the city, which passed as a prismatic blur beneath him. The Tower soon loomed before him, cold and dim in astral space, but recognizable by its shape and location. Dim patches of life could be seen emanating from within it, but the non-living obviously dominated.

Kyle shot toward the penthouse and entered through the lakeside windows that opened into what the Trumans used as their family room. Seated on the central couches were Melissa and her sister Madeleine, whom Kyle had met only in passing at the hospital. She was older by nearly a decade than either Melissa or Mitchell, and was lighter of complexion as well as build.

Entering the room, he hovered there as Charlotte also entered from the floor below. She braked to a quick stop in front of him.

"Master," came the reverberations of her voice through astral space. *"The watcher found you!"*

"What happened?" Kyle asked her.

"The area you told me to guard was entered by another spirit," the elemental told him. *"I sensed it and moved to strike at it, but it sensed me also and fled before I could reach it. I did not pursue, as you did not instruct me to."*

"No, you did well. Did you see what it was?"

"I could not," Charlotte replied. *"Its coloration was dark."*

"Dark?" asked Kyle. *"It was weak?"*

"No, it was powerful, but its colors were dark."

That puzzled Kyle. He'd never heard of any spirit with dark coloration. Then again, there were many things about this that he—

Something was wrong. The two women had stood up and were backing away across the room, frightened by something in his vicinity. He turned and looked behind, but saw only the dark opacity of the plasteel windows. He and Charlotte were the only beings present in the room beside Melissa and Madeleine.

Of course. He was unmasked and radiating power, which meant he was probably leaking some of that energy into the physical world, and Charlotte's presence was probably compounding the problem. The result was undoubtedly an area of haze or distortion hanging in the room. Between the two of them they might even be dumping off enough energy into the physical world to make the area glow slightly.

"We need to manifest," he told Charlotte.

"Very well," the spirit said grudgingly.

Kyle willed his astral form into synchrony with the physical world, and then allowed himself to appear there, ghostly and insubstantial. It was the best he could manage while he was a spirit without body.

The women were startled, and began to race toward the nearest doorway. Kyle held out his hand. *"Melissa, Madeleine!"* he called. *"It's all right. It's Kyle Teller!"*

They paused a moment as the more familiar form, at least for Melissa, of Charlotte appeared next to him. Slowly, recognition dawned on Melissa's face, though Madeleine still seemed frightened.

"Jesus fraggin' Christ!" Melissa said. "You scared the drek out of us!"

Kyle smiled and shrugged. *"Sorry. I didn't realize you'd be able to see signs of Charlotte and me. Manifesting seemed to be the only thing to do once you noticed us."*

Melissa turned toward her sister. "Maddy, you remember Mr. Teller from the hospital."

Madeleine Truman nodded. "Yes. Yes, I do. Of course, he looked slightly different then."

Melissa laughed. "Yes, I suppose he did."

Kyle started when he realized what was going on. His astral form, glowing and sparking with energy, was quite nude and quite idealized. He reached out and grabbed Charlotte and pulled the spirit down in front of his waist.

"Sorry," he said.

"Please," said Madeleine, "don't be modest on our account."

"Yes," said Melissa, "we had no idea." She smiled. "I mean there are all sorts of stories about orks and trolls, and even dwarfs, but I'd never heard of magicians being so, um, gifted."

"Unfortunately, it's not quite like that." Kyle was about to explain, then realized he didn't really want to. Let them think what they pleased. *"There's no change in your brother's condition, but I wanted to check on you and the rest of the family."*

"We're fine," said Melissa. "My mother and father are packing some clothes so they can stay at the hospital with Mitchell until you and the doctors can figure out what's wrong with him."

"Have you had any luck?" Madeleine asked.

"No, not really. Some theories, but nothing more than that."

Melissa broke in suddenly. "Oh! There was a message waiting here when we got back. The staff said some woman had called looking for Mitch. She sounded upset."

"Did she leave her name?"

Melissa shook her head. "No. She hung up when the maid said he was in the hospital."

"Damn," said Kyle. Now whoever it was, probably Linda Hayward, knew Mitchell was in the hands of his family. *"Does Facile know about the phone call?"*

"Yes, Hanna told him right away."

"Good. Tell Hanna to instruct the staff not to give out any more information."

"She's already done that."

"Good. I'm going back to the hospital. I'll let you know if anything changes."

"Thanks," said Melissa.

"Hope to see you again," added Madeleine.

Kyle smiled. *"I suspect you will."* He returned to astral space. *"Charlotte, resume your duties. But make sure Lieutenant Facile of Knight Errant knows that another spirit was here."*

"Yes, Master," the spirit replied.

And Kyle flew off back to the hospital.

He sat up and blinked, stretching out the slight lethargy that had begun to seep into his limbs. He'd been separated from his body for less than half an hour, a fraction of the time he was able to spend disassociated, but the body always showed some effects regardless.

"Everything is well?" Seeks-the-Moon asked.

Kyle nodded. "Some kind of spirit . . ." His words trailed off as he saw Delta, the watcher spirit, still hovering at the far side of the room. He sighed. "Delta," he said.

"Yes!" It bounced to life and began circling him.

"Go back to Charlotte and do what she tells you," he told it.

"Yes!" it cried jubilantly and then vanished.

Seeks-the-Moon shrugged. "I tried to tell it the same thing, but it wouldn't listen."

"Doesn't matter now. What's important is that some kind of spirit visited the apartment. Charlotte couldn't recognize it, but she noticed something very strange. The spirit was dark."

"Dark?" both Seeks-the-Moon and Doctor Douglas said in unison.

"Dark. I don't really know what that means either."

Seeks-the-Moon turned toward Mitchell. "He's dark . . ."

Kyle nodded. "I thought of that. What if Mitch's astral self has somehow gotten separated from his body? What if it was off, lost somewhere, while his body slowly died?"

"That's a possibility," the doctor said.

"Except," said Seeks-the-Moon, "that his aura isn't weakening. It's dim, nearly dead, but stable."

Kyle sighed. "I know." He stood and looked at Mitchell Truman's still form. "We've got to find out what's going on in case he gets worse."

"Worse?" asked Doctor Douglas. "Pardon my pessimism, but this boy isn't going to get better. His mind is simply gone."

"I know, but there's always a chance." Kyle turned to Seeks-the-Moon. "Go back to the Truman residence and stay there in case another one of those spirits shows up. If it does, see what you can learn."

The spirit nodded. "I will."

"Also, while you're there, find an empty room and set up a full ritual circle."

"How big?"

Kyle paused and thought. "Nine meters across."

"And the spell?"

Kyle flashed the spirit a mental image of the spell. "This one. The same as before."

Kyle turned toward the doctor. "In the meantime, and with your permission, I'd like to leave two elementals here to guard Mitch."

"That's fine, as long as they stay in this room and don't disturb the other patients."

Kyle laughed. "No, these two are pretty calm." He turned and shifted his perceptions until they synchronized with the harmonics of the elemental metaplane of water.

"Elliot, Richard," he said, and two water elementals came into existence before him. "Guard the boy in the bed and this room. Allow no one and no magics into this room without the permission of Doctor Douglas."

The two spirits looked at the doctor, and then back at Kyle.

"Got it," said the first.

"If I have to," said the second.

Kyle turned to Seeks-the-Moon. "Go ahead."

Seeks-the-Moon bowed and disappeared. The two spirits also faded away, back into astral space.

Kyle turned toward Dr. Douglas. "Do you have a syringe?"

She raised an eyebrow. "Behind on your medication?"

Kyle smiled, but shook his head. "No, but I'd like to get a real ritual sample from him." He gestured to the body. "Just in case."

The doctor pulled a small case from the test cart still parked in the corner of the room and handed it to him. "Here. A blood sample kit."

Kyle unlatched the case and removed the pistol-gripped sampler, pulling clear the self-sterilizing protective cap.

"How much will you take?"

"I don't need much," he said, bending closer and laying his hand on the boy's arm. Again he focused his magical power to infuse the blood sample he was about to take with enough secondary energy to allow it to remain fresh for some time. He placed the tip of the sampler against the arm and moved it until the sensors indicated he was above a suitable vein. Kyle pulled the trigger and simultaneously released the energy of his ad hoc spell. The small ampoule at the rear of the grip quickly filled, and Kyle could sense that it had taken the power he'd fed it. He set the gun down, removed the ampoule, and placed it inside the protective container the sampler pouch provided.

"You have my personal telecom numbers," he told the doctor. "If anything changes, call me immediately." Then he left, heading for the hospital lobby.

The building was quiet, the morning rounds just beginning. Just as Kyle was coming out of the elevator on the ground floor, he heard some commotion down one of the corridors. Following the noise, he was led straight to the administative information center, the computer heart of the facility.

The disturbance was coming from inside the main computer room, where the staff monitored the hospital's various systems. Before Kyle could enter, one of the facility's private guards, flanked by a Knight Errant officer, stopped him. Knight Errant had been assisting with hospital security ever since Mitchell Truman had been transferred here. "What's going on?" Kyle asked them. The hospital guard merely looked at him, but the Knight Errant officer recognized Kyle. His name patch said Leventhal.

"It looks to me like a decker, sir," the man said, while the hospital guard shot him a cold look.

Kyle tried to get a better view into the room, but couldn't see much.

"The computer system's internal security programs noted a load anomaly a few minutes ago," the Knight Errant guard explained. "They've been trying to figure out what's going on, but it looks like someone's decked into the computer from outside and is searching the database."

"Admittance records?" asked Kyle.

"Seems that way, sir."

Kyle sighed. If this was related to Mitchell Truman's presence, it was more than probable that whoever was cracking the computer had found his admittance records and knew he was here. "We probably shouldn't move him again," Kyle told the officer. "But let's at least change his room once the decker is either out, dumped, or they finally get smart enough to crash the system. This way whoever it is won't know Mitchell's exact whereabouts in the building. It might give us a few minutes."

The officer nodded. "I'll pass your recommendations on to Lieutenant Facile."

Kyle smiled. "You do that." He turned and walked slowly from the lobby, lost in thought. He was in luck, almost immediately able to find a taxi back to the hotel.

Back in his suite, and finally able to get some sleep, Kyle was soon dreaming of thunderstorms.

11

There were two messages awaiting Kyle when he woke nearly eight hours later. He didn't remember leaving a Do Not Disturb notice on anything but the door, but considering how much better he felt, he felt no need to complain. The first message was from Beth. She wanted him to call. He did, using his pocket telecom. The Fuchi logo appeared, floating and barely opaque, visible in his field of vision thanks to his display-link cyberware.

Kyle felt strangely uneasy calling her at work. It still felt wrong for her to be doing this job, but he'd lost the option of doing anything about it years ago. He felt a twinge as he connected into Fuchi America's internal communications network and then was routed to Beth. She picked up immediately. Her hair was styled differently then when they'd had dinner a day ago. He barely recognized her.

"John Mikayama's office, Elizabeth Breman speaking," she said crisply.

"Hoi," he said.

She paused when she saw his face. "Hoi. Are you all right?"

"Sure," he said, surprised at the question. "Why wouldn't it be?"

She pursed her lips. "I got a little worried when you didn't call."

"Sorry. I know this won't surprise you, but things got more complicated then I'd expected."

Beth nodded, glanced at something Kyle couldn't see, and then spoke again. "You're right. It doesn't surprise me. But did you get a chance to speak to Ellen?"

"No," Kyle said slowly. "But I will."

Beth looked away again. "I haven't been able to reach her. I tried all day yesterday."

"How long has it been since you've talked to her?"

"Two days."

"You've checked with her friends?"

She shook her head. "I don't know any of them—if she has any."

"I'll stop by and see her today. Is she still at her old address?"

Beth nodded.

"Don't worry. I'll call you as soon as I find out anything."

"Thanks," she said.

Kyle reached for the Disconnect, but paused for one last thought. "By the way, I like your hair."

She smiled self-consciously and reached up to smooth a nonexistent disarray. "No you don't. You're still a terrible liar." The screen jumped to black.

Checking the time, which was just after midday, Kyle thought the odds of Ellen being home were minute. Then he suddenly remembered that she didn't work—wasn't able to yet, according to the psych evaluations—and was living on settlement money the government had distributed from the seized Universal Brotherhood coffers. It was a good bet she'd be there.

The second message was, somewhat surprisingly, from Dave Strevich at the FBI. Considering their last conversation, Kyle was almost reluctant to return the call. But he did.

"Dave Strevich," the burly man said as he made the connection. "Teller! Sure took your fraggin' time getting back to me."

Kyle shrugged. "Man's gotta sleep."

"Really? Well, that explains it." Strevich held up his hand, indicating that Kyle shouldn't speak, and then tapped a few commands into his telecom keyboard. After a moment, Kyle heard a series of three low beeps come from Strevich's console. The older man nodded. "Good. We're clear."

"No bugs, eh?" said Kyle, and was surprised by the way

his friend's eyes hardened just for a moment before he laughed forcibly.

"No, nobody's listening in."

"What's going on?" Kyle asked him.

"Look, I'm not telling you this," said Strevich tersely. "Nobody did, got it?"

"Got it."

"Red alarms started going off all over Ares Macro-technology and Knight Errant some hours ago. We figured they were gearing up over some intercorporate drek, but it turns out their interest seems to be in Chicago."

Kyle was startled. "Chicago? Ares doesn't have any major offices or facilities here, at least none that I know of."

Strevich nodded. "You're right. Their interest is in you."

"Me?"

Strevich nodded. "Maybe not in you personally, but at least in what you're involved in."

"I don't understand."

Strevich shrugged. "I don't either, but Knight Errant has moved, or is in the process of moving, various key personnel and assets into Chicago."

"Assets?"

"We have it on good authority that Knight Errant has sent what they call one of their 'Firewatch' teams into the city. They have three of them. Six to a team, a hard mix of combat cybernetics and magic. Combat strike teams."

"Great Coyote," Kyle said.

"Whatever," said Strevich. "There's more. This is Team Two, and it's been operating either in Barcelona for the European trade summit or in Azania down around Cape Town, depending on which source we believe." Strevich paused. "More important is who commands it."

Kyle waited. "Who's that?"

"Anne Ravenheart," Strevich said, "*Captain* Anne Ravenheart, formerly of the Sioux Special Forces and a former classmate of yours at Columbia, if I'm not mistaken."

"That's impossible," Kyle said, trying to remember what he could about his old acquaintance, and on one drunken night, lover. "She was there on a Sioux government scholarship."

"Military scholarship."

"It can't be," Kyle insisted irrationally. What he remembered of her wasn't military, nothing hard or unyielding. Just the opposite. It was true she had an edge to her, but he had taken the source of that to be the same as his own—being born into poverty.

"Think again," Strevich said. "She's a known quantity in military circles, no question about it."

"This doesn't make sense. I've seen nothing here on a scale large enough to mobilize Knight Errant like they're gearing up for corporate war. Sure, there are some weird things, but . . ."

"Maybe you should tell me what those weird things are," said Strevich.

"Only if you'll answer my questions."

"I'll answer what I can," his friend said, "and anything I can't answer I'll see if I can get you cleared for. Don't expect much, though. Senator Birch is on the Oversight Committee these days. I'm sure he still remembers you fondly. I know his wife does."

"Thanks," said Kyle. "You always did know exactly the right thing to say."

"Your frag-up, chummer, not mine."

"Look," Kyle said, "let me fill you in on what's going on here and then maybe we can figure it all out."

"Deal," said Strevich.

"Deal," said Kyle, and then he began to give Dave Strevich the whole scan.

Strevich was quiet for most of Kyle's briefing, but it was obvious that the FBI man didn't want to be hearing any of this. The farther along Kyle got with the story, the more agitated Strevich seemed to become, though he fought unsuccessfully to hide it.

"The nature of this spirit remains unclear. I don't recognize it offhand, but I also haven't had time to do any research," Kyle said in conclusion.

Strevich was silent, leaning back in his chair, staring away at something. "Kyle," he said, after a long pause, "we've been friends for a long time."

Kyle felt himself grow cold. He didn't like either the preamble or Strevich's quiet tone.

"Listen to me when I tell you—get away from the Truman boy."

"Why?" asked Kyle. "Why?"

"I can't say."

Kyle slammed his fist on the desk, and the trideo image of Strevich jittered. "*God damn it!* You've got to tell me something!"

Strevich shook his head. "I can't. I swear to God I wish I could, but this is wrapped up so tight it scares me."

"You've got to tell me something."

"I am, Kyle—stay away from the Truman boy. What's going on there is bad, maybe as bad as it gets. You've walked straight into the middle of it. Disassociate yourself from the Trumans and disassociate yourself from your sister-in-law."

"*My sister-in-law?*" Kyle said. "What the frag does she have to do with—"

"I can't tell you any more," Strevich said. "If you've ever trusted my word, listen to me now. Get clear."

"I can't. Not without knowing more."

"I can't tell you more. You've got to understand."

Kyle nodded. "Yeah, I do," he said. "Goodbye, Dave." He reached out to hit the Disconnect, then sat there for some time staring at the blank screen. Finally he picked up his portable phone and connected it to the datajack behind his left ear. A fraction of a second later he'd called up the number he needed and entered it. It rang twice, but there was no image. Like his own, Hanna Uljakën's cellular phone had no trideo pick-up.

"This is Hanna Uljakën," she said.

"Hanna, Kyle Teller."

"Hello!" Her voice was bright and cheerful, and it sounded like she'd gotten even more sleep than he had. "There's been no word of any change at the hospital."

"That's good, I suppose. But that's not why I'm calling. I

need your help with some research. How quickly can you get over to my hotel room?"

She paused to think. "Twenty minutes?"

"Good. I'll see you then."

He disconnected and then eyed the mess the room had devolved into. He'd have to get it cleaned up before she arrived. That, and he'd need a shower.

Invoking the Truman named had Housekeeping in his room and working feverishly within five minutes of his call down to the front desk. The outer sitting room was fairly clean, just strewn with datapads and other such tech, but he wanted them to do a good job on the bedroom. He really didn't think about why.

Hanna arrived dressed in a smart blue and black Raphael business suit. Probably cost her ten times what Beth had paid for hers, he thought.

"What's going on?" she asked.

"Something big, but I don't know what it is," he said. "My sources aren't telling me much. But they know something. And if they do, someone else does too. I want to see what we can find."

"Of course."

"You use the terminal"—he motioned toward the desk—"and I'll set up my datapad on the other table and use its cellular link."

Hanna set her briefcase on the couch and removed her suit jacket, dropping it down there as well. She sat down at the telecom terminal and immediately began setting it up to search the various online and national databases.

Kyle picked up a pad off the desk and wrote some telecom numbers and passcodes on it. "Here are some that I've still got access to. Federal Data Repository, Smithsonian-Rand WorldFacts. Try these first."

"What am I looking for?"

"Do a multi-criteria search. We're looking for key words like 'spirit', 'free spirit', 'anima', and related terms. Also 'essence draining', 'neuropsychological damage', and the like. Anything similar to Mitch Truman's case."

She nodded. "That shouldn't be too hard."

"And once you get that up and running, I want to see if you can find Shadowland."

"You're joking."

"No, I'm not. I'm afraid the only way we'll get anything of real value is from the illegal databases, not the government and corp-supported boards."

"I haven't a clue how to get into it."

He smiled. "I know what's-his-name Devress does most of the 'independent personnel' hiring for the Truman family, but I'll bet you've got some connections of your own."

She smiled. "Maybe I do."

"Use them to find the local Shadowland node."

"And then?"

"Same multi-criteria search, but this time add in a few more. Add in 'Universal Brotherhood', 'Knight Errant', and anything else you can think of."

"Why the Brotherhood?"

He shrugged. "There might be a connection between what's going on here and them, but I don't know."

"All right. I can at least try," she said. "Where will you be searching?"

"Magicknet," he said.

"Never heard of it."

"No reason you should have. It's like Shadowland for magicians. I think I know where to access it, but it might take a little work."

She nodded, then began tapping in commands at the terminal.

A moment later Kyle was busy doing the same.

It took him just over an hour to track down the access number for Magicknet's Chicago node. It wasn't a public board, but one used by those interested in pirated spell information, formulae, and other non-public information on the subject of magic. He knew there were several continuously updated databases there on the subject of spirits, their abilities, and origins. If anyone who'd ever accessed the board had encountered anything even remotely similar, it would be noted in the archives. Unless he was dealing with a unique, or possibly small group of virtually unique spirits, Kyle figured his chances would be pretty good. But considering that the total database of Magicknet was measured in terabytes, trillions of bytes of data, that search could take hours . . . But that's what computers were for.

Across the room, Hanna was working her way diligently toward finding the more mundane Shadowland system. She was in mid-call, trying to cajole a news-snoop acquaintance of hers into giving her the telecom number of a data fiend who might know Shadowland's current access number. Not wanting to interrupt her, he simply waved, pointed to the door, and quietly left. Intent on her efforts, she barely noticed.

Ellen Shaw's apartment was on Chicago's west side, in the neighborhood known as Cicero. Kyle was surprised to find a parking spot so easily; he'd planned to double-park and let Truman worry about the five-hundred nuyen fine. Instead, he switched to manual control and guided the car into an ample spot one door down from where Ellen Shaw lived.

It was late afternoon, but the block was quiet. Further up the street, a group of kids were playing with some kind of remote-control aircraft that buzzed in and out of a courtyard apartment. Two nearly white squirrels eyed him expectantly, waiting for some offering of food. He waved at them and kept walking.

His sister-in-law's apartment house was a deep U-shape, with four entrances and about six times that number of units. It was run-down, the courtyard choked with weeds and roving bits of trash caught in the breeze. He pressed the apartment buzzer, but couldn't tell if it worked since there was no answer and he heard no sound of it from the window two stories above. He tried to remember if he had heard the bell the only other time he was here.

Stepping back from the door, he looked upward at the closed and curtained windows of Ellen's apartment. There was no sign of movement, and on an August afternoon, he'd have expected at least one of the windows to be open to catch the courtyard breeze. He stepped forward again and examined the entrance door. The lock was old, mechanical. That was good.

He pressed the buzzer once more, then placed his hand over the lock. Senses extended, he focused the forces of magic through him, his hand, and into the lock. He wove them together until the lock was infused with mystical energy, ready to obey his command. He willed it open. The door swung inward.

The inner door had once also carried a lock, but it was long gone, with only a shabby hole remaining. He moved through it, up the broken and musty staircase to the second floor. He stopped in front of the door at the top of the stairs, apartment 2S.

Kyle listened at the door, but heard nothing. He knocked firmly, and was surprised to hear a sudden scrambling from inside. The sound moved quickly toward him, snapping and clicking across the hardwood floor of the apartment. He stepped backward, a barrier spell ready, but the noise seemed to stop at the door.

He waited, and then whatever it was scratched, almost quietly, at the bottom of the door, near the frame. It scratched again and Kyle focused his magic and his senses, specifically his vision, projecting it forward, past the door and into the apartment. He looked down.

And the gray and white cat, as such small creatures are inexplicably wont to do, looked up at him. It was panting, thin, and starving, its nose dry and cracked from dehydration. It seemed to be trying to make a noise, but Kyle, on the far side of the door, heard nothing.

He disintegrated the lock with a carefully aimed dart of focused violet power. The cat, whose name he knew to be Grendel, scooted away as fast as it could, slipping and skidding across the floor as it disappeared around the corner.

Kyle expected a terrible smell when he entered, but the short hall was only musty, hot, and dry. Bits of metal lock and wooden door were scattered down the hall and into the living room, but he closed the door behind him, pushing at the twisted wood until it shut. The main room was as spartan as he remembered it, and showed no signs of anything out of the ordinary. A single red light flashed repeatedly on the telecom.

He ignored it for the moment and pulled aside one of the heavy curtains, letting light spill into the apartment. Kyle then cautiously entered the next room, the dining room, turning right and following the path of the cat. It was nowhere to be seen, and the room was unremarkable. The kitchen to the left was the same, except that the trash can showed signs of having been rifled and raided. The cat's empty bowls were near the door to the rear stair, next to its obviously used litter box and a compacted bag of trash.

Kyle walked across the room and into the short hall that led to the bathroom at the end and the bedroom across from it. He checked the latter first. The bed was unmade. A small fan on a nearby night stand blew warm air across the sheets. The room, except for its furniture, was empty. A pair of dull eyes stared at him from under the bed. Grendel.

A quick sweep of the rest of the apartment: the bathroom and various closets revealed nothing. He filled the water and food bowls in the kitchen, and Grendel, needing no coaxing, attacked them with renewed energy.

Except for some sad-looking plants in the living room, that cat, Kyle suspected, was the only living thing that had been in that apartment in close to a week.

Of the seven messages, six were from Beth. The seventh was a wrong number.

He searched the apartment and found little, save a small cache of secreted Universal Brotherhood literature and chips in a small box in the closet. Then, in a plastic tray in the topmost drawer of the dresser, he found Ellen's house keys and wallet, with her credstick slipped neatly into its holder in the wallet's spine. Also stuffed in there was a small wad of about a hundred and twenty dollars' worth of paper money. Unless these were all spares, Ellen Shaw had gone out a week ago without her money, her ID, or her keys, and never returned.

Kyle poked through the apartment for another hour or so, eventually refusing to feed Grendel after the cat begged for a fourth bowl of food. When he finally left, Kyle could do little about the door lock, so he used his magic to warp the wood slightly once the door was closed. The door would open, but someone would have to use his shoulder to do so. He'd let Beth know about the cat.

Outside, the kids had moved closer to this end of the street, and an Eagle Security patrol car had pulled up alongside a white minivan parked in front of a fire hydrant near where the kids had originally been playing. One officer, a young Chinese man, was obviously scanning the license plate and running it through his portacomp. His partner, a woman, Kyle suspected, though he couldn't tell much more about her, was on the driver's side talking to someone he couldn't see through the tint on the windscreen. As he came out, they both turned and looked at him.

His pocket phone rang.

Kyle let it ring twice more as he slipped into astral perception and carefully scanned the area. It looked normal, completely and utterly normal, including the van, the patrol car, and the two officers. He reached into his pocket on the fourth ring and slowly extended the interface cable and plugged it behind his left ear.

"Yes," he said to the caller, eyeing the white minivan.

Hanna Uljakën's voice echoed in his ear just as the plug clicked home in his datajack and her image sprang up in his view.

"Kyle, it's me." She was obviously still in his hotel room.

"Are you all right?" he asked.

She seemed puzzled. "I'm fine. How about you?"

"So far, so good."

She was suddenly alert and cautious. "Devress just called me. I'm wanted back at the Truman apartment immediately. He wouldn't say, but something was definitely up. He asked where you were. I told him I'd let you know."

Still listening, Kyle watched the two police officers casually move away from the van and climb back into their own car. Though the street was two-way, the police car went in reverse until it reached the end of the block, then backed into a turn before moving forward again and out of sight. The minivan didn't move.

"I'll be there as fast as I can, but it'll be about twenty minutes," he told her. "I'm at the edge of the city." For some reason, he didn't feel like telling her even generally where he was.

He saw her nod. "I'll let them know," she said, "Oh, and I found—"

He cut her off. "Wait and tell me when you see me. And ask the front desk to put extra security on my room. Have them bill your boss."

She nodded again. "I will."

"Copy any information you might have off the room's computer and take it with you. If the search is finished on my datapad, take that with you too."

"I will."

"And have Knight Errant come pick you up. Call Facile right away, even before you start copying files."

Hanna was obviously disturbed by his tone and the content of his requests, but she agreed. "I'll see you in twenty minutes at the Tower."

She disconnected.

Kyle did the same, got into his car, and quickly pulled away, making a U-turn so as to drive past the minivan. He couldn't see inside as he went by, but he did note the registration plate.

The van did not follow him.

12

"Kyle Teller," said Daniel Truman, "this is Captain Anne Ravenheart of Knight Errant. She's a personal security expert sent in to help with the situation."

Kyle stepped forward and took the offered hand of his former classmate and accidental lover of a decade ago. She hadn't changed that much, but some differences were noticeable. The long black hair that he remembered so well had become a ragged, ear-length military cut. Gone, too, were the dangling earrings she'd favored, replaced by a pair of chrome datajacks below each ear. Her eyes were still green, but they glistened differently, oddly. Kyle didn't think they were real. But when she smiled, that was exactly as he remembered it.

"Hello, Kyle," she said, squeezing his hand.

"How've you been, Anne?" He tried to keep his tone utterly casual. "This is quite a surprise."

She shrugged and widened her smile. "For me too."

Anne Ravenheart's arrival signaled some other changes that Kyle had noticed even before entering the building. Changes mainly to do with beefed-up security and a much more visible presence for Knight Errant. It had been a Knight Errant officer rather than the usual doorman who met his car. Kyle had also noticed a perimeter drone about half the size of a man sitting under a gray tarp in a niche near the doorway. At the elevator bank the guards were obviously armed and cybered, their body armor equally evident. Then the elevator had asked for re-verification of Kyle's vocal pattern by repeating the random words it said to him. There was even an armed guard in the hall outside the Truman apartment.

Anne Ravenheart and two other Knight Errant officers were with the Trumans on the patio near the pool, Mr. Truman looking tense and Mrs. Truman tired and distracted. Melissa and Madeleine were there too, both showing visible relief at Kyle's arrival. Hanna Uljakën looked just as relieved. The other assistant, Devress, who had hired Kyle, was also present. He gave Kyle a slight smile when their eyes met. No other staff members were present. Nor was Lieutenant Facile, who Kyle had not seen anywhere on the way up either.

The three Knight Errant officers were garbed in what he took to be casual field dress. One-piece gray and white urban camouflage jumpsuits and darker bulky jackets bearing their rank insignia and red and black corporate logos. Each carried a heavy sidearm, and Kyle guessed that the tall, thin, hawk-faced man with thin brown hair peeking out from under his black beret was, like Anne Ravenheart, also a magician.

"You know each other?" Daniel Truman asked, glancing from Kyle to Anne and back.

"Yes, sir," Anne said. "Kyle and I went to school together longer ago than I'd care to admit."

Truman laughed. "Well, Mr. Teller is probably wondering how he comes to meet you again here. Why don't you tell him?"

Ravenheart turned to Kyle. "As you know, Mr. Truman is a good friend of Damien Knight, CEO of Ares Macrotechnology. When Mr. Knight heard about the disappearance of Mitchell Truman, he ordered Knight Errant's assets placed at Mr. Truman's disposal.

"And I've been sent in to handle Knight Errant's investigation of who's responsible and what we might do to restore the boy to health."

Kyle hazarded a glance at Hanna Uljakën, whose eyes showed concern.

"Well, your assistance is certainly appreciated," Kyle said. "With Knight Errant helping out I'm sure we can—"

"They want to take over," Melissa said suddenly, her gaze darting between Kyle and the frown her father was giving her.

Ravenheart was also frowning. "As Mr. Truman and I were discussing when you arrived, Knight Errant would prefer to handle the investigation and security exclusively. To do otherwise might slow down critical communication and hinder the operation—regardless of the other talent involved." She gave Kyle a slight smile. "Nothing personal."

He shrugged. "None taken. I agree it would be a good idea to combine forces, but I'd argue for your people to assist *us*." He let his gaze travel briefly around the assembled group. "Things are already happening. I'd be reluctant to lose any time transferring command and information.

"And, truthfully, I've been exploring some avenues that I'd rather not reveal due to the confidentiality of the sources. Knight Errant's assistance is certainly appreciated, but it seems to make more sense for them to support the existing structure than trying to rebuild it."

Ravenheart was about to protest, when Daniel Truman cut in. "I tend to agree with Mr. Teller. Ms. Uljakën tells me that the two of them have been making progress toward identifying the people responsible."

"People?" asked Ravenheart, turning back to Kyle. She seemed about to continue her line of thought, but a flick of her eyes at Mrs. Truman apparently decided her otherwise. Instead, she said, "That's good news. Whatever your decision, Mr. Truman, Knight Errant is at your disposal."

"Excellent," he said. "Mr. Teller is still looking into this for me and my family, and your prior acquaintance should make it all the easier for him to get what he needs from your team."

"I'm sure it will."

"For anything else," Truman told her, "please liase through my assistant Ms. Uljakën, who is also working with Mr. Teller."

"I'll do that, sir. In the meantime would it be possible for Mr. Teller to brief us on his progress?"

"Now's as good a time as any." Daniel Truman motioned

his family toward the doors leading back inside. They obediently followed his lead, though Melissa gave Kyle another strained look as she disappeared from view. This time Hanna saw it too, but he didn't react to the questioning on her face. Devress also stayed behind, but melted farther back from the discussion.

"First I'd like to apologize for not introducing the other two members of my team," Ravenheart said immediately. She gestured to the burly man, who Kyle was fairly certain was not a mage. "This is Sergeant Keith Vathoss," she said.

Vathoss nodded, and Kyle could almost hear the flatmotors and microhydraulics of his cyberware rev up as he did. His hair was buzz-cut and bright red, his chin square and neck bulky from the chemicals he was taking to boost whatever natural muscles his body still had. His eyes were dark and translucent, a protective shield grafted over what Kyle was sure were equally artificial vision and related sensory systems.

Vathoss smiled. "Sir," he said.

"And this is Lieutenant Paul Gersten." Ravenheart gestured to the other man. "My second in command."

Gersten stuck out his hand and Kyle shook it. "Pleased to meet you," he said, noting that Gersten's grip was strong, but cold.

Ravenheart turned back to Kyle. Her posture was formal and her eyes set while she spoke. "We've got a somewhat awkward situation here because we know each other." He nodded agreement. "But we're going to have to ignore that, even if it means things might ultimately get more awkward."

Kyle could see Hanna watching the exchange with intense interest.

"Now don't take this wrong," Ravenheart went on, "because I have the greatest respect for you and your talent, but you're way out of your league this time."

"Thank you for pointing that out," Kyle said.

She sighed. "I'm sorry to be so blunt, but you probably didn't know that Knight Errant has been conducting its own investigation concurrently with your own."

Kyle glanced at Hanna, who seemed surprised. Beyond her, Devress was expressionless.

"And we've turned up a few interesting things." She turned to Gersten. "Lieutenant?"

Gersten cleared his throat and took a small step closer to them. "We know that we're dealing with a covert group of anima spirits operating in the guise of five women, Dierdre Reinmann, Karyn Moffit, Mary Hauser, Gwen Pitvorec, and Linda Hayward. They're a conspiratorial group whose motivations are unclear except that they are apparently directed toward the gain and advancement of the group."

"How does Mitchell Truman fit into this?" asked Kyle. "It sounds like some kind of women-only group, probably with pretty hard-line strictures. They couldn't have been trying to recruit him."

Ravenheart shook her head. "We believe they were trying to possess him," she said, "but slotted up royally."

"How could they hope to pull that off? If they're anima spirits, they've got pronounced 'female' characteristics. It would have been difficult for any of them to pretend to be Mitch Truman."

"The boy was bisexual," said Gersten, and Kyle saw Ravenheart wince.

Kyle glared at the man. "I won't even bother responding to that."

"I'm with you," Ravenheart said. "I think the Hayward-spirit targeted or stumbled across Mitchell, established a romantic connection, maybe through magic, and was going to use him." She paused. "And then something went wrong."

Kyle nodded. "Something in the relationship changed. Who knows? Maybe he found out something, and they had to act."

"What you don't know, Kyle, is that the night Mitchell Truman was found, his sister Melissa was on her way to meet with him."

"What?"

"She'd received a call from her brother earlier that evening and had sneaked off to meet him. We intercepted the call and so knew where to go when she shook off the two guards with her. She made it, but her brother never showed up."

"Do you think your people might have scared him off?"

Both Gersten and Vathoss seemed to bristle slightly, but Ravenheart just shrugged. "Hard to tell. Our team was pretty well concealed, but anything is possible. The point is simply that he called his sister and asked her to meet him secretly."

Kyle frowned. "You think they were switching targets and going for Melissa?"

Devress didn't flinch, but Hanna gasped. "It would make sense," Ravenheart said. "If they saw they were losing control over Mitchell, it would have been logical to try to get direct control over another member of the family."

"Through possession," said Kyle.

Raven nodded. "Through possession. In the same manner they control the bodies they now inhabit."

"So what do you recommend as our next step?"

"Maintain level one security on the whole Truman family and their immediate staff," Ravenheart said. "It's unlikely the group will try again, especially now that we're alerted, but we want to play it safe. Once we've got that in place, we continue our pursuit of the Desolation Angels."

"Got any leads?" Kyle asked.

Ravenheart smiled. "Oh yes, but our sources are confidential, so I can't reveal the status of any just yet."

Kyle returned the smile. "Of course."

"Suffice it to say we're close."

"Good. Then I won't keep you." Kyle reached into his pocket for one of his business cards. "Let me give you my portable telecom number . . ."

"I have it," Ravenheart said.

He stopped searching. "Well, then, can I have yours?"

"Ms. Uljakën's got it. You can reach me directly at that number or through the command post we've established in the building's security office."

"That should make it easy."

"Good. Then everything's settled for now." Ravenheart turned and, much to Kyle's surprise, gestured her teammates toward a walkway that led along the patio and out of sight toward the building area. "I'll be in touch as soon as we learn anything further."

Ravenheart turned to follow the other two Knight Errant troopers away, but looked over her shoulder just before passing out of sight. "We should talk too," she said.

Kyle smiled. "We will."

She returned the smile and vanished around the corner.

"Where are they going?" he asked Hanna, who was walking quickly toward him. Behind her, Devress was scanning the patio area slowly. He seemed very intent on something.

"They arrived in a tilt-rotor. I presume they're going back to the helipad."

Kyle nodded, then called for Charlotte.

The spirit was instantly at his side, and had probably been waiting directly alongside him in astral space. "Watch them and make sure they all leave. Return to me if they don't go straight to the aircraft, and return to me if they depart in it."

"I will," Charlotte said as she vanished.

Kyle looked around the pool area. "Seeks-the-Moon?" he said.

Devress looked up. "Yes?" he said, his features and clothing melting, flowing against gravity into the form of Seeks-the-Moon.

"I'll be damned," said Kyle.

"Quiet possibly," agreed the spirit, "but I suspect your old friend Captain Ravenheart will be receiving her fitting punishment a few circles below your own."

"Oh?" said Kyle.

"You will, of course, find yourself head turned backward with the others of your kind in the seventh pouch of Malebolge," said the spirit, quoting Dante, "while she will be found three below you, in the tenth pouch, with the other liars."

"You think she lied to us?" asked Hanna.

"Nearly every word," Kyle said.

Hanna looked back and forth between Kyle and the spirit. "How do you know?"

"Timing," said Kyle. "Everything she said here and the things we already know imply that Knight Errant was inves-

tigating the case long before the Truman family actively re-
cruited them."

"I don't follow."

"We know Knight Errant bought out your previous security provider's contract about three months ago. Why?"

Hanna shrugged. "Prestige, market position. Any number
of reasons."

"Three months ago was about the time Mitchell Truman
first met Linda Hayward, or whoever she is."

"True, but I don't see how you can be sure there's a connection," Hanna told him.

"I also know that Knight Errant is throwing mega assets
into the Chicago area. In fact they've been doing that for
some time now. For about the past three months, to be exact."

"They're gearing up to be a force in the Chicago market,"
Hanna told him. "They were very clear and direct about
that."

Kyle shook his head. "Wrong kinds of assets. You don't
move military-grade combat teams into a city if you only intend to beef up your image."

Hanna's eyes widened. "Military? You think that Captain
Ravenheart and her people are military?"

"Knight Errant's equivalent, certainly."

A dull whine began to echo overhead, quickly building to
a powerful roar of jet turbine engines. Seeks-the-Moon was
a blur as he moved out of sight, passing through the patio
doors and into the sanctuary of the condoplex. Over their
heads, visible through the armored glass skylight, a Knight
Errant tilt-wing cleared the building and began accelerating
away quickly, its engines rotating into position for forward
flight. It was going west.

"Heading to O'Hare," said Kyle.

Hanna nodded. "Ares has a small enclave out there. We
understand that's where Knight Errant has its base."

Kyle turned as the patio doors slid open. Seeks-the-Moon
stepped through, an odd smile on his face. Close behind
came a sour-faced Daniel Truman, who stood watching the

receding tilt-wing craft. At that moment, Charlotte also reappeared next to Kyle.

"*Master,*" she said. "*They all departed on the aircraft.*"

"Thank you, Charlotte. Resume your patrols." The spirit vanished.

"What kind of game do you think they're playing?" Truman asked him.

Kyle shrugged. "Truthfully, I'm not sure."

"But you agree something's going on?"

"Most definitely," Kyle said. "They obviously have their own agenda here. I'm just not sure what it is."

"Pardon me for saying so," said Hanna to them both, "but I still don't quite see why you're so sure Knight Errant is up to something."

"I've met Damien Knight twice, Hanna," Daniel Truman told her. "I could repeat to you verbatim all twelve words we've exchanged. Yes, my firm has some dealings with his. But the two of us? We aren't friends. Especially not the kind of friends who give the other a billion nuyen worth of help without being asked."

Kyle gasped. "A billion? What did they offer you?"

Truman smiled lightly. "They said if things got particularly unpleasant—and they subtly warned me they might—I might want to think about taking a vacation with my family off-planet."

"*Off*-planet?"

Truman nodded. "They offered me a free orbit-lift and luxury quarters on their *Daedalus* space station."

Kyle was nearly speechless. "That seems more than a little . . ."

"Yes, doesn't it?" Truman said. "Of course, they said that would be a worst-case option, but they wouldn't elaborate on what that worst case might be."

Kyle shook his head. "Knight Errant is up to something. Do you feel comfortable releasing them from your service?"

Truman frowned. "No . . . for better or for worse, they're the best at protecting me and my family. I think they have ulterior motives for doing so, but I don't think they wish my family ill."

"I suspect you're right. Though I don't think we can assume they wouldn't be against sacrificing one of you to get whatever it is they want."

Truman's eyes were hard. "Like they might have done with Mitch."

Hanna's eyes widened. "I don't understand . . ."

"If they were watching him and my family for months," Truman said, "why didn't they step in and do something when Mitch got grabbed? Hell, they may even have known where he was."

"I don't think so," Kyle said. "Otherwise they'd have had no reason to be watching Melissa the night Mitch was found."

"They were watching Melissa?" Truman was obviously surprised. "Who the hell told you that?"

"It came up during the talk I had with Captain Ravenheart. The night Mitch was found, Melissa sneaked away to meet with him. She'd received a telecom call or some other contact that Knight Errant monitored from Mitch. I think they deliberately let her think she'd ducked them and then shadowed her. Mitch, however, never showed."

"You have proof of this?" Truman asked.

"Just circumstantial. Knight Errant was supposedly using ritual sorcery to trace her. They even had a ritual sample, which should have made it incredibly easy to track a nonmagically protected target like Melissa. It would have taken no more than the minimum time for the ritual—say an hour or two."

"But they said they didn't find her until she was back at the condoplex," Hanna said. "Nearly five hours later."

"Exactly," said Kyle.

"Goddamn them," said Daniel Truman, staring off in the direction of the long-gone tilt-rotor.

Seeks-the-Moon quietly stepped forward. "It would also seem that they have some information regarding the women-spirits."

Hanna started. "I nearly forgot. My search didn't really

turn up anything useful"—she turned to Kyle—"but yours did."

"Oh?" he said.

She shrugged. "I looked when I grabbed your datapad . . ."

"What did it find?"

"You got a couple of search requests indicating that Knight Errant and Ares were both willing to pay for information regarding something called 'aberrant spirits'."

"What does that mean?" asked Truman.

"Spirits they don't understand," said Seeks-the-Moon. "Or perhaps a type that contradicts what they believe they know about spirits."

"Aberrant spirits," echoed Kyle. "That could be almost anything." He looked at Hanna. "Do you remember when it said Ares first started looking for that kind of data?"

Hanna closed her eyes and tilted her head, trying to recall. "Early February twenty fifty-one," she said after a moment. "About four years ago."

"It could be a coincidence," Truman pointed out.

"Yes, but too many coincidences aren't likely either," Kyle said. "Did the searches turn up anything on their findings?"

Hanna shook her head. "No, not directly, but you and I combined did get about two and a half gigapulses of data on the various subjects."

"Great. The answers could be somewhere among all that data, but we might never find it."

"I can set up a search program with a finer filter to run through the data we have. Index and cross-reference it. Then we can just scan the topic list," Hanna offered.

"Do that," Kyle said, then turned to Truman. "In the meantime, I'd like to—"

Somewhere, deep inside of him, the echo of a part of his being that had been sent elsewhere twisted. He felt it burn, and then an instant later, dissolve as potential unexpectedly freed returned to him.

He gasped.

Seeks-the-Moon was suddenly alongside him. "What is

it?" Concern also showed on the faces of both Hanna Uljakën and Dan Truman.

"One of the elementals I left guarding Mitch has been destroyed," Kyle said. He turned to look out across the city in the direction of the Handlemann Institute. "And that means the hospital is under attack."

Dan Truman turned white. "Oh my god . . ."

"I've got to get over there," Kyle told Seeks-the-Moon, who nodded but seemed surprised. "Charlotte!" Kyle called, and the air elemental appeared alongside him.

"Help her," he told the spirit, pointing at Hanna. "Gather the rest of the Truman family inside. Then do anything and everything Seeks-the-Moon tells you."

If air spirits could scowl, Charlotte did so, but all she said was, *"I will do as you say."*

"You'll need my help at the hospital," said Seeks-the-Moon.

"No, it could be a trick," Kyle said, quickly sitting down in one of the pool chairs. "Excuse me. I need to get over there."

Working as fast as he could, Kyle turned his perception inward and allowed his spirit freedom from its physical body. He separated, then looked over the quiet area of astral space around the pool, the mundanes Dan Truman and Hanna Uljakën, though she still wore her scintillating earring, and the spirits Seeks-the-Moon and Charlotte. The mundanes stared at his body while the two spirits watched where Kyle floated a meter or so above the ground. Only Hanna seemed to catch on that Seeks-the-Moon was looking somewhere else than she was.

Kyle nodded at the spirits, turned, and shot outward over the city. The Handlemann Institute was not far, about twenty blocks north of the Truman Tower. He was there even before his physical body had collapsed fully in the chair.

A sense of despair filled him as he entered the hospital—emotional overflow from the sick and the dying. But there was something else he could feel as he dropped quickly through the man-made floors, taking as straight a path toward Mitchell Truman's room as he could. There was pain,

active and sharp, echoing upward at him, and some odd
metaphysical aroma, pungent, cold, and *alien*.

He dropped into the Truman boy's room, and almost
leaped out again in revulsion. The room was splattered in
blood and gore, the bed torn and twisted, slammed against
one wall. But Mitchell Truman was not in it. The blood,
Kyle saw, came from the bodies of a disemboweled guard—
Knight Errant by the tattered shards of his uniform—and
what seemed to be only the torso of a small woman in a doctor's coat. Parts of her were lodged between the blinds on
the window.

Kyle cursed, and felt another twinge—his other elemental.
Its cry came from below him again, deeper in the bowels of
the building. He willed himself down toward it, and felt the
reverberations of a powerful spell echo through astral space.
He homed in on it.

He emerged in a corridor as the final wisps of unleashed
mystic energy washed through it, illuminating it in shifting
astral colors of green and blue. There were four beings present. Two of them human and two of them spirits.

The two humans were probably from Knight Errant, but
from astral space Kyle could not read the markings or colors
of their uniforms. Their clothing was a simple, non-living
dull gray. One, however, was a mage, and his aura sparkled
with the residual energy of the powerful spell he'd just
tossed at one of the spirits. The mage stumbled backward,
pained by the force of that spell, while his companion, by
his size and form apparently an ork, opened fire on the
larger of the two spirits with his assault rifle.

The dark spirit, twice man-sized, barely noticed as the
rounds of gunfire passed through its shadowy body and tore
up the wall behind it.

Kyle stared, unable to suppress a gasp. The thing before
him was huge, with six sharp legs and a long, flattened body
of a shiny leathery brown. A terrible scent, horribly pungent
and one that could only be described as an *odor*, reached
Kyle in astral space. The spirit lashed out with one of those
legs, a smaller front one, and caught the mage across the up-

per part of his right arm. Blood jutted from the wound, spraying the other guard and the spirit.

The second spirit, Kyle's elemental, sputtered near the floor, dim and weakened from an obvious clash with this many-legged thing. Oblivious to Kyle's arrival, the dark spirit moved in on the collapsing mage.

Kyle acted quickly, thinking to attack the spirit while it was distracted. His choices were simple—attack it directly with the raw energy of his own form or through a spell. Both were dangerous.

He enacted the spell, pulling the energies of astral space together with blinding speed. The spirit looked up at him, though its form seemed to have no true eyes. Kyle had no doubt it could sense him quite clearly. It began to hiss.

The energy flowed, violet, white, and blue, into him as the final pieces of the spell came together in his mind, and the spirit leaped, spreading its short, apparently vestigial wings, as he released the spell.

The spell caught the spirit square on, a bolt of astral power that impacted against the creature's head and splashed backward along nearly the whole length of its dark, shiny body. It squealed, the sound of its cry alien and painful in astral space, then seemed to shake its form as though to trying throw off the remaining energies of the spell tearing at it. As it thrashed, its legs flashed about, ripping tears in the walls and threatening to dismember the others in the hall. Its long feelers slapped against Kyle.

He reeled. The pain from casting the powerful spell in astral space, raw and unanchored to the physical world, was tremendous. He was also nearly suffocated by a putrid, nearly overpowering odor. He fought off the red mist that filled his mind as the spirit steadied itself. Tendrils of astral smoke rose from its hideous form as it leaped at him again.

Kyle barely had time to react. As an FBI man he'd learned quick and dirty hand-to-hand combat from a UCAS Marine Corps specialist, and that training came back to him now. He turned his body aside violently as the spirit shot forward. The lead claws missed, and then Kyle was inside them, close to the spirit's head. Grappling at the thing for leverage with his left hand, he focused as much raw energy as possible into his right as he brought it up under what he thought was the spirit's head.

The energy of his astral body clashed with that of the spirit's in a flash of gold and black power. Kyle felt resistance, the spirit's form seeming armored even in astral space. He forced his hand upward. Pain raked across his back as one of the second set of legs struck him.

The spirit reared, uttering another of its awful shrieks, and Kyle saw his injured water elemental stab upward into the creature's underside. The thing bucked and spun, slamming against the wall and dragging Kyle off his feet. It squealed hideously again, and Kyle struck down with his own feet against its distended belly, pushing with all his might while grabbing what he could of the spirit's head with his right hand.

The spirit curled up all its legs when the head finally gave way. The head, such as it was, tore free of the body. The force of the separation, induced by Kyle's own will, threw him to the side, past the striking legs and on to the floor.

The spirit writhed, its body tossing about uncontrolled, the stench even stronger now, until its movement began to lessen and its form dissolve, streaming and floating off through astral space. In agony, Kyle looked at the head-thing in his hand as it too dispersed, its coherency lost with its life. Suddenly, he realized what he was looking at, and what he'd just fought.

His mind fought against the truth. The legs, the head, the short wings, the long, twitching antennae, the strange shape of the body. Here in the bowels of the hospital, Kyle had just done combat with a vicious, magically powerful spirit. And that spirit had the form of an enormous, hideous, stinking brown cockroach.

13

Kyle lay there in astral space, his back wracked with pain from the slashing by the cockroach spirit's legs. The pain was severe, but the injuries didn't feel life-threatening. His body, back in the Truman condoplex, had manifested the physical effects of the spirit's astral attack, but Kyle had the pain all to himself. The spirit itself was gone, destroyed. He turned his head to look at the two Knight Errant troopers.

The ork had applied a trauma patch to the mage's shoulder in an attempt to stop the heavy bleeding. Kyle could see the man's aura flickering; he was unconscious and unable to help heal his own body. Kyle didn't know if he himself had enough energy merely to try and stabilize him. If he'd been physically present and this injured, he wouldn't give it a second thought. Being present only in astral space was another matter, for he risked injury to himself if he tried to heal another.

But Kyle didn't have to heal the man, only stop him from dying. He willed himself to float toward the injured mage to examine him more closely.

There. A power focus in the form of a bracelet on the magician's left hand. Without that link from the astral world to the physical one—the circuit of power from astral space, through the focus, into the mage—Kyle wouldn't have been able to help him. But the active focus made all the difference.

Kyle reached out and placed one hand on the man's heart, the other on his left hand at the focus. He would have to slow the man's metabolism, slow his respiration and heart beat, slow his body down to where critical seconds became critical minutes. Kyle picked a rhythm in astral space, the slow beat of ambient energy, and slowed his to match it.

The ork realized something was happening, and stepped back, pulling his sidearm clear as a dull halo of green energy began to surround the injured man. The ork's eyes searched the area, but he could see no target, nothing against which to protect his friend. Then, as the energy flowed around the mage, the ork's radio crackled to life.

Kyle couldn't make out the words that came over it; they were an electronic signal, cold, lifeless, and meaningless to his perceptions in astral space. But the ork's reply was clear.

"Roger, roger!" he shouted into his throat mike. "Officer down, ground floor near the loading dock. I need a trauma alert and another mage. Something's happening down here!"

Kyle felt the injured man respond, his body sliding into synchrony with the rhythm Kyle was providing it. The blood flow slowed, nearly stopping. If Knight Errant could get a medic or another magician with healing spells here in time, he would survive.

"Roger that!" said the ork trooper. "One bug down here. Repeat one bug down!" The radio crackled in reply, and the ork returned his attention to his companion. Kyle backed away. There was little chance the ork would notice him. The emotions and lingering energy from the fight with the spirit were dampening any of Kyle's own aura that might have leaked into the physical world, but he still didn't relish the sensation of being pushed aside by the trooper's significantly greater mass.

He looked around. There were no physical signs of the magical battle that had just taken place, only the physical effects of the weapons fire and sprayed blood. He heard footsteps running toward him from where the cockroach spirit had been standing. Kyle shot in that direction, wincing at the pain that coursed through him. He quickly passed a field medic and another trooper. Far beyond them, way down the hall, he could see another trooper covering their movement.

Kyle willed himself in that direction, and found the trooper also guarding an injured hospital guard who sat in a small pool of blood. Continuing on, he passed through a pair of swinging doors, and into the what seemed to be the hospital's shipping and receiving area.

There had been a fight here, a pitched battle, from the look of it. Kyle saw six bodies, two were Knight Errant and two seemed to be hospital employees probably caught in the crossfire. The last two looked human at first glance, but even though they were dead and their auras long vanished, Kyle could sense something wrong about them.

"Secure the site!" a familiar voice yelled, "Cover the bodies!"

Kyle turned and saw Lieutenant Facile in full combat gear, one arm bandaged and bloody, leaning against a pile of boxes. A doctor or nurse—Kyle couldn't tell which—tended him. Despite his injury, Facile's aura seemed strong. Kyle quickly floated over to him and slowly made himself visible.

Across the room, a half-dozen weapons instantly turned on him. None fired as he held his hands in a submissive raised position.

"Facile," Kyle said, as the lieutenant stepped in front of the woman assisting him and used his good arm to draw his heavy pistol. "It's Kyle Teller."

"Son of a bitch!" Facile said. "What the frag are you doing—"

"I killed one of the roach spirits down the hall from here." Kyle pointed back in the direction he'd come. *"One of your mages got torn up pretty bad, but I was able to stabilize him."* He paused to let those words sink in. *"Mind telling me what's going on?"*

Facile had turned to look in the direction Kyle had pointed, then relaxed and reholstered the weapon. It was another few moments before the frightened nurse resumed work on his arm. "Fraggin' bugs attacked the hospital in force," he told Kyle, gesturing at the two strange bodies now being covered. "At least four true forms and a half-dozen or so of these clean flesh forms."

"Flesh forms? True forms?" Kyle asked him. *"What's the difference?"*

Facile gestured again at the pair of now covered bodies. "We call these pieces of trash flesh forms. They're possessed by bug spirits, but they look human. Most that get possessed aren't this lucky. True forms just look like fraggin' big versions of the real bug."

"Where's the boy?" Kyle asked.

Facile pointed toward where Kyle took the loading dock door to be. The physical details of the concrete and metal room were nearly indistinguishable to him. "Took him away in a car waiting out there."

Kyle was about to head in that direction, but Facile stopped him. "Don't bother! I don't even have a make on the car." He pointed at the dead troopers. "They're the only ones who saw it."

"No idea which way it went?"

"None."

"Security tapes?" Kyle looked around the room to see whether it contained any dull machinery that might be a camera.

Facile shook his head as the woman administering to him stepped away. "They hit the security room first after eating our sentry spirits. Trashed all the digital storage. Backups were in the same room."

Kyle nodded. *"I'm at the Truman condoplex. Let me know right away if anything else turns up."*

Facile almost seemed to laugh. "I'm sure Captain Ravenheart will call you once she's done chewing us up here."

Kyle shifted out of his physical manifestation and accelerated at maximum speed across the short space of city.

Back at the Truman house the patio area around his body was quite a mess. Apparently the roach spirit had hit Kyle hard, not only on the back but on his left leg as well. His body had apparently thrashed, sending blood pouring from the sudden wounds. Hanna was seated across the patio being assisted by one of the other staff members. Kyle also noticed that Dan Truman was standing watch over his physical body, along with Seeks-the-Moon and two of Truman's personal—not Knight Errant—guards. Someone had already administered emergency first aid to his body. In spirit form, he'd barely felt it.

Kyle called out mentally, *"Moon!"*

"Yes!" came the clear reply as the spirit looked up at him. "Are you well?"

"Well enough. How bad do I look?"

"You've been worse," Moon said. "You've made quite a mess of the patio, though, and I'm afraid your friend Ms. Uljakën was a little unprepared for your spontaneous wounding."

Kyle laughed, and then commanded Charlotte, who immediately appeared in astral space.

"The two are dead?" she asked him. Kyle nodded, recognizing the empty spaces within himself for both spirits, the second apparently destroyed when it moved to help him against the roach spirit.

"We're fighting what seem to be some kind of insect spirits." With those words, Kyle saw Seeks-the-Moon's face blanch and his powerful aura waver, for just a fraction of an instant. Even the air elemental, normally supremely detached, seemed to shudder. Kyle was surprised; he'd never heard of such spirits before either.

"I understand," said Charlotte. *"I will try to serve you well."*

Again, Kyle was surprised by the tone of near finality in the spirit's words. *"Good,"* he said. *"Stay alert."*

"They will not pass me," Charlotte assured him, then vanished.

Kyle willed himself back into his body, re-forming flesh and spirit into one, but instantly regretted the decision. The pain was terrible, and he felt his body spasm as he reacted to it.

Dan Truman started to speak, probably wanting to know what had happened at the hospital, but Kyle held up his hand. Seeks-the-Moon also reached out and placed a hand on Truman's arm to still him. His body wanted to sleep, but Kyle knew he couldn't.

He sat up slowly and felt Seeks-the-Moon's strong hands under him, helping him into a chair. "Thank you," Kyle said.

"What's happening?" Truman asked, unable to restrain himself any longer. "Your spirit here wouldn't tell me a thing."

"I'm afraid your son's been kidnapped."

"Oh my god . . ." said Truman.

Looking pale and shaky, Hanna had also joined them. "Why?" she said. "Why would they take him now?"

"All I know is that they did. Knight Errant couldn't stop them. It's a real mess over there."

"How did it happen?" she asked.

"Remember Ares was looking for information on 'aberrant spirits'?"

Hanna nodded.

"Well, they found some," Kyle told her.

"What do you mean?"

"I fought one. A powerful thing. I'm lucky there was only one. Fraggin' thing looked like a huge insect. You won't believe this—like a giant cockroach."

Seeks-the-Moon paled, and his existence seemed to flicker in the physical world for the briefest instant. Both Truman and Hanna also drew back in silent revulsion.

"That's all I know," Kyle said. "It was bigger than I am, and looked just like an enormous roach. The Knight Errant troopers seemed to know what they were and referred to them as 'bugs'."

Truman's eyes were fire-bright. "I don't really know what you're talking about, Mr. Teller, but it scares me cold. I'm going to call Damien Knight about this. Let's see just how good a pair of friends he and I really are."

Kyle held up his hand. "If I could suggest something . . ."

Truman stopped and turned back. "Yes?"

"Knight Errant now knows that I know at least something about these 'bugs'," Kyle said, "and that I've probably told you. Let's see what they do. Let's see what they decide to tell us."

Truman nodded. "All right. I see your logic. Their hand's been shown. Let's see if they still insist on bluffing. Fair enough." His gaze turned back toward the interior of the condoplex. Beyond the dark plastiglass of the patio door

Kyle could see a couple of vague shapes waiting impatiently. "In the meantime, I'd better go tell my wife."

Kyle nodded and leaned back, closing his eyes, thinking Truman had walked away. He opened them quickly when he heard Daniel Truman's cold voice again. "Don't get me wrong, Mr. Teller—I want my son back, and I want him whole. And I don't give a damn if I piss on anybody doing it."

"I understand," Kyle said, and Truman walked over to the patio doors. Someone on the other side, one of Truman's own guards, opened them. Kyle could see Mrs. Truman and at least one of her daughters waiting on the other side.

Kyle turned to Hanna Uljakën. "Are there guest rooms here?"

She nodded, looking slightly disheveled. He wondered for a moment if she'd actually fainted when he'd begun spurting blood. "I want to move closer to the family."

"Of course," she said. "I can have a room ready immediately and a car sent over to the hotel for your things."

"Thanks," he said, "but I'd better go for them myself. There are a few items there I'd rather not have anyone else touching."

"Fine. A car and an escort will be waiting downstairs in five minutes."

"No, don't bother. There's something I've got to do first, and fast."

"The ritual circle is complete, as you requested," Seeks-the-Moon told him. "I'm afraid I have inconvenienced them somewhat."

"Oh?"

Hanna laughed. "You could say that."

Kyle sighed. "Let me see it." Then he followed Hanna and Moon into a section of the condoplex where Kyle hadn't been before.

"Seeks-the-Moon took over the dining room," Hanna explained. "It was the only room big enough for what he said he wanted to do." She threw open the dark wood double doors.

The room inside was long, with a wide view east to the

lake. It was, however, barely wide enough to accommodate the intricate, multilayered circle now drawn in the center of the room. Kyle looked down at its three concentric rings and the dozens of signs and symbols that filled it, some astrological, some alchemical, but all of them occult. Thirteen unlit candles circled the outer ring, seven the middle, and three the smallest, inner ring. All of it had been drawn on the hardwood floor in paints of silver and gold.

Seeks-the-Moon looked proud.

"Very impressive," Kyle said, removing his coat and shoulder holster and setting them on the dining room table, which had been shoved to one end of the room and covered with sheets. "And how unlike you. I wasn't expecting this symbol-set."

"Thank you," said Seeks-the-Moon. "I knew it had to be both formidable and comfortable for you."

Kyle nodded. "Let's get started."

"You don't want to rest?" Seeks-the-Moon asked.

"Good point," Kyle said, the pains in his body flaring up as a reminder. He stilled himself and focused his magical energies inward. His injuries weren't serious, but if not dealt with, they might hinder him in the ritual he was about to attempt. He could sense the damage, feel the very physical tearing and ripping of his body that mimicked the damage his spirit had taken in astral space. But it was that very spirit that would allow him to heal himself. Deep within, at the very center of his being, was his True Self, the core of his existence. It was the essence of Kyle Teller's body and soul, a template of who he was and how he should be. By channeling his magical power through his Self, he could rebuild his body, heal his wounds, and restore himself to health. He did, taking minutes to coax the flesh into wholeness. It was a process that would not be rushed.

When he was done, and his weight back on his left leg without pain, he opened his eyes. Seeks-the-Moon was walking the edge of the ritual circle one last time, eyeing his handiwork. Hanna Uljakën was staring at Kyle, an odd, fascinated look on her face as the last visible traces of the magical energy he'd used drifted away from his body in wisps.

Kyle smiled at her, and she managed a tiny smile in return. "Much better," he said.

Seeks-the-Moon looked up. "You're ready then?"

Kyle nodded.

"Will you need the shirt?" Hanna asked quietly. "I can have a car sent . . ."

Kyle shook his head. "No need." He reached into his pocket and pulled out the small red and white sample container. "This time we can do it right."

He turned to Seeks-the-Moon. "Odds are something's going to come after me if I can't do this fast enough. I'm going to call Winston in for extra protection."

"If you must," Seeks-the-Moon said, shrugging.

"Winston?" asked Hanna.

Kyle held up his hand and shifted the frequencies of part of his spirit until they matched those of the elemental metaplane of fire. "Winston?" he called into astral space. In front of him, over the center of the circles, a spark leapt into life, and then quickly grew into a ball of flame half Kyle's own size.

"Good afternoon," the newly called fire elemental said. *"You look well."*

"Thank you," Kyle said. "You will remain here under Seeks-the-Moon's command, Winston, and work with Charlotte to guard this place and the people dwelling in it."

The spirit nodded, but seemed amused. *"That one is not the smartest of your servants,"* it said.

"With great power comes great sarcasm," said Kyle. "Do as I say."

The spirit seemed to nod again. *"Of course,"* it said, and vanished.

"Do you think it was referring to you or Charlotte?" Kyle asked Seeks-the-Moon, but his ally spirit didn't answer. He stood looking at the ritual circle, lost in thought. "Seeks-the-Moon, are you all right?"

"Yes, yes," Moon said, "I'm fine. I was only thinking."

Kyle walked slowly into the center of the circle, careful not to disturb any of the markings. At its heart, he could clearly see its power. Seeks-the-Moon had inscribed a pow-

erful circle, perhaps even better than Kyle could have done.
It was a disturbing thought, considering Seeks-the-Moon's
origins.

Kyle turned completely in place, waving his hand across
the plane of the circle, the candles springing to life as he
gestured at them. Even with the windows wide open, the
powerful aura of the circle was evident. It was warm and
solid and fit him perfectly.

He removed the ampoule of blood from its protective
case, opened it, and poured half into his outstretched hand.
Immediately, he felt the vibrations of Mitchell Truman's life
echoing through it. Kyle closed his eyes, centered himself,
and when he opened them again, eight metallic wheels circled him, spinning at different rates and angles to one another. Each glowed with power and rang with a musical tone
that echoed its nature.

The power was Kyle's, and he changed the rotation of the
copper wheel until it matched the vibrations of Mitchell
Truman's blood pooled in his hand. The blood vibrated in
response. Kyle willed the silver circle into position parallel
to the copper one and slowed it until both spun at the same
speed. Just as they did, the copper circle pulsed and began
to rotate through its axis around him. Kyle closed his hand
around the blood, and the copper wheel ran with red, crimson dancing along its edges. The wheel flashed again, and a
translucent image of it expanded outward in all directions,
drawn to Mitchell Truman's physical existence.

Kyle felt the forces of the wheel traveling outward, ex-
panding from him in an ever-growing sphere. If left to continue, bound by no other constraints, it would grow
infinitely, weakening as it did, but never quite ceasing to ex-
ist.

Some part of Kyle was with the leading edge of the magic
as it rushed across the city, searching for the exact harmony
that would match it. The blood in his hand was hot, burning
with the power he focused. The wheels circled him, singing
with energy, building upon the simple energies within.

The blood flamed, coursing through his fingertips, but not
burning him. The copper wheel resounded, and its tone in-

creased in pitch. It had found its source. It had found Mitchell Truman.

Kyle worked quickly. The argent circle shifted perpendicular to him, and an image of it closed around him until it reached his outstretched hand, blood-red flame leaping from between his fingers. The magical energies met there, and a flash of argent leaped in two directions. One into Kyle, merging with his aura so that he might see what lay at the other end of the ritual sending. And the other, the Sending itself, lanced outward beyond the circle, reaching for the conjunction of the mystical forces on Mitch Truman. It was only a matter of time.

But Kyle could feel a ripple in the Sending as it surged outward. Alerted perhaps by the ritual's connection to the Truman boy, something was following his magic back through astral space. He could not sense what it was, only its approach, fast and strong.

He pushed his casting, willing it forward, toward Mitchell. A flash of mystical energy coursed around the edges of the ritual circle. Whatever was coming, it was projecting before it, testing, probing.

The wheels sang, their tones changing to harmony. Kyle's Sending engulfed its target, spreading across and around Mitchell Truman. He felt resistance there as whatever magical forces shielding the boy strove to disrupt his magics. But blood was to blood. Kyle's spell locked on to the boy's body, and then washed outward, writing its location into Kyle's mind. He could not see Mitchell Truman, nor anything of where he was, but the magic told him *where* he was. Kyle felt the location within him and knew he could find it again.

The ritual circle flashed once more, and Kyle felt the presence coming against him grow. It was almost upon him when he collapsed the ritual, the blood in his hand burning away, reduced to ash and smoke. The wheels faded, the connection, the path to Mitchell Truman's body dissolving.

In his mind and far off in the distance, Kyle then heard a wail. A terrible, alien cry of anger. Frustrated at the dispersing of the bridge it had been following, leaving it nothing to travel. The howl died away, fading with the magic.

Kyle stood, his left hand smoking, the final traces of the ritual folding in on itself. The candles around the ritual circle faded, and Kyle nodded to himself, satisfied.

"I found him," he said.

14

The ride to his hotel was uneventful, and escorted by Daniel Truman's own corporate guards. Despite the assurances of the driver of his car, Kyle had no doubt he and his group had somehow been followed. He'd seen how much interest the Knight Errant guards around Truman Tower had shown in watching their little motorcade of three cars form up.

He was sure Knight Errant would not delay in responding to Daniel Truman's decision to take matters into his own hands. When Kyle had told Truman that he'd discovered Mitchell's location, the man hadn't hesitated even a heartbeat in telling Kyle to take care of it. Then he and his wife had walked slowly out of the room, Truman with the air of someone who'd lost what was most precious to him. He didn't understand everything that was going on, least of all the nature of what had destroyed his son, but he wanted some kind of retribution, some kind of justice. Kyle was more than willing to oblige him.

To do so meant taking action, and fast, but Kyle was reluctant to call on Knight Errant for help. Not only did they seem to have their own agenda, but the organization's forces, at least those he wanted to deal with, were almost exclusively trained for site protection, not field work. That left only one choice in Kyle's mind, a force that was standing and ready, and probably more than willing to jump at the bidding of Truman Technologies—the Chicago law enforcement organization, Eagle Security.

At the moment, Kyle knew only the vague direction and distance of Mitchell's location: north, farther than North Avenue, but not as far as Foster. He left Hanna to contact Eagle and to use all the political clout Truman had to get them moving, *fast*. Kyle suggested a staging area in the vicinity of North and Western. He'd meet them there after retrieving some things still at his hotel.

At the Marriott, the staff was all sweetness and light as he asked for access to his security strongbox. One of the managers led him to the secure area and then went to retrieve the box, but only after Kyle had him repeat the password three times to be sure he got it right. He did, and returned with the box a few minutes later. The man handed it over without a word, though Kyle thought the single bead of sweat running down from his temple statement enough.

Kyle let the box scan his thumb print and retinal pattern before keying in the special code to open the box. About the size of a briefcase, but much deeper, the box had a simple latching lid that lifted completely off. Inside, Kyle found his magical accessories still wrapped in black silk and velvet, exactly as he'd left them.

There were two metal bracelets braided from heavy wires of silver, copper, and the mystical metal orichalcum. Kyle slipped one around each wrist. Over the middle and next fingers of his left hand he slid silver rings set with a diamond and sapphire, respectively. On his right hand in like positions he put on silver rings, one set with a ruby and one with an emerald.

Around his neck and under his clothing he hung an amulet made of golden-coppery metals and dominated by a large opal. And finally, he placed an ornate silver and orichalcum-bladed knife, inlaid with jewels of all kinds and designed in the Egyptian style, into a custom black leather sheath that fit under the arm not girded with his shoulder holster. Feeling overburdened and somewhat foolish, he headed up to his room.

"The hotel assures me that the scrambling on my line is just about the best that money can buy," Kyle told Dave Strevich.

"I'm sure it is," Strevich said. "My system says yours is

saying the right things, but that doesn't mean I'm going to answer any questions."

"I switching to encryption now." Kyle leaned forward, typing the command into the keyboard. Strevich's image blurred as the man cursed, and it remained distorted and unviewable for a few moments until he put his system into like mode and the two machines had agreed on how to talk to each other. When the image returned, it was no longer three-dimensional and it lacked color fidelity, but Kyle had no doubt that for a short while at least the signal was indecipherable.

"You insist on getting into trouble, don't you?" Strevich said. "Do you have any idea how many alarms your actions in Chicago are setting off?"

"I can imagine," Kyle said. "All things considered."

Strevich's eyes narrowed. "The drek's gonna hit the pavement real soon now. The suits upstairs aren't happy with Knight Errant's activities in Chicago, despite the fact that they're real friendly with Ares Macrotech these days."

"Why not?" Kyle asked innocently. "Knight Errant hasn't done anything wrong."

"Don't play dumb, Kyle."

"I wouldn't have to if you'd given me the scan straight up."

"I couldn't. Still can't, you know that."

"Tell me about the bugs," Kyle said.

Strevich's face hardened. "Jam it, Kyle."

"Tell me about the true forms."

Strevich didn't answer.

"Tell me about the flesh forms."

"I don't know what you're talking about."

"Dammit, Dave, you're leaving me disconnected here! You've got to tell me something."

"I don't have to do anything of the kind. The problem is being addressed, in our own way. It takes time, but we're handling it."

"Really?" said Kyle, the word coming out a little harsher than he'd intended. "It doesn't look that way from here."

"Walk away, Kyle," Strevich said. "You still can. When

the big red, white, and blue scooper comes along to clean up all the drek, it's going to scrape you up too if you're not careful."

"No."

"Walk away. Take Beth and Natalie on a vacation," Strevich told him. "Stop worrying about everything. Watch some simsense."

"You're frizzed."

Strevich spoke in a very deliberate manner, seeming to choose his words very carefully. "I saw an interesting sim the other night. Story was unbelievable, but the effects were wizzer. You'd almost swear it was real."

Kyle eyed him suspiciously. "Do you remember the name?"

"Nah," Strevich said. "I didn't see it from the beginning, but it was by that simsense chica. The one that Bettleman liked when we were all at Quantico for extended weapons training that time. Remember?"

Kyle nodded. It was years ago, but he thought he did.

"Anyway," Strevich went on, "you should sense it. Real wiz. Real hype. I think it was her last one."

"I'll try and find it." Kyle recalled the simsense star Strevich was talking about, a beautiful dark-haired girl named Euphoria. Kyle wasn't a big simsense fan, but he remembered her. He had no idea which sim Strevich was talking about, though. Or why he was going on about it at the moment.

"Good," Strevich told him. "You do that, and I'll talk to you some other time."

Kyle nodded, still suspicious. "Later."

Strevich waved, and then disconnected. Kyle stared at the blank screen a moment, then switched the telecom system over to the hotel's own entertainment library. According to the information he'd seen, it contained thousands of new, hot, and classic simsense programs on demand for immediate viewing. He keyed in the name "Euphoria" and requested a list of her titles in the system. He had a feeling that if Strevich had been trying to tell him something, he'd know as soon as he saw the title. He never quite got the chance to see the list.

"It's called *Against the Hive,*" came a woman's voice behind him.

Kyle threw himself forward violently and then kicked himself sideways beyond an oversized chair and down to the floor behind it. He came up quickly, Ceska vz/120 pistol in one hand, jeweled knife in the other, and half a dozen combat spells flooding his mind.

The woman was crouched low to the floor, one hand across her knee and the other on the floor for balance. Even as she was, Kyle could tell she was tall, with shoulder-length black hair and bright silver-blue eyes that reflected the window light back at him. She wore black leather pants, a tight, midriff-revealing black leather halter top, an a long-sleeved green leather jacket. When she smiled, Kyle felt more than a little fear. She was painfully beautiful, and he had little doubt who she was.

Her bright, unblinking gaze locked with his. "Apparently, some lucky simsense producer happened to be in the right place at the right time and got footage of Knight Errant attacking a real ant spirit hive. Saved them quite a bit of money on special effects, I'd say.

"Of course, why present the truth when you can make money selling it as fiction?" she said, standing up slowly, gracefully unfolding herself. "Not that anyone would have believed it."

"Please don't come any closer," Kyle said.

"I don't intend to. I was simply tired of crouching there."

Kyle clenched the pistol tighter and risked slipping his perception into astral space. Her aura was powerful, and odd. Its shape didn't seem to match that of the body she wore. She smiled again, and he willed his foci to life, mentally triggering the final mystical connections that empowered them. He felt the energy, the potential, arise within him as each activated in turn.

Linda Hayward stopped smiling, tensing slightly as she eyed the additions to his now unmasked aura.

He stood up carefully too, but with none of her other-worldly grace. He holstered his pistol, freeing up his hand. The knife remained drawn, but held loosely at his side.

"There," he said, as casually as he could, "thought I'd balance things out a bit."

"You are an initiate," she said.

Kyle nodded. "For some time now."

"I'm impressed." She smiled a little. "Preening for me?"

"Hardly," he told her, "since I know what you really look like."

"No," she said gravely, "you don't."

"Really?"

"I'm not at all like those things you fought at the hospital."

"No?"

She laughed, almost sadly. "I didn't take you for a monosyllabic mutterer, Mr. Teller. But your kind frequently disappoint." She looked directly at him. "Would you like me to show you what I truly am?"

"Not particularly," he said. "There, I said two words. Happy?"

"Rarely," she said. "But I think you need to be shown."

Kyle raised his blade and held it across his chest.

"Don't worry," she told him. "I'll stay over here." And she changed. Gone was her human form, in its place a giant glistening green and black insect, taller than Kyle, but lighter of build with a long, thin body and delicate legs that were almost as long. She'd become a powerful and majestic praying mantis. When she smiled, Kyle felt an almost overpowering wave of desire rush over him. He braced his body and spirit against her as she resumed her human form.

"Sorry," she said. "An instinctive reaction."

"So, you're a different kind of bug."

She winced and seemed sad again. "Mantid, if you must, Mr. Teller. And though you won't believe me, we're actually on the same side."

"Tell Mitch Truman that."

Her eyes hardened, and Kyle felt another emotion wash over him, this one far different from the last. He took an involuntary step backward and choked back the little food in his stomach as it rose. "I did, and he believed me," she told him.

"That," Kyle said, "*I* find hard to believe."

"I and my sisters are not responsible for what happened to Mitchell Truman. We are enemies of the ones you seek, the ones who have him."

"Then tell me what happened."

"I'll tell you enough to send you on your way and leave all this to us."

"People keep telling me that, and I haven't listened yet."

She laughed. "You should."

"Go on."

"Generally, I and my kind find yours to be shallow, weak, ill-mannered, fearful, and devoid of worth," she told him. "We come here when the level of magic is right so that we can breed. We come here because there is more space. There are too many of us back home."

"So, don't breed."

"Ah, but Mr. Teller, it's what we do best." She winked, and Kyle began to feel a strange sensation of warmth.

"Those that you saw in the hospital, and perhaps later, use humanity as cattle. They see the possibility of using human flesh as humanity's only redeeming feature."

"Don't tell me you're different," Kyle said. "Mantids often eat their mates, if I remember my biology right."

"From consumption comes new life," she told him.

"Did Mitch know about that part?"

"He did," she told him, "but he was safe."

"Oh?"

She nodded. "I discovered, much to my own dismay, that when it came time to invest him with a male spirit I did not want to. I had grown too fond of him."

When Kyle said nothing, it seemed to make her angry. "I really don't care what you think. I'm here to tell you to stop interfering. The queens took Mitch from us so that they could learn what forms we took and what our plans were. The queens destroyed Mitchell Truman, and I intend to destroy them for it."

"The queens?"

"Think about it," she said.

"If they, whoever they are, and not you, did that to him in the first place, why would they want to grab him back? His mind was gone. There was nothing they could learn from him."

"I don't think they knew that," she told him. "I think he refused to talk. I think he wouldn't tell them about us or where we could be found." Her voice became sad and quiet for a moment. "That was stupid. He should have told them."

He watched her, surprised in some ways at how human she seemed. "When he wouldn't betray us, they tried to possess him. They tried to invest him with one of their own larvae *spiritis,* hoping the merge would be good and his memories would be relatively intact. Then he would be theirs and they'd know everything they needed to know."

"He tried to meet with his sister the night he was found with his mind gone."

Her head tilted oddly. "Really? I didn't know that. Perhaps he broke free and they tried to invest him as punishment."

"But why grab him again?"

"They may not have known the final outcome," she said. "In fact, they probably assumed he'd retained his mind. How else could he have run away again?"

"Indeed," Kyle said.

"I saw him after the police found him, at the first hospital. There were fragments of his mind still there. Tiny twisted flames sputtering in the darkness. He actually seemed to recognize me. I doused the fragments so that he might rest."

"How kind of you."

She grew angry again. "Yes, actually. Uncommonly kind of me. I think he resisted the investiture and fled, his mind unraveling and disintegrating as he did. I gave him release."

Again Kyle said nothing.

She paused, seeming to be gathering up her composure. "I've told you why I came here. You have no need to pursue Mitch's flesh body. They probably ate it once they found his mind was gone. Perhaps they even tried another investiture into the empty host. I don't know. The point is, your con-

cerns and the Truman family's concerns are at an end. I will
avenge Mitchell Truman."

"I'll pass on your message."

"You do that," she said. "And remember, Mr. Teller, you
and your kind are mine whenever I want you. And want you
I will if you get in my way again." With that she turned and
passed through the door without opening it.

Kyle stood there blankly for a few moments and then sat
down slowly in the chair that had been positioned between
him and Linda Hayward. He knew he had to center himself
and calm his body. It took a long time.

15

As Kyle and the two cars escorting his pulled into the supermarket parking lot at Western and North, an Eagle Security helicopter was dropping into the area that had been cordoned off by a phalanx of police and security vehicles. Enough Truman guards were mixed in with the Eagle troopers that Kyle's motorcade was waved directly into the center of the area, alongside a huge armored police command van.

Kyle jumped out even before the vehicle had stopped, protecting his eyes against the bits of flying debris kicked up by the landing helicopter. Beyond it, Eagle officers were attempting to clear away the small crowd of gawkers that had begun to gather. Kyle wondered if any of them were secretly from Knight Errant.

The side door of the command van slid open sideways, and Hanna Uljakën waved from inside. Kyle hurried over and climbed into the red-lit interior. Cramped together within were a small technical staff and four Eagle officers. One bore the clear insignia and simple uniform of a chief, but Kyle's untrained eyes could not decipher the ranks of the other three, who were decked out in dark, close-fitting body armor and associated weaponry and gear.

The chief stepped forward and extended his hand. "Mr. Teller, I'm Chief Lekas of Eagle Special Operations." He gestured at the other three. "This is Commander Joshua Malley, leader of the Special Ops team," he said, working his way from left to right, "and Sergeants Peter Woodhouse and Kenneth Walsh, also of Special Ops." Each nodded in turn.

Kyle shook all of their hands. "Thank you for responding so quickly."

"It's quite a tale your Ms. Uljakën has been telling us," Malley said. "You don't mind if we ask a few clarifying questions, do you?"

Kyle shook his head. "No, not at all, but I'm concerned about time. They may have already moved on."

Malley turned to the other two men. "Go ahead," he said.

Walsh spoke first. "We haven't had time to verify any of the story. Can you tell us your qualifications to assess the situation?" Walsh gestured vaguely to Hanna Uljakën. "Ms. Uljakën has told us some of your background, but we'd like to know more."

Kyle frowned slightly, wondering whether they were going to start playing "who's the boss" games with him. Aloud, he said, "Of course. I have a degree in comparative metaphysics from Columbia-Manhattan with a minor in behavioral psychology. My practical experience includes seven years as a field agent and special investigator with the UCAS Federal Bureau of Investigation, Department of Paranormal Affairs. If you're so stuck on my cred, I can give—"

Woodhouse held up his hand in a halt gesture. "That won't be necessary," he said. "You're the one found Wilhemina Keene, aren't you?"

Kyle paused. "Yes." Keene had been a registered nurse and adept mage performing ritual sacrifices with newborn babies stolen from hospitals throughout New England. She killed twelve before the FBI finally caught up with her on the verge of murdering her thirteenth, the final element in whatever bizarre ritual she'd been performing. Her ultimate goal had never been determined. That was five years ago. "Maybe I should say I led the team."

"We saw the locked file last year as part of a special training program," Woodhouse said. "Can you tell me what her primary ritual instrument was?"

"Now what the frag does this have to do—"

Chief Lekas cut him off. "Mr. Teller, Truman Technologies is asking quite a bit from Eagle on this. And most of it has to be taken on faith, if you will. We'd like to confirm that you are who you say you are. If so, we're ready to roll. If not, well . . ." Lekas let his voice trail off. "The boys tell me that the Keene woman's actual methods were never disclosed to the public, but you, of course, would know."

Kyle sighed and glanced at Hanna.

She smiled weakly. "Please, don't spare any details on my account."

Kyle drew in a breath. "All right, you win. She used a surgical scalpel to drain some of her own blood and the child's into a tub of water. Just before the baby got too weak, she drowned him in it and then burned the body."

The four men looked at each other and nodded. Hanna had gone pale and seemed to be struggling to hang on to her composure.

"Happy now?" Kyle asked.

"Look," Walsh said, "you seem to be forgetting that—"

Kyle cut him off angrily. "No, you've forgotten that every second we stand here playing games might be the one by which we miss them."

The two junior officers looked like they wanted to continue the argument, but Commander Malley silenced them with a glare. "You're right, Mr. Teller," he said. "Sergeants Walsh and Woodhouse are the magicians on the team. Sometimes we all get a little territorial. Why don't you give us the tactical situation as you see it?"

Kyle nodded. "No offense taken," he said, though no one had offered an apology. "A force of unknown number, consisting of powerful spirits, has kidnapped the son of my client. From everything that I've seen and heard, these spirits resemble insects and they breed using human hosts. I've specifically seen one in the form of a cockroach."

Walsh blanched slightly, as did Malley, who said, "We've had the occasional unexplained contact with insect-like spirits before, but nothing we could categorize or build any information from. They seemed to be anomalies rather than something we needed to be concerned about."

"Aberrations," Kyle said, "Well, I'm afraid we might be dealing with entire nests or hives, or however they group themselves, including queen spirits and Coyote knows what else. There might even be more than one type of insect spirit present."

"So we're facing significant opposition?" asked Malley.

"You'd better believe it. And most normal tactics won't work against them because they're spirits. How experienced are your people in fighting spirits?"

Malley frowned. "Trained against them, but not experienced."

"The one I fought was pretty powerful, but if your people keep their heads, I think they'll manage."

"But we don't even know where they are," said Chief Lekas.

"I know where they are," said Kyle. "I just haven't found it yet."

"Ritual?" asked Walsh.

Kyle nodded, pointing north and west. "That way, not too far. Can your people take me up in a helicopter? I can find it faster that way than trying to reconnoiter on the ground."

"Makes sense," said Malley. "I'll head my team in that direction, and once you find the location, we can go straight there instead of blindly driving around."

"Excuse me, sir," said Woodhouse. "I've got a suggestion."

Malley raised an eyebrow. "Of course, Sergeant. Speak up."

"Mr. Teller could recon astrally. It would be a lot faster than the helicopter."

Kyle shook his head. "Thought of that, but I don't know Chicago well enough to recognize where I am by positions of roads and buildings." He turned to explain to Hanna. "You can't read signs from astral space, only sense emotions associated with the information on them. If they're anything, road signs are unemotional."

Hanna nodded, giving him a wan smile. She seemed lost, out of her element with tactical and mystical matters she barely understood. But he could see that she was taking it all in, absorbing it, and most likely learning from it.

"One of us will go with you," said Walsh.

Kyle paused to think. "That would work."

"If you stay in view, I shouldn't have any trouble follow-ing you," the sergeant said. "We can leave our bodies in the truck and then start north along Western."

Malley nodded. "Sounds good to me, if you agree, Mr. Teller."

"Yes. It'll speed things up."

The commander gestured to two observation chairs near the truck's telecommunications suite. As Kyle and Walsh settled into them, Malley jacked into the tactical system and began issuing orders.

"If you need me while I'm out, slap me as hard as you can," Kyle told Hanna.

"I . . ." she said, obviously surprised. "If you say so."

"If you hit me hard enough, it'll jerk my spirit back into my body. Otherwise, there's no way to get in touch with me."

"I should warn you, I'm pretty strong," Hanna said.

Kyle smiled. "Great." He looked at Walsh, but the mage had already lapsed into unconsciousness, his astral form probably floating free. "Gotta go," said Kyle, and he leaned back, relaxing his body, shifting his focus, and finally slipped free of his body as the tone and texture of the com-mand van shifted.

Walsh was waiting there, standing next to his body, sur-rounded by a nimbus of blue and gold energy. Otherwise, except for Woodhouse and the mundane auras of the others present, the command van interior was cold and sterile, and reeked faintly of hard emotions like anger and fear.

"Lead on, Mr. Teller," Walsh said. "Though you might want to dampen yourself somewhat."

Kyle nodded, realizing that his foci were radiating consid-erable magical energy, energy that would serve as a flare to anyone or anything looking for them. With a quick thought, he subsumed the radiating power into his own aura, masking the overflow. It was uncomfortable, but bearable. Walsh nodded approval.

Kyle turned toward what he knew to be the direction in which Mitch Truman's body had been just over an hour ago.

He slipped through the walls of the command van, Walsh drifting after him, and then shot off, as quickly as he could, toward the lake.

Walsh followed on his tail along the dim, life-accented, careening track of North Avenue and then finally out over the bright lake itself. "I thought you said the site was to the northwest," the sergeant said, drawing abreast of Kyle's floating astral form.

"It is. I'm concerned about pursuit or surveillance."

The two hung there for several heartbeats, but saw no sign of any other astral presences.

Kyle signaled, and they dropped down to the surface of the lake and skirted its edge, skimming over the various sunbathers, bike-riders, strutters, dog-walkers, and other denizens of Chicago out to enjoy the afternoon sun. As the coastline changed at where Kyle believed Fullerton to be, he soared inland, Walsh close behind.

The effects of the earlier ritual pulled at Kyle, guiding him ever farther north and west. He pushed on, passing across the breadth of Chicago's northside in a few blinks of an eye. Then, sensing he was near, he slowed and dropped closer to the ground. Walsh drew up alongside him.

"Any idea where we are?" Kyle asked him. "I sure as drek don't."

Walsh nodded. "Near Harlem and Irving Park."

"I'm going to go low and coast. I don't want to suddenly be on top of this place."

Kyle drifted down to just above the level of the cars passing on the major road beneath them. He tried to judge the distance carefully to keep from being brushed aside or sent spinning by the physical mass of the people in those cars. At the approach to a major intersection, he could sense a surge of emotion as the light changed and a slight gridlock developed. When Kyle finally came down to the ground, he chose to land in a trash barrel so no one would bump into him. Walsh dropped down a short distance behind him, pressed half into a storefront. They both hoped the auras of the mundanes passing by would conceal them from anything that happened to look their way.

"We there?" asked Walsh.

"Yes," said Kyle, pointing north along the intersecting street. "It's right up there, third one in." There was little that could be seen, just a dim storefront. Nothing magical. Nothing extraordinary.

"Looks normal," said Walsh. "They could be gone already."

"Let's hope not."

"Why don't you head back and tell them where," Walsh said. "I'll stand guard here."

"All right," Kyle said, and lifted off to the south, traveling in that direction for a while, then turning west to find the intersection with Western, where the police convoy would be. From there he turned south again, following what he believed to be Western.

Then, seconds later, he passed over an interstate highway, which he was certain was Interstate 90/94 headed in toward the Noose. But that, he thought, was too far south. Kyle paused and hung in the air trying to remember if Western crossed 90/94 north or south of North Avenue. He continued on, watching for the presence of the large command vans and the helicopter that would be flying cover.

He paused again when he came to another expressway, one he knew to be Interstate 290 heading directly east into the city from the western suburbs. That told him he'd gone too far south. Not for the first time in his life, Kyle cursed the fact that there was no simple way to follow the connection with his body back to it.

Kyle shot east, to the lake, arriving there in a fraction of a second. He then followed the shoreline north, looking for the lakeshore at North Avenue, where he and Walsh had passed over it. He continued north, finally stopping at the break in the shoreline which he knew to be Fullerton. He was now too far north.

Kyle cursed again, knowing that his stupidity was costing him valuable time that he couldn't afford to waste, when he felt a shock, a short, quick pain in his left arm. His perception blurred, and he felt himself pulled back to his body by the force of what he took to be Hanna Uljakën's blow. Then he felt the sensation again, harder across his neck, and he slammed into his body and a wave of pain.

His physical senses returned and he was on the floor, covered in something warm. A man yelled. "Grab him! Grab him!"

Kyle rolled over, pushing against a booted leg near him, just as another spray of blood exploded from Sergeant Walsh's neck. Still in the chair, pinned there by another Eagle officer, Walsh's body thrashed and the side of his head darkened as blood vessels ruptured and bone shattered. Still on the floor, Kyle cast a web of protective magical energies around Walsh. He could do nothing to stop what he took to be a vicious assault on the mage's astral form, but he was suddenly afraid that any magicians present at the other end could use the connection between Walsh's spirit body and physical form to "ground" a spell directly into the command van. The best he could hope for was to disrupt those energies if they leaped through.

Walsh's body jerked again, and his bloodied eyes flew open as he screamed and pitched forward even against the strength of the two officers holding him. He fell across Kyle's legs and onto the floor. Kyle immediately dropped the protective energies and placed his hand on the man's neck in an effort to staunch the arterial flow.

The thrashing subsided as Walsh's resistance collapsed and his body slipped rapidly into shock. His eyes glazed and his breath faltered.

"Harlem, north of Irving!" Kyle screamed, and then focused his magical talents on the dying mage. He quickly synchronized their two auras and began channeling living energy directly into Walsh's being. Kyle felt the other mage's spirit faltering when it needed to be strong, at least strong enough, if he was going to be able to continue healing him.

Walsh's spirit flickered, slipping from Kyle's control. There, just as Kyle's essence meshed with his, Kenneth Walsh died, his True Self dissolving into chaos, back into the dance of energy from which it came.

Kyle leaned back, releasing his grip and allowing the last

spurts of blood from the man's sputtering heart to arc across the room. He was covered in Walsh's blood, as was Malley and the other trooper who'd tried to restrain his thrashings. Beyond them, and equally as stunned, Hanna Uljakën stood ashen, except for the spray of crimson across her face and blouse. Kyle collapsed back against the cold wall of the van.

"Harlem, north of Irving," he said again. "That's where they are . . ."

16

The storefront, when Kyle finally got a clear look at it, was simple and drab. As he and half a dozen Eagle troopers moved toward it from an alley across the street, he could see paint peeling from the door and window frames, the view inside blocked by old newspapers and plastic garbage bags hanging in the windows. A lopsided sign still hung over the entrance, the letters themselves long gone, but the ghostly outline of the words were still visible—UNIVERSAL BROTHERHOOD: FOR THE NEXT STAGE OF YOUR LIFE.

Thoughts of Beth's sister Ellen rushed into Kyle's mind. And Strevich's warnings, Mitch Truman's destroyed mind, the true form of Linda Hayward, and the vicious roach spirit he'd killed in the hospital. The Brotherhood was somehow mixed up in this. But he couldn't think about it now, there was no time as the strike team rushed forward from the alley, steps behind a two-man team coming in from the side.

The lead trooper dropped into position covering the closed door as Kyle's group reached the middle of the street, the traffic stopped in both directions by Eagle troopers at the flanking intersections. Kyle was just reaching the curb when the second trooper slammed his heavy riot shotgun against the door lock mechanism and pulled the trigger.

Kyle's group reached the doorway moments after the shot splintered the doorframe and sent the metal lock hurling inside. The lead trooper in Kyle's group hit the door hard, his solid metal riot shield braced in front of him.

The rest of the door shattered under his weight, and the team moved inside. Kyle could hear similar noises as the team led by Malley and Woodhouse entered through the rear. Some of the troopers were armed for urban combat, carrying riot guns firing high-velocity flechette or SABOT rounds designed to cut lightly armored targets to bits. Others were armed with more conventional assault weapons and submachine guns. A couple were armed primarily with nonlethal weaponry—riot guns firing gel rounds, stun batons and gloves, shock/concussion grenades, and net guns in case they met "questionable" targets. It was they who fired first on the two men who rushed forward against the onslaught. The pair fell quickly, knocked off their feet by a barrage of gel rounds, and then subdued by the skillful application of shock batons.

The interior of the storefront was a large waiting room filled with plastic chairs and tattered propaganda posters. Twin rows of rusted fluorescent lights supplemented what little light crept in through the dirty, partially covered windows. Of the six people—men, women, and a child—in that outer waiting room, all but the two who attacked immediately did not resist the police rush.

On a small desk at one end of the room was a notepad computer and some piles of paper now strewn about or fallen onto the floor. Beyond that, against the wall, was a small table holding a soykaf maker and a three-dispenser sodapak machine adjoining a closed door.

The baby began to scream as Kyle reached the middle of the room and the trooper immediately ahead of him took up position covering the door. Kyle moved in opposite him and twisted the door handle open, turning away as he did.

The door swung open quickly, pushed wide by the rush of six brown and black shapes the size of large dogs that darted into the room with lightning speed. They were roach spirits, much smaller than the one Kyle had fought at the hospital, but unquestionably deadly. Three of them, drawn to the odor of power reeking from Kyle and his foci, immediately turned on him.

They stayed low, scuttling close to the ground, and Kyle crouched to meet their attack. The first two came at him, their long, threadlike antennae vibrating wildly, but the third took a vicious stamping kick from one of the other troopers. The thing let out an unearthly squeal and the man's impact with its shell made a crackling sound that was terrifying, but the kick only sent it flying to the side.

Kyle slashed at the first with his blade, catching the hideous thing across the head, severing it completely and dissipating the spirit in one blow. Surprised, Kyle continued the slash against the other spirit, which tried to twist aside now that it had seen the deadly touch of the knife. It was fast, but Kyle's blow came faster, raking across the gleaming carapace, splitting it open. The roach spirit tried to dart aside, shrieking amid a gush of yellow-green fluid, but was stopped dead by a hail of flechettes from one of the Eagle troopers. The spirit thrashed, its legs twitching furiously as its body ricocheted into the air among a cloud of flying splinters. Unable to withstand the dual assault, it too disintegrated. The stink of its foul odor did not.

Kyle stood and immediately moved toward the door.

"That seemed too easy," the trooper said, coming abreast.

Kyle nodded. "Babies," he said.

The trooper blinked, and then covered Kyle passing quickly through the door. There were a series of offices here, little more than partitions and desks. Empty, except for the presence of two Eagle troopers at the far end of the long room.

"Anything?" Woodhouse shouted.

"Six roach babies rushed us," Kyle called back as he advanced.

High-velocity gunfire erupted from the floor above, and Kyle guessed that Malley's group had found a stair or some other access. Together, he, Woodhouse, and the other troopers who had converged on the area from the front and back scoured the rooms, finding nothing.

Then came the excited shout of one of the troopers. "A passage!"

Kyle turned from the desk he was examining and saw that a portion of panelboard wall had swung inward. Two troopers moved to cover it. One of them dropped into position alongside the door, but then the trooper was spinning suddenly, his body armor tearing as a huge clawed leg lashed out through the passageway. Even before the man's body hit the floor, the enormous roach spirit, bigger and even more loathsome than the first one Kyle had seen, had somehow made it through the narrow opening and into the room.

The troopers, numbering a dozen at least, opened up on the thing. Surprised by the ferocity of the assault, it staggered back on its spiny, jointed legs, mouth parts working furiously but wildly as it gave a long, ear-splitting screech. Then the thing began to fade, attempting to flee into astral space.

Kyle called to mind the formula for a quick and dirty spell of raw physical power and performed it. Power arced from his body, crossed the distance between him and the bug spirit in astral space, and then exploded back into the physical world through the spirit's still-manifest form. The spirit all but exploded as the spell discharged, chunks and smears of its rapidly dissolving ectoplasmic form blowing across the room.

The trooper who'd been struck was injured, but not seriously. Another trooper pulled him clear as the team medic rushed up.

"It went down fast," said Woodhouse. "Maybe they're not that tough."

Kyle looked at him. "There were, what, fourteen of us?"

Woodhouse nodded reluctantly. "Good point."

Troopers moved through the passage, one of them suddenly calling out, "Stairs down!"

Malley came up alongside Woodhouse and Kyle. "Assume we've got only hostiles," he said. "These things are too fraggin' fast. I don't want us caught with our pants down."

Kyle thought for an instant of his sister-in-law and the apparent humans cowering in the front room, but nodded slowly. Malley stepped forward and pulled a grenade from his pocket, one of the stun loads. "Fire in the hole!" he shouted, tossing it down the stairs.

The grenade's confined explosion, stun round or not,

shook the whole building, and echoed under them for some
distance.

Kyle moved up alongside Malley, who was peering into
the dim, now smoke-and-debris filled stairway. "Grenades
won't affect the spirits," Kyle said, hoping the officer remembered his limited training. Only directed attacks, those
that carried the immediate force of living will behind them,
were effective against spirits. Intentless things like explosives were useless against them, while hand-to-hand and
armed weapons and spells were the most effective. Gunfire
fell somewhere in the middle, effective due to its sheer de-
structive power.

Malley nodded. "I know. But they're bugs. It might still
confuse them." He turned to the troopers immediately
around him. "Down we go."

Each one reached up and pulled light-magnifying and
thermal-sensing goggles over his eyes and followed Malley
down the stairs.

"Why the frag did he do that?" Kyle asked Woodhouse,
who'd just come up. "He could have taken out the stairway!"

Woodhouse shrugged. "He's a good tactical commander,
but in the field he's a little crazy. Unfortunately, he's well
connected."

Kyle smiled. "You must be too to talk like that."

The other mage only shrugged as gunfire and screams
erupted from below. Rushing forward, Kyle activated one of
the spells locked into the focus on his left wrist. A barely
visible blue-silver field opened around him a few centimeters from his body. At the same time a similar magical field
had erected itself around Woodhouse. Kyle's own was a barrier spell designed to repel magic and living energy. It was
useless against bullets and the like, but those weren't his
biggest concern.

Magical power lanced from Woodhouse's outstretched
hand as they peered down into the large space at the bottom
of the stairs, seeing more insect spirits than troopers. The
sight of so many writhing insect spirits was grisly, the
screams and shrieks deafening, the stink of the roaches all

but unbearable. And so tightly packed was the combat that neither Kyle nor Woodhouse could use a spell with an effect radius and not catch troopers. Kyle glanced over his shoulder and checked that there was wood paneling behind him. The natural wood barrier would prevent the spirits from slipping past him astrally, so his back was protected.

With Woodhouse still on the stair, Kyle's only recourse was to use magic against the bugs. Writhed in black and red flame from Woodhouse's spell, one roach spirit was already staggering away, apparently dragging its huge brown shell. Kyle released another bolt of magic of the same type that he'd used upstairs, and the spirit disintegrated in a splatter of greenish blood. Woodhouse rushed forward to stand over the trooper the spirit had been tearing into, his submachine gun opening up at something Kyle couldn't see.

He jumped over the remaining steps and came down in a crouch, twisting to look at the room. It was long, probably the length of the entire series of stores along the street, and wide open with only the occasional support column. Dozens of roach spirits of varying sizes were everywhere, rushing the besieged troopers, striking as they passed, then disappearing back into astral space, only to reappear elsewhere and attack again.

The racket was deafening, the sickening sound of roach legs skittering madly across the floor, the shouts and screams of the troopers, and always accompanied by that now unmistakable, disgusting smell.

There were other things in the room too, large, swollen shapes sitting on the floor at the far end of the basement. Kyle saw perhaps a score of them, with the two largest roach spirits standing guard over them, only their long antennae moving as they calmly observed the carnage their fellows were creating. A bundle seemed to move, to shudder, and one of the big roaches turned slightly, its long, thin feelers twitching in idle interest.

Another roach thing flashed by Kyle, barely centimeters from his head, but he twisted away in time. The troopers were holding their own, covering each other enough that the insect spirits couldn't swarm all over them, but they were

taking plenty of punishment all the same. Unless they with-
drew, it would be only a matter of time. And if the roach
spirits pursued them there wouldn't be much hope.

Woodhouse's magic flashed again as a spinning disk of
energy that sliced the legs clean off a leaping roach. It
twisted in the air, and landed hard against one of its brethren, knocking them both down.

The insects and troopers were still too tightly packed for
Kyle to risk a powerful area spell. He was thinking fast, trying to come up with something that might lure the insects
into clusters that could be blasted. Perhaps an attack against
whatever the large roaches were guarding? It was probably
suicide, and he didn't know if Woodhouse had a spell powerful enough to deal with the spirits en masse. He also didn't
know if the roach spirits, considering the size of the two
guardians, would consider him a threat.

Linda Hayward's words suddenly filled his head. A threat.
Kyle thought he knew one that might be enough to distract
the roaches.

He pictured Hayward in his mind, not clad in her green
and black biker leather, but as she claimed she truly was.
Two meters of deadly, insect-devouring mantid spirit.

He wove his spell, imprinting the energy of the magic
with the image from his mind. He shaped it into her form,
detailed it as best he could remember her, and then colored
it in the same glistening greens, browns, and blacks.

Without warning, a giant screeching mantid came into existence halfway between the troopers and the huge guardian
roaches. It screeched again, and the two guard spirits answered, immediately moving to protect their charges.

The remaining roach spirits wheeled, summoned by the
battle call of the larger spirits. They surged forward, a mad,
blind rush against the towering mantid. Clawed legs flashed
and snapped as they smashed into each other where the mantid stood braced for the attack, but insubstantial. A few of
the roaches passed straight through her to bounce and skitter
near the larger bugs.

Kyle released his illusion of the mantid, which instantly
began to fade. The mass of roach spirits tore into itself as

Woodhouse's first spell struck, erupting in a huge fireball.
Roaches squealed and began to scuttle away, some attempting to flee into astral space, but Kyle hit them again.
The ruby ring on his finger and the amulet around his neck
flashed as he released the spell, wincing in pain as the energy flowed through him. It exploded in a near-silent spray
of white and green shards of energy that tore into the spirits,
cutting them to pieces.

Troopers opened up on the bugs that remained, most of
them maimed or burning. Still gasping from the strain the
powerful spell had put on his body, Kyle slipped his perceptions into astral space, quickly bringing up his mystical
knife to ward off any attacks now that he was present and
vulnerable in that realm.

The astral echoed with the resonations of the power released in the room and the disruption of the insect spirits
that had succumbed to that power. Kyle immediately saw
that most of them had fled, escaped up and away through a
patch of ceiling that looked different in the astral. The floors
of most of the buildings were probably impassable wood,
except for some space cleared for just such passage.

A handful of injured spirits lingered in astral space, darting around the still physically manifest and barely touched
larger guardian roaches. Wincing again, Kyle tossed a low-
powered ball of energy across the room. He centered it on
one of the bug things present only in astral space. The spell
struck it and exploded, sending searing energy into the group
in astral space and cutting into the two larger bugs present
in both realms. Three of the cultures dispersed, unable to
maintain their existence.

A tremendous flash of magic filled that end of the room
as another of Woodhouse's fireballs ignited. Waves of fire
lashed out from its center over one of the huge guardians,
and washed over the rows of now quivering bundles on the
ground. The large bugs shrieked both in pain and apparent
fear for their charges. The bug on which the spell had been
centered was badly injured and engulfed in flame. It leaped
forward toward the nearest trooper, catching his arm and
tearing it clean off in passing. The trooper spun, his assault

rifle still tracking and firing at the burning spirit as he fell. The bug collided with the far brick wall and flipped onto its back, its huge, spiny legs flailing in the air.

Kyle turned as the second bug, its carapace smoking, leaped at Woodhouse. Its legs scraped against the magical barrier that surrounded him, sending sparks of black energy across the room. But it was getting through and into him; Kyle could see a tear deep into the armor on Woodhouse's side.

Kyle ran forward and leaped, his perceptions still in astral space, striking with his enchanted weapon. He drove it at the creature's middle back, the place on its body that seemed the most damaged. The knife dug in deep, flashing gold as it did, burying Kyle's hands up to his wrists inside the thing. The mystical shield around his body flashed azure against the bug as it screeched and reared back off Woodhouse, who instantly stepped away, and fell backward, all the while spraying the thing with a burst from his submachine gun. Jerked into the air by the bug's thrashing, Kyle felt a sharp pain across his right arm as one of the bullets sliced into him. That hand spasmed, and he let go of the blade and felt himself twist again, hanging on only by his left hand. His weight, now suspended off one side of the roach's back, dragged the knife down, pulling and cutting deep across the thing's back.

It turned in the direction of the pain as more bullets tore into it, then landed on its back across Kyle. He pushed upward with the knife as hard as he could, felt something give, and then his hand and knife cut into the air, bursting out of the roach's underside. The creature thrashed and immediately began to dissipate, its weight vanishing with its dissolving form.

Kyle wrenched his arm free and quickly rolled to his feet, striking a leaping smaller roach as it passed. Its legs sparked against the shield surrounding his head as it spun madly off to one side, catching a hail of flechettes as it did.

Kyle turned to survey the room, and saw that the bug spirit he'd just inadvertently diverted was among the last left in the room. With the deaths of the big guardian roaches, the rest seemed to have fled. None remained solely in astral space, and the few that fought on manifest were being quickly dispatched by the remaining troopers.

Within moments, it was over.

The terrible sounds of gunfire, magic, and the screams of dying men and spirits still ringing in his ears, Kyle walked slowly across the basement to the clusters of swollen shapes the larger roach spirits had been guarding. He approached cautiously, his senses still existing primarily in astral space.

They were alive, somewhat, pulsing with energy and existence, but there was an alienness about them. Some of the auras leaking from the meter-and-a-half-long objects were cool and constant, others flickered as if fighting something unseen, and the remainder showed echoes of duality, of two spirits overlapped. All, it seemed, were very slowly fading.

Kyle reached the first cluster, six of the objects piled almost haphazardly on top of each other, the bottom one all but buried. He touched it, and felt coolness, a rough skin, and the faint wisps of fear, longing, and despair echoing from inside it. And something was inside it—it lurched at his presence, thrashing, the sensation of fear growing from it. The clear outline of a hand, a child's, pushed against the outer covering.

Kyle stood, bile and horror catching in his throat. Woodhouse came up silently alongside him.

"Are these . . . cocoons?" he asked quietly.

Kyle nodded, looking slowly around the basement at the dozens of piles. There were over a hundred cocoons. Did each one hold a human being?

"Jesus Christ," someone muttered softly.

"Is there anything we can do?" Woodhouse said, unable to take his eyes from the terrible sight.

"I don't know," said Kyle. "But we've got to try . . ."

17

But there wasn't anything that could be done.

Hours later, Kyle sat against one of the basement walls drinking tepid soykaf from a plastic cup. The cheery fast-food logo seemed to jeer at him from the side of the container. He watched as Woodhouse, another Eagle Security magician, a young woman who'd arrived with the reinforcements, and some paramedics tried to save a girl, barely out of her teens, from the terrible death that overcame most of the cocooned once they were removed. Physical death came quickly, but the mental anguish seemed to echo long past the body's final spasm.

Some, by strict medical definition, survived. One by one, mindless and still the way Mitch Truman had been, they were carried away in ambulances for extended treatment elsewhere, but no one held any hope for them.

The girl, swathed in some almost embryonic blue-white gauze shrieked and pushed against the gentle hands that tried to help her. Mucus flowed from her mouth in a great rush, down her neck and shoulders and across her exposed body. As they had done with all the others, the magicians tried to heal her, to stave off whatever biological reaction was forcing the body into collapse.

As Kyle watched, she gave one last gasp, then went limp, her body releasing whatever other fluids it contained. He could see that her body would not live. He'd become an expert at telling such things. She became quiet, and the four eased her back inside the cocoon.

Woodhouse stepped away, the muscles in his arms quiv-

ering from the exertion to which he was subjecting his body.
He looked at Kyle, eyes helpless.

"There's nothing we can do," Kyle said.

Woodhouse nodded, but the other mage turned on them.
"That's right. We can't do anything for them here. Let's
move them. Let's take them somewhere we can—"

"It won't work," Kyle said wearily.

The mage was angry. "We're just not set up here to help
them. We need to—"

Kyle interrupted her again, this time by standing. "It's not
us. It's them. They're dying even without our interfering."
He pointed to a pile of cocoons in the farthest corner.
"Those are dead already. And we haven't touched them."

While Woodhouse was spelling Kyle in their attempts to
resuscitate the insect spirit victims, Kyle sat watching as the
auras of all the cocoons slowly but inevitably began to dim.
They were simply dying.

The mage had turned and Kyle could tell she was using
her astral senses to examine the piles he'd pointed out.
"Maybe if we moved them all closer together," she said.
"And left them alone. It might be our presence that's killing
them."

This time it was Woodhouse who spoke up. "I think it's
that we killed the females."

Kyle nodded. "That's what I think too. The two biggest
ones."

"Yes."

The younger mage seemed perplexed. Kyle walked toward her between the piles. "All the cocoons started showing signs of agitation once the big ones began to get hurt,"
he said. "I think a couple of the bodies in them died even as
the mothers were being killed. The mother roaches were
doing something to sustain them, feeding them energy, I
don't know. With the mothers gone . . ."

"We've got to do something," she insisted.

"We can kill them quickly," Woodhouse said.

Kyle turned toward him. "That might be rash."

"You think so?"

Kyle sighed, thinking of his sister-in-law Ellen and Mitch

Truman. He'd already casually examined all the cocoons and satisfied himself that none of the forms inside was either one of them, but many of the human bodies had already become, or were becoming, half insect. If Ellen or Mitch were one of those, they might as well be dead. "No, I don't," he said reluctantly.

"We can't make that decision," the mage said. She was as exhausted and disheveled as either one of them. Kyle didn't even know her name.

"If we don't, these people will linger for hours, maybe even days, in agony," Woodhouse said. He turned to one of the paramedics who was now resting in the spot where Kyle had been. "Are you familiar with the Illinois euthanasia statutes?" Woodhouse asked him.

Kyle saw the man's body tense, but then his shoulders slumped with resignation. "I am," the man replied, nodding slowly.

"Do you agree that these people are beyond the point of recovery to a reasonable life and that only heroic measures could possibly save them now?"

"I do."

"Are you certified to make that decision?" Woodhouse asked, now letting his gaze run slowly over the remaining cocoons.

"I am."

"Would you please state your name for the record."

"Paul Michael Davidson, certification number RST002-1992-128-02-IL."

"And I, Sergeant Peter Walsh, Eagle Security ident number 203-272-12819 EFG, concur."

The woman was staring at Woodhouse, tired and angry, but powerless against the quiet despair in her senior officer's eyes.

Woodhouse looked at the other troopers and paramedics present. "Let's clear the space," he said.

Slowly, some understanding, others torn by what was occurring, gathered their gear and moved slowly up the stairs. After a moment of indecision, without further protest, the woman climbed the stairs after them.

"It won't take much," said Kyle.

Woodhouse nodded, and unsnapped the strap holding the pistol at his belt. He looked at Kyle, waiting for an offer of help, for some of the burden to be lifted, but it didn't come. Kyle only nodded slightly. He understood, but he would not kill these people.

Woodhouse returned the nod. Kyle turned and walked to the stairs. He was only halfway when the first shot rang out.

Upstairs, their work punctuated by the slow, deliberate rhythm of the shots from the basement, an Eagle Security forensics team was going over the offices and adjoining storerooms. Chief Lekas was walking toward the basement stairs as Kyle came up. Kyle shook his head and held the man back.

"Let him be," he said.

Lekas opened his mouth to speak, then stopped. He'd seen the basement. He understood. The two walked slowly over to where Commander Malley's rent body lay, covered by a dull, dark-stained blanket.

From there Kyle went on alone, passing through the offices and out into the waiting area. There, as the shots continued, he collapsed into one of the plastic chairs. Part of his mind wanted to count the shots, but he wouldn't let himself.

Only a few Eagle troopers were present, all looking from one to another as the shots continued. Kyle stood up and walked toward the front of the room, stepping through the shattered door and out into the sunshine. The late afternoon glare blinded him, but he let himself stare against it for a moment.

There were dozens of police, security, and medical vehicles parked in every direction on the street. A score of uniformed Eagle troopers held the crowd back at over a block away. Eagle wasn't taking any chances on any of the general public catching even a glimpse of what was going on. "Terrorists" was the word being circulated as a cover for the attack on the stores. The people could accept that; it happened all the time. The truth was another matter entirely.

Kyle stepped back into the doorway and slowly pulled his

portaphone out of his pocket. Part of its case caught on the
Eagle body armor he was wearing, but he carefully worked
it free. He didn't jack into it, certain he looked like drek and
not wanting her to see him that way. It didn't even occur to
him that his portable phone didn't transmit a picture. He was
beyond such subtleties.

He flipped open its sleek black and gray case and activated the address book display. He found the number he
wanted and instructed it to dial. It rang three times before
she answered. She'd been laughing.

"John Mikayama's office. Elizabeth Breman speaking."
Her voice was airy and almost breathless.

"Hoi," Kyle said.

She paused. "Kyle?"

"Yeah, it's me."

"Are you all right?" Sometimes, it seemed she always
asked him that.

"Uh-huh," he said. "Mostly tired."

"Where are you? There's so much noise . . ."

"I'm on the street. Nothing to worry about."

"Sure . . ."

He coughed. "Look, I called to tell you to stop over at
your sister's on your way home if you can."

Her voice rose excitedly. "Is she there?"

"No." He heard her exhale sharply. "At least she wasn't
earlier, before lunch. You have keys, right?"

"Yes, I do. Is something wrong?"

"Truthfully," he said, "I don't know. She's not there, but
her cat is. You might want to pick him up."

"Oh my god."

"I don't know if anything's wrong. She's just not there.
That's all I'm saying."

"Please tell me."

"Beth, there's nothing to tell you," Kyle said, letting himself squint against the sun. "I don't know anything more
than that."

"Please tell me."

He dipped his head forward away from the light. He

shouldn't have called. "You're going to be home tonight, yes?"

"Yes, I'll be home."

"Good. I'll try and stop by. Maybe help Natalie with her homework or something."

"She won't be here. She's staying at her friend Pammy's with some of the other girls from the computer club. They're finishing off a class presentation on Pammy's father's system. He's a media programmer."

"Then maybe tomorrow."

"Come by anyway. Let me know if you'll make it for dinner. If you do, I'll cook again."

He smiled. "Such treatment."

"Yeah, well," she said, "I've been practicing."

"I'll call and let you know."

"Please call, will you?"

"Yes," he said. "Bye."

"Bye."

He disconnected and folded the phone shut, slipping it back into his pocket.

Back inside, Kyle walked slowly through the rooms. The gunfire had stopped, but there was no sign of Woodhouse. A few officers were making their way carefully down the stairs. Then Woodhouse came up, blank-faced. He looked at Kyle and walked toward the rear door. Kyle let him go.

The detectives were searching every corner, examining every scrap of paper or file they could find. Kyle watched them and listened. The papers said nothing. The files were innocuous, revealing nothing. There was information on bill payment, and one of the detectives thought they might be able to find out more by tracing the bank accounts. Kyle doubted it. This had been a Universal Brotherhood storefront, apparently keeping up some level of operation despite the official government shutdown months ago. There would be no traces to anything.

Kyle shuddered and wondered if all the Universal Brotherhood sites had been like this. Was this what had prompted the government crackdown? Was this the drek Strevich had tried to warn him away from? Part of him wished he'd listened.

After speaking briefly with Chief Lekas, he walked back outside to return the body armor to the officer watching over the command van. They arranged for a police car to drive him back to his hotel.

Ignoring the odd, almost frightened looks of hotel security and other patrons, Kyle went up to his suite, stripped off his clothing and foci, and sat in the shower under the water running as hot as he could stand for as long as he dared. He didn't even think that Linda Hayward might come back. He thought about sleeping, but knew he couldn't do that yet.

He used his shaving gel to remove the day's growth of stubble on his face, then put on a pair of jeans and the old pullover sweatshirt he reserved for the rare times he bothered to jog. He almost walked out without his foci, but remembered them at the last minute.

Kyle couldn't remember where his car was, and checked with the hotel valet. No, they told him, it wasn't there. They called him a cab instead.

Two and half hours later, when Elizabeth Breman finally came home carrying her sister's cat Grendel in her arms, she found Kyle sitting on the front porch in the same FBI pullover he'd been wearing on the day she'd first met him. He was fast asleep. She took the cat inside and then came back. After a moment's thought, she led Kyle half-awake up the stairs to the second floor and the master bedroom. He didn't notice as she gently pulled off his shoes, followed by his pants and sweatshirt. He didn't even notice when she removed his foci and placed them carefully on the nightstand, just within reach, and then draped a blanket over him. He didn't even notice when she leaned in and kissed him softly on the temple, next to the long, dark scratch that only now seemed to be closing over. He was fast asleep, safe among the fluffy quilts and pillows that smelled faintly of flowers and leaves.

When a chill breeze slipping in through the partially open bedroom window woke him sometime in the middle of the

night, she was curled against him, her new short haircut
pushed askew by his shoulder. Though covered by the blanket, she seemed cold, wearing only one of the long night-
shirts she favored. As he pulled her closer, she opened her
eyes. She said nothing for a long moment, then clung to him
and he felt her body begin to shudder as she choked backed
the tears she'd never wanted him to see.

She was cold, and he held her tighter against both the
night and the sadness. His own emotions of the last days
came rushing up on him, and he felt her sadness, almost undeniable, flow over him. But then she moved against him,
and suddenly in the near darkness their lips met, carefully,
and he tasted them washed in her tears.

They turned slightly and sat up, her legs spreading around
him, nightshirt pushed high up on her hips. She gasped, and he
wanted the feel of all of her body beneath his hands, the smell
of her hair, the brush of her warming skin, and the rush of their
mingled breath as he entered her roughly. He wanted it all.
Then. Now. Immediately. But as she closed her eyes and arced
her body away from him, he pulled her shirt off slowly, forcing
himself to linger over every curve, every revealed shadow.

Calmly, slowly, he turned them both, letting her lie on her
back. He lowered himself to where their bodies nearly
touched and kissed her gently high on the forehead. He
moved down from there, against the soft curve of her ear,
across the strong line of her jaw, beneath her chin, and
lower, below her breasts, and then carefully around and back
up again to their hard, dark tips. And he did this slowly, deliberately, thinking only of her and her body. Every inch. Ignoring everything else. Forgetting everything else. For as
long as he could.

18

He awoke again toward morning, he and Beth safely beneath the covers, protected from the surprising morning chill that had crept in. The light outside, slipping in through the partially open window, was a brightening blue-gray, tinged with the promise of another day of bright sun. He breathed in heavily and squinted against that unexpected glare. Beth moved too, pushing away from him slightly, and making an unintelligible noise. He shifted his arm into a more comfortable position across her back. For a long, strange moment, he was caught in a physical and emotional limbo where three years had vanished and foolish mistakes were forgiven. It was familiar territory, someplace safe, where he'd least expected to be—

Familiar territory. Someplace safe. Last place you expected to be.

Kyle knew then where to look for Beth's sister, and for Mitch Truman.

He carefully untangled his arms and legs from Beth's, trying not to wake her. She slept on, hearing nothing as he pulled on his pants and walked silently downstairs. Grendel regarded him from a strategic position near the front windows, but did nothing except watch with wide, unblinking eyes.

He crept into the room where Natalie played, taking more care than needed since she wasn't there. Her computer booted up quickly, shifting through the start-up of the spinning, prismatic Apple logo and then showing the floating iconic interface Natalie had designed, with his and a program's considerable help, a year ago. He ignored it, instead

tarting a program keyword search. From the list he was
hen presented, he found the program he wanted and loaded
t.

Within moments, he was inside the gateway to the public
ibrary datanets. He scanned for the Archives section and requested access to the last ten years of local Chicago telecom
nd address listings. Adding them to his search list, he then
acked out of the Archives and pulled up the current
elecom and address listings. Adding that to the search list,
e instituted a global search through those eleven files for
eferences to the Universal Brotherhood.

Two hundred and nineteen references were generated. He
efined the list by excluding duplicates, and then instructed
he program to indicate which listings were not duplicated.

Twenty-nine listings appeared more than once in various
volumes, six appeared only once.

Thirty-five places to look. One, however, stood out—
partially because of its absurdity, and partially because the
address had stopped being listed eight years ago even though
ts telecom number was listed in every directory. The Universal Brotherhood Merchandising Center had been at Mad-
son and Sangamon, not too far from Interstate 90/94. The
other locations would also have to be checked, but Kyle suspected that an old, familiar location that hadn't been listed in
he directories for more than eight years should be high on
his list.

He then imported the addresses into the mapping and display subset connected to the listings and asked for a printout
of all the locations on a map of Chicago. Once the colored
map had scrolled out the side of the machine, and he'd confirmed that all the info he wanted was there, Kyle disconnected from the library and shut the computer down. It very
politely wished him a good night as he walked away already
studying the new map.

Kyle thought about going back upstairs and slipping back
into bed with Beth before traveling astrally to scout out the
locations on the list, but changed his mind. He didn't want
her to wake up to find him next to her, seemingly unconscious. Instead, he went into the living room with a piece of

paper and a marking pen. He sat down on the couch and
wrote "Gone traveling" on the paper, folded it into a little
sign, and sat it on the couch next to him.

Another thought struck him, and he realized that he didn't
have either his portable telecom or his datapad. He'd been
out of touch with the Trumans for some hours, and even if
they knew he had an ex-wife in Chicago, they probably
wouldn't think to try him at her number. He'd have to make
one stop before beginning his search.

After studying the map one last time, he called up a simple spell that would keep the map's image crisp in his memory for a few hours. He'd still have some trouble finding the
locations from astral space, but he could compare the image
in his mind to what he saw by counting from recognizable
intersections or landmarks. Not being able to read street
signs would be a problem, but he had a solution for that.

His astral self slipped free easily, and he felt renewed and
rejuvenated. He glided quickly up the stairs of the old
wooden house and into the master bedroom. Beth had spread
out in his absence, arms and legs askew, her face half-buried
in one of the pillows. He slipped out through the window,
twisting to pass through the frame and into the now golden
morning.

Heartbeats later, Kyle was approaching the dull, lifeless
Truman Tower and then moments after that angling himself
in toward the patio of the condo. As he alighted on the
ground, Charlotte, Winston, and Seeks-the-Moon appeared.

"*Boss,*" said Winston.

"*Master,*" said Charlotte.

"Where the hell have you been?" Moon bellowed.

Kyle shrugged and smiled. "Busy. I needed some time to
myself."

The two elemental spirits hung there motionless, but
Moon nodded understanding. "Ms. Uljakën briefed Mr.
Truman on what Eagle found. It apparently took considerable effort on her part to get the information since you had
wandered off."

"Yeah, I'll need to apologize."

Moon nodded again. "It might be wise." he said. "All things considered."

"What do you mean?"

"The young lady was apparently quite worried that you'd been injured or gotten into some trouble."

The information surprised Kyle somewhat, coming as and when it did, and considering the events of the previous night. "Then I'll make sure I do," he said. "I take it she's home sleeping?"

Moon shook his head. "No, she's here in one of the guest rooms."

"Then let her sleep for now," Kyle said. "When she wakes up, tell her I checked in and that everything is fine and I'm continuing with my investigation."

"The things she said happened seemed quite terrible," Moon said.

"They were."

The spirit looked like he wanted to ask more, but he didn't.

"I'll come by physically in a few hours, especially if all my clothes are here now," Kyle told him. "I assume they picked up my portable and datapad?"

Seeks-the-Moon nodded. "They did, as Ms. Uljakën discovered when she tried to call you and your telecom rang two rooms away. She seemed disturbed by the fact that you were not carrying it. I tried to reassure her that you were fine, but she didn't quite understand that I would know if anything had happened to you."

"Understandable," Kyle said. "I'm going to be scouting possible locations of hives or nests or whatever they are, and I'd like you to come with me."

"Really?" said Moon. "I'm no longer the home guard?"

"No," Kyle told him. "I need someone who can read."

The first site Moon and Kyle checked was empty, abandoned, but from astral space Kyle could sense the echoes and resonances of power that had been present there. They were dulling, fading with time, but enough was present for him to recognize many of the same sensations he had expe-

rienced in the roach nest. The lingering astral smell was un
mistakable.

They moved on to the next, and the ones after that, Moon
guiding them through the physical world by reading the
street signs and address numbers when Kyle's dead reckon
ing in astral space wasn't good enough.

Finally, after examining a dozen closer sites, they closed
in on the one Kyle had initially thought was most promising
of all, the Universal Brotherhood Merchandising Center a
Madison and Sangamon. They alighted on the roof of a taller
building a few blocks away and studied the small warehouse
from astral space. It seemed quiet, inert, a dog sitting in the
shade of the receiving dock the only sign of activity.

"Do you think it's a guard dog?" asked Moon.

"I don't know," said Kyle. "It could be a watch dog. I
could be a stray. There's no way to tell from here."

"Let me see if I can get a better look from the physical
world," Moon said, and Kyle saw the spirit's form shift
slightly, become more solid, as it took physical form. "No,"
he said in Kyle's mind. "I can't see any better. There is—"

Moon quieted as the lone normal-sized door opened and a
man stepped out. He had a strong aura, extreme strongly, but
Kyle couldn't tell if he was a magician, or something else,
at this distance.

"How does he look?" Kyle asked.

"He's wearing work clothes, one-piece cover-alls," Moon
said. "And he's bald."

The man threw something that looked like a large white
garbage bag onto a pile of similar objects near a dumpster. The dog watched idly and then dropped its head back
down. The man stepped back inside. Up on the roof, blocks
away, Seeks-the-Moon slowly turned and looked over his
shoulder.

Kyle turned too, but saw nothing that would attract the
spirit's interest, only the dull grays and black of the roof and
assorted air conditioning and heating machinery.

"I heard something," Moon said, stepping back from the
edge, this time looking slightly upward at the small metal
structure that supported a half-dozen old and rusted micro-

wave dishes. Moon circled the tower, approached it, and then began to climb.

"What is it?" Kyle asked. "I can't see anything."

"Wait. Wait," said Moon. He climbed about his own height from the roof and leaned in. After a moment, he slipped into astral space and floated down to Kyle's side.

"It's a camera of some sort, pointed at the warehouse. I don't know technology well, but I heard it move to follow the man."

"Someone's watching the building." Kyle looked up at the tower even though he couldn't distinguish the small device among the other metal and electronics up there.

"So it would seem," Seeks-the-Moon said. "Who do you think?"

"Well, Eagle wouldn't bother with anything that fancy. They'd simply assign some slag to sit up here with binoculars or a camera. Which leaves only Knight Errant, unless there's someone else involved or this has nothing to do with anything."

"Is that likely?"

Kyle shook his head. "Not in the least. But if it's Knight Errant, they've got to be around here somewhere in order to get the transmission from the camera."

"Won't they simply come up here now?" Moon asked.

"Why?"

Moon shrugged. "Someone would have seen me standing at the edge of the building when I became physical."

"No, probably not. Cameras that can see that far have a very narrow field of view. You'd have to stand almost in front of it for them to see you."

"Ah, I'd thought maybe we could follow them if they came up here."

"We can still do that," Kyle said, and began looking around the roof. "Do you see any pieces of paper or newsprint or heavy cardboard?"

"Yes," the spirit said, having returned to manifest form. "There's a bag over there. It says 'McHughs'."

Kyle chuckled, imagining a crumpled, greasy, fast-food bag. "That'll do."

"I'm confused." Seeks-the-Moon said. "What will it do for?"

"Pick it up and put it on the camera, blocking the lens," Kyle said.

"Ah. Then they'll come to fix it."

Kyle smiled. "We can hope."

The bag in place, Kyle and Seeks-the-Moon quickly retreated into a nearby ventilation duct, passing easily through the machined metal and plastic of its construction, and then descended to slightly below roof level. There, Kyle carefully constructed a spell that would project his vision into the physical world and allow him to observe the tower and the camera. Compensating for the drain the effort put on his body, he surveyed the area.

Finally able to see the camera, he confirmed Seeks-the-Moon's report. But his own experience also told him some things. It was quite small, very concealable, and of a kind often used by corporate or government surveillance teams. He had, in fact, worked a number of times with a very similar model in his FBI days. Like that one, this unit also has a small shotgun microphone attachment that, with the proper filtering software, could easily pick up any conversations that might take place on the loading dock.

A shadow loomed over the tower, and Kyle shifted the spell's point of view back and around to view the source. A thick, flat dish, slightly larger than a garbage can lid, hung in space over the edge of the building. It was a drone, some sort of remotely piloted vehicle, equipped with a camera system and other sensors, undoubtedly sent to determine the cause of the camera outage. It slid in closer, angling the protected rotor blades that made up much of its center, until it got a better look at the camera and the obstruction blocking the lens.

Kyle immediately knew what the operator would do once he or she saw what the problem was, and he quickly began to cast another spell. The strain was greater; the distraction of maintaining the far-seeing spell combined with being in astral space made the casting harder than it should have been. But as the drone's pilot angled the craft to blow the offending bag off the camera, Kyle's spell applied force of its own, holding the bag in place. The pilot swung the drone quickly around to the far side, hoping to blow the bag off with a gust of air from that direction while minimizing the vehicle's exposure to view from the warehouse. But Kyle held the bag in place. The drone backed off, hovering for a moment, and then zipped away out of view. Kyle tried to follow it with the vision spell, but the drone was too fast and the range of the spell too short.

A short time passed, and Kyle was becoming concerned about the amount of time he'd spent in astral space. His body, back on Beth's couch, could only support itself for so long without its spirit, and based on the sun's position in the sky, he'd already been traveling astrally for some time. He decided to risk it, waiting to see whether he was experiencing the telltale weakness that would be a warning of danger. In the meantime, he combined a spell that let him hear what was going on up on the roof with the one that let him see. Just as he completed the combination, the sound of scraping metal attracted his attention.

He shifted the point of view of the spells and saw a well-built man climbing up through the access door and onto the roof. He quickly approached the tower, vaulted up onto it, and deftly yanked the bag clear of the camera.

"Repairman's here," Kyle told Moon, using the mental speech they shared.

"About time." The spirit, it seemed, was slightly claustrophobic.

The camera now unobstructed, the man leaped nimbly down and headed for the trap door.

"All right. You know the plan," Kyle said. With his sight and hearing extended through the spells, there was no way he was going to be able to guide himself through astral space. Moon would do that for both of them, responding to Kyle's mental instructions.

Kyle waited while the man climbed down, then shifted the point of view of his spells to follow him. The trap door opened onto a ladder leading to a stairwell that seemed to extend down through the building.

Kyle followed the man down as far as the spell's range, and then told Moon, "Take us down."

The spirit, holding Kyle's astral body carefully, began to descend through the ventilation shaft. At Kyle's prompting, Moon paced their descent so that the man stayed just inside the edge of the spell's effect.

They followed him, using the buildings along the street as cover, until the man made a turn at Randolph. But from their position, Kyle could clearly see a pair of large tractor-trailers, casually surrounded by a half-dozen nondescript light vans and trucks parked a few blocks down. The area was a mix of commercial and light industrial, so the vehicles almost seemed part of the environment.

"Got 'em," said Kyle.

"Good. Now what?"

"Now, we pay them a visit." Kyle told him. "But first I get my body."

19

Kyle opened his eyes, and immediately began the stretching exercises he used to rid his body of the cramping and lethargy that came with a prolonged jaunt in astral space. That was why it took a few moments before he noticed the large easel and the crayon-scrawled words "I'VE GONE TO WORK." There was nothing else; no other words, no signature, no sign-off to signify with what emotions she'd written the words. Kyle slipped back into astral space and examined the easel and the now indecipherable writing. He sensed a slight annoyance attached to the words, but there was something else. A touch of brightness, though tempered by the darker emotion.

He sighed. He should have kept better track of the time, should have been there when she woke up. Beth would have been irritated by the time she came downstairs, and seeing him sprawled on the couch, his spirit and attention elsewhere, would only have made it worse. If true to form, she'd have calmed down by the time she got to work. He'd call her there later, after he dealt with Knight Errant.

Finding his clothes in a pile on the now re-made bed, he dressed and went back downstairs to call the Truman condplex. A servant answered, and moments later, he was speaking to Hanna Uljakën. She was wearing a white business suit over a mandarin-collared silk shirt that matched her eyes. She was trying very hard not to show her anger.

"Where have you been?" she demanded. "Are you all right?"

Kyle started to ask her if Seeks-the-Moon had given her his message, but then realized that he'd taken Moon with him. The spirit was probably only now returning to the Tower as Kyle had instructed.

"Yes, I'm fine," he said. "I'm sorry I didn't let you know what was going on. I stopped by late last night, left a message with Moon, and then took him with me to help check something out."

"Well, that wasn't very smart." Kyle could tell she was still angry despite her smile and attempt at a bantering tone. Her reaction implied many things, but none of them he could deal with immediately.

"Is my car still at the staging area from yesterday?" he asked.

"Assuming it hasn't been stolen."

"I'll be back at the Tower in about an hour," he said. "I'll see you then."

"Don't you want to know what's been happening here?"

He tensed. "Anything critical?"

She shook her head. "No."

"Then I'd rather talk in person."

Her eyes softened. "Fine. Will you need Mr. Truman?"

"No. At least not right away."

"He's trying a full business load today."

"Good." Kyle started to reach for the Disconnect, then thought of something else. "Has Knight Errant reported in or briefed him?"

She shook her head again. "Not to my knowledge."

"If by chance they show up before I get there, stall them."

She nodded. "I will."

"Thanks. See you in an hour."

Kyle called a cab, and twenty minutes later was heading down Interstate 90/94 toward the Core. He looked to his right as they passed the Washington off-ramp, but the warehouse and Knight Errant's surveillance caravan were blocks from the highway. Minutes later he was at the Truman Tower, and being met by the normal retinue. Hovering in the background were a half-dozen Knight Errant troopers, though the security was markedly reduced. It seemed Knight

Errant was less worried about the safety of the Truman family than previously.

He went directly upstairs, passed no extra Knight Errant guards along the way, and found Hanna sitting opposite Seeks-the-Moon in the large family room. A wooden board cross-hatched with lines and littered with dozens of rounded white and black stones sat between them.

"Who, dare I ask, is teaching whom how to play Go?" he asked.

Moon seemed pensive and his attention was focused on the board. Hanna, however, smiled and looked up. "I'm teaching him," she said. "He's very good."

Kyle laughed, but was surprised again. He'd tried a number of times to master the Japanese game during his student days, but had never quite managed it. She was probably exaggerating Seeks-the-Moon's abilities.

"Well, he seems to be deep in thought, so I'd be eternally grateful if you'd show me where I can clean up and change clothes."

Hanna stood up, straightening her jacket. "I'll be right back," she told Moon, who nodded, but did not look up from the board. Kyle followed her out into the corridor on this level. "That reminds me," she said to him, turning slightly, "does he ever change his clothes?"

"Moon?" Kyle asked.

"Yes, Moon."

"No. What he's wearing is part of his form. He knows a couple of spells. You saw him use the disguise spell when the Knight Errant combat team was here. But otherwise the clothes he's wearing are the ones I created him with."

"Here." She stopped in front of a door along the hall. "This is yours."

"Great." Kyle opened the door and stepped inside, then turned to her. "Come in for a minute."

She seemed to hesitate briefly, but following him in. Kyle closed the door and looked around. The room reminded him of a luxury hotel. There was a single, king-sized bed, night stands, dresser, and wardrobe, desk and telecom, and a small sitting area off to one side, all modeled in the currently fash-

ionable avante-Asian style. His datapad and portable
telecom were sitting on the desk, and he assumed his clothes
were already organized neatly in the dresser and adjoining
wardrobe, but his interest was drawn to the gold and white
marble bathroom he could glimpse through an adjoining
door. He glanced in and confirmed the presence of a small
whirlpool bath and shower.

"Very nice," he said.

"Glad you like it."

"I'm going to shower and change while we talk. Do you
mind?"

"No, not at all." Hanna sat down on the edge of the bed.

"Good." He went to the dresser, searched through the
drawers, and pulled out a pair of pale blue briefs.

Hanna flushed slightly and quickly looked away, but Kyle
didn't let her see his smile. He went into the bathroom, closing the door partly. As he showered, he loudly told her what
he knew about what had transpired at the first Brotherhood
location at Harlem and Irving, and about his and Seek-the-
Moon's investigations at the other sites. He told her they had
not checked any of the other Brotherhood sites on the list,
since the in-force presence of Knight Errant troops seemed
a good indication that they'd found the point of interest.

"So you're hoping that nothing happens before you get
back there?" she called out as he finished both his shower
and the story.

"Yes and no," he said, toweling off. He could hear her
moving around in the other room. "If they've already moved
in by the time I get back, great. It'll be over and there'll be
a scene to investigate."

"What if they won't let you?" she asked.

"Then I call in Eagle Security and they take over the situation. Knight Errant doesn't have the jurisdiction to override Eagle here in Chicago."

"They could still say no."

"They could, but that might provoke publicity they don't
want." He slipped the briefs on and wrapped a towel around
his waist. "They're operating in the city of Chicago, not on
corporate territory."

He walked out into the main room and found her standing near the window, looking out across the city. If Hanna was embarrassed, she tried to hide it as Kyle stood obviously looking for something in the room. "Flat black case," he said, "A little larger than a briefcase."

She pointed at the wardrobe. "In there."

He took it out, and dropped it on the bed. Opening it quickly, he began pulling out items of heavy, white, semi-rigid partial clothing.

"What's that?" she asked.

"Form-fitting body armor. I had it made for me some years ago. Pretty expensive, so it's a valuable incentive not to gain weight." Maneuvering the towel, he pulled on a pair of long shorts with what seemed to be additional padding in the front and rear thighs. Those in place, he let the towel drop and began strapping other pieces onto his body, covering and protecting vital organs.

"You seem to be expecting trouble," she said, almost casually.

Kyle had gone to retrieve his magical foci from the bathroom. "I guess I am." He slipped them on and activated them. "All things considered."

Just over an hour later, he pulled into the intersection of Sangamon and Randolph and confirmed that the Knight Errant trucks were still present. Some of them had moved since earlier in the day, but the main Citymasters were still there. He'd gone past the Brotherhood warehouse too. Except for the absence of the dog, nothing seemed to have changed there either.

He made a left onto Randolph, taking the center lane to avoid the many trucks that dominated the one-way inner roadway. Three men, husky and dressed far too warmly for the weather loitered near the trucks, eyeing everyone who passed. Kyle continued on another block and turned into the inner roadway, stopping a dozen meters shy of the trucks. The three men watched him, then one broke away from the group and headed toward Kyle as he was climbing out of the car.

"Hey there," the man said when close enough to talk. "We're gonna have to back this thing up outta here in a couple minutes. You better not park there."

Kyle smiled. "Thanks. I'll keep that in mind," he said. "Tell Captain Ravenheart that Kyle Teller would like to talk with her."

If the man was surprised he didn't show it. He merely nodded and turned away slightly, his mouth and throat moving, an obvious sign that he was subvocalizing, probably into a hidden microradio or cybernetic headware system. Within moments, he turned back to Kyle and said, "You're clear. Lead truck."

Kyle nodded. "Do I still need to move my car?"

"Not yet. We'll let you know."

"Thanks." Kyle walked forward, past the second truck, casually noticing the structural reinforcing, the barest signs of armor plating, and the flat mesh of military antenna in a strip near the roof. As he came to the front truck, one of its doors opened, a small stair folded out, and a casually garbed, buzz-cut man stepped out.

He nodded to Kyle and motioned him up the stairs.

"Not going to frisk me?" Kyle said.

"No, sir."

"Appreciate it." Kyle climbed the stair, and pushed carefully past the black curtains that hung just beyond the doorway. The interior was lit with flat green lighting, but where the Eagle Security command van had been cramped and overcrowded, the Knight Errant vehicles were spacious and efficient, as testified by the obvious comfort of the six individuals present. He saw computer consoles with large touchscreen displays that served double duty as control and data and trideo monitors. A long bank of them showed the exterior of the gathered Citymasters and the surrounding neighborhood, including multiple views of the Brotherhood warehouse. Another showed a truck full of troopers, dim figures in black body armor, waiting. From the way they were arming up, Kyle didn't think they'd be waiting long.

"Looks like I got here just in time," Kyle said.

None of the occupants of the command and control area seemed amused, save one.

"You owe me fifty, Vathoss," Anne Ravenheart said, smiling slightly as she turned in one of the console chairs. She was already geared up in her black body armor. A tactical helmet hung from the side of the chair. Beyond her, Sergeant Vathoss frowned at both her and Kyle.

"I left my credstick in my other pants," he said sourly.

"Null sweat," she told him, glancing over her shoulder at him and then back at Kyle. "I know you know Sergeant Vathoss," she said, "and Lieutenant Gersten." Vathoss didn't acknowledge the mention and continued working the combat data console he was prepping. Gersten, however, seated to the rear of the cabin and apparently doing nothing more useful than scratching under the collar of his combat armor, nodded.

"Across from me"—she gestured to the tall Japanese woman on the opposite side of the cabin—"is Sergeant Sakai." The woman didn't directly acknowledge the mention either, but Kyle wasn't surprised. Three hyper-speed optical cables ran from the base of her neck and plugged into her chair, which was, in turn, part of and directly connected to her console. What he could see of her eyes were focused on something invisible to anyone else. She was the tac-ops officer, in charge of coordinating and tracking unit and individual movement once an operation began. Again, from the intense look on her face and the visible activity on her console, the preliminary stages were already underway.

"And lastly," Ravenheart said, indicating with her eyes the older and at least partially Amerindian man standing directly behind her, "I'd like to introduce you to Roger Soaring Owl, CEO of Knight Errant."

Soaring Owl, who looked more like an accountant despite his combat armor, nodded at Kyle. "I'll have you know that I came very close to losing that bet myself," he said in an almost deliberately slowed voice. "Fortunately, I changed my mind."

Kyle stepped forward and hesitantly extended his hand. The shorter man shook it vigorously. Kyle didn't know much about Roger Soaring Owl, but he did know the man answered only to Damien Knight, himself the CEO of Ares Macrotechnology. For him to be here, and fully geared, actually frightened Kyle. He hadn't heard that Soaring Owl was any kind of adrenaline junkie or even a hands-on manager, and that meant this operation was very important to Ares.

"You're not going, by the way," Soaring Owl said in the moment of silence after they shook hands. Kyle saw Ravenheart smile and spin back to her console.

"Going?" asked Kyle.

"On the raid."

"I should think you'd want all the help you could get."

Sergeant Sakai's voice interrupted them. "Astral teams report they're staging point one."

"Thank you," said Ravenheart just as Soaring Owl was telling Kyle, "We appreciate the offer, but we're all set." He smiled slightly. "We've done this before."

"So have I," Kyle said.

"Yes, the Eagle raid. We have it all recorded if you'd ever like to see it. Many men and women died there for no reason. We had the situation in hand."

Kyle felt cold. "The cocoons . . .?"

"No," Soaring Owl said. "The troopers. Those poor souls who were cocooned are lost. Nothing could be done for them."

"Based on what I saw in that raid, you need all the magical help you can get," Kyle said. "Conventional weaponry is only of limited use, grenades and rockets are useless, and considering the metaphysics, I can't see drone or remote weaponry being of any real help either."

Soaring Owl nodded. "You're right, but we're prepared. Eighty percent of the assault force is magically active—either full-blooded magicians, sorcerers, or physical adepts. They'll have drone cover against the flesh forms, which gunfire seems to cut down just fine. They'll also be supported by a cadre of elementals and watcher spirits inside, and a circle of them outside as backup and to catch any that try to break free. We've also got four shamans, all combat-trained, who will turn the place inside out magically. There's going to be a world of drek flying into that building in thirty minutes, Mr. Teller, but you're not going to part of it."

Kyle scowled, but knew it was useless trying to change Soaring Owl's mind.

Then the older man smiled and gestured to the multitudes of display monitors. "You can, of course, watch."

20

Sergeant Sakai's voice was calm and soothing as she coordinated the staging and interaction of the thirty-two different elements comprising the Knight Errant raid on the Brotherhood warehouse. Kyle understood her words, but little of what she was saying as she related custom map coordinates and abbreviated sequencing information. She, one other coordinator, two technicians, and Roger Soaring Owl were the only Knight Errant troopers present in the command cabin. The rest were staged for combat.

"All units at start point," Sakai said loudly. At the rear of the cabin, Soaring Owl quickly finished off a private telecom call that Kyle believed was to Damien Knight himself. After disconnecting, he walked over to Sakai and placed his hand on her shoulder, "We're green," he said.

She nodded and her hands flashed over the console, a dozen indicators turning green. "Stage green go," she said. "Good luck."

Things suddenly began to happen on every monitor in the cabin. Kyle could barely follow it all, but seeing that Soaring Owl seemed to know exactly where to look next, Kyle let his attention follow the older man's. Any doubt that Soaring Owl was simply a data-mover out for a rush among the troops was laid to rest during these final preparations. As Ravenheart was rattling off last-minute changes and amendments to the battle plan, Soaring Owl's questions and concerns were coming just as rapid-fire.

"Rocket's away," Sakai said.

Soaring Owl turned to the monitors showing the exterior of the Brotherhood warehouse, and as a score of black-clad

troopers rushed forward, even faster streaks of light hit
the various doors and windows, blowing them open.
Immediately, a second wave of rockets soared through the
open windows and exploded inside the structure, spreading
huge, billowing clouds of foul-smelling gas specifically designed to overpower the insect spirit's dominant sense—
smell.

Three armored hover drones zipped past the troopers and
in through the ruptured cargo door. Kyle searched the monitors for a view from them, and found it just as a trio of half-
men, half-something-else figures were cut to pieces in a
barrage of high-velocity gunfire. The troopers swarmed in
after the drones, and flashes of magical power began to
dominate the viewscreens.

Now Kyle could see real insect spirits appearing, and not
just roaches. A giant wasp flashed in against the troopers but
banged against a barely visible wall of force that suddenly
appeared in front of it. Gunfire had no problem passing
through the barrier, however, and the wasp vanished back
into astral space.

The lead troopers moved forward into the main area of the
warehouse, which was open and virtually empty. The huge
room contained almost nothing but scattered piles of small
boxes. Then other insect spirits quickly began to appear, engaging the lead troopers.

Now came the elemental spirits, intercepting the huge ants
and flies as they fell upon the raiders. The troopers began to
make their way to where the building plan showed large
stairways and elevator shafts leading to the lower storage
depths. It was there Knight Errant expected to find the hive
itself, and its queen. To speed that penetration, three teams
of demolitions experts began placing excavation charges on
the concrete floor while other troopers defended them from
the insect onslaught.

"There are a lot of different kinds of bugs there. . ." Kyle
said.

"I have to admit we weren't expecting that," Soaring Owl
said. "The different insect hives apparently don't get along,
but the Brotherhood leaders were somehow able to keep

them from going after each other for many years. When the Brotherhood collapsed, we figured inter-hive warfare was inevitable."

"And that is cause for concern?" said Kyle.

Soaring Owl nodded. "Yes it is."

The battle in the warehouse raged on, but Kyle felt numb as he watched, drained of emotion. There were too many insect spirits, of all kinds, too many troopers, too much magic, and too much gunfire. The scene was beyond the realm of comprehension. And, displayed as it was on banks of trideo monitors, it began to lose any sense of reality.

"Chemsniffers are registering alerts," Sakai said suddenly. "PVMH and C-6 off the scale."

"Where?" Soaring Owl asked, turning toward her. "Is it our stuff?"

"Main floor. But it's not ours."

"Drek!" he said, turning back to the main monitors showing the views from the drones. To Kyle's amazement, Knight Errant casualties were minimal so far, even though the wave after wave of maddened insects seemed endless. Soaring Owl's face paled and he reached out to touch the monitor image where one pile of small boxes had been scattered to reveal bundles of smaller packages, and wire. . .

"Oh my god," he said just before the bundles exploded.

Plastic explosives all around the main room detonated, sending shockwaves and a wall of nails and other small bits of metal shooting through the assembled troopers. The bugs, creatures of magic, were untouched by the random, undirected explosions, but the troopers were another matter.

Caught in intersecting blasts, many were simply torn to shreds. The rest were either knocked from their feet or stunned, while the insects wasted no time descending upon them in force.

"God fragging damn!" Soaring Owl screamed. "Second and third teams in! Booby trap alerts!"

"Second Team alert advance. Third Team alert advance. Explosive trap warning in effect," Sakai said calmly. "Repeat, Second and Third Team advance. Explosive traps are present."

Other troopers entered the fray, some engaging the furious ants and flies and wasps directly, while others attempted to pull the injured from the main area of battle. Then more explosions suddenly tore open the ceiling, rocket hits blasting holes big enough for more combat drones to enter. Kyle saw one firing repeated bursts of green-white laser beams that cut deadly swaths through the swarming, flying, crawling, shrieking wave of deadly insect spirits.

"Demolition charge one firing," Sakai said.

And another explosion rocked the building, but this one was shaped downward and shattered a huge section of floor. The drones moved quickly to descend as teams of troopers struggled to assemble at the edges of the hole, prepared to drop into the smoky darkness below.

Then, without warning, the gates of hell opened.

A horde of insect spirits, scores, maybe hundreds, exploded out of the hole. Ants, roaches, beetles, wasps, flies, nearly every creeping or flying kind Kyle had ever seen came forth from the hole. Many resembled the actual insect, but far more were half-creatures catapulted into the main room by the force of the others' flight and leap from the hole.

And the swarm didn't stop.

Kyle turned his head and looked at one of the monitors showing the outside of the warehouse and the black stream of insect spirits pouring out from the ruptured roof.

"Mother of god . . ." said Soaring Owl.

Once outside, the bug spirits scattered in all directions, some flying, some darting and skittering down off the roof or through the broken, smoking windows.

Inside, the troopers were overwhelmed. Maybe a hundred flesh forms attacked them, with more crawling up out of the hole or now coming up the stairways. The creatures couldn't hold against the Knight Errant firepower, but there were too many, moving too quickly. The aerial drones seemed to be the most successful at decimating the force of attacking flesh forms.

Soaring Owl was shaken. The sheer number of ungodly creatures pouring from the hive was tremendous, far more than the picket line of spirits could ever hope to restrain. He turned to Sakai.

"Signal we have a break out situation," he said, his voice cracking. "And note for the record that I am preparing Damocles."

Sakai flinched and her eyes flicked in his general direction, but all she said was, "Yes, sir." And then into the communications net: "All units, we are under break out situation. Repeat, break out situation. Initiate Plan Centerpoint. Repeat, initiate Centerpoint. All commands signal acknowledgment."

Kyle was watching Sakai, but then turned back to Soaring Owl as the man pulled his head back from what could only have been a retinal print scanner. Immediately, three monitors that had been showing redundant trideo images changed. One showed black, and the other two gave technical information and displays that Kyle didn't recognize. One of them, though, seemed to be the status for a vehicle of some kind.

All the monitors showed the Knight Errant troopers obviously withdrawing. And taking the wounded with them. The chittering, buzzing, hissing horde of vile things continued to attack.

The van suddenly shook as something hammered against it. More hammering followed, and a couple of monitors began to flicker.

Soaring Owl looked up for a moment, then pulled a long optical cable from the console in front of him and connected it to his datajack. The displays changed, and the black screen brightened, giving the camera view of a drone inside a launch bay of some kind. The unit designator "Damocles" appeared on the monitor as did a fuel display.

"Signal command that we have found the primary hive," Soaring Owl said as indicators on one of the monitors changed. The drone was powering up. "As per instructions I have initiated Damocles and am solely responsible for its detonation."

"Detonation?" Kyle spun to face him.

The man's hands were shaking. "We've found, god help us, the central hive. The main North American hive. Who the frag would have thought they'd have hid it in a city?"

"I don't understand."

"This is it. The most powerful queens are here. All the others are commanded from here. We must destroy it."

Kyle shook his head. "You can't know that. We've got to withdraw. Those bug things are all over the city by now. Eagle's going to need all your—"

"If we can kill the queens, the rest of the hive is lost. Directionless. We have to kill the queens. Now." Daylight was appearing on the drone monitor; the bay doors were opening.

"There's no way you can get down there. Your people are stopped cold. If the queens are on the bottom level, you're not even going to get close before the sheer number and weight of those bugs ground your drone."

"Close, Mr. Teller," Soaring Owl said, "only counts in horseshoes, hand grenades, and thermonuclear weapons."

"Mother of god, you can't be serious."

Soaring Owl finally turned toward him slightly as the drone lifted from its cradle and rose up out of the bay. "We have no choice. It's small, tactical, less than a kiloton, but it will reach them. That's what counts."

Kyle stepped forward. "I can't let you do this."

"It's got to be done."

Kyle took a step toward Soaring Owl, one hand extended, as the Knight Errant technicians in the cabin began drawing their sidearms. Kyle was faster—the spell forming in his mind, the energy shaped, channeled through his body—when the truck suddenly lurched to one side, knocking both him and Soaring Owl down.

Metal screamed as it was peeled away, and the living biomatter lining that had kept the spirits at bay tore away with it. Kyle's spell unraveled and he reached for his weapon focus as the beetle spirit that had torn open the roof of the truck screeched and dove inside, followed by the gleaming bodies of its brethren.

Kyle screamed too and fought for his life as the horde dove at them amid their own wild shrieking. His voice was drowned by their sounds.

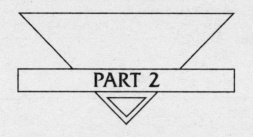

PART 2

Inside the Chicago Containment Area After 22 August 2055

21

There was gunfire, and Kyle awoke suddenly into darkness. Cold, hungry, and filled with pain that shot through him like electricity, beginning somewhere deep in his left leg and ripping through and across his hip, and then up into his back. He tried to cry out, but the only sound that came from his parched throat was a harsh, guttural cough. His hand lay in warm water, and he dragged his body to it, painfully, slowly, finally rolling into its soothing warmth with a final grunt.

There came the sound of more gunfire, nearby, and he tried to open his eyes, but couldn't. Touching them with the one hand he could lift that high, he felt the lids sealed shut by what felt like clotted blood. He worked to clear them with the warm water, and that brought more pain but also faint glimpses of dim light.

Two more shots echoed through the air, and then a scream. It wasn't a scream of pain, but one of final, inevitable death. Kyle could see now, just barely, and discovered he was wedged behind a tipped metal garbage dumpster and lying in a pool of rain water spilling off from a roof edge high overhead. It was night.

His body armor was torn, soggy from the recent rain, and stiff in places where his own blood had clotted. He tried to stand, but couldn't—the pain in his leg stopped him. Even trying to pull himself up using the dumpster was more than he could stand. Kyle let himself slide back into the pool of water and lay there for a moment as a soft irregular drip from high above splashed his skin. He shifted so that it fell on his face.

Kyle was sure his leg was broken in at least two places.

Most of the rest of his body hurt too, but those pains seemed to be from wounds, tears deep through his body armor and into his flesh. He remembered the beetle spirit ripping open the roof of the Knight Errant command truck, and he remembered fighting against it and another spirit that flew with brilliant green iridescent wings, but he couldn't recall anything clearer than that.

He tried to focus his magic on his own body, drawing it through his True Self to begin the healing, but where the magic should have come as a torrent it only sparked, his command of it distorted by pain. He tried again, but this time his coordination of the forces unraveled even quicker. Kyle was too hurt to concentrate, even with the help of his foci. They were all there, he was surprised to discover—the bracelets, the rings, and the amulet around his neck. Only his knife wasn't immediately at hand, but he could sense that his intangible connection to it was still intact. It was still active, somewhere.

It was then he felt another loss that was more an empty space where things had been. Kyle suddenly realized with utter certainty that he had no spirits, no elementals, bound to him. They were all gone, more than likely destroyed, though he couldn't be sure now. Then came the awareness of an even greater absence that almost swallowed him whole. Seeks-the-Moon was gone, lost. Their connection, omnipresent since the moment of the spirit's creation, was obliterated.

Kyle did not know how long he lay there, but it was some time before he felt the rain begin to pick up again, strong and warm. His body was weak, hungry, and on the verge of dehydration, but he needed to get to better shelter. If he was going to find it, though, it wouldn't be with the help of his nearly immobile body.

He relaxed as best he could, and after a moment his astral form slipped free of his pain-wracked physical being. Though he could still feel the pain, it was separate from him, distant enough that he could all but ignore it. Cautiously, he rose above the dumpster, rancid even in astral space, and extended his senses outward.

The streets were dark, dead, and cold, but splashed with

the flickering lights and shadows of a number of fires blazing nearby. From the look of the area, he seemed still to be on Randolph, but across the road from the Knight Errant trucks, or rather what remained of them. Both were wrecked, and one of them still burned, a beacon of white energy in astral space. There was no other life to be seen, so he drifted cautiously toward the vehicles until he could see the dozen or so bodies among the wreckage, mangled and torn by either the attacking insect spirits or the explosion of the truck.

Turning, Kyle flew toward the intersection with Sangamon, where he saw more fires below—the Brotherhood warehouse was burning, along with a number of nearby buildings. Though it was hard to tell from astral space, it looked as though the fires had been going for some time and were nearly spent. He saw no life visible and did not go any closer. Kyle had no desire to see the death there.

Not wishing to leave his defenseless body for too long, Kyle searched the immediate area quickly, but found neither signs of human life nor the source of the gunfire heard earlier. The streets were desolate, scattered with debris and the occasional live fire or the embers of other ones. He wondered how long he'd been unconscious.

Kyle returned to the area near his body and searched the vicinity. The dumpster that hid his flesh was near a storefront that had been blasted partially inward, perhaps by one of the trucks exploding. That suddenly made him remember something, and he shot back across the street to search the twisted remains of the truck for a dimly remembered, half-launched drone, but he couldn't make much sense of the broken metal from astral space.

Returning to his body, Kyle fought back the wave of pain that wracked him as his limbs gave a slight involuntary jerk with the return of his spirit. He searched himself carefully, and found only his ID and credstick, his portable telecom and datacable, and his foci. His pistol was gone from its shoulder holster, as was the spare magazine. He was sure, though, that there were plenty of weapons and ammunition to be had in the carnage across the street.

He tried to sit up again, but immediately collapsed back

into the water. Kyle knew he was too weak for a complex, difficult working like healing magic, but perhaps he could get what he needed with a simpler spell than healing. He constructed the magic carefully, pacing himself to limit the strain on his body. He created a lattice of energy around his leg, holding it rigid. Then he extended elements of that field along his body, and then outward, pushing against the ground and the dumpster.

Slowly, Kyle lifted off the ground and rotated to a nearly upright position. Despite his best efforts, the pain and stress on his body were tremendous as he propelled himself through the already shattered storefront window with more force than he'd intended, desperate to end the spell and the pain.

In the dim light, he picked out what seemed to be a relatively clear portion of the floor and lowered himself carefully onto it. Down, and wincing from the jolt of pain, he used the last remnants of the spell to clear more of the area around him, pushing the piles of hardware and painting supplies away.

He sat back against the wall, satisfied that he was out of sight of any casual passerby or observer. There was no way of knowing who, or what, might look into the store and he was too weak to take any chances.

Next, he pulled the portaphone from his pocket and activated it. Immediately, a terrible, distorted squeal came from the small speaker, and he quickly turned it off. It was obviously broken, perhaps by his fall, or from the water, or . . .

Kyle turned it on again and listened to the squeal once more, carefully. There was nothing wrong with the telecom, he realized. It was being jammed—the squeal was the effect of a very powerful electronic countermeasure signal that was filling the airwaves. He wondered how localized the jamming was.

Kyle sighed and put the phone away, the stress of his exertions and his body's continuing fatigue pushing him toward sleep. He knew he could fight it and stay awake, but there seemed little point. His body needed both rest and healing before he could get away from there. And if any threat should come along, he wasn't currently in any shape to defend himself. And so Kyle slept, barely noticing the increasing throb in his leg and the growing warmth of his own body.

He awoke sometime later, too cold and too warm, sweating and unable to ignore the pain in his leg. But it wasn't that which woke him. Somewhere, off in the distance, something was exploding. He could hear the quick series of detonations, and even felt the muffled rumble of the shockwaves. Kyle didn't know what it was, and didn't care as he slipped back toward what passed for sleep.

When he next awoke, the light was blinding, but Kyle couldn't move or muster even the energy to open his eyes beyond painful slits. Outside, very close, perhaps on the street just beyond the storefront, he could hear the steady beat of helicopter blades. He even thought he could feel a slight rush of warm air.

But it was too bright, he was too cold, and he need to sleep more. Only to sleep.

He slid deeper into the cooling darkness, suspended there, waiting for change . . .

He saw haze. A gunshot sounded, echoing in his head, slowing, drawing itself out into a terrible drone. Incessant, it tore gashes in him, sending waves of pain through his body.

A girl's voice spoke, Natalie's. *"Daddy, can you make it dance again? Can you make it spin more?"*

Kyle fought, won, and opened his eyes, blinking against the perspiration that stung them. She was nearby, sitting in a pool of rusty water and wearing the dark dress they had bought her for her grandmother's funeral. She was trying to spin a delicate glass figurine; it would twirl for a moment and then begin to fall. But she'd catch it before it touched the ground and make it spin again.

She didn't move, but he heard her say, *"Do you see the colors? The colors spin like she does."*

"Natalie," he thought he said, and the glass dancer spun, twirling the light it caught. And she turned too, slower, as the figurine faltered, one leg dipping and cutting the dirty water. Half her face smiled, lit with joy at seeing him. The other half rippled, thousands of dark shapes crawling and surging across it. She started to speak, to laugh or cry, and the bugs fell from her mouth, tumbled down and struck the glass dancer as it tilted too far.

Light exploded from it, forcing his eyes shut and him away into a far deeper place.

"NATALIE!" he heard Beth scream as he felt the brush of wings and air moving past him. He reached out and touched silk, hair, warm skin, a deepening wetness, and then nothing.

Glass shattered, red and black shards fell around him. He felt the wings again, but this time they were dark and musty. Kyle opened his eyes and saw the bird. Ebony and sleek, its power stolen him from, sharp blue eyes in a face wrinkled from age. Its head tilted as it regarded him. He reached for it, but could not see his hand, could not touch it.

The bird flew into the darkness, revealing a light that grew beyond Kyle's understanding, too bright too see, too strong to contain. It enveloped him, consumed him, and he screamed, his voice echoing out into the darkness that returned . . .

He heard voices next, close by, and then the hard press of hands against him. He knew he should cry out, protect himself, but he was so tired and his body so numb. He thought his mouth moved, though he couldn't hear his own voice. And then he did, but it wasn't his own voice, though very close, very familiar, and something sparked deep within him and gave him unlooked for hope against the darkness.

"Don't worry." Seeks-the-Moon said, "you're safe now. I found you."

Kyle slept again, and dreamed of quiet laughter.

22

There was a breeze, and it brought to him the smell of food. Cheese, he thought, and maybe bread. And there was softness beneath him, and he was dry. Kyle opened his eyes slowly and blinked against the thin shafts of light slipping in through the curtains. Someone in the room moved, and he heard a voice: "You're awake?" It was Seeks-the-Moon.

"I think so . . ." Kyle remembered—or had he dreamed it?—of spinning and of a place cold and wet. "Where am I?" He felt sore and tired, but whole.

"An obvious question," the spirit answered slowly, the timbre of his voice deep and strange. "You are in someone's home. I know not whose."

"I take it the owner isn't home?" Kyle turned his head slightly and saw the spirit sunk deep in a large, old chair, the light from the window cutting a bright slit from his eye to his knee. He seemed older. But also seemed to fit somehow with the shabby, sparse furnishings of the room and the fine cracks that ran down its walls. An open door revealed a narrow hallway and a faded, threadbare rug.

The longer Kyle studied Seeks-the-Moon, the more he could see that the spirit was different. His face seemed older, harder, but the eyes were brighter, more blue than he remembered. And his clothes were different, subtly; darker and more beat-up, but at the same time the colors truer.

"The owner is dead," the spirit said. "I believe it was she I found down the hall."

"The bug spirits?"

"No, her own kind." Moon's face betrayed no emotion. "She did not die well."

Kyle tried to sit up slightly, but he was too weak. The pain in his leg was only a dull throb, but the rest of his body felt like it was made of wet clay. Two dogs barked at each other somewhere outside.

"You have been very sick," Seeks-the-Moon told him. "I attempted to heal you as best as I could, but I'm afraid what you taught me wasn't enough to restore you to full health."

"How long have I been out?"

"It's been two days since I found you. You were on the street for at least four days."

"A week?" Kyle said. "It's been a week?"

"Six days." There was an odd stillness in Seeks-the-Moon, a tension Kyle could not place.

Kyle tried to sit up again, and this time the pain in his leg made itself known, shooting through him and collapsing him back onto the creaking bed. "Beth," he said, "do you know what . . ."

"No, I don't," the spirit said quietly.

Kyle propped himself painfully up on one elbow. Even that simple exertion left him weak and nearly faint. "I have to find out if she and Natalie are all right."

The spirit didn't move, but a slight touch of sadness slipped into his expression. "You are far from where they might be, and too weak to travel. You wouldn't survive the journey."

Angry, Kyle tried to shout at the spirit in his mind, but the cry went nowhere. There was no connection between them. No channel, no empathy, nothing. Kyle stared at Seeks-the-Moon, and remembered the emptiness he'd felt behind the dumpster. And the emptiness he felt now . . .

"You're free . . ." he said, slowly.

Seeks-the-Moon glanced away, and then nodded. "Your injuries were great. I believe you came as close to death as someone could without dying. You lived," he said, "but I became free."

"I see," said Kyle, and the spirit tilted his head slightly, moving his eye out of the shaft of light. It still gleamed back at Kyle, reflecting the light that reached it.

"What will you do?" Seeks-the-Moon asked him after a moment.

"What will I do? I don't understand."

"Will you attempt to regain control of me?"

Kyle stared as the spirit went on speaking. "You created me. You have the right."

"I don't think I could."

"That doesn't matter. What matters is whether you want to."

Kyle lay back down on the bed and brought his arm up across his eyes. What did he want? What could he do? What had happened? "I don't know,' he said. "I need time to think." He needed real sleep.

"And the longer you think, the more you will heal, and the stronger you will be," said Seeks-the-Moon.

"Yes," said Kyle. And I'll have gained the strength to contest you, Kyle thought. And you know that.

But there was silence, and the spirit allowed him to sleep.

The next time he awoke, suddenly, his mind rushing blindly between the last pieces of a dream and reality, there was a woman sitting in the chair Seeks-the-Moon had been occupying. She seemed familiar, and in the confusion and the dim reddened light that slipped in from outside, she was Beth. He moved toward her, and she faded away, slipping into the shadows of the chair as he woke fully.

Kyle shook his head and ran his fingers through the days of beard growth on his face and through the dirty, greasy tangle that was his hair. He felt rested, but there was still a dull ache through his body, but only that. He turned his senses inward and examined himself. He was immediately surprised. The deep wounds he had felt while lying on the street were gone, healed, no longer anything more than sharp echoes in his flesh. Even his leg was healed, the bone joined and solid again. He could tell, though, that it would still be painful for a few more days at the very least.

He felt strong, or at least stronger, and very hungry. From outside came the sound of gunshots, three of them in quick succession, coming from perhaps a block or two away. Mov-

ing as carefully and quietly as he could, Kyle swung his legs
off the bed and stood.

Again, he was surprised at the strength in his limbs. Looking down at his body, he noticed for the first time that he
was wearing somebody else's clothes, but he felt each of his
magical foci present, except for the knife. Despite his apparent strength and health, he moved carefully to the window
and parted the dulled and dirty blinds. It was sunset, nearly
twilight, and the street was empty but for the blackened and
charred wreck of a Honda minicar turned on its side against
the far curb. That, and dozens of bright red sheets of paper
that caught the wind and swirled.

If this side of the street matched the one opposite, Kyle
thought he must be in a room on the second floor over a
small storefront. The ones he could see across the way
showed signs of major looting and destruction, their windows smashed and doors flung open.

"You don't want to stand there too long," came the voice
of Seeks-the-Moon behind him.

Kyle let the blinds close and turned toward the spirit.

Moon was standing next to the chair. "How do you feel?"

"Better than I should, I suspect," Kyle said. "Like I've
been through a car crash, but I walked away."

He nodded. "It's been a few days."

"How long since I last woke up?"

Seeks-the-Moon frowned slightly and looked away, thinking. "Two days."

Kyle sat down on the edge of the bed. He glanced toward
the window and then back at the spirit. "What the frag is going on?" he asked quietly.

"You found the main nest, certainly for the region, maybe
even for the whole continent," he said. "When you attacked
they . . ." The spirit looked away for a moment.

Kyle leaned closer. "What?"

"They spread," said Seeks-the-Moon, still looking away.

"What do you mean?"

Seeks-the-Moon shrugged. "They're insects. Their nest
was disturbed. They sought shelter elsewhere."

"Oh Jesus . . ."

The spirit nodded. "They're all over the city, and many people are dead or else wish they were."

"Aren't the police or corps able to control them?" Kyle asked him.

"There are thousands."

"What about the government?"

"They have done something," said Seeks-the-Moon. "They have sealed off the city."

"*What?* That doesn't make sense," said Kyle.

Seeks-the-Moon pointed at a folded, water-stained sheet of bright red paper sitting on the bedstand. "They dropped those all over the city."

Kyle took the sheet and carefully unfolded it, suddenly afraid. It said:

People of Chicago!
By order of the federal government This city has
been quarantined until further notice. Remain in
your homes. Stay off the streets unless absolutely
necessary. Watch for food and supply drops in your
area.
Please do not try to leave the area. The government is taking every measure to control the creatures that threaten you. Until your safety can be
guaranteed please remain in your homes and follow
all instructions.

Kyle shook his head. It made no sense. Why weren't government troops patrolling the streets? "Why haven't they declared martial law and moved in?" he asked. "Why did they
seal it off?"

"How were they to fight?" Seeks-the-Moon asked. "These
things are not of this world. Spirits have nothing to fear
from bullets or hand grenades. The soldiers could not defeat
what they were not strong enough to even fight."

"The Eagle Security troopers I was with fought them,"
Kyle said angrily. "The Knight Errant troops were fighting

them."

"There were many more of the police than there were of the spirits," Seeks-the-Moon said. "And the Knight Errant soldiers are dead."

Kyle started and stared at him.

The spirit nodded. "You, and maybe some others, though I didn't see them, survived."

"How many have gotten out?" Kyle asked.

"None—the soldiers are dead."

"No, I mean how many people have gotten out through the lines?"

"Few."

"Few?"

"The government isn't letting anyone out. They're afraid of contamination."

Kyle started to reply, but then shut his mouth quickly as the truth sank in. "They can't tell who's been possessed by the bugs," he said slowly. "They have no way of knowing who's clean and who's not ..."

"A magician could tell," said Seeks-the-Moon. "As we did. But how many do they have? How good are they? Can they trust the results? What if they're wrong?"

"This is insane ..."

The spirit shrugged. "They're afraid."

Kyle turned his eyes toward the window and the city outside. "We have to be sure they know what's happened." He looked at Seeks-the-Moon. "You could fly through astral space to the lines and talk to them."

"No, I cannot do that."

Kyle stared at him.

"I am at risk, even now," Moon said. "And in some ways I am a risk to you as well. The insects can smell me. If I were to attempt to fly through astral space, they would sense me and be on me in an instant." The spirit paused, and then said, "I have tried."

Kyle was astounded. "There are that many?"

Seeks-the-Moon nodded. "There are stories of the insect spirits grabbing people and taking them away. Nobody knows where, but they're not killing them. At least not right away."

"So they have a new nest."

Seeks-the-Moon nodded. "And soon, within days perhaps, there will be many, many more of them."

23

The spirit would say little more, his expression growing troubled when he spoke about it at all. Seeks-the-Moon and Hanna Uljakën had still been playing Go when Kyle had taken his nearly mortal injuries. From that moment, and for what Moon believed were hours afterward, the spirit knew only the terrible pains of freedom and rebirth. He could not, or would not, describe what he passed through. The most he would say was "You wouldn't understand."

Moon said he remembered little from that time except the pain and a few images. He recalled looking to the north of Truman Tower as a black cloud rose skyward from out of the earth and spread across the city. He also remembered hearing, or feeling, the presence of aircraft on or near the Tower. And then there were the bug spirits.

They attacked the building a short time after the departure of the aircraft, taking with it most of the life in the building. He knew there were still people there—he could hear the voices—and perhaps they'd even been speaking to him. But by then he hadn't yet found the strength to respond.

When the insect spirits attacked, Seeks-the-Moon fled. And as he spoke of this, Kyle could almost sense the emotions the spirit was trying to control. When the bug creatures came, Seeks-the-Moon had abandoned the people still in the building because he was helpless, his form and power reduced to little more than pain and turmoil.

He hid himself away somewhere, he didn't know where, and when he regained control of himself, realized truly what had become of him, Seeks-the-Moon returned briefly to the building. It was deserted, but he'd found a message to him and Kyle in the main room of the Truman condoplex. It was from Hanna Uljakën and said that the Truman family had fled in a Knight Errant tilt-wing aircraft. Daniel Truman, his wife, and their daughter Madelaine had flown to apparent safety, but Melissa was missing again. She was gone from the condo, out with Knight Errant guards who couldn't be raised on the radio when the word had come through that the Trumans and key staff were being evacuated.

Hanna had stayed behind by choice, coordinating the Truman organization's feeble attempts to find Melissa. But even before that could be begun, the Truman Tower itself was invaded. The message ended with word that Hanna and the others were leaving via the building's state-of-the-art fire evacuation system to get clear. That was the only sign of her Seeks-the-Moon could find, and that was when the spirit had set out to find Kyle.

All of which had happened a week ago.

"I have to try," Kyle told him. Seeks-the-Moon merely stared back. "I have some influence," he said. "I might be able to find out what's really going on."

"They'll shoot you."

"No, they won't. They're not shooting anybody."

"People on the street have said that the government is shooting people who are trying to get out."

"I don't believe that; people are scared and when that happens all sorts of stories start," Kyle said. "Besides, I need to go north."

"Your wife."

"My ex-wife," Kyle said, "and my daughter."

"Where will you look?" said Seeks-the-Moon. "At her office? At the apartment? Your daughter's school? The odds of them still being at any of those places is very small."

Kyle nodded slowly. "I know, but if Beth had any way of leaving me a message, she would have."

He stood up. "I have to try. And I'd like your help. I have no reason to expect it," he said, "and I certainly won't demand it."

The spirit frowned, but a moment later he nodded. "I will help you," he said. "Because you asked."

Kyle nodded back. "Thank you."

They gathered what supplies they had, the food the spirit had raided or gathered, and the weapons taken from the ruins of the Knight Errant assault. Kyle could see that a lot of weapons and armor had apparently been looted from the site, but he hoped that having state-of-the-art weapons evened the odds somewhat between the local populace and the marauding bug spirits.

When they were ready, Kyle thought he must look like a refugee from some second-rate post-nuclear holocaust sim-show. He was careful, though, to remove any obvious Knight Errant markings from the gear, especially the body armor. There was no telling what the city's politics had de-generated into. Seeks-the-Moon looked the same, except for the heavy backpack slung over one shoulder. It was all he could really carry since he might need to slip quickly into astral space. He could take nothing "real" with him, and needed to be able to drop any belongings quickly.

They'd discussed the possibility of Kyle summoning up more elementals or watchers, but had rejected the idea. The time and effort needed to create a conjuring circle to sum-mon the elementals was impractical, and Seeks-the-Moon counseled against any summonings at all until they knew more about the hordes of insect spirits. He was concerned, and Kyle reluctantly agreed, that any summoning might be tantamount to turning on a porch light of a hot summer eve-ning. The last thing they wanted was to attract the attention of the bugs.

Despite the heat, Kyle wore a heavy long coat liberated from a thrift shop over his combat gear. While the visible presence of military-grade firearms and armor might per-suade some that the price for messing with him and Moon was too high, others probably wouldn't be able to resist the temptation of grabbing up some choice hardware.

With his newfound freedom, Seeks-the-Moon had gained the ability to mask his aura, hiding his spirit-nature and con-

tinual presence in astral space from all but the most percep-
tive astral observer. Kyle's foci were another story. He could
mask some of them, subsuming their auras into his own, but
he couldn't conceal them all. So instead of being in a constant state of worry about attack from astral space, he decided to travel with the foci temporarily deactivated.

Throughout their preparations Kyle wondered about the
continued presence of Seeks-the-Moon. The spirit was free,
liberated, and beyond Kyle's direct control. He had no reason to remain—could, no doubt, easily escape the besieged
city. And yet, Seeks-the-Moon wanted to stay. Kyle wanted
to know why, but his growing pangs of guilt over having
kept the spirit in virtual thrall for years instead of freeing
him, stopped his tongue. Seeks-the-Moon seemed to sense
Kyle's distress, but he did or said nothing to ease it.

The apartment where Seeks-the-Moon had taken Kyle was
a few blocks north of the Randolph and Sangamon intersection. Before setting out across the city they climbed to the
roof of a tall nearby building that had once held offices.
Abandoned and looted, the building probably housed some
squatters, but those residents concealed themselves well and
had nothing to gain from antagonizing the pair. Once, during
their climb up to the roof, Seeks-the-Moon lamented the irony
of the fact that he was now free and newly empowered but
virtually impotent for fear of attracting insect spirits.

On the roof, Kyle used the pair of high-power binoculars
they'd scavenged from the Knight Errant site. It was morning.

Looking south, they could see the tall, thin spires of the
downtown Core. At least three of the buildings were on fire,
and uncontrolled. From their position he could also see the
gleaming upper half of the Truman Tower. There were no
signs of insect spirits, or any other life, but most of the
building's windows were broken or cracked. A small trail of
smoke drifted up from the roof. A rogue fire, he wondered,
or someone's plea for help?

Beyond the building, Kyle suddenly saw movement.
Three black and armed attack helicopters arced quickly
around the structure. They cut across the Core, dodging

buildings as they moved from east to west, their UCAS Army markings easily visible in the morning light. Then they fired, unleashing a powerful barrage of rockets against the upper stories of a copper-colored office building at the southern edge of the Core. Seeks-the-Moon made a noise deep in his throat: even without the binoculars he could see the flash of weapons and the huge fireballs that erupted from the building.

The helicopters continued their lightning volley as dozens of dark shapes bolted from the growing inferno. Most fell quickly, either unable or too injured to fly, but some, a half-dozen forms of what seemed to be wasps, shot toward the helicopters. Three of them suddenly broke off their attack, bouncing in different directions in a glittering blur of wings and sparks of astral energy. Kyle was still unwilling to use his astral senses and expose himself to attack, but he was sure those three had run into other spirits, elementals or watchers, guarding the helicopters. The three remaining insect spirits continued their mad rush at the choppers.

The helicopters jinked, turning away from the bugs and accelerating. The lead helicopter dipped, and caught the first insect spirit in its rotor blades, hurling it away but damaging the blades. The second helicopter avoided its attacker and tired to evade, but Kyle knew the wasp spirits would be much, much faster than the machines. The third wasp caught its prey, and began to attack the cockpit.

Kyle wondered, but only for a moment, if the cockpit would hold. Then he saw the armored glass shatter and peel away. The helicopter immediately yawed to the right and began to lose altitude. It would hit the ground in a matter of seconds.

He looked for the second copter, and saw it maneuvering vainly to avoid its attacker. Regardless of how good the pilot, it would not be able to hold out much longer. Kyle took a deep breath and called on his power. Raw astral energy focused through him and the formula he assembled in his mind. He reached out with his astral senses and synchronized the energy of the spell with the insect's, then released it. The energy flashed between them in astral space, a blue-gray spark of power that exploded against the thing like a bolt of lightning. It spun to one side, its wings torn, and began to fall, still writhing in blue energy as it dissipated. The helicopter dropped below the tops of the buildings and fled west, using the streets as cover. Kyle quickly scanned for the first helicopter, but did not see it. A ribbon of smoke rose into the air to tell him where the third had fallen.

Within a minute of their sighting, they were gone. A handful of dark shapes lurked in the area of the office building, whose upper stories were ablaze. Soon the ominous shapes descended toward the streets.

"It would seem your government is actually doing something," said Seeks-the-Moon.

Kyle nodded. "Keep a lookout. Someone or some of the bug spirits may have seen my spell."

"I have been," said Seeks-the-Moon.

"Did that first helicopter get away?" Kyle asked. "I couldn't tell."

"I couldn't either."

Kyle looked back toward the Core. Light gunfire echoed up from the streets near them, but he still saw nothing. Kyle then looked east toward the lake. The sky was virtually cloudless, reflecting cleanly off what he could see of the still waters of the lake.

There were boats out there, arrayed in a north-south line about three kilometers from the shore. He could make out the shapes of what seemed like Coast Guard cutters, and what may have been a regular Navy vessel or two. The rest seemed to be merchant vessels, probably impressed into service. There were a few smaller white pleasure boats out there as well, but those seemed to be keeping clear of the blockade. An orange and white helicopter hovered in the air near one. After a moment, the two parted and the sailboats headed back toward shore.

Kyle turned his attention inland. There was little change visible in the already half-abandoned Noose, and he wondered if the vagrants and squatters living there might not survive this best of all. There was little else to see, with the exception of some smoke northeast and near to the lake.

Looking west of the city, he could see more smoke, a half-dozen thin plumes, and signs of a land blockade around the city. Off some distance, helicopters and what seemed to be at least one light combat vehicle, maybe a scout LAV, patrolled the line of demarcation, which street rumor said was either as far west as Interstate 294, or as close as Harlem Avenue. The binoculars' rangefinder placed them at about fourteen kilometers, which made Harlem far more likely than the interstate some twenty plus kilometers away.

Beyond the helicopters Kyle could see a glint of light from something big and elongated that hung in the air. A lighter-than-air craft, he thought, probably housing high-resolution radar for monitoring the sky over the city. He wondered if it was powerful enough to pick up the insect spirits when they moved about in physical form. He also wondered about the vulnerability of the craft, hanging there in plain sight. He knew that he could easily have struck it with a powerful spell, and assumed that others in the city could do the same. He also knew the military would have thought of that too.

Then, finally, he looked north. Again, there was smoke, a particularly dense cloud billowing upward along the lake. He could barely make out the demarcation line, and wondered how far north it was. They'd been told Belmont Avenue, and he hoped that was true, as it would place Beth's apartment and Natalie's school out of the containment area. But the helicopters seemed farther away than that; the rangefinder on the binoculars was estimating fourteen kilometers, which seemed too far.

Without a map there was no way to tell, so Kyle and Seeks-the-Moon began walking northward.

24

To make the best time, and to avoid getting ambushed by someone who might want to relieve them of their weaponry, Kyle and Seeks-the-Moon headed north along Interstate 90/94. It meant they were more exposed, more vulnerable, than if traveling one of the main streets, but it also put them less at risk. Kyle hoped that with the advantage of Seeks-the-Moon's always active astral senses, they would have advance warning of anything coming.

As they headed down to the highway via the Lake Street exit ramp, a battered delivery truck sped past them, the older ork male in the passenger seat keeping his eye, and the barrel of his shotgun, trained on them. The truck didn't slow, but continued north, weaving once to avoid the burned wreck of a bus in the passing lane.

They saw only one other car, a Toyota Elite speeding south on the other side of the highway. When its driver saw them, he slowed down and screamed out "What are you fraggin' nuts!" before zooming away again.

The city was quiet around them as the roadbed rose slowly from below street level near the old Loop, to above street level a distance beyond Hubbard's Cave. At that point, Kyle and Moon could see more smoke and some obvious fires that still raged uncontrolled. They ducked once into cover as a swarm of insect spirits, dragonflies, appeared over the rooftops, and then quickly banked away down toward the streets. It was like the sudden passage of a heavy dark cloud that blocked the sun and deafened the ears with the whirring of giant wings. Kyle thought again about casting a spell that would make the two of them invisible, then decided against it since they didn't yet know how the creatures perceived. It might not do any good.

Once, a possibly stray bullet kicked up dirt near them, but they could see no sign of a gunman. They kept walking, but Kyle readied the formula for a spell that he could cast quickly that ought to—he hoped—slow a bullet down, if not stop it completely.

The two walked mostly in silence, each one lost in his own thoughts. Approaching the Ashland exit they passed the remains of a minivan that had apparently struck the guard rail and turned on its side before bursting into flames. There were six people inside. Four of them children. They'd obviously been dead for some days.

At Ashland, Kyle and Seeks-the-Moon left the highway and took that street north, gradually starting to see more signs of life. They passed people clustered in doorways, who eyed them with concern or fear. They passed a bar that seemed open, music with a heavy synthetic beat leaking through the boarded windows. They also began to see more cars, but there were still very few of them. Then they came upon a large parking lot filled with scores of torn-open wood and fiberglass cases—food and supplies apparently dropped there by the government within the last few days. There were four bodies lying on the ground as well, lined up in a row alongside an Eagle Security patrol car. A young black officer sat atop the car, shotgun in hand.

Kyle waved to him, and considered approaching, but then thought better of it when he spotted two other bodies a short distance away. One was an older woman, the other a young troll boy. Both had been killed by shotgun blasts. Kyle also saw boxes of food stuffed into the back of the patrol car. The patrolman eyed them warily and they continued walking.

Near Oakdale, a huge, blackened beetle with hints of red on its carapace sat watching them from a storefront. Mucus and bits of flesh dripped from its mandibles as its odd head pivoted slowly to follow them. Kyle nodded to Seeks-the-Moon, and they both dropped their masking just for a moment. The beetle reacted as they'd hoped, moving further back into the shattered interior.

A few blocks later, just north of Belmont, Moon noticed a car following them some distance behind. Kyle glanced back and saw it too: a large tan car with old tires roped to it was pacing them five blocks behind. He and Moon moved out of the streets and began to hug closer to the storefronts.

A block later, the car accelerated, drawing closer. When it was only a short distance away, a young man in dark leathers leaned out the shattered window, waving a heavy revolver at them.

"This is Rager turf!" he howled. One of his eyes was covered over by dark-stained gauze. "Rager turf!"

"We're just passing through," Kyle called back. "On our way to somewhere else."

The car stopped, and all the doors opened. Seven men in torn denim and leathers piled out, each carrying a rifle or submachine gun. Four of them also carried bats. Kyle looked at Seeks-the-Moon, who was watching them impassively.

"I don't think you heard me," the first ganger said as he walked up. "This is our turf, Rager land. Nobody just *passes through.*"

"Look," Kyle told him, moving his arm slightly so the high-velocity Ares combat gun was clearly visible. "We're not looking for trouble. We're just gonna keep walking and then we're gone. No hassle. No trouble."

The first ganger smiled, and a couple of the others laughed. Kyle was amazed at their bravado. He also knew that up close neither he nor Moon would seem threatening. Kyle was trying to appear calm and capable, as well as armed and armored. Seeks-the-Moon seemed the more calm, and almost slightly amused.

"Tribute, chummer," said one of the others. "Taxes, you know. You live here, you pass through here, you pay us. You don't have nothing to pay, we take you instead. We can always find some use." A couple of them sniggered.

Kyle sighed, and started to reply, but Seeks-the-Moon cut him off. "You have a lot of confidence in your magician," he said loudly.

The group stopped laughing and looked at him. Two of them glanced nervously across the street.

"He's a whelp," the spirit continued. "Barely able to count. Already he sweats, trying to decide how to kill us quickly without taking you to boot."

Kyle looked off in the same direction as the gangers, but saw nothing. Seeks-the-Moon glanced at him. "Their magician is nothing more than a bug," he told Kyle. "We should treat him as such."

Kyle nodded. "All right." And he dropped his masking again, believing Seeks-the-Moon was doing the same.

Immediately, there was commotion from an abandoned lot that looked like it had been used for parking. A lone figure, a girl wearing the same colors as the gangers, darted from behind a pile of garbage and dashed away beyond some buildings.

The gangers were distracted by this, and Kyle quickly added to their confusion. A globe of gray-green energy sprung up around him and Seeks-the-Moon as he released the energy for the barrier spell he'd prepared earlier. Then, he raised his own weapon.

All seven gangers took an involuntary step back. Kyle smiled. "Now," he said "I think it's time you took off."

The first ganger was angry. "Nobody tells us what to—" A protoplasmic mass of dark purple suddenly covered his head, and he staggered backward and fell to his knees. Kyle shifted his eyes toward Seeks-the-Moon just in time to see the last vestiges of the spell's energy dissipate from the spirit's hands. He knew it was Moon—the spell was one he'd designed himself.

The ganger began to gag. "Get him out of here or he will die," Seeks-the-Moon said. Another of the gang members raised his rifle and pointed it at the spirit, but Kyle turned his weapon toward him.

"Please do as he says," Kyle said. "I don't know how to use this rifle well enough to only wound you."

The ganger blinked, and turned toward the one on the ground, and then began to back toward the car. The others took this as the sign they'd been waiting for, and began dragging their gagging and hacking leader back and into the car. They all piled in quickly, and the car jerked forward even before all of them were fully inside. The last ganger fired a couple of random shots toward them, but they went wide and impacted in the storefront behind them. Kyle waited until they were at least a block away and then gathered the power for a small, showy spell he'd known since school. It was harder to cast while maintaining the barrier spell, but it was well within his ability. A split second later, a flash of blue and silver fireworks erupted at the rear of the car. It was only light and sound, and did no damage, but the car jerked as it accelerated again, then quickly turned down a side street heading west.

Kyle dropped the barrier spell, and turned to look in the direction the beetle spirit had been. There was no way the creature could have missed the display of magic, and that, plus the clustering of people, might have been enough to send it for others. He and Moon turned down the nearest street and made their way quickly past the row of houses along it. In a few places they saw signs of movement from behind partially shuttered or boarded windows, but for the most part there was only silence. One block farther east they turned north again, watching for signs of pursuit and seeing none. Then, Kyle realized, they were only a few blocks from Beth's house.

He stood outside for a moment and stared at the building. It looked the same, little changed from when he'd fallen asleep on the small porch. Beth's car was several doors down, one of its windows smashed and some of the dashboard electronics taken. One of the tires had been punctured too. A house three doors away looked like it had caught fire and either burned itself out, or been put out. The buildings next to it were only slightly damaged.

Kyle climbed the short steps to the porch, Seeks-the-Moon directly behind him. He looked in the front windows, and saw the living room as he'd left it more than a week ago. There were no signs of anyone inside.

He went to the door and keyed in the access code. The locked clicked and the indicator turned green. It was open.

Slinging his rifle to leave both hands free for magic, he then pushed the door open and stepped inside. The air was stale and musty except for a sweet smell of something rotting. He immediately recognized the odor—garbage not emptied for a few days.

He glanced up the stairs, and then walked slowly toward the kitchen, glancing into the living room and dining area as he did. There was no movement. Only silence.

In the kitchen, he found evidence of activity. The cabinets had been looted, and it was obvious that most of the canned and nonperishable foods were gone. He immediately turned and rushed past Seeks-the-Moon, then bounded up the stairs.

In Beth's room, he found the dresser drawers hanging open, with various items of clothing half hanging out of them. He searched through the piles on the floor and what was still in the drawers. Satisfied, he dashed back downstairs again and into Natalie's room. Her clothes were similarly strewn about, and Kyle searched through them too. When he'd confirmed his suspicion, he stood up to find Seek-the-Moon staring at him from the doorway.

"They're not here," Kyle said, slightly out of breath. "But they were."

Seeks-the-Moon nodded. "I saw the kitchen."

Kyle shook his head. "That could have been anyone. But some of their clothes are gone too. None of Natalie's underwear is here, and only some of Beth's is upstairs. They obviously packed before leaving."

"Ah," said Seeks-the-Moon, shaking his head as he walked toward the living room.

"What?" Kyle asked loudly, but got no reply.

Looking down at the mess of clothes and toys, he felt a wave of relief at the signs that Beth and Natalie had been here and gone elsewhere. Beyond the lines to safety, he hoped, though he'd seen nothing to tell him that.

"Kyle," Seeks-the-Moon called out from the front of the house. "There's a message here for you."

Kyle rushed out into the hall and into the living room.

Seeks-the-Moon was pointing at an easel that had been propped up against the far wall. It bore a large pad of plain white paper on which a message had been written in green crayon. It read:

Kyle—
We're fine! We're going with Ellen and some of her friends to find a safe place to stay. I'll come back and leave a message when we know where we'll be. We're safe!

Beth

It was dated five days ago.

Kyle, suddenly unable to stand, collapsed onto the couch. He'd never warned Beth about her sister, and now she and Natalie had gone for safety with people who were quite possibly the very creatures that had the city living in fear.

He read the message again, and then a third time, before he buried his face in his hands and wept.

25

The stores and homes along Irving Park Road, from Lake Michigan out to the Des Plaines River, had been dynamited or bulldozed to mark the northern edge of the Chicago Containment Zone. Beyond the piles of debris, backed by powerful searchlights on makeshift towers, sat elements of Eagle Security, the Illinois National Guard, and the United Canadian and American States Army.

The lights cut bright slices through the night air and played across the wide open area that had been a main street, picking out the desperate and foolhardy as they tried to sneak or dash across the exposed area. As he watched the roving searchlights, Kyle wondered if the fugitives truly believed they'd find sanctuary or reprieve when they reached the barricades. From what he could see, they found neither. Anyone who made it across was forcibly subdued by men in heavy combat armor and unceremoniously escorted back the way he'd come. Sometimes, depending on exactly who made it across, the troopers would open up with tear gas or stun rounds until the transgressor retreated. Sometimes, as testified by the occasional limp body on or near the barricade, the offender was simply shot. Kyle noted that almost invariably, of the half-dozen or so he'd seen while walking the line from Ashland to Sheridan, the dead were orks or trolls. The troopers were afraid these people might actually be able to get past the wall of debris.

There were thousands, maybe tens of thousands, gathered along the line. They were packed and stacked deep into the side streets that intersected the demarcation line. People were camped where they could, others overrunning and occupying houses. Most simply slept in any empty spot, atop what worldly possessions they dared carry with them. People shouted, argued, and cried as the spotlights panned over them and the helicopters roared overhead. Through powerful speakers, the soldiers ordered the people to pull back. The government wanted them to go home, but they couldn't— they had nowhere to go. Their homes were infested.

Draped in a bright yellow rain poncho he'd pulled from Beth's closet, Kyle walked the line, searching carefully through the side streets, looking for Beth and Natalie. He showed pictures of them to anyone who would stop and listen. Most just stared back at him glassy-eyed. Some cursed him in the name of one of their own lost loved ones. A few smiled sympathetically and looked at the pictures. But no one had seen the child or her mother. Seeks-the-Moon was busy doing the same.

It had been raining since sundown, and one man fought another for the right to have his child sleep under the eaves of a building. Finally someone yelled out that the men should just let the children sleep together. They agreed, for now—the rain was only light.

There were gunshots two blocks or so over; small-caliber, not the army. Moving among the refugees and showing his pictures, Kyle wondered briefly what might have caused it.

A rumor spread like lightning—the government was dropping food over the line down near the lake. There was a rush. People gathering up what they could and then taking off east toward the lakeshore. Maybe there'd be food there, maybe it was rumor. They couldn't take the chance.

Kyle let the tide of people flow around him. If Beth and Natalie were there he'd never find them now. His best hope was that the group she'd hooked up with had staked a claim to some space nearby, though with the line so close to her actual apartment it would have made more sense for Natalie to stay home. Kyle and Seeks-the-Moon had found enough food in the house, even with what had been stolen, to last about a week if rationed. Beth and Natalie could have hidden there until he came for them. But they hadn't. Instead they'd gone looking for safety somewhere else.

Just then there was a commotion behind him. A little group of men and women were gathered in the debris that was all that remained of a store on the south side of the street, opposite the barricades. They were tense, agitated, and kept glancing toward the line of troops. Kyle looked too, and saw the troopers' attention on the flow of people eastward. They were distracted, and in that moment the small group of men and women rushed the barricade.

Kyle almost screamed out in warning and had to choke back the power that rose inside him, but the concussion grenades were already detonating. A water hose started up on one of the towers and it tore into the group just as they reached the barricade. Several were stopped cold or went limping away after the grenade blasts. The rest stormed the barricade.

They were not unprepared. A pair of smoke grenades lighted, filling the area quickly with green haze. There were gunshots from this side of the barricade as well; snipers from the southside debris. They were light, but accurate— Kyle saw one group of guards pinned down by the shots. A portion of the barricade began to move as the people tore at it, ignoring the growing fusillade of stun rounds being fired blindly into the smoke.

Then, the helicopter was overhead. A jet black Hughes Stallion with its huge rotor downwash and powerful searchlight. The smoke dissipated as fast as it came, and suddenly the people began to fall, clutching at their knees and thighs. Somewhere on the line a government sniper was systematically disabling them. Within moments, under obvious fire from the watchtowers and the sniper, they began to haltingly withdraw, dragging most of their fallen behind them. Kyle saw blood on the street. Not all the rounds were gel.

He watched the little group gather together again, cursing and moaning. Two went off trying to round up others for another try. They were confident the barricade could be breached. But then what? Kyle wondered. Did they think that past the line there was nothing? No army camp, no armored personnel carriers, no light tanks? Only freedom?

Suddenly, there were screams from behind him, a block,

maybe two away. He spun, and saw bugs. A swarm of them,
roaches and ants, had erupted from a sewer and flashed into
existence among the crowd pushing toward the rumored
food. Kyle pushed to get closer, but the surge of the crowd
was against him. He wanted a clear view of the insect spirits, but there were people in front of him, hands in his face,
screams in his ears.

A woman with a young boy still clinging to her was
dragged forcibly into the sewer. Five or six wasps appeared.
Buzzing angrily, they dived into the crowd, swooping to
pick people up with their front legs, then lifting them skyward in a shower of blood and out of sight over the houses
to the south. The army opened fire. Bugs were hit; the spirits
didn't care. People were hit; they began to die.

Two elementals appeared, and were immediately consumed by a swarm of insect spirits. The bugs climbed across
the people on their sharp, jointed legs, reaching down into
their midst to pull some free and then skitter off with them.
There were more gunfire and explosions.

Kyle saw an opening, prepared a spell, and was knocked
to the ground. The fleeing tide rushed over him, stepping,
smashing. Desperate, he cast a quick spell and a gray-green
bubble appeared around him, pushing the people aside. The
ones nearby, those still thinking clearly enough to grasp
what was happening, screamed and rushed away. Some pan-
icked and ran straight toward the bug spirits.

Kyle stood and let the spell fall. There were fewer insects,
fewer people. One wasp, caught in the air by a hail of gunfire that would have reduced a tank to scrap, was slowly
whittled away until it could absorb no more and fled into astral space.

The crowd fell back from the line as two helicopters arrived overhead, blanketing the area in wind and light. But
there was nothing for them to do. The marauding spirits
were gone, and with them maybe a score of people, probably
more. Off in the side streets, between the homes and inside
them, the wailing began.

Kyle watched as he leaned back against a tree half uprooted by the press of a bulldozer. How could this be happening? How could this be—

Vathoss.

Sergeant Keith Vathoss, cyber-soldier for Knight Errant Security, was standing a half-dozen meters away. Next to him was another man, similarly garbed in a bulky long coat. Both had military buzz-cuts, and both seemed tense as they eyed the demarcation line with the gaze of skilled professionals gauging another journeyman's work. Satisfied, they stood in the shadows and talked quietly. Kyle slipped around the tree to watch them, fairly certain they hadn't seen him.

After a moment, and some more discussion, they headed west, past him, parallel to Irving Park Road. Kyle thought about simply calling out to them, but didn't. There was something about their manner, the way their gazes searched the crowd ahead for threats, that put him off. He realized he didn't trust them. Only if they were with Anne Ravenheart would he make contact.

Kyle followed them carefully as they continued on. Keeping to the shadows, he deactivated the rest of his power foci. There were two spells he wanted to cast on himself, but he'd need all of his masking ability to conceal those auras. No way could he could handle the spell auras and the auras of power coming off the foci at the same time. He thought about trying to contact Seeks-the-Moon, but didn't know where the spirit had ended up after the insect attack. They'd arranged to meet later at Beth's house, but Kyle had no other way of contacting him.

He paused, and quickly cast the spell, running through the four levels of formula in his head. His view of the world shifted slightly, becoming fuzzier and slightly bluer, almost like pure moonlight. He was invisible to anyone who stepped within the area of the spell, but the spell didn't bend light around him and so wouldn't work against the heat-sensors Vathoss probably had in his eyes. What the spell did was insist to any onlookers in range that Kyle simply was not there. And, if he was lucky, they'd believe it.

Then, before the two Knight Errant troopers could get too far ahead, he cast the second spell, which blanketed him in near silence. The outside world sounded to him like he was underwater, but Kyle's own noises would be inaudible. He sprinted forward to catch up to them, making the internal adjustments necessary to mask the aura of the two spells. Again, if he was lucky, he'd be all but undetectable.

He followed them past Ashland until they came to some elevated rail tracks that had been dynamited and sealed. They turned south away from the demarcation line; the street sign read Ravenswood. Then, he noticed that the two men grew cautious. Though trying to appear natural as they carefully moved through the mass of people camped there, they continually changed their positions relative to each other, casually circling each other as if in animated conversation. All the while they scanned the area.

Kyle cursed. Until that point he'd been able to follow them by walking in the cleared area, away from the people. Now, the two cyber-soldiers were moving directly through the throng, forcing him to do the same. And though the people couldn't see him or hear him, they'd certainly feel him as he passed. Kyle would have to risk casting a third spell.

Fortunately, Vathoss and the other trooper were walking slowly, giving Kyle the extra time he needed. He marshaled the energy carefully; the fact that he was still sustaining the other two spells made casting this one extremely difficult. But when he'd completed it, feeling only a slight weakening from the strain, he floated upward, high enough to pass over the camped refugees.

He glided forward to within a half-dozen meters of the two troopers, who had relaxed their vigilance, satisfied that no one was following. After another four or five blocks, they passed Ravenswood's intersection with Addison and the angled Lincoln Avenue, and continued on for another half-block. Then Vathoss paused and casually finished his cigarette, which he tossed into the street, using the pretext to look around. Meanwhile the other trooper climbed the short stairs of what looked like it had been a small warehouse or perhaps self-storage company. Vathoss followed him up the stairs onto the short loading dock, then the pair pushed aside one of the large double doors and went in.

Kyle willed himself up onto the platform and then dropped the levitation spell. The door they'd gone through had yielded too easily to the troopers' touch to be locked. If they were keeping at least one major exit clear and unlocked in case they needed to make a quick exit, Kyle would use it to his advantage.

Stepping up to the door, he reached out carefully and grasped the handle. With only the slightest tug it slid aside noiselessly, the sound absorbed by his still active silence spell. Quickly, he darted through and scanned the area. It was a small-crate or large-package handling area. Seeing no one about, he slid the door shut. Had anyone been around, Kyle would have left the door open to make the guard wonder how it had done so on its own.

There were two doors leading out of the darker area. One accessed an office, the other apparently opened into a larger storage or handling area. He moved toward the door.

Before going through, Kyle waited and listened, but heard nothing he could identify through the silence spell. Beyond the open door was semidarkness; only the faintest light leaked through from distant windows.

As Kyle stepped through the door, movement to his left immediately attracted his attention. He turned and began to duck reflexively as a matte-black weapon pivoted toward him, the flat plate of its main sensory array covered in dark mesh.

Kyle raised his hands and shouted for it not to shoot, but the machine heard nothing past the silence spell. And even if it did, it knew its target wasn't carrying the right transponder chip and hadn't given the right verbal override. All it knew was what its sensors told it:

It fired.

26

"That was pretty fraggin' stupid," Anne Ravenheart said as she leaned over Kyle and adjusted the bandage on his side. His wound was now only minor; she'd healed most of it within moments of the hypervelocity autofire burst tearing into him, but enough wound and soreness remained to remind him of how close it had been. "Lucky for you the fire-control system on that sentry gun is fragged."

"Yeah," said Kyle, grinning slightly as he pulled himself up into a more comfortable position. "My lucky day."

Ravenheart's eyes narrowed. "Damn straight. That weapon fires six rounds of armor-piercing discarding-sabot ammunition per fire command with barely any recoil. You *are* lucky."

Kyle nodded and motioned for her to let up on the lecture. "I know, I know. I'm sorry I sneaked up on you."

"Why the frag did you?" she demanded. "Why didn't you flag Vathoss down on the street?"

"Caution . . . paranoia," Kyle told her. "These aren't the most stable of times, in case you hadn't noticed. I didn't know if he was still with you or out on his own."

"Fair enough," she said, then stood, offering him a hand to rise to his feet. He took it, and stood up alongside her. She looked like drek, her skin pale and drawn, her normally bright eyes dulled with fatigue, the body armor underpadding she wore over a T-shirt and shorts battered and stained. Seeing him take it all in, she managed a smile.

"Life in the field," she said, turning to lead him into a different part of the room, out from among the piles of stored boxes where she'd laid him down. There, casually seated around a jumbled pile of arms, armor, and supplies were five other Knight Errant troopers. Kyle paused and half-turned toward Ravenheart. "Don't tell me this is all that survived," he whispered.

She looked over at them, and then back at him, matching his gaze. There was a coldness there that he hoped was an effort to block out the pain of having lost so many. "No," she whispered back. "About two dozen were medivacced, and I have another three guarding this building and another four out reconning the city."

"Twelve," Kyle said.

"Thirteen. Don't forget me." Then her voice became even softer. "Lucky thirteen."

They started walking again, and Kyle resumed his normal conversational tone. "Can you tell me what happened?"

She shrugged. "We got crammed, pure and straight."

The other five troopers looked up at their approach, and a few of them, especially Vathoss, shifted angrily at the remark. "Too fraggin' many of them," she went on. "And they got smart just when we got lazy."

Kyle said nothing, but watched the body language of the five troopers. He could tell they'd heard this before, and he wasn't sure if the controlled anger they showed had to do with memories of the massacre or if it was directed at Ravenheart herself.

"Were you in the command van?" she asked Kyle.

"That's the last place I remember being," he told her. "I saw a giant, screeching beetle tearing the roof off like it was opening a can of soup, and then nothing. I woke up beaten to drek behind a dumpster."

She nodded. "Do you know if Soaring Owl got out?"

He shrugged. "I have no idea. He was in the van with me, but I don't remember seeing him at all. Did you search the wreckage?"

Ravenheart nodded again. "We"—she motioned to the other five—"were pinned down for most of a day near the hive. We heard choppers that night, but couldn't get free because of all the fraggin' bugs. We couldn't even raise anybody on the secure channels.

"By the time we got clear, the emergency pickup had come and gone. We searched around the vehicles some, picked up a few stragglers, and then moved out." She grinned and shrugged. "I guess we missed you."

"Somewhat understandable," he said. "I hear I was pretty close to buying it."

"Before we moved out, we swept the area, cleaned out any critical gear, and moved out to an in-city safehouse."

"Here?"

"No." She shook her head. "Closer to the Shattergraves, and actually not far from where the nest was."

"Were you able to get in touch with anyone?"

She eyed him suspiciously.

"I presume there was a communication rig in the safehouse," he said.

"You're right. There was."

"And?"

"We were told to hold our position pending further orders. Then the jamming started and we haven't been able to punch through it since."

"Do they think they'll send in a team to contact you?"

She eyed him again. "Maybe."

Kyle looked around the large storage room. "I take it this is another safehouse?"

Vathoss slammed a full clip into the automatic rifle he'd been cleaning. He didn't look at Kyle, but instead began to polish the barrel. Kyle had no doubt the gesture had been directed at him.

Ravenheart ignored the display. "Yes. The other one was lost to the bugs. We're lucky this was still inside the containment area."

"More interesting luck," Kyle said.

She nodded, and the two of them sat down on one of the crates. One of the other troopers, an Asian man with a fresh scar on his face, offered them both cigarettes. Ravenheart accepted, as did Kyle, even though he'd quit nearly a decade before.

"So, what are your plans?"

Ravenheart regarded him for a few moments. "I'd say I should be asking *you* that."

Kyle dragged on his cigarette, the smoke scorching his throat. "My plan is simple. I want to find my ex-wife and my daughter and get the frag out of this mess."

"You think they're still inside?"

"I don't know. I can't assume they're not."

"Is anyone with you?"

"Seeks-the-Moon, my former ally spirit."

"Former ally spirit?" she said, eyes widening slightly. Being a mage, Ravenheart understood the full import of that statement.

"Former," Kyle repeated. "I told you I was pretty close to buying it."

"And he didn't tear your head off once he was free?"

"No," Kyle said. "He didn't."

Ravenheart blew out a plume of smoke with an emphatic puff. "Lucky day? Frag, it's been your lucky week."

Vathoss looked over. "We're not running a refugee center here, Teller."

Ravenheart scowled at him. "Just keep cleaning your gun," she muttered ominously, then turned back to Kyle. "It would be a good idea if both you and your spirit were here."

Kyle nodded. Anne Ravenheart knew the potential power of a free spirit like Seeks-the-Moon and wanted it under her control. Kyle was willing to set up the situation, but only Moon could decide what he would or wouldn't do.

"How tight is the army's blockage?" he asked, shifting his body to include all the other troopers in the conversation. Everyone responded, except for Vathoss, though they first glanced at Ravenheart for permission before actually joining in.

"Pretty tight," said Asian. "They're doing it by brute force, the way it has to be done. Zero tolerance—nothing in or out."

"They've got a couple of surface-to-air missile batteries along each flank," another officer said, a tall, thin, Hispanic man with thick brown-red hair. "They're shooting down anything that isn't cleared, regardless of why it might be gong in. The only mercy flights are the ones they stage. Evrything else gets grounded."

"They send in the occasional hunter-killer flight of choppers, or more recently drones, gunning for suspected new ests or gathering spots," the Asian added. "The drones are retty ineffectual."

Kyle looked around at them. "Gathering spots?"

The trooper looked uncomfortable, as did Ravenheart, hough he could see some of the anger and coldness had returned to her eyes. "It would seem that human, or human-appearing, agents of the insect spirits, maybe insect hamans, are gathering people into groups."

"What the frag for?"

"We know the bug spirits are kidnapping people for the new hives," Ravenheart explained. "But they've got to be careful about the rate they grab host-bodies since the nests can only convert a finite number at a time."

"So they're herding people into holding areas," said Vathoss, looking up again. "That way they're all ready and waiting when it comes time to take them to the nest."

Kyle was shocked. "Spirits! How are they managing that? How can they control the people? Force?"

"Food," said Ravenheart. "Some of the fragging things, ike the ants, can secrete an edible substance. They lure the refugees in with promises of food, give it to them, and then keep them there. Naturally, the sites are safe since it's the bugs themselves that control them."

"Jesus fragging Christ."

She nodded. "We've disrupted six of these sites already, and we think we have leads on two more. If we can't handle t we pass word over the barricades and let the army send in choppers."

Kyle shook his head. It was all monstrous. And somewhere out there, maybe even in one of those sites, were Beth and Natalie. Kyle reached into his pocket and pulled out the holopix of the two that he'd been showing among the refugees. The troopers passed them around.

"Do you remember either of them at any of the sites you broke up?" he asked.

They all shook their heads.

"Even if we did," Ravenheart put in, "we probably wouldn't remember. We weren't paying that much attention to human faces."

"Have you tried any conjuring?" Kyle asked her.

"Just minor stuff, a couple of watchers," she said. "I haven't had the time or the materials to try anything bigger. We did hear about a shaman who got himself torn to pieces while trying to summon up a nature spirit. Apparently the bugs are particularly sensitive to that."

"Makes sense," Kyle said. "Seeks-the-Moon indicated that they were very sensitive to him as well. He's been walking around physical and masked the whole time."

"Bet that thrills him."

Kyle grinned. "Yeah, I bet it does." He was about to ask her if she knew of any specific spells or magical techniques to which the bug spirits were vulnerable when one of the piles of gear in front of him began to emit a series of loud electronic beeps.

"Son of a bitch!" said the Asian trooper as he kneeled down in front of it. He opened the casing, and Kyle saw that it was a compact field communication unit. Its three liquid crystal displays were active, showing data that he couldn't read and three-dimensional wave and field matrices that he didn't understand. "Mr. Cryptographer strikes again," the trooper said with a smile.

"What's the ident code?" Ravenheart asked.

"Operations HQ. This one's from the top of the drek chain. The box is verifying the codes." He leaned in and re-read the data display, then turned to Ravenheart. "It's 'eyes only'," he said. "Yours."

"Can we reply?" she asked him.

"No. It's a hyperburst transmission, and it looks like UCAS has already changed their jamming algorithms." He shook his head. "I for one would never have believed they'd have anything we couldn't breach."

This time Kyle grinned. "What? You don't think that's been a priority at the National Security Agency for at least thirty years?"

"Point taken," the trooper said, then stood up and gestured to the communications rig. "It's all yours, Captain."

"Thanks," Ravenheart squatted down next to it, shifting it slightly for a better view. As she did, Kyle spotted the lightweight optical cable attached to its back. His eyes followed it through the pile of gear, up a support column, and out the room through a perfectly round hole in the ceiling. He guessed the hole was recent, and that the cable led to a field satellite dish on the roof.

Ravenheart typed in her personal ident code, and then pulled a small cupped device from a panel on the side of the case. Another optical cable led from it into the case. She placed it against her right eye and held it there for a few moments until the communication rig beeped its approval. It began verifying her retinal pattern.

"Doesn't Ares have any satellites with laser downlink capability?" he asked. "That would eliminate the jamming problem."

Ravenheart sighed and shook her head. "Sure we do, but we're not getting any replies on the linkup. I don't know if it's us or them."

The machine beeped again, and Kyle saw the data display change, and a couple of words on it began to flash.

"Tox," Ravenheart said, her eyes widening slightly. "The message is cyber-encoded." She reached down and pulled out the retinal scanner unit, but detached the optical cable from it. From the same compartment she removed a small adapter plug with a round swivel-pad attached. She connected it to the end of the optical cable and then slotted the entire attachment into a jack behind her right ear, from which it hung. That done, the displays on the communication rig changed, and Ravenheart's eyes became unfocused. Her jaw, though, suddenly clenched.

Kyle turned toward the Asian trooper. "Induction link?" he asked.

The trooper nodded. "Easier to interface with helmet gear and the like."

Kyle nodded and then leaned in toward the man, extending his hand. "Kyle Teller," he said.

The trooper shook Kyle's hand. "Corporal David Lim."

While Ravenheart stared into nowhere, Kyle exchanged introductions with the rest of the troopers present. Vathos merely gave him a grim smile when Kyle came to him. "Yes, I suppose we do already know each other," Kyle said, turning away just as Ravenheart yanked the cable out and stood up quickly. Her body was tense, and her eyes hard. She looked around at the other troopers, and then at Kyle. "I need to talk with my team," she told him tersely. "Why don't you go get your friend?"

Kyle nodded and turned to leave the room. "Soaring Owl did get out," he just barely heard Ravenheart say. "The message was from him. He sends his condolences that we survived."

27

Seeks-the-Moon was waiting on Beth's porch when Kyle finally returned. The sight of the spirit standing there in the slowly growing morning light somehow reminded him of his father. Stern and silent, conveying everything with a glance and a tilt of the head, expecting everyone to understand him implicitly. The spirit said nothing as Kyle climbed the short stair and began describing what he'd seen and where he'd been.

"But you don't trust them," the spirit said as soon as he'd finished.

Kyle sighed. "No . . . I . . ." He looked away, seeing nothing. "I just don't know. I'm beginning to think that their mysterious behavior was them trying to conceal the fact that they were hunting the insect nest."

"Why would they do that?"

Kyle shrugged. "I don't know. They're a megacorp—who knows why the frag they do anything? When I was with the FBI it baffled the drek out of us half the time. We rarely had enough information to evaluate their actions, so a lot of it seemed to come from nowhere. It will be interesting to see whether or not Ravenheart tells us what the message from her boss was."

Just over an hour later, Kyle and Seeks-the-Moon reached the Knight Errant safehouse. This time Kyle knocked.

When they entered, and Kyle began introducing the spirit around, he noticed a decided tension in the group and a remoteness in Ravenheart. The watch shift had changed and there were two new troopers there he hadn't met before. One

was an ork, Trooper Allen Douglas, and the other a black elf
woman, Trooper Deena Reaves. Kyle also noticed that some
of the heavier weapons, most of which he recognized by
type rather than name, were being field-stripped or serviced.

Once the introductions were over, Ravenheart wandered
up alongside him and said in a low voice, "We need to talk."

Kyle nodded, and followed her into a small office in the
rear of the storage area. From the looks of things, she apparently claimed it as her own. "Soykaf?" she asked, stepping
up to the maker and dispensing a cup.

"No, thanks."

Blowing on the hot liquid, she sat down, not behind the
desk as he'd have expected, but on a metal folding chair
near the far corner. She placed the steaming cup on an adjacent file cabinet, then pulled a pill dispenser from a vest
pocket, shaking two small round green ones into her hand.
She popped them in her mouth and saw Kyle looking at her.
"You don't want to know," she said, then took a slug of
soykaf to wash them down.

"What's going on?" he asked her.

Ravenheart held her hand up for him to wait a second, and
took another drink of the hot liquid. "I wasn't sure what
would happen when the soykaf and those pills hit my stomach together. They're only supposed to be taken with water.
But frag it."

Kyle meanwhile had pulled up another folding chair
alongside her and settled into it. Finally, after a few moments of silence, she said, "According to Soaring Owl, the
government is paralyzed. Everyone is advising something
different.

"Disease Control in Charlottesville has given the go-
ahead to start bringing refugees through the line, but the
Army says its people think that would be suicide for the rest
of the country. Amazingly, there's been enough disinforma-
tion spread about that the public still doesn't have an accurate or truthful picture of what's going on here. The National
Security Agency's worried about the long-term social impact
of the truth that the government can't handle a magical
threat of this nature."

"Great," said Kyle. "So nothing's been decided, and in the meantime more people die and the hive gets stronger."

"Wait," she said. "It gets worse."

Kyle stiffened. Anne Ravenheart was staring straight at him without the slightest trace of emotion in her eyes. He could hear some in her voice, but it was as if she'd put it there purely for his benefit.

"Two days ago," she continued, "a joint delegation from the elven nations of Tir Tairngire, led by Prince Ehran the Scribe, and Tir na nÓg, led by Caoimhe O'Dunn, daughter of the High Steward, had a private audience with President Steele that lasted six hours."

"I suppose Ares has a transcript."

Her face betrayed no sign she'd heard the jibe. "Sometime during the meeting the White House received a call from the great dragon Lofwyr. What I've been told is that the joint delegation, and Lofwyr, recommended to Steele that the area inside the Containment Zone be saturated with ANVAR-TFM, Saeder-Krupp's most powerful pesticide, which will turn the area into a toxic waste zone for centuries."

Kyle froze. "But the people . . ."

"Dead," she said. "Like most pesticides, ANVAR-TFM is a nerve agent, except this one will kill most living things within a few seconds, and the rest within a few minutes. People, I'm told, take two to six minutes."

"But . . . that's absurd," Kyle sputtered. "How the frag can they believe that *pesticides*, fraggin' *chemicals*, will kill an insect spirit."

"As below, so above," came a voice from the shadows.

Both Kyle and Ravenheart jumped up and pulled their pistols, aiming in the direction of the voice. Standing in a darkened corner, Seeks-the-Moon stared back at them. Kyle immediately flipped his line of fire away from the spirit, but Ravenheart kept hers trained on him. The small subdued lights on the side of the combat pistol told him it was armed and ready to fire. Her hand shook slightly, and Kyle gently reached out to grasp her wrist. That motion alone, even before his hand actually touched hers, was apparently enough to break her out of whatever fugue state she'd entered.

Cursing, she snapped her hands and the pistol away, pointing it at the ceiling. Kyle expected her to say something, but she just glared at the spirit. He noticed, though, that her weapon's status lights indicated that the firing mechanism had been disarmed. Kyle holstered his own weapon.

"What did you just say?" he asked, as calmly as he could.

"I believe I was paraphrasing an axiom of magical theory you once taught me," the spirit replied. "These creatures look like insects native to this plane, yet they are from somewhere else. Fire elementals are vulnerable to water, as natural fire is, so maybe these spirits are vulnerable to the things that natural insects are."

Barely listening to what Seeks-the-Moon was saying, Ravenheart holstered her weapon, dropped back into the chair, and ran one hand through her dark hair. She was running the razor's edge and completely exhausted. Kyle squatted down next to her. He knew she needed to rest and that he probably shouldn't press her, but he also knew that time was running out for Beth and Natalie.

"What time frame did they suggest?" he asked her.

She looked at him, now bleary-eyed and tired. He was glad to see some real emotion in her eyes. "The nerve agent is already being shipped to the area," she said, "so it can be used as soon as Steele decides to do so. The elves and the dragon told him that it wasn't used within seventy-two hours, the new cocoons would hatch."

"Does that sound right?" he asked her.

She nodded. "Based on what we know, yes. The process of investing the host with an insect spirit larva takes a couple of weeks, and more, depending on the power of the spirit in question. If they started a new 'crop' right away, the weak spirits could be ready to leave the cocoons any day now."

Kyle slowly sat back down in his chair. "Then we've got less than forty-eight hours."

"Probably closer to thirty-six," she said.

"We must find the main nest again," Seeks-the-Moon said. "Quickly."

Kyle shook his head. "They'd be stupid to re-form another main nest. If they were smart they'd create dozens of smaller nests to keep Knight Errant or anyone else from finding them all before the cocoons are ready."

"You'd be right," Ravenheart said, "except they don't trust each other."

Kyle looked at her. "What do you mean?"

"We've been tracking insect hives for about four years now. The first ones were nearly always single-type hives or nests. There was very little intermingling of insect types. In fact, it seemed that for the most part the different types didn't get along. Half the time the only reason we were able to find new nests was because interhive fighting broke out. The ants or the wasps usually start it.

"Then we learned about the Universal Brotherhood."

Kyle nodded. The same organization of which his sister-in-law Ellen had been a member and the one Dave Strevich at the FBI had refused to give him any information about. He glanced at Seeks-the-Moon, but the spirit was standing quietly in the corner, listening.

"The frightening thing," Ravenheart said, "the thing that defied everything we thought we knew about the slotting bugs, was that the UB was a collective, a cooperation of a bunch of different types of insect spirits. Somewhere along the line some of the bug queens must have realized it was stupid for them to fight each other.

"Anyway, the Chicago hive we attacked north of the Core was, we now think, the primary Brotherhood hive in North America. We'd already dusted what we thought was the main hive in the Rocky Mountains a few months ago, after the Project Hope fiasco almost blew the lid off the whole thing."

"Project Hope?" Kyle echoed. He didn't remember hearing the name before.

She waved away his question. "Doesn't matter, long story. The point is that the UCAS government knew about the Brotherhood, and what they really were. That meant we had to work quickly, about eight months ahead of our plan, to deal with them."

Surprised, Kyle said, "Wait, the UCAS government knew

about the Brotherhood, about the bugs, *before* this happened."

She nodded. "Chip-truth. Did they do anything except argue about what they should do? No. Were they working under a deadline now that the Brotherhood knew their secret was out? You bet your fraggin' hide they were. The best the government could agree to do was shut the Brotherhood down as a fiscal entity. Sure, they staged some raids, but they couldn't be convinced this wasn't a small, easily manageable problem."

"But if you people at Ares knew, why didn't you brief them earlier?" Kyle could barely control his anger.

Ravenheart's eyes hardened. "Do you really think their response would have been different? Please. With a wonderfully blind eye to its own history, the UCAS government barely acknowledges the fact that there's magic in the world, let alone that it's a real threat to national security on this kind of scale. Plus, if we'd told them, they'd have probably started taking steps to prevent us from dealing with the problem. You know how touchy they are about multinational strike teams hitting civilian targets."

"So now it's all gone to slot," Kyle said. "The bugs have torn this city apart and in less than two days everything in it is going to die. Why the frag didn't you at least tell them when you found the nest? And why the frag didn't you just roll in a couple trillion liters of that nerve agent instead of going in guns blazing?"

Ravenheart paused, visibly trying to calm herself. Kyle knew he was provoking her, but he didn't care. The bulldrek and the games that her company had been playing for years had cost untold thousands of lives, two of which were potentially more important to him than anything else in this world.

"I didn't know about the effectiveness of the pesticides until a few hours ago," she said in measured tones. "I presume our people were thinking like you had been, that chemicals wouldn't be a threat against spirits. As for why we didn't alert the government about the presence of a huge nest in a major urban center . . ." Ravenheart stopped, seeming to reflect for a moment. "I couldn't say. I've wondered myself, but you'd have to ask Roger Soaring Owl or Damien Knight. All I know is I had my orders then, and god help us all, I have my orders now."

Kyle glanced at Seeks-the-Moon, who returned the look with a tilt of the head. "And those orders are?"

She looked away and said nothing, but Kyle could see she was thinking. Her orders were probably confidential and she was debating whether to reveal them.

"Look," he said. "Something has to be done. If we're going to—'

She nodded vigorously and waved her hand at him. "I know. I know. I agree." She sighed and shook her head. "The pleasures of field command," she said half under her breath, and then shifted in her seat to more directly face Kyle.

"Soaring Owl believes, as we've discussed, that if this was the main nest, it will re-form for the same reasons that brought it into being in the first place. He wants us to find it and do something about it before the deadline."

"How the frag are we supposed to find it?" Kyle asked her, and then the answer hit him. "The gathering spots," he said slowly.

She nodded. "We've been disrupting them as we find them, but if we watch them instead, we can follow a group as they're taken for investiture. That should lead us to the main hive."

"You're betting a lot on the hope that one of the spots you're watching will be tapped before time runs out."

She nodded again. "Yes, we are. But while you were gone we added two more sites to our list, and one of those is pretty much overloaded. I think that one will go next."

"Then what?"

"Then," she said, "then we deal with the fraggin' nest."

"How?" Kyle asked. "You had a small army before, and failed. How can you expect to take them on again with less than two dozen people?"

She tensed slightly. "We have a weapon . . ."

"Damocles?" Kyle asked, a numbness beginning in his stomach.

Her eyes widened and he saw her arm flinch toward her pistol. "How the frag do you know—"

"I was in the command van, remember?" he said. "Soaring Owl activated it just before the van got torn apart."

She looked away, nodding. "I thought it looked like it had been prepping for launch."

"I take it the drone was in a truck a few blocks away from the main trucks?"

She nodded again. "Yes. We recovered it and the launch system when we moved to the first safehouse."

"It's operational?"

"The payload is, and I've been ordered to use it," Ravenheart said. "I've been ordered to find the new main hive and nuke the thing straight to hell."

28

"Give me some other choice," Anne Ravenheart said. "Anything at all—I'll take it. By all the gods I swear I'll take it." She was agitated, pacing before the gathered troopers. Kyle and Seeks-the-Moon had convinced her that this was a situation that went beyond corporate loyalty, beyond chains of command and "eyes-only" orders. Reluctantly, she'd agreed.

Kyle had been startled by the reaction of the group once the full situation, in all its terrible details, was presented to them. Most of the Ares troopers seemed not to question the need to use a nuclear weapon against the main hive.

A few seemed nervous and not so sure after Kyle pointed out that a nuclear weapon had been detonated only five times in anger since its invention over a century ago—the two dropped on Japan in 1945 and the three on Libya by the Israelis in 2004. Then the ork trooper, Douglas, brought up another disturbing point. Ever since the Great Ghost Dance that had broken the back of the old United States and forced the return of most of western North America to Native American control, there was no guarantee a nuclear weapon would detonate at all.

"What about, what was it, the *Lone Eagle*?" the ork asked, looking about the group for confirmation. "Those Indian terrorists launched a nuclear missile at Russia, but it didn't go off. How do we know this one will?"

Kyle turned toward Ravenheart. "I heard other rumors too when I was with the government. More recent stuff. Any ideas?"

She shrugged, but didn't answer right away. "Not really. All I can say for sure is that test nuclear weapons *have* been successfully detonated since the Ghost Dance, and I can only presume that Ares wouldn't have built a last-ditch defense around an untried weapon."

"It'll blow," said the Asian trooper, Lim. "I don't think even magic can selectively dampen a subatomic reaction based on whether or not it came from a weapon."

"But we don't know for sure," said Douglas, looking directly at Ravenheart. Kyle could see that the thought of using a nuke frightened the ork as much as it did him. They seemed to be in the minority, however, which was not too surprising, considering the nature of the group.

"How much damage are we talking about?" he asked Ravenheart.

She sighed. "It's just about the smallest yield you can achieve, half a kiloton. Significantly smaller than what was dropped on Hiroshima, fourteen kilotons, or what the Israelis used on Libya, about a hundred kilotons per warhead."

"How much damage?" he asked again.

Ravenheart scowled, obviously trying to remember facts learned long ago. She started to speak, but Vathoss cut in.

"Everyone exposed to the unimpeded blast, out to about one to two hundred meters, will be killed instantly. The full blast itself will carry to about twelve hundred meters or so—breaking windows, starting fires, tossing light debris, and immediately killing about a third of the people exposed. Roughly a third of that number will die later."

He paused for a moment and let that settle in. "Since we're talking about a ground burst, there will be long-term radiation effects within about a five-hundred meter area around the blast. The ground burst may lessen immediate casualties, but it will increase long-term fatalities. There's also the problem of ground-water contamination and prolonged fallout."

"How many dead?" Kyle asked.

Vathoss shrugged. "Thousands. Tens of thousands. Depends on where it detonates."

Ravenheart, hands on hips, had been looking down at the ground while her subordinate was speaking. Finally, she looked up. "Thank you, Sergeant," she said coldly. "I didn't know you were such an expert."

Vathoss matched her stare. "I know what I need to know."

"Then it depends on where the nest is, doesn't it?" said Douglas, ignoring the stare-down. "If it's in a populated area, we've got to find some other way."

"It's too late," Ravenheart said, turning toward him. "We're out of time and we're out of options. The nest may be closer to opening its cocoons then we think. All our numbers are just guesses. Even if we knew where the nest was and went directly there from here, we could still be too late."

Kyle shook his head. "But we can't be the ones to decide this. It affects too many people."

"Then who?" asked Ravenheart.

"The government."

"They *have* decided—they're going to spray the city."

"Then we have to advise them of the alternatives," Kyle said. "Has your boss told them that the hive might regroup? That you're in position to do something?"

Ravenheart shook her head and smiled lightly. "And said what? Mr. President, we have an elite strike team in position in Chicago prepared to detonate a nuclear weapon. All you have to do is give the word." She shook her head again. "Pardon me, but I don't think Thomas Steele is going to give a megacorp permission to nuke one of his cities."

Ravenheart let her gaze take in the whole group. "Like I said, show me another alternative and I'll take it."

Kyle nodded. "Believe me, If I can think of something, you'll know in a tick. Meanwhile we should probably be preparing as if we were going to use the drone." He looked around and saw resignation in the eyes of everyone gathered around him. Seeks-the-Moon stood silently off to one side. Kyle regarded him for a moment. "What about you? Do you have an opinion on this?"

The spirit blinked and laughed lightly. "I do, but it is of no matter."

"Why not?"

"Because this is your land, your city, your people," he said. "Not mine. Regardless of what happens, I can leave."

"True enough," Kyle said. "But I'd still like to know what you think."

The spirit stared at him for a few moments, then finally said, "I think your people have often chosen one terrible solution to combat another. It is your way of things, something you understand."

"So then you think this is a bad idea."

"I didn't say that. If the birthing is not interrupted, it may be unstoppable. Already there are thousands dead in the city. What is the price of a few thousand more against what you fear?"

"Will you help us?"

Seeks-the-Moon paused again before turning away to stare at nothing.

"Will you help us?" Kyle repeated.

"I don't know."

"While you're deciding, will you at least help me find my wife and daughter?"

The spirit looked back at him. "That I will do."

The walk out to Ellen Shaw's apartment would have been a long one, so Kyle and Seeks-the-Moon borrowed the talents of one of the Knight Errant troopers and commandeered a dirty, beat-up Chrysler-Nissan Jackrabbit that was sitting in the building's parking lot. The car's battery charge was three-quarters full, so it took almost another half hour to top it off using the building's still-active power system. Kyle had heard of power outages occurring in parts of the city where power lines or poles had fallen, but so far most of the containment area still enjoyed basic utilities. Natural gas service, though, had been discontinued to much of the area, presumably for fear of fires and explosions.

Kyle and Seeks-the-Moon took the car quickly along Addison to Western, not wanting a repeat of the gang confrontation on Ashland. There, they turned south. The traffic lights still worked, for the most part, but Kyle ignored them. Down the length of the major north-south artery, they saw only four other cars in use. Each, packed with youths, eyed them suspiciously but otherwise left them alone.

"How long before they think of raising barricades to control their land?" Seeks-the-Moon asked.

Kyle had no answer, though he'd been wondering exactly same thing.

They continued south, past a stretch of streets near Chicago Avenue that was just charred rubble. It reminded Kyle of pictures he'd seen from wartime. Not a single soul was in sight.

Without any warning, the car suddenly lurched as the sloped rear of the Jackrabbit buckled and shattered. Kyle slammed on the brakes, and turned to look as a sickly sweet odor reached him and the insect spirit began to chitter at a terrible pitch. Metal shrieked and tore as the back of the car peeled away easily, one of the ant's long, gleaming black legs kicking it in. The braking car had thrown the creature off balance, and its sharp leg cut between Kyle and Seeks-the-Moon, ripping the seat and shattering the windshield.

The ant spirit thrust its head forward, tearing more of the car and itself in an attempt to get its mandibles near its prey. Neither Kyle nor Seeks-the-Moon could get a spell off as the car skidded to a halt, turning and sliding to the left. The ant, beginning to spit some glossy, semi-liquid spume, surged forward again, bending the top of the car. Both Kyle and Moon dove from the car.

Chittering and frenzied, the black ant pulled back, free of the car, a piece of the rear seat dangling from one of its mandibles. Its head moved side to side, looking from Kyle to Seeks-the-Moon, then it backed up slightly as it saw the power gathering around both of them.

Twin bolts of crimson energy, one slightly darker than the other, struck the ant simultaneously. It stepped back again, screeching and twisting its head and spraying drops of the greenish fluid that now oozed from it. Then it seemed to recover and rushed directly at Kyle.

But Kyle was ready. His foci were all active, and none of his attention was diverted to their masking. The spirit lunged, and Kyle released a different spell—a simple, focused dart of power backed by everything he had. It caught the charging ant head-on, penetrating deep in a flash of power. In the same instant, the rear of the ant's form was engulfed in a sickly green substance that pulled it to the ground, stopping its rush and slamming its head down onto the pavement. Kyle stepped back as the creature thrashed, its big head cracked and oozing. He readied another spell, felt Seeks-the-Moon doing the same, and then watched as the ant spirit thrust itself upward in a final act of defiance before suddenly losing cohesion, its form drifting apart and streaming away in an unfelt breeze.

Kyle and Seeks-the-Moon stared at the creature until its form was completely gone. "Come on!" Kyle shouted, rushing back to the still running car. He threw himself behind the wheel and had the vehicle gunned and accelerating away even before Moon had shut the door behind him. When they were clear and saw no other signs of insect spirits, Kyle turned to Seeks-the-Moon. "Why didn't you just slip into astral space?" he asked.

"What?"

"When the ant attacked, why did you wait until the car had stopped and you could use the door."

The spirit stared at him blankly and then Kyle saw quick realization dawn on the spirit's face. His eyes widening, Seeks-the-Moon laughed. Very loudly.

"I think you are a bad influence on me," he said, continuing to laugh as they drove on.

Turning at the intersection of Ogden with Western, they headed southwest into the township of Cicero, which was not part of the city of Chicago, but was still within the Containment Zone. Kyle knew the area fairly well and was able to find his sister-in-law's apartment quickly. The street was as quiet as the last time, but now he could see signs of abandonment. Only one house, a structure across the street from Ellen Shaw's apartment building, still looked inhabited, and now resembled a fortress.

Kyle pulled up onto the curb and into the courtyard of the building, scraping the passenger side of the car against part of the iron fence that used to stand there. Then he turned the car off and let the engine wind down. He considered leaving it running in case they needed a fast getaway, but decided that the risk of theft was potentially greater than the likelihood of quick flight.

"Do you wish me to check inside?" Seeks-the-Moon asked Kyle as they studied the section of the building where Ellen Shaw had her apartment.

"Wait one second," Kyle said as he stepped forward and pushed against the front door. It swung open easily, both lock and frame smashed.

"Drek," Kyle said, looking up toward the apartment.

"Looters?" asked Seeks-the-Moon.

"Maybe. Do you want to check ahead?"

The spirit grinned slightly. "It was you who reminded me of my abilities, remember?"

Kyle nodded. "Go ahead, but step into the foyer so that anyone watching won't see you disappear. Ellen's apartment is on this side"—he pointed south—"two floors up."

The spirit nodded and stepped through the door, with Kyle close behind. Even before completely entering the trash-strewn entranceway, Seeks-the-Moon faded from view. Kyle pulled his gun, an Ares Predator II heavy pistol Ravenheart had given him, and waited. But the gun was only clear of the holster a moment before the spirit returned.

Seeks-the-Moon was shaking his head. "The apartment is empty and looks like it's been ransacked."

"Looters."

Kyle and the spirit climbed the old staircase to the first door on the second landing. Here too the lock and frame had been shattered, and then Kyle remembered that he'd done the damage himself with one of his own spells the last time. It didn't look like anyone had tried to repair the damage, even temporarily, in the interim.

Kyle pushed the door open, holstering his pistol as he entered. The apartment had indeed been looted, with little of value left behind. Most of the appliances were gone, as were the electronics and the food from the kitchen. In the bedroom, Kyle saw that clothes had been pulled from the closets and dresser. He couldn't tell if any of their contents were missing, but the bedclothes were gone.

Then, in one corner of the dining room, where random trash and debris had apparently been pushed, Kyle found a small padded chip-book carrier. It was identical to the one he'd given Natalie two years ago for Christmas, and the more he stared at it and turned it over in his hands, the more certain he was that it was hers.

"I think they may have been here," Kyle said to Seeks-the-Moon, who'd quietly followed him in. The spirit nodded.

They continued to search, but turned up nothing of further interest except some dishes in the dishwasher. Kyle counted them and paired them with utensils and drinking glasses also sitting there. One partial set was smaller, as if someone had deliberately been given a smaller portion of what looked like prepackaged lasagna. The drinking glass was even a tumbler, not full-sized. The food was hard, but hadn't yet begun to turn bad, probably not more than a day or two old.

Kyle nodded. "They've been here."

Seeks-the-Moon called out to him. "Then you should look at this." He was back in the living room.

Kyle walked out there and found Moon pushing a small tack into the wall. A tattered and torn sheet of paper dangled from it.

"What's that?" Kyle asked.

"It was on the floor. I think it was hanging here and someone ripped it down."

Kyle looked at the paper, but it was only a fragment obviously torn from a larger sheet. "Is the rest of it around?"

Seeks-the-Moon shook his head. "I haven't found it."

Kyle nodded, also looking this way and that. "If the whole sheet was torn down by looters, why isn't it here?"

"You think they would have torn it down and left it on the floor?"

"Why do anything else? Why take it if it had no value?"

"Depending on what it said, they may have perceived it as having value to someone else."

Kyle stared at him. "That's hard to believe."

"You don't believe your people are capable of such things?"

Kyle looked away. "It doesn't make any sense."

The spirit shrugged. "The people your wife and daughter are with may have taken it down themselves."

"What do you mean?"

"They wouldn't want anyone to know where they were going," Seeks-the-Moon said, "but they also would not want to alarm your wife by refusing to let her post a note to you."

"So after Beth and Natalie left, someone or something pulled the note down."

The spirit nodded.

Kyle turned and looked at where the fragment of paper hung. "I think I prefer your other suggestion," he said.

After quickly checking some of the other apartments in the building, and finding nothing, Kyle and Seeks-the-Moon went back to the car. It was exactly as they'd left it, but Kyle stood there looking across the street at the barricaded house. "I want to see if they know anything," he said.

"They don't seem very sociable," Seeks-the-Moon said.

"Maybe." Kyle unslung the submachine gun from under the long coat and passed it to the spirit. "They're probably just scared."

"Fear does not promote rational thought."

"I know," Kyle said, "but I have to ask."

Seeks-the-Moon walked with Kyle to the edge of the curb, then Kyle continued alone toward the house, his arms held out, palms open.

"Hoi!" he called out as he reached the far curb. There was no response, so he continued forward a few more steps. "Is anyone home?"

Kyle saw a piece of wood pull away from one of the windows, and then he dimly made out a face—he thought it was a woman's—and the muzzle of a shotgun. Both were looking at him.

"What do you want?" the woman shouted. She sounded young, barely more than a teenager.

"I'm looking for my sister-in-law, Ellen Shaw. She lived across the street in that apartment." He pointed back at the building. "I think my wife and daughter are with her, and I'm trying to find them."

The shadowed face pulled away, but the shotgun remained. The woman returned in a few moments. "They're gone," she said. "There were about a dozen of them, but they're gone."

"How long ago?"

"Day before yesterday."

"Do you know where they went?" he asked.

"They said they were going to some relief camp."

"Relief camp? Do you know where?"

"No, they didn't say."

Kyle cursed under his breath. "Did you see which way they went?"

"Down that way. But I didn't really watch."

"Was there a little girl with them?"

He could see the woman nod. "Two of them. One was carrying a cat."

Kyle nodded. "Thanks," he said, and started to turn away, but the woman called out to him.

"Has he come yet?" she yelled.

Kyle turned back. "I'm sorry?" he replied.

"Has he come yet?"

"Who?"

"Jesus."

Kyle paused and looked deep into the shadows through the window. The shotgun was there, and so was the faint outline of a woman's head, but he could see nothing else. He allowed his perceptions to slip into astral space for just a moment, and he could see her aura, flickering madly about her, a torrent of emotions.

"No," Kyle said evenly. "I don't think he has."

"Don't despair," she said. "He'll come soon. Then you'll find your wife and child."

Kyle nodded again, stepping back. "Thank you. I'll keep an eye out for him."

The wood slid back into place as Kyle turned back toward Seeks-the-Moon, shaking his head. Seeks-the-Moon merely shrugged. "We all seek something," he said, and together they walked slowly back to the car.

29

Returning north, Kyle drove the rapidly disintegrating Jackrabbit along Cicero Avenue. About halfway, just north of Division, they passed through the site of what must have been a gang battle. At least a dozen lay dead in the street, such that Kyle couldn't help but roll slowly over one with the car. A pack of dogs, themselves fighting over the bodies, scattered as he passed. Neither he nor Seeks-the-Moon said a word.

When they finally made it back to the Knight Errant safehouse, Vathoss introduced them to three "new" team members—Knight Errant security guards caught inside when the Containment Zone was established. Kyle questioned them, but neither had been at the Truman Tower or knew where any of its occupants might have gone.

Anne Ravenheart was gone too. According to Vathoss, she and some of the other troopers were out investigating a surveillance post near a gathering point that had reported some activity. Kyle tried to get more information, but the sergeant wasn't talking. No one was, and Kyle sensed a growing unease among the troopers. Time was passing and nothing was happening.

As twilight came, one of the troopers that had gone out with Captain Ravenheart returned with the message that she wanted Kyle to join her at the surveillance post—the people at the gathering point seemed to be preparing to move to another location.

The trooper, a rookie named Canelli, was driving an "appropriated" Honda Viking heavy motorcycle, which could carry one additional person. Seeks-the-Moon reluctantly suggested he follow the cycle in astral space, despite his continuing concern about attracting the attention of the bugs.

Kyle had a better idea. Seeks-the-Moon would climb on behind Canelli, while Kyle, held aloft by a levitation spell, held on for dear life. The three of them set off like that, Kyle hoping he understood the properties of the spell as good as he thought he did.

The cycle made its way west, and then south, heading so far in that direction that Kyle thought they were going to the Cicero area where his sister-in-law's apartment was located. But Canelli turned the bike east before they got that far, coming to a stop near Chicago and Kedzie. After hiding the bike behind an overturned garbage dumpster and under the watchful eye of a nearby half-hidden Knight Errant trooper, Canelli led them through the back entrance of what looked like an old warehouse or storage building. Kyle dropped his levitation spell, not wanting to attract astral attention.

Inside, they found Ravenheart, Lim, and two other troopers clustered around a small closed-circuit video monitor. The image showed another building similar to this one, with a crisscross of train tracks and uncoupled railroad cars in the background. From what he'd seen on approach Kyle suspected the area was almost directly across the street. He could see movement on the screen, some figures clustered around one of the doors, given away by the telltale glow of cigarettes. Beyond them, Kyle could just barely make out the front end of what seemed to be a Chicago Transit Authority bus.

"What's going on?" he asked, squatting down next to Ravenheart.

"About an hour ago two men arrived in a car and I popped up and risked a peek at them astrally," she said. "Let's just say they were looking a little fuzzy around the edges."

Kyle nodded. He knew that the use of electronic surveillance was common when watching potentially magically active targets since a human observer could be detected by his aura, which was how he'd spotted the woman in the house across from Ellen's. It was safer to pop up, astrally active, for a quick, hopefully detailed look, than risk detection.

"They went inside, and soon after there was a lot of activity," she continued. "It looked to me like they were starting to pack up. About a half-hour later two buses arrived. The first one loaded up pretty quick and headed out. We weren't in position to follow it, so we let it go. When this one leaves, we're going to tail it."

"How many guards or people do you think might be possessed, or whatever it is they are," Kyle asked, squinting at the monitor.

She shrugged. "Can't tell. We've seen six different people with wrong auras. So there are at least that many."

"Any idea how many more are inside?"

"No. Maybe forty or so, but that's a real out of my butt guess," she said with a shrug. "Any luck with your wife?"

"No. They've been to the apartment, but according to a neighbor they went off to some 'relief camp'. The neighbor didn't know where."

"Sorry," Ravenheart said, touching his arm for a moment.

Kyle looked toward the monitor. "Is this the closest gathering spot you know to the Cicero area?" he asked.

Her eyes widened slightly. "That we know of. Cicero—I assume you mean the township—is only a couple of kilometers to the southeast."

"So this might be where they ended up," Kyle said slowly.

"'Possible."

"There is one very powerful out there," Seeks-the-Moon said suddenly.

Kyle and Ravenheart both turned toward him. "What do you mean?" she asked.

"There is a very powerful spirit out there," he said, looking away as he seemed to stare through the wall. "I can smell him."

"Can he sense you?" Kyle asked.

Seeks-the-Moon shrugged. "I don't know, but I hope I do not smell as bad as it does."

Ravenheart turned to Kyle. "Makes sense that they'd send a powerful one to guard the buses if they were transferring the people."

Kyle nodded. "I know you've got to follow them, but first I've got to find out if Beth and Natalie are in there."

Ravenheart looked away. "I can't let you do that. I can't let you jeopardize our chances of finding the main nest." She turned back and stared at him. "If they were here, they may have already left in the other bus."

"I have to find out, Anne," Kyle said, matching her stare.

She frowned. "There's only one way I'll let you do it. Take yourself a couple of blocks from here and astrally project. Check out the bus that way. If anything chases you, get the frag out of there and lose it. If they only see one idiot human, they might not panic."

"Gee, thanks," he said.

"Better get a move on it. That bus'll be loaded soon."

Kyle stood up and shook out the cramps in his legs. He turned toward Seeks-the-Moon. "Watch my body?"

The spirit simply nodded and followed him out the back door.

Enveloped in the warm flow of astral space, Kyle watched the bus from two blocks to the south. He could tell that it was almost full—the glow emanating from the auras of the people packed into it almost flowed out into the street.

Waiting until he no longer saw anyone outside the building, he shot forward, gliding a few millimeters off the ground, and slipped through the sheet-metal and plastic walls of the building. As he passed through, he immediately willed himself upward, hoping to get lost in the rafters of the building, assuming there were any.

There were, barely, a meter or two of clearance filled with pipes and support beams. Below him, seemingly unaware of his presence, were a dozen or so men and women, the auras of two-thirds of them rife with dark streaks and bursts of confusion. They all stood around a figure lying on one of the many cots in the room. He could hear the conversation, and gathered from it that her family—the four other normal-seeming auras—feared that she was too weak to travel. Some others were attempting to explain to the family that the bus was waiting. The family wasn't listening.

He recognized none of them by their auras or what he could make out of their physical forms, and willed himself upward, hoping to pass through the roof. His astral body couldn't, though. There were planks of wood across the roof, and he couldn't pass astrally through that once-living material. Staying as close to the ceiling as possible, Kyle began to drift forward toward the far wall, hoping to slip out there. As he went he noticed that three of the insect-possessed humans had moved off and were having a hushed argument. He also noticed that the old woman seemed to be watching him. Her head, at least, turned as he drifted forward, seemingly tracking his movement. He thought about pausing to get a better look at her, but decided against it, and instead accelerated his motion.

He reached the wall, and easily slipped his head through the inorganic metal there. Talking quietly among themselves near the door of the bus were three of what Kyle took to be guards. From the bus streamed some light, but Kyle saw no one inside it. Nor did he sense any sign of the powerful spirit that Seeks-the-Moon had detected.

He was concerned about reaching the bus without detection, but could think of no simple way of creating a diversion while in astral form. He watched them for a moment, and when they all seemed to glance down or look away, he shot over to the roof of the bus with the speed of thought.

Just as he brought himself to a stop flush against the metal roof, Kyle heard a door of the warehouse slam shut and a pair of voices begin an indiscernible conversation. More voices quickly joined in. Kyle took that as his chance to shift position to where his head dropped down through the roof of the bus.

There were dozens of people inside, men, women, and children. Propelling himself forward he looked quickly at each of their auras, hoping to recognize one. All were unfamiliar.

As he came to the last one at the front of the bus, a tall man with short dark hair and a crumpled long coat stepped into the bus, his aura bearing no resemblance to anything

human. He immediately stopped, surprised, and then lunged
up at Kyle's head, his face and aura instantly turning dark.

Unrestrained by the confines of the flesh, Kyle was far
faster. Before the newcomer could move even two steps, let
alone try to seize his astral head, Kyle was gone, moving at
the speed of thought toward the railway yard. He shot between cars, keeping himself a meter or two off the ground to
use them as cover. He turned quickly, once, twice, and then
back toward the bus. From cover inside one of the freight
cars he could see the bus pulling away quickly.

Staying out of its view, he crossed between more cars and
then accelerated back to where his body was. He reached it,
slipped back inside, and almost leaped to his feet in one motion. Seeks-the-Moon, seated in an old wooden chair in the
back room they'd broken into, eyed him expectantly.

"They weren't there," Kyle said, picking up the Ares assault rifle he'd been carrying. "But I did see your spirit
buddy."

The spirit raised an eyebrow.

"I think he was like the others, an insect spirit possessing
a human body, but he was a powerful fragger," Kyle told
him, "and I think he could mask his aura."

The spirit seemed surprised. "How well?"

"Don't know," Kyle said as they left the building, "but I
think I caught him with his guard down. He could see me in
astral space, even took a swipe at me, but he didn't pursue.
I think he was stuck in the flesh." They began jogging toward where the Knight Errant troopers had been. Kyle could
hear engines beginning to recede in the distance.

"How distasteful," Seeks-the-Moon said

Kyle didn't answer, but as the two reached the alley behind the building Ravenheart and the others had been using
for surveillance of the gathering site, he could see that the
guard and Canelli's motorcycle were missing.

"Drek!" Kyle cursed. "They better not have moved out already."

The two dashed into the building and up the short flight
of stairs to the room where the trooper had been. It was
empty.

Kyle slammed his fist into empty air. "God-frag-it!"

"The bus can't have gotten far," Seeks-the-Moon said. "I can still almost hear the motor."

"Yeah, but we're on foot. And to travel fast enough we'd either have to go astral or use magic, which that fraggin' man-bug-spirit thing will notice like a flare going off." Kyle was pacing the room as he spoke, then suddenly stopped at one of the partially broken windows. A man was sprinting toward the warehouse.

"Come on!" Kyle said, and dashed toward a different stairwell that seemed to lead down toward the front of the building. It did, and ended near a partially broken-open front door. Kyle shouldered his way through the door, then he and Moon dashed across the street toward the warehouse, Kyle quickly activating all his foci as they went.

"Wait!" said the spirit. "You don't know what might still be there!"

Kyle ignored him and rushed toward the rear door he'd seen the sprinter heading toward. Approaching, he could hear it locking shut and a man's voice on the other side beginning to shout. Kyle slowed, slung the rifle, and ran the formula for a powerful blast of raw physical power through his head. He released the spell, barely pausing in his dash, and watched with some satisfaction as the weak wooden door disintegrated in front of him.

"Keep at least one alive!" Kyle called out as he rushed in, the spell for a physical shield racing through his mind. It sprung into being, a transparent rectangle of shimmering blue energy, as the man, who'd ducked to one side of the door, threw a skillful martial arts kick at Kyle's head.

The blow smashed against the magical shield and pushed Kyle to one side, clearing the door for Seeks-the-Moon, who quickly stepped in. The man turned to meet him, and Kyle saw a slash of red energy cut across him as Seeks-the-Moon's own hand shot out. Blood and ichor immediately burst from the man's neck as he stumbled back, clutching at the wound. He fell backward over a crate and crashed down onto the floor. Seeks-the-Moon maneuvered himself between the man and Kyle as Kyle rushed forward into the main room.

The four family members were dead, their bodies twisted and tossed aside. As Kyle rushed in, one of the men, the larger of the two remaining, had just finished snapping the neck of a teenage boy. He let the body drop at his feet and charged at Kyle.

The man was quick for his size, but Kyle let the shield spell dissipate and quickly reworked the energy. It flowed together through his fingers and extended toward the man, almost solidifying into a shaft of physical energy. The man tried to turn, but couldn't, hitting the end of the shaft head on. The energy burst around him like water from a hose, tearing into him and arcing around him.

As the man stumbled, Kyle sidestepped and then lashed out with his own kick, catching him on the side of the knee. Kyle felt the leg snap, and the man twisted, screaming with more pain. He fell, crashing down headfirst onto the concrete floor.

Pain surged through Kyle's side as the other man hit him blind-side. He stumbled, most of the breath getting knocked out of him as the man hit him again across the side of the head. A wave of pain and nausea washed over Kyle as he turned away, trying to protect himself. The man struck again, and this time Kyle felt the blow slice by close to his ear.

Kyle jabbed up with his fist and caught the man's forearm, slamming it away. Expecting another blow, Kyle spun aside, his arms moving in what he knew would be a futile attempt to protect his head. But the blow didn't come. Instead, his attacker stopped suddenly, a look of surprise crossing his face as a bolt of flame chewed its way out his chest to explode across the front of his body. Blood and fire poured from his mouth as he pitched forward to land at Kyle's feet. Beyond him, in the door, the last energy from Seeks-the-Moon's spell faded away, dissipating off the spirit's hand.

"Thanks," Kyle said.

The spirit shrugged. "Are you hurt?"

"No, just banged up. Nothing we can't deal with."

"That one is alive," the spirit said, pointing at the man Kyle had speared. "I don't feel so bad about killing these other two."

"I knew you'd come back," said a frail woman's voice.

Both Kyle and Seeks-the-Moon turned toward the sound. On one of the cots, where Kyle had seen her earlier, was the old woman. She was staring at him. Her voice had barely enough breath to create words.

Kyle walked over toward her. "I thought you were going to leave me like this," she said.

"I'm sorry, I don't know what you . . ."

The old woman looked away at the bodies scattered around the large room. "Or did you come back for them?" she asked, her attention drifting.

Kyle glanced at Seeks-the-Moon, who seemed equally perplexed, and then turned back. The woman had grown very still, except for her mouth, which was moving slightly. Kyle leaned down closer, and she said as she died, "No, you came to take all of us."

Kyle stood up slowly and looked back at Seeks-the-Moon, but neither said anything. There was a moan from the man Kyle had speared. He moved, and Kyle grabbed him, lifting him up and flipping him onto one of the cots. Kyle shifted his senses into astral space and studied the man.

His aura was wrong, twisted, laced with dark streaks, and with his astral senses Kyle could almost smell a stench coming from him. The man, clutching his leg in pain, hissed up at Kyle.

"The bus was going to the main hive," Kyle said. "Where is it?"

The man spat, a glob of blood and greenish fluid that Kyle turned slightly to avoid.

Kyle smacked the side of the man's shattered knee with an open palm, and the man choked back a howl of pain.

"Here's the chip truth—I know what you are, and I know that the spirit that used to inhabit that body is dead. That means I don't have the slightest pang of guilt about doing whatever I need to do to you to make you talk."

The man only sneered. Kyle could see, though, that sweat

had broken out across his face. He couldn't tell if it was from pain or fear.

"It's a simple spell really," Kyle said as a small swirl of black and red energy appeared floating above his now outstretched hand. "As the energy covers you, it'll feel like thousands of tiny red-hot needles jabbing into your body. Nothing immediately serious . . . But now imagine if that energy covered your own body and I could make it hurt more and more until all you had was the pain. No body, no mind, just the pain."

The man shrank back as Kyle spoke and the swirl of energy began to drift toward him.

"Then," Kyle went on, "it'll use any opening it can to get inside your body . . ."

"Cermak and Racine," the man hissed suddenly, holding out his hand to ward off the slowly approaching spell. "The power plant!"

Kyle nodded and stood, confident from the man's expression and attitude that he spoke the truth. "Good." Kyle unslung his Ares combat rifle and aimed it at the man. "I'd have hated to create a spell like that on the fly."

He fired a burst of three bullets, deciding the creature's death was worth the waste.

30

They approached the vicinity of Cermak and Racine carefully. Kyle didn't know the area, except by mentally following the path of both streets from where he knew them to where they had to intersect. The neighborhood, southwest of the devastated Noose and northwest of the rebuilt downtown Core, was fairly rundown. In the years following the destruction of the IBM Building, it had gone from being an ethnic enclave to the only sanctuary for many displaced by the disaster.

Kyle and Seeks-the-Moon walked cautiously down Cermak from Ashland looking for signs of the insect hive. It was hard to miss. About three-quarters of a kilometer east of Ashland the two could clearly make out the tall exhaust stack of the power plant where the insect-spirit-inhabited man had told them it would be. It was mostly dark, except for some slowly blinking lights on the tower and around the plant building itself.

They stayed on the opposite side of the street, trying to act casual and avoid detection. As they got closer, and could see the site better, they began to make out some additional smaller buildings and power distribution towers to the right of the main plant building, which stood about six or seven stories high just behind the towering hundred-and-fifty-meter smokestack. There was activity around the building; a few cars sat scattered in the wide-open grassed and rail-tracked area that fronted the building. A dozen meters or so from the only large warehouse doors that Kyle could see, a row of three Chicago Transit Authority buses were lined up, their motors running but lights out. As he and Seeks-the-

Moon watched, the large doors were closing, hiding a set of bus taillights inside. There seemed to be guards, but they were milling around the line of buses almost nonchalantly—Kyle guessed that they were relying on spirits in astral space that he could not see.

"Anything?" Kyle asked Seeks-the-Moon, who's own astral senses were always active.

"This is the hive."

"You're sure?"

"There is no question. The air reeks of it."

"Can you see any spirit guards?"

"No."

"No?"

The spirit scowled. "That's what I said. The men and women standing around the bus all seem to be like those we killed at the warehouse, but I see no true form spirits." Seeks-the-Moon told him. "They are here, though."

"In the building?"

"In the main building, and in the smaller ones. Maybe underneath them too. It feels as if there are many hives and nests here. But they're all quiet."

"Any idea why?"

"Perhaps the time is near and the queens are distracted."

"So no one's telling them to do anything."

The spirit nodded. "I'm only guessing."

"Let's turn at the next street and look for Knight Errant," Kyle said. "They can't be too far."

The two turned north at the rubble of what looked like it had once been the site of a restaurant or cafe that had later become home to a group of particularly incompetent bombmakers. They also passed a row of rundown and apparently abandoned houses. There was, in fact, almost no sign of life.

"Do you think they were smart enough to take the people who lived in the area first?" Seeks-the-Moon said.

"I don't know if they were smart enough," Kyle replied. "but they are certainly savage enough."

Seeks-the-Moon started to speak, then stopped and gestured up the street with his head. "There," he said quietly. "A large truck and a moment ago a group of people near it."

"Knight Errant."

"Most likely."

Instead of turning east again as they'd intended, Kyle and Seeks-the-Moon continued along the street toward the shapes the spirit had seen. As they got within half a block they could see someone walking toward them. It was the ork trooper, Douglas. He nodded as they stopped a few feet from each other.

"You can't shake us that easily," Kyle said.

Douglas smiled. "No, Captain Ravenheart said she thought you'd show up before kickoff. She's over here." He gestured toward what seemed to Kyle just another deteriorated building, this one a walkup with a long front stair.

"Kickoff?"

Douglas' face clouded and he looked away as he escorted them up the steps. "We've found the hive," he said quietly.

Kyle nodded and said, "I understand," as Douglas pushed open the battered front door and made way for them to enter. Inside, another trooper stood, weapon ready, covering the front door. The building had once held apartments, and Douglas directed them toward the partially open door of one just beyond the lobby.

Inside, Ravenheart and two other troopers were studying a small display Kyle recognized as a remote control deck, undoubtedly for the drone. Sergeant Vathoss stood nearby and frowned slightly as Kyle and Seeks-the-Moon entered.

"Glad you could make it," Ravenheart said. "Sorry we had to cut and run on you like that, but when the bus bolted I was afraid we'd lose it."

Kyle nodded and shrugged. "No harm done. Like I told Douglas—you can't shake us that easily."

For no reason Kyle could guess, Ravenheart glanced at Seeks-the-Moon. "I suspect you're right."

"What's the plan?"

She turned back to the remote control deck. "Well, once we get the reprogramming done, which shouldn't be much longer,"—she stressed the words for the benefit of the other two troopers working the display—"we're going to set it on autopilot, get it airborne, give us some time to get clear, and thread it like a needle through one of those windows over there. After that, we cut power, it loses altitude, drops as far as it can, and . . ." She let her voice trail off. "Well, then it explodes."

"How far off can you remote pilot it from?" Kyle asked her.

Ravenheart smiled and shook her head in mock disbelief. "You are sharp, Teller, I'll give you that. With the deck we have here, and with the minor damage to the drone—"

"It's damaged?"

"Slightly. It apparently hit something while Soaring Owl was trying to launch it. Probably the sides of the bay or the cover doors. Anyway, with that and everything else factored in, our guess is about a kilometer and a half for any reliability."

"Just at the edge of the blast radius."

She nodded. "Just beyond it, we hope."

"What's your timetable?"

She looked back at the display. "I hope to detonate within the hour."

"That is good," Seeks-the-Moon said suddenly. "It is beginning."

Nearly everyone in the room turned their attention to him. He was staring off in the direction of the power plant, and to Kyle he looked wan and drawn.

"You feel something?" Kyle asked.

The spirit nodded. "Power is being drawn away from here, everywhere, into there," he said. "I can feel it; I am weaker."

"How soon?" asked Ravenheart.

"Soon."

"Then we have little time." Kyle turned to Ravenheart. "I want to get the people out."

"What?"

"As many as we can, just before the bomb goes off. There are buses there. We can use them to carry people away." Before Ravenheart could answer, he turned slightly and addressed the others in the room. "Any idea how quickly they're taking the buses inside?"

One of the troopers, a short woman with dirty-red hair, said, "There were three other buses here when the one we were following arrived. It got in line, and about a half-hour later, just before you got here, one pulled out from inside and the other pulled in to take its place."

"Going in is suicide," said Ravenheart angrily.

"I didn't say we'd go in," Kyle told her. "I don't like it, but from the look of things and from what Seeks-the-Moon senses now, and the fact that it seemed to him that there were many, many more spirits inside the building, I think you're right."

"Then what?"

"The buses outside. Few seem to be guarding them. If we hit them hard and fast we could gain control of the buses within the space of a few minutes. There's plenty of room to turn them around." Kyle shifted his attention to the others in the room. He noticed that the trooper who had been watching in the hall was standing in the doorway listening. "If we do this right, we could get us and the buses clear before the bomb goes off."

"They'll come after the buses," Ravenheart said. "And the bugs'll tear them apart."

"But what will they do?" Seeks-the-Moon asked. "What will happen when the bomb detonates?"

Ravenheart turned toward him, scowling. "The buses will be sardine cans in a microwave."

"No," said the spirit, evening his tone. "What will happen to the spirits when their queens are dead?"

Her face blanked. "I don't know."

"Nor do I."

"What have they done in the past?" Kyle asked Ravenheart.

"What do you mean?"

"You said you've destroyed hives and nests before. What happened to the spirits when the queen died?"

She frowned and looked away for a moment, thinking. "It depends on which kind they are. Roaches don't care. They really don't have queens. Same for flies and beetles and the others that have 'nests' rather than hives. The true hivers, with real queens, they usually go nuts and either mill around the queen's body or start attacking each other. I think the ants tend to do that."

Kyle nodded. "Then we have to hope it's true hivers chasing the buses."

"You're insane," she said. "I can't jeopardize the mission doing this."

"You won't be. The drone'll be airborne and the clock will be ticking. No matter what happens, the drone goes in and detonates. Freeing the buses and targeting the drone aren't related; the drone mission won't be compromised, no matter what happens to the bus mission."

"I can't give you any of my people," Ravenheart told him evenly. He could see, though, that she was fighting to control her anger.

"I'd like your help," he told her, "but I don't need it. I can do this alone."

Now her eyes widened and she shook her head. "You're truly insane. There's no way you can do it."

"I'll bet I can."

She pointed at him, and Kyle could hear the edge in her voice. "You aren't thinking clearly. The only reason you want to do this is because you think your wife and daughter were on that last bus. What about the other two buses, Kyle?

"Assuming you take out the guards quickly, assuming there aren't too many inside the buses that we can't see, and assuming that you don't immediately attract the attention of the billion or so bugs that are in the fraggin' building, what then? How are you going to drive all three buses?"

"You're right about me not thinking clearly, and I'm glad I'm not," Kyle retorted. "I'm glad I haven't become some emotionless robot ready to kill maybe thousands but too cowardly to save maybe a hundred."

Her eyes lit up and she stepped closer, jabbing at him with her finger. "Don't you dare tell me—"

Douglas' voice from the doorway cut her off. "I'll drive the other bus."

There was silence as Ravenheart, startled, turned toward

the ork trooper who'd just entered the room. "Excuse me?" she asked.

"I'll drive the other bus," he said. "We know we can save those people. We have to do it."

Ravenheart was furious. "There's too much risk! I won't allow it. The destruction of the hives has to come first. There's no other alternative."

"I'll drive the third bus," said Sergeant Vathoss from where he leaned against the wall.

Ravenheart spun to look at him. *"What?"* she all but screamed.

"What we're doing is something terrible, and awful, and necessary," he said to her. "But I won't kill those people, people who can still be saved, just because it's risky for us to try and save them. If we don't try, what's the fraggin' point? We destroy hives to save people. Well, Captain, I got bad news for you—the people on those buses are literally the people we're doing this for. That's the chip truth."

Ravenheart began to slowly look around the room, and Kyle did the same. It seemed most, if not all, of the Knight Errant troopers had come in or were standing in the hall within earshot. Many looked fearful, yet were nodding at the sentiments Sergeant Vathoss had unexpectedly voiced. The consensus was evident.

Ravenheart closed her eyes and shook her head violently. "You're all fraggin' glitched," she muttered, but she looked and sound very, very tired. "All right," she said, turning to Kyle. "Let's do it."

31

"The wacker is," Anne Ravenheart said as they stood alone in a large, loft-like warehouse space some blocks away from the insect hive, "that we don't even really know if the nuke will hurt them."

Kyle nodded, but said, "I'm pretty sure it will. We're talking about one hellacious blast of energy."

"Conventional blasts don't harm them," she countered. "No real mystic, human impetus behind them. No emotion, no energy."

"You're right, but a nuclear blast, despite the way it's achieved, is one of the most primal effects you can get. If they're immune to that, we'd be better off at ground zero ourselves."

She smiled and nodded. "Yeah, I suppose so." She looked around the space quickly and then back at Kyle. "You sure this is a good idea? One or two of the little bastards is bad enough, but close to a dozen . . ."

He laughed. "Why do I suspect you'll never have children?"

Ravenheart mocked a flinch. "Ugh. Fraggin' right. I just don't have the tolerance for them."

"Then let me do all the talking. You just echo it to your brood."

"Deal," she said. "I'll guard you first."

Kyle nodded and took a few steps away from her, turning as he did. With that slow spin, he shifted his senses into astral space. It was warm and cool at the same time, and he felt the careful radiance that flowed from Anne Ravenheart's aura as well as his own. The rest of the loft space was peaceful and quiet. That would soon change.

He reached out a hand, and focusing his power, swept it through the ambient energy of astral space. It scooped into his palm and condensed as he swept it again, building more energy into his cupped hand. The energy of astral space pulled together. It was the energy given off by all living things, the power of the planet's biosphere, and as he compressed it, formed it, shaped it, it began to take on a life of its own.

He wouldn't need it long, just an hour or two, so he allowed it to form some degree of loose structure. Its weave didn't need to be tight enough to last for any real length of time. He folded the energy in on itself as a piece of astral origami sculpture. Then, barely a few heartbeats after he'd begun, the molded energy gained and retained its own form (not unlike yogurt floating weightless in space). A pair of impossibly big eyes opened in the form and blinked at him. Then it grinned, big wide, ragged, and dumb.

"Hoi," it said, almost shyly. *"Are you gonna play with me?"*

Behind him, Anne Ravenheart groaned. Kyle had created a watcher spirit—incredibly fast in both astral space and in the physical world, with the fighting spirit of a pit bull, and the brains to match. It was one of nearly a dozen he and Ravenheart would create before they attacked the nest.

"The plan," Ravenheart told the group who'd be participating in the raid to capture the buses, "is straightforward, and not without its risks."

The Knight Errant troopers were all garbed in assembled pieces of hard combat armor and softer body armor. All carried helmets equipped with some sort of vision-enhancing system and a tactical communication system strong enough to punch through the UCAS government jamming for a short distance at least. And they were all armed, most with Ares Alpha combat guns, a few with the newer HVAR high-velocity assault rifles, and two with Mossberg SM-CMDT combat shotguns equipped with under-barrel mini-grenade launchers. They all also carried—trained to use it or not—the biggest knife, combat, survival, or kitchen, they could find. Kyle had suggested it, and Ravenheart quickly ordered it, both knowing that if an insect spirit got in close enough to the trooper to strike with its claws or mandibles, assault weapons would be of little use. Even in untrained hands, a physical, direct attack with a knife, or even an unarmed one, carried more emotional, mystical power than a firearm did. A firearm, though, tore into the bugs before they got too close. An undeniable advantage.

With them sat a dour Seeks-the-Moon who stared off unblinking in the direction of the power plant. Whatever magic was working in the power plant was affecting him, though he refused to admit it. Near him, and possibly a contributor to his mood, was what one of the Knight Errant troopers had dubbed "the crib"—a low-power mana barrier that kept the ten watcher spirits Kyle and Ravenheart had summoned contained and hopefully protected from the unknown capabilities of the insect spirits' senses. Inside the hemisphere of dull blue energy, the ten globs of protoplasm chased each other gleefully, more than occasionally plastering themselves flat against the barrier, only to rebound in the other direction with even more force. At Seeks-the-Moon's request, Kyle had placed a silence spell over the area to cut off the cacophony of squeals.

"Our main goal," continued Ravenheart, "is to get those buses, with the people inside them, out of that plant. There's enough room to turn them around, and even if the gates are closed, as I expect them to be, the first bus will be able to get up enough speed to tear through it.

"Six of you will actually participate in the assault. Three of you, Douglas, Quess, and Keith, will drive the buses, tagged alpha, beta, and delta, respectively, from first in line to last." Once the consensus had been reached that Ravenheart and her team would back Kyle in his attempt to rescue the bus passengers, it was quickly agreed that his best use, as a mage, would be to accompany and provide magical support for the assault. Kyle had readily agreed; he really didn't know how to drive anything bigger than a commuter car.

"We're going to come in from the south, through the boat yard that abuts it off the river." She recapped for them. "There's nothing special about the fence, just aluminum alloy; Vathoss and Douglas will use the acid strips on them. No sparks, little noise.

"By that time, I suspect," she said, "we'll have trouble."

"Excuse the interruption," Seeks-the-Moon said unexpectedly, "but I am suddenly afraid I know what they're doing." He stood up from the crate on which he'd been sitting.

"What?" Kyle asked.

Seeks-the-Moon started walking toward one of the room's few exits. They'd gathered and commenced the briefing in a small extension to the rear of the building that sat across from the power plant. It was old and derelict, probably abandoned years before, but it served. Kyle and Ravenheart followed as Moon said, "We must look."

"Vathoss!" Ravenheart gestured at the sergeant. "Begin a weapons check, and let Conner know to prep the drone." Vathoss nodded as his only reply.

The spirit led the two mages on a fairly involved path through the building they'd mapped out earlier. Squatters, at some point in the building's history, had punched holes in the walls connecting originally isolated sections. They climbed to the fourth floor, second from the top, via a rusty ladder in an elevator shaft. Reaching the warehouse space there, they crept forward, keeping to the inner wall. Halfway, Seeks-the-Moon held up his hand and the other two stopped.

"We can see from here," he said.

Kyle could clearly see the power plant's enormous, dormant tower and the top of what he took to be the generator building. Much of it, however, was dark and barely highlighted by the silver of moon in the sky.

"Do you see it?" the spirit asked quietly.

Kyle couldn't see anything with his eyes, and a quick glance at Ravenheart confirmed that she didn't either. Shifting his senses into astral space, he immediately gasped.

The power plant grounds, including all of the main facility and most of the outlying ones, were covered in a slowly building dome of green energy. The forming power drifted down over the gradually defining sides like fingers of smoke, pale and nauseating. The energy flowed from the center of the building, from deep in its bowels, Kyle felt, as it fed the burgeoning ward.

"What the . . .?" whispered Ravenheart.

"Do not look too long," Seeks-the-Moon said even more softly. "We don't wish to be noticed."

Kyle looked at the growing lattice of power one last time before he let his senses return exclusively to the physical world. "How long have we got?" he asked Seeks-the-Moon.

The free spirit shrugged. "Less than an hour, maybe minutes. I do not know the strength of the magic."

"Are they erecting a ward?" Ravenheart asked, almost stunned.

Kyle nodded. "A fraggin' powerful one—based on the waves coming off it. The bastards have to be using a ritual; that thing's too powerful for one magician to cast."

"Even for a queen of the insect spirits?" Seeks-the-Moon asked.

"I don't know, but I fraggin' well hope not," Kyle said. "The point is, though, that it's almost done. The ward is forming—that's the Sending we're seeing—and it's directed against the casting place itself. It'll come together in no time."

"What do we do?" Ravenheart asked, her gaze snapping back and forth between both Kyle and the spirit.

"Ready or not," Kyle replied, "we attack now."

32

The light-amplification system in the goggles Kyle held over his eyes lit up the grounds of the power plant like daylight. The others hidden with him in the shadows near the boatyard were using low-light and thermographic systems integrated into their own helmets. Kyle, being a mage, couldn't cast magic through those systems since they translated what few photons of light they gathered and amplified into another form, that of a viewable electronic display. The goggles impeded him too, as he needed a direct, untranslated view of any potential target, but those he could flip up or toss aside if needed.

Right now, Kyle could see the three buses, none of which had moved, and the four guards standing casually around them.

"I have two more, plus your four, to make six," came Ravenheart's slightly garbled voice over his helmet headset. He keyed the response pad built into his left glove twice to signal a positive response. Ravenheart and all the troopers except those commanding the drone were positioned in the five-story building from which she, Kyle, and Seeks-the-Moon had observed the coalescing magical ward some minutes before. The location was closer than they'd have liked, but time was against them and the placement at least gave a clear view of the grounds.

Kyle nodded to Vathoss, and the sergeant, barely visible though only a few steps away, nodded in reply. A quick series of clicks came in through his headset, the coded communication used by the Knight Errant troopers. There'd been no time for Kyle to learn the code, but he knew from the timing of the message that Vathoss was signaling Ravenheart to begin the second phase of the operation. The first phase had brought them within striking distance of the building, and now it was time for the fireworks to begin. Somewhere, maybe high overhead, maybe a few blocks away, the fateful drone circled nearly silently, waiting for either a cue from Conner on the ground or the programming in its computer brain to tell it to begin its descent.

Ravenheart responded by click-code instead of voice, two chirps. Two seconds later came the blast. It happened a few blocks away, a line-of-sight, laser-beam-detonated charge that had been placed in the derelict restaurant. The blast was only big enough to blow out the remaining windows and storefront bracings, but the noise carried for blocks and sounded like a war breaking out.

It also immediately produced the desired effect as the four guards visible to Kyle quickly moved to the far side of the bus to get a glimpse of what remained of the blast cloud, or more likely, the glow from any after-blast fires. If all went well, the guards would stand gaping, perhaps even wondering if it was one of the increasingly common gas explosions, while the Knight Errant team began their assault.

On Ravenheart's signal, troopers Quess and Douglas sprinted forward under cover of Vathoss and Keith's guns and Kyle's readiness to unravel any spells that might be directed at them. At the same time, Kyle quickly began activating his powerful foci, and masking as much of their aura as he could. No use in tipping the bugs off early or making himself an especially inviting target.

Quess and Douglas reached the fence and quickly strung a sticky gray rope that resembled primer cord across the fence, forming roughly the shape of a large door. One end terminated in a set of wires and a small plug. As Quess severed the end that curled outward from the small roll he held, Douglas attached the wires to a small box. Without a word spoken between them, Quess stepped back and Douglas pressed a button on the box.

There was no spark or light, but smoke suddenly sprang up along the length of the rope where it adhered to the fence. Kyle knew that the electrical charge provided by the box disrupted the barrier between two substances in the rope. When they merged, there was acid, and as Kyle watched, it quickly ate through the thin metal of the fence. Both Quess and Douglas, wearing bulky, oversized gloves, held on to the section of the fence so it wouldn't fall. It didn't, and as it bowed and pulled away, they yanked it clear, carefully laying it down on the grass.

The stench off the fence was terrible, and there were still wisps of smoke rising from the edge of the hole. But it was there and the troopers around him were quickly moving toward it.

Suddenly, three muffled shots rang out. Kyle knew the sounds from experience, but wondered how many others would know what they were—high-powered sniper fire. If he and the others were lucky as they passed through the fence, three of the six guards would already dead. The second volley would come quickly, though probably only fast enough to catch two of the three remaining. Odds were the third would dash around the bus for cover, and straight into the sights of Sergeant Vathoss.

As they moved quickly and quietly, the second volley rang out, but Kyle saw no guard dart around the bus.

"Six on the ground," said Ravenheart in his ear. Vathoss, down on one knee, gun braced and ready, stood quickly and moved to cover the rear of the line.

They were just under one hundred meters from the buses and there was little doubt that the queens and nest-mothers now knew they were under attack—six of their own were dead or dying.

"Brood released!" Ravenheart said suddenly, and Kyle shifted his attention into astral space, slowing his pace, his perceptions of the physical world becoming blurred. The "brood" was the gaggle of watcher spirits, and the plan was to release them when Seeks-the-Moon, temporarily positioned next to Ravenheart, saw signs of bug spirits responding from the depths of the building.

Looking ghostly in the physical world, the ten spirits exploded into the area, screaming and shouting at the top of their lungs. They darted into view from between the smaller buildings to the east and the power array beyond them. They were, even to Kyle at about a hundred and fifty meters away, quite loud.

A dozen insect spirits, a mix of buzzing wasps and flies and skittering ants and roaches, darted through the big metal doors that led deep into the building. Immediately, the watcher spirits banked, continuing to scream, and in at least one case, sing as loud as they could. The bugs darted apart, unsure of the strength of their attackers. The watchers were small, and deadly fast, and would ultimately be no match for the more powerful insect creatures. But they didn't need to win, only delay.

As Kyle's group rushed toward the buses, Kyle saw the faint glow of a spell in front of the building. If things were still proceeding according to plan, Ravenheart had just cast a wall of energy against the metal power plant doors. The bugs would be able to batter it aside, but it was another way of gaining an additional few seconds.

Visible only in astral space, three wasp spirits burst out of the building through the an upper window. Kyle watched for an instant as the first two turned quickly, angling for the front of the plant. The third, however, jerked itself in mid-flight and dove down toward the assault group.

If it saw them, then it also saw clearly that Kyle was a mage and astrally active and vulnerable to attack there. He stopped himself suddenly. Quess, running immediately behind him, twisted to avoid Kyle as he ran past.

The bug shot toward him at blinding speed while Kyle pushed the formula for the spell through his mind and then cast it, the blur of the spirit's form barely meters away. The energy, backed by the full power of Kyle's foci, flashed between the two in astral space, striking the bug as it tried to turn aside. The flash, red and brilliant white in the astral, was so powerful it even flared slightly in the physical world. The spirit, not as large or powerful as the others Kyle had faced, disintegrated, clouds of its dissipating energy engulfing Kyle.

His spell had been powerful, he and Ravenheart having

decided that the personal risk of throwing high-powered spells was worth the strain. If a bug got through or close enough to either one of them or Seeks-the-Moon, the whole plan could fail. On the downside, the spell's power also mean that nearby insect spirits had probably perceived it and would be swarming his way within moments.

But there was little he could do. Almost immediately Kyle saw a pair of ant spirits clamber around the lead bus, half running across its side. He could now also hear screams and shrieks of fear from within the bus. He hoped, and prayed, the people would stay where they were. But that was Seeks-the-Moon's job.

Two of the troopers paused and opened fire on the onrushing ants, while Kyle and the others rushed forward, shifting their run slightly to avoid the ants and the hail of gunfire. The ants jerked to one side as the hypersonic bursts struck them. The shots were precise and deadly, but the two ants were tough.

A flash of fire erupted between them suddenly, pitching them both to one side. The spell could have come from either Ravenheart or Seeks-the-Moon, depending on whether or not the latter had begun moving toward the buses. One of the ants was torn to pieces; the other stumbled, two of its legs sheared off or broken. It screeched terribly, probably calling to its hive-mates.

Kyle and Quess reached the side of the second bus and immediately began calling out to the occupants to stay inside. Kyle could hear screaming, a smashing noise as if someone was trying to pound a window, and terrified shouts. Quess suddenly shoved Kyle's shoulder, spinning him and pointing him toward the river. Beetles, tens of them, black and shiny but barely visible in the shadows of the building, were pouring into view. He didn't dare count, but there had to be dozens, maybe even scores.

He keyed the voice circuit in his headset radio. "Barrier! *Now!*" he said on Ravenheart's channel.

The horde of beetles rushed forward at an impossible speed, their huge claws tearing up the turf as they ran.

Traces of light glinted off their hard-shelled bodies, and Kyle prepared the heaviest area-effect spell he could muster.

Suddenly, a wall of gray and blue energy sprung up between the swarm of beetles and the bus. It arced quickly over Kyle and dropped down the other side, encasing the buses in a hemisphere of energy.

The front line of beetles struck the barrier, and immediately flashes of energy ripped through them, knocking them back and turning them away. It was a powerful spell, a custom design the Ares magicians had created specifically for use against insect spirits. The barrier blocked them, and contact with it was hideously, maybe even fatally, painful. It was one of various hard-core designs that Ravenheart knew. Kyle would have been happy to know even half of them.

All of the troopers were within the barriers and quickly began moving to their assigned buses. Kyle reached the doors of the first one, just as Douglas and his powerful ork strength pulled the side door open. The ork dashed inside, ducking low under the protection of the panel along the half-steps that led up to the deck of the bus. He glances quickly down the length of the vehicle, and then stood, turned, and fired two quick shots from his combat rifle. Kyle pulled himself up behind the ork trooper just in time to see a man with a twisted dark aura and a gun in his slackening hand begin to fall, a trail of blood arcing through the air from his head. A young girl, barely a teenager, and just second a ago the man's hostage, dove forward screaming.

Kyle turned, looking at the occupants of the bus, who ducked and cowered in fear. He did not or could not see Beth or Natalie. He cursed, and vaulted back down the stairs as Keith entered, covering Douglas's move to the front of the bus while shouting for everyone aboard to keep their heads down. Kyle doubted there would be any problem with that.

But he was supposed to be on the last bus, the rear one where he could see the rest and provide them magical aid if needed. He dashed down the line of buses and was about to run through the open doors of the second bus when a flash of light lit the area.

He spun as dozens of bugs threw themselves blindly against the shield, blasting and searing themselves in a maddening effort to breach it. And Kyle could see that the shield was weakening, fading in spots. Ravenheart's voice confirmed it: "Get ready to move! The shield's only got a few seconds!"

Kyle turned back and looked up at the shapes and forms of people he could barely make out in the bus. One of the troopers was moving among them, and he heard the engine of the first bus spring to life.

"Come on!" Vathoss yelled at hm from the rear bus.

Kyle glanced over and saw the sergeant hanging out the rear door, waving him forward to the third bus. Beyond him, Seeks-the-Moon stepped out through the wall of the bus and manifested physically. Kyle wanted to catch his eye, to see if Moon had seen Beth or Natalie as he'd manifested in turn in each bus, advising the passengers to stay low as the assault began.

But Seeks-the-Moon was turned away, looking up at the dimming, now almost flickering shield. Kyle saw that and dashed for the third bus. Time was up.

Vathoss leapt inside and into the driver's seat, and Kyle quickly followed him, both men slamming their hands down on the flat yellow button that closed the doors. The key was in place, so Vathoss depressed the ignition switch, and the bus' engine surged into life.

Seeks-the-Moon appeared as a blur of motion next to Kyle. "We're out of time!" he said. "The shield is solidifying."

"What?" Kyle yelled, barely able to hear him over the gunning of the bus engine. He wanted to scan the crowd on the bus, look for Beth and Natalie's auras, but Seeks-the-Moon had moved in front of him, blocking his view.

"The shield is nearly complete," the spirit told him.

"It'll fall in a second!" Kyle said, trying to move past him.

"No, not Ravenheart's," said Seeks-the-Moon. "The other shield, the one around the hive, is almost complete."

Kyle stopped and turned, leaning to look out the slightly

bubbled front window of the bus. Vathoss wanted to move, to get clear, but Ravenheart's barrier was still up, though flickering dangerously. Beyond it, obvious to his still astral senses, Kyle could see the ward that was being erected around the grounds of the power plant. Seeks-the-Moon was right; the energy lattice was nearly ready, nearly complete.

Kyle keyed his communication link. "Anne!" he shouted unnecessarily. "The hive's ward is nearly completed!"

"I know." Her voice was ragged with stress. "I'm releasing my barrier . . . *now!*"

The gray and blue barrier, barely existent and now crawling with bugs powerful enough to resist the burning arcs of power, exploded in a flash and spray of energy. Bugs, dozens of them of all types were tossed aside by the dissolution of the barrier. Immediately, grenades began detonating in the midst of the swarm of insects that had fallen back from the exploding barrier. The grenades did little damage, but it did scatter the creatures. Both Kyle and Seeks-the-Moon threw explosive spells of their own into the chaos.

"Go! Go! Go!" screamed Ravenheart. "We're out of time—I'm sending the drone in!"

Vathoss's body jerked as he heard the words, and he turned to look at Kyle. If Ravenheart had ordered to drone in, they had maybe a minute, maybe slightly more, before it exploded.

The headset in Kyle's helmet crackled. "Negative! Negative!" it was Quess' frantic voice. "My key isn't here and the hot-wire won't jump it!"

Kyle flexed his finger to respond, but Ravenheart's was faster. "No choice!" she yelled. "Run if you have to!"

Ahead of them all, the first bus lurched forward, turning hard to the right. A whirring, keening, skittering mass of bugs rushed it, climbing madly over the front. A barrage of magical darts of power rained down on them from Ravenheart; Kyle was amazed that her position across the street was still safe.

"Rockets!" she yelled over the open channel, and Kyle saw four flashes of light from the darkness beyond the edge of the plant grounds, followed quickly by three barely visible streaks. The four high-explosive rockets shot through the re-grouping mass of bugs, probably a dozen in that area alone, and continued on toward the front of the building.

The rockets struck the large metal doors as Ravenheart's shield was dropped. They detonated in rapid succession, sending shockwaves through the building and out across the open ground, where it rocked the buses.

Vathoss slammed the transmission of Kyle's bus into motion, jerking forward and crashing into the rear of the second bus. The throttle was wide open, and its tires spun for a second on the concrete, but then it began to push the other bus forward.

The first bus was covered in a wall of bugs; there was no way Douglas could see past them, but he only needed to head toward the outer fence or gate. His helmet system displayed a compass bearing; if necessary he could navigate by that, turning right after he struck the fence. Assuming the bugs didn't tear the bus apart first.

"I will help them," Seeks-the-Moon said, flashing through astral space toward the first bus. The writhing swarm of bugs on the bus was so dense that Kyle wondered if the spirit would be able to find a way through them. Then, Kyle could hear the sound of tearing metal despite the distance and the roaring of the bus engines. The bugs were peeling the heavy plastic and metal sides and top of the bus away.

Another wave of missiles arced in through the now blasted open doorway. This time, their path unimpeded, they exploded deep inside the plant. Kyle saw the flashes in the building's upper windows.

Almost immediately, dozens of the bug spirits began to leap from the first bus and rush toward the building: the queens were under attack, they must be defended. It wouldn't be too long, however, before either the queens themselves or any human insect shamans inside would realize the true nature of the threat and respond accordingly.

Kyle's bus lurched, and window to the rear shattered in a spray of safety glass. He turned as the powerful mandibles of a beetle thrust inside, catching a man who was springing away, tearing his head and shoulder completely off. Kyle called up and released a missile of magic power that struck the bug in the head and made it pull back, squealing. He felt a slight twinge in his neck muscles, his body beginning to protest the strain.

The translucent skylight and emergency exit on top of the bus were torn free, and a pair of ants tried to thrust their way in simultaneously. Their odor was unmistakable, and Kyle unslung the hypervelocity assault rifle he'd been given. He stepped under the skylight as one of the ants finally made room for the other, and fired before the other's head was clear. The weapon fired, spraying twelve quick rounds of exploding ammo at the ant spirits. Most of the shots hit the first, the bug that was trying to push inside, but some also hit the second. Neither was badly hurt, but each was thrown off enough that as the bus lurched again and sent Kyle sprawling, both insects slid from view. Kyle thought he saw their bodies tumble off outside as he fell hard against his shoulder.

Hands immediately reached down to help up. As he stood, leaving the rifle behind and his upper arm throbbing in pain, Kyle saw that his bus had turned away from the second bus and was beginning to accelerate. Kyle stumbled forward and practically collapsed against the safety cage that protected the drive.

"What are you doing?" Kyle yelled at Vathoss. "What about Quess?"

The sergeant shook his head, cursing. "I can't push him! Some of the fraggin' bugs are jammed up in his wheels!"

Kyle leaned down to look back toward the second bus as a group of ants, apparently unable or unwilling to run after the moving buses, turned on the unmoving one. Kyle rushed to the back of his bus, pulling a powerful spell to mind. He cast it, and it lanced out in a series of white-green bands that wove into a loose web and flashed over a group of rushing bugs. They lurched to a halt, pinned to the ground beneath the web of energy, and then began to attack the strands that held them.

He realized that he had not heard a message from Quess in nearly a minute, but a quick check of the heads-up display projected on the inside of his helmet faceshield showed that only the command circuit, the channel to Ravenheart, was active. Using her remote command ability, she had, for some reason, locked him out of the channels the other—

The rear windows exploded inward, showering Kyle in a spray of rapidly fragmenting safety glass. A black and brown roach, Kyle's height and twice his width, thrust itself through the broken window. Its front legs dug into the metal and plastic, as its long antennae whipped nearly two meters into the bus. Kyle was knocked back onto the floor, landing flat on his back.

The roach, reeking of something foul, pulled itself forward, and dug one of its front legs into Kyle's abdomen, pressing down sharply against his body armor. Its mouth clicked open and shut as it leaned down toward him. Kyle kicked up with his right leg, wincing against the pain in his abdomen and shoulder, catching the creature in the soft, wet part just below its mouth. The roach yanked back, letting up on the pressure and Kyle rolled to one side. Just as he did, a wild burst of automatic weapons from inside the bus tore into the bug. Kyle looked up and saw a man, his eyes huge and mouth wide, holding down the trigger of the assault rifle. Stray rounds tore into the rear of the bus, clipping the bug and another passenger.

The roach thrust forward, whipping a feeler across the man's face, leaving a long, bloody cut. The man spun away, the gun still firing wildly across the side windows, blowing them out. Most of the roach was in the bus, its legs braced, pushing and tearing at the screaming passengers. It reached the man and slashed into him with his front legs, then bringing him toward its mouth. Kyle herd a loud crunch and the man's body began to jerk even more.

The bug was less than a meter away, and Kyle reached out with his hand and a spell and touched its sleek body. The roach jerked, and Kyle released the spell. The roach's body began to darken in an area radiating outward from where Kyle's hand was, and the creature began to thrash, its long spiny legs tearing into the side of the bus and the passengers.

Blood and ichor burst from the weakened body of the creature as it began to screech. The bus lurched again, and Kyle
heard the distinct crash of metal against metal, and then the
bus bounced harshly across what Kyle took to be the railroad
tracks paralleling the street. The bug twisted away from Kyle,
turning to one side, but Kyle's hand was already sinking into
the weakened, liquefying skin, down onto the creature's un-
derbelly.

One of the roach's thrashing legs caught him in the head,
knocking him to one side. Dazed, Kyle curled and tried to
roll away as the thing hit him again, tearing into his body armor.

The bus turned, tilting radically to the right as it bounced
off the tracks. The engine surged again, but Kyle also heard
what sounded like plastiglass cracking at the front of the bus.
The screams got louder as the roach righted itself, drenched
in a spray of blood from someone's leg.

Kyle tried to clear his vision as another spiny leg shot
down at him. Before it could get him, he twisted aside and
the leg tore through the plastic seat next to him. He released
another spell, directly into the roach's looming underside.
The force of the spell lifted the bug and slammed it against
the roof of the bus, arcs of power rippling around. Single-shot
gunfire sounded from the front of the bus, and as Kyle tried
to pull himself to his feet, the ground outside, back toward
the plant, was illumined in a red-orange glow, quickly followed by an explosion and a shockwave. The second bus,
still where Vathoss' push had left it, blew open in a flash of
light and fire.

The bug dropped down to the deck of the bus, its legs flailing out again. The bus hit another series of bumps, and Kyle
was knocked back onto the floor. The roach screeched and
came at him, pinning him to the partially shattered rear seat.
Kyle pulled the combat knife from his boot sheath and
stabbed it upward into the bug's lower body with all his
strength. The bus bounced again, but this time its motion
helped him, slamming the rear of the bug's body harder onto
the blade.

One hand on the blade, one hand now on top of the creature's jerking back, Kyle cast another spell, wincing as a wave of hot red pain washed over him. Power arced between his hands, cutting the insect spirit's body like a band saw. Kyle and the rear of the bus were bathed in a sudden wash of ichor, but then the creature's form began to unravel, its energy returning to astral space as it died. The bus jerked, and Kyle was knocked to his right as it struck on that side, sending up a shower of sparks and sheared plastic and metal.

A single, loud tone sounded in Kyle's headset. The bus continued on, smashing heavily into something. Kyle sprawled forward screaming, *"GET DOWN! GET DOWN!"* as he tried to grab anyone and everyone near him and pull them down to the bus' deck.

There was a light behind them. Unstoppable and searing, it burned bright white, bathing everything, even the shadows, in the blazing light of the sun. Heat washed over them, and then the bus was pushed forward, twisting, turning on its side. As he spun, the bus flipping, Kyle could see back toward the plant just for a second.

The light was blinding, but it was dampened and dimmed by the cracking shield of green-purple energy that contained it for the briefest moment. There was a point of light inside the dome of energy, surging, straining against it. The sky lit with a second sun.

The bus rolled, and Kyle was slammed against the side as another wave of light, this one laced with purple, washed over the bus. There was pain everywhere in his body as the bus slid on its side and slammed into something far harder than itself.

The light dimmed, and there was no other noise, no other shockwave, only a powerful rush of wind back toward the power plant.

The bus stopped, tilted, and then settled. People cried and screamed. Some began to fight to get out. Kyle struggled with them, his right arm virtually useless.

It was dark again outside, and warm. Warmer than it had been. A red-white glow lit parts of the surrounding buildings and the now shattered roadway and abutment that had apparently shielded them from most of the blast. Kyle staggered a few steps out onto the road and looked back. He could dimly make out a plume of black smoke that rose into the air, lit from below by a terrible fire. He knew where he was—he was at the point where the 90/94 interstate crossed Cermak Road. They hadn't gotten clear; he was within the blast radius. But he was alive. He was alive.

He turned, barely able to keep himself from falling over. His bus, almost unrecognizable now, lay on its side, slammed into the front of a building. Far beyond it, on the bridge that crossed the south branch of the Chicago River, he could see the first bus, twisted and bent and crammed into the metal supports of the bridge. There were people milling, stunned, near each vehicle. There were no bugs to be seen.

From around the rear of the last bus, Seeks-the-Moon came walking slowly. Even through Kyle's pain he could see that the spirit was weakened, maybe irrevocably—he'd fought one of the insect spirits toe to toe and maybe won, barely.

"Beth . . . Natalie . . ." Kyle gasped, his legs suddenly giving way. Seeks-the-Moon reached out to hold him up, saying, "They weren't on the bus."

Not on the bus. They weren't on Seeks-the-Moon's bus, the first bus. They weren't on Kyle's bus, the last one. That meant they'd been on the second bus. The bus that had exploded.

Kyle collapsed, falling forward and barely supported by the spirit. There was nothing. Nothing to feel, only the pain.

"They weren't on any of the buses," the spirit whispered. "I was on all of them."

Kyle turned his head slightly and was startled by what he saw. The depth of compassion in the eyes of his former ally spirit was unfathomable. "None of the buses . . . ?" Kyle mumbled, almost unable to speak. His right leg wanted to collapse, but he wouldn't let it.

"They were on none of the three buses. I didn't see them."

Kyle nodded. He needed to heal himself, but carefully; there were pains in his stomach that were dangerous. He tried to key his communication link with Ravenheart and then stopped, realizing his helmet had been torn from his head by the bug or during the crash.

"We have to lead these people away from here," the spirit said.

"Yes, there might be radiation . . ." Kyle pulled himself up and stood again on his own. "That way." He pointed across the bridge past the other bus. "Toward Chinatown."

"There's no radiation," said Seeks-the-Moon.

Kyle looked at the spirit again, trying to place what was so different about him. "There's got to be radiation. The bomb went off."

"Obviously," the spirit said. "But there is no radiation." He fingered a small badge of plastic dangling from Kyle's body armor. It was battered, but it was still green. "See."

Kyle looked down at it. "How the frag . . ."

"The bomb went off *inside* the insect's ward. And I think most of it was held there."

Kyle turned to look back that way and saw a woman standing a few meters distant. She was battered and bruised, her once-stylish short blond hair matted with drying blood, the left side of her pale face dark and swollen. She was pulling a long, torn purple raincoat tight about her and Kyle could see she was favoring her left arm.

"Kyle?" She said in a hoarse voice, taking a half-step forward.

"Oh my God . . ." he said, reaching out his good arm toward her. She stumbled against him and he ignored the pain in his arm and shoulder as he wrapped it around her and pulled her close. Hanna Uljakën began to cry, and after a moment he did too.